SOMETIMES IT LOOKS LIKE THAT

Jessie Dorin

This is a work of fiction. While some characters may be composites of persons I have known, no character is representative of a single person. Except that Mary Estes is Stella. Always, she is Stella. It is inevitable in 14 years of teaching high school that former students may find their names in this book. However, all student characters are composites, and names are used because of their fit to a composite character, not because they are the name of an actual student from any of my classes. The chapter describing Metta Annie's workshop is entirely fictional, though based on the work of Byron Katie.

ISBN: 1977869548
ISBN 13: 9781977869548

DEDICATION

*Dedicated to my students. You matter. You have
always mattered. You always will matter.*

CONTENTS

CHAPTER 1
AUGUST. EFFING RULES.

One minute to the bell. A cold trickle of dread spelled out what Ava didn't want to admit: I am going to fail.

In a secondhand blouse that had seemed like a good idea that morning, she now saw herself as she appeared: Shabby, and, what was the word? White.

The room was small for a high school, or maybe these teenagers took up more space—voices louder, gestures bigger. Amid tables that still bore the indelible marks of old graffiti, students flashed gold veneers when they spoke, boys dangled price tags from their ball caps, and girls strutted in stiletto heels. Ava looked as if she should be ringing up customers at Wal-Mart.

Open your mind. You wanted diversity. You wanted different. But the different she'd envisioned included different skin tones and different foods. These students used slang words and gestures she didn't understand. They were confident insiders, name-dropping neighborhoods she didn't know, people she'd never heard of, and the numbers of bus lines as if referencing old friends: "49 be crackin' this morning." She hadn't anticipated she'd be the one who was different. She glanced at the carpet, oddly dirty for the start of a school year. Her eyes traced an unraveling seam down the center of the room. What if they saw right through her?

"You want first and last name?" Charnikka bent over her name-etag, her short braids pulled into tight rows.

"Just your first. Or whatever you like to be called."

Charnikka grunted. "You need more room on these." She paused to give Ava a look. "I'ma be late to school sometimes. The lady tell you? She said it was fine." Her eyes narrowed. "I best not be getting no truancy letters."

"For being late to school?" Wasn't that the definition of truant? "I'll ask. What lady was that? The principal?"

"White lady. One who signed me up. My momma can't be watching my daughter Tuesdays and Wednesdays. I gotta take three busses to my auntie house to drop her off. She in South San Francisco, so I'ma be late."

"Tuesdays and Wednesdays. Got it." A baby, white lady, busses. At 28, Ava Llewellyn didn't have any children. She'd never taught in a place where students distinguished themselves from staff by the single word *white*. And what would Charnikka say if she knew her new teacher was terrified of riding the city bus, afraid the driver or other passengers would berate her when she got it wrong? Ava had had enough of yelling.

Thirty seconds until the bell. To her left, a small student sat quietly, his face obscured under an oversize hoodie. Here was the calm that she so clearly lacked. His nametag read: *The General.*

Behind him, sunlight fought through rows of tangled blinds, letting in the heat along with glimpses of San Francisco's famous Victorians across the street. It had only been an hour since Ava had looked out over that view, the sun rising on an empty classroom, and felt a sense of hope and confidence.

She was a fool.

She saw now that the past three years teaching in the backwoods of Washington State didn't mean anything. She knew cows on the baseball field. Students' hands raw from shifts at the dairy. The only busses there were school busses, and vehicles that drove the dirt roads were a patchwork of junkyard parts. Cars here were all the same color. They had a shine. These kids had shine. She was a rusted Impala with blue and green doors.

Another girl held out her course schedule. Ava peered at the paper, then pointed to the girl's name. "How do you pronounce it?"

"Kabernay."

Like the wine? That couldn't be right. "I'm sorry—Will you say your name again, please?"

The girl put a hand on her hip. "Cab-er-nay."

It was right. "Glad to have you in class. Here's a nametag. Just write whatever you like to be called."

Any other start of school, she'd recount her adrenaline and students' personalities to Dan over dinner. He'd laugh at the parts where she confessed her anxiety, and on good days she could find the humor too. Then they'd take a walk out back among the towering evergreens, earthy moss mingling with the scent of minty gum that was as much a part of Dan as his trickle-down demeanor. But neither Dan nor the evergreens were in San Francisco, and he wouldn't share a stick of gum with her now if she paid him. She'd wanted different, and she got it. And there was no way to get back what she had.

Kabernay stared at her.

"Just your first name on the nametag."

"I need my schedule back."

"Right. Sorry."

A kid with a round, shaved head glanced over. Still wearing a puffy jacket, he fiddled with the fan, trying to get it to work. "Never say you're sorry, Ms. L. That's some weak shit." Beads of sweat ran down his forehead. His nametag read: *Sean*.

Ava nodded. "Got it. Sorr—"

The fan started. Sean smiled. He leaned in toward the blades. "Ms. L, I aaaaaaaaamm yoooooooourrrrr faaaaaathaaaaaaaaaa."

Star Wars. She gazed at his dark, billiard-ball forehead, slick with sweat. *Star Wars.* Something in common. She smiled. "I thought you looked familiar."

Sean turned to Charnikka, who had taken a seat to his left. "Charnikka, I'm glad I'm nooooot yooooooourrr maaaaaaaathaaa aaaaaaa."

"Fuck you, Sean," said Charnikka. Her nametag now read: *Head Bitch In Charge.*

Ava's words echoed in her mind: Whatever you like to be called.

The bell rang.

Her stomach clenched. There was no one else to do this. "All right, folks. Let's find your seats and get started."

Grumbling, students ended their conversations. They grouped themselves at tables according to ethnicity—black, Asian, Latino. The room was full and, despite the fan, overly warm. Shifting uncomfortably in their seats, kids sized up their classmates and this new school. The class was for students aged sixteen to nineteen who hadn't passed the English portion of the High School Exit Exam, one of California's requirements for graduation.

"Good morning," Ava said. She pointed to the seven rules she'd meticulously written on the whiteboard. It was the usual beginning-of-school litany about respectful language, bathroom passes, and turning off cell phones during class. "I've written down the rules here so we can go over them together. Does anyone want to read out the first rule? Anyone? Any readers here?"

Silence.

"Okay," she said. "So. Rule Number One—no swearing."

"Oh, hell naw!" said a kid to her right. He had a full beard and the word *Norteño* tattooed on his neck. Tagging scrawled across the table in front of him identified him as "Francisco."

"Is she fucking kidding me?" Kabernay seconded.

"Fuck that shit," said a tiny girl, hiding behind a SpongeBob Square Pants backpack.

A tall student rose from his chair. "I'm sorry, Ms. Llewellyn, but if that's the rule, I'm out of here right now."

Ava's mouth went dry. *Shit*. Now what?

In an unexpected nod to classroom etiquette, Francisco raised his hand.

"Yes?"

"I'm just telling you now I'm not going follow that rule. That's fucking bullshit. No one can tell me what to say."

Ava was confused. In a classroom full of layman lawyers, how had she become the nut job arguing to stifle free speech? She edged nearer to The General, pretending his silence made him an ally.

The masses agreed. "Fucking rules." The kids shifted in their seats. Some closed their notebooks and put them back into their backpacks.

Ava took a deep breath, searching for why it was that that rule had come up first. "But what about in a job situation? Don't you have to watch your language there? We're in a professional space. We need to act like professionals."

"I ain't no fucking professional," said SpongeBob. Dark hair bulged under a florescent pink scarf. Her nametag read "Paris."

"I'm a professional gangsta," Sean said. He smiled and looked around, sweat beads forming on his perfect billiard-ball forehead.

"You're professionally stupid," said Francisco.

Sean raised his voice. "You wanna see stupid? I can do stupid. In fact, I'll *show* you stupid." He rose from his seat.

"I'm gonna professionally slap you if you don't sit back down," Charnikka said.

Ava let out her breath. I'm so glad you're in charge.

"Yo, Ms. L.! I'm a professional," said a tiny kid near the back. His eyes were impish. His nametag read simply, "Melvin."

Finally. Thank you.

Melvin said, "I'm professionally sexy."

The kids laughed. Melvin turned to a quiet girl on his right. "Karen," he sang, "Once you go Filipino, you never go Latino…."

Charnikka snorted.

"It's K-Ron, not Karen," said the girl, her expression as severe as the hair shellacked to her skull. She'd drawn her eyeliner into thick cat's eyes, lips outlined the color of congealed blood.

"K-Ron…." Melvin sang.

Ava looked at her watch: 8:59. Class had been going for fewer than five minutes. "Fine, fine. New rule," she said. "No swearing *at* someone." She looked around. The kids were listening. To sound more authoritative, she added, "Swearing too much lessens the effect you were after anyway. Anyone have a problem with that?"

"Fine."

"Whatever."

"Fuck it," said SpongeBob.

"I ain't trippin,'" said Francisco.

The General remained silent. Ava took it as approval.

She amended the rule on the whiteboard, feeling an *Animal Farm*-like familiarity in doing so. In the novel, Squealer the pig had amended the Animalism rule of *No Animal Shall Kill Another Animal* to include the words *Without Cause*. Ava similarly found herself amending Classroom Rule #1: *No Swearing* to include the words *At Someone*. "Good," she said, as if she'd planned the morning to proceed in just this way.

She glanced at rest of the rules, many of which were being broken this very second and in plain sight: No texting, no playing on your phones, no leaving for the bathroom without permission. "Let's save the rest of the rules for tomorrow. Now I'll assign you your grammar books."

The students groaned, but settled back into their seats. Ava handed out a tattered set of *Perspectives on Grammar*, copyright

1987. Many books had tagging along the edges of the pages, the most common being variations on the words "bitch." Quite a few had belonged to someone with the last name of Meoff, first name: Jack. Ava asked the students to write their names inside the book covers just so: Last name first. This showed that she was in charge. She knew best. She was a professional. Her first attempts at this school had not failed.

A voice in her head said, *Fucking coward.*

CHAPTER 2
GETTING TO KNOW YOU

Near the end of the day, Ava prepared for homeroom. Unsure what that entailed, she had asked the teacher across the hall, Cheryl Wilson, what exactly she was supposed to do with the daily fifteen minutes spent with her homeroom kids. Cheryl handed her a box of blue folders containing transcripts for each of Ava's twenty-five students. Her colleague gave an encouraging smile. "We schedule their classes, keep track of their credits, handle any problems between students and teachers, call home. We put homeroom later in the day to catch kids who always skip the first few periods…got it?"

"Got it," Ava said. She didn't address the high-pitched voice in her head that protested, Yes, but what am I supposed to do during Homeroom?

The bell rang. She looked at her students, a number of whom she had met in her Test Prep English class earlier. Charnikka was reading a novel entitled *Gettin' Buck Wild: Sex Chronicles II*. The General slumped low in his seat, blending into the background of hoodies and caps. Paris was texting as though it were her job. Sean, still in his puffy jacket, worked homeroom like a politician, chatting up a student in a Giants tee shirt.

"All right, everybody," Ava called, "let's get started. I have a get-to-know-your-neighbor activity for us."

Charnikka looked up, eyes black, scowling.

Ava remembered donning a similar scowl years ago during 3rd period English, Ms. Wendell's class. Fifteen, in glasses and braces, Ava had sat hunched like an armadillo, her mouth set in a grim line. Dread and anxiety bled into a lonely sadness: Another long weekend ahead with her dad. The rest of the class buzzed around her. Then Ms. Wendell walked by. She looked past Ava's scowl, saw the tears, and handed her a Kleenex. On Monday Ms. Wendell said, "I was thinking about you. I was worried." And Ava joined humanity.

Sean sauntered over to a slender girl named Lexus. Her dark skin gleamed in contrast to the white scarf wound round her hair.

"You look like a cotton picker," Sean said, gesturing to the scarf.

Ava gasped.

Lexus lunged. "Nigga, don't you ever say that to a dark-skinned Black woman."

Charnikka glared over her book. "Dumb-ass."

Ava's stomach contents liquefied. She had never seen a race riot before, but she was pretty sure this is how they started, even among persons of the same race. "Ok folks, I don't want to hear anyone using the N-word, and Sean, you shouldn't—"

"Why you cock-blockin'?" Lexus waved her away. Her voice took on an instructional tone. "We was having a conversation."

Oh, God. She just said "cock." Ava stared at the worksheets clutched in her hand. This is how kids court each other? Oh, God. I just said "court."

Lexus turned back to Sean. "So, dumb-ass, you go to Wallenberg High School?"

He nodded. "But I didn't have no credits, so the counselor sent me here."

"I got kicked out for fighting." Lexus gestured with her thumb to a student sitting hear her. "The Chinese kid went there too."

"I'm not Chinese, I'm Korean," the kid mumbled. His nametag read: *Jason.*

"You look Chinese," Francisco observed. He was working a pen-knife into the wood of the table.

Ava stared. "Francisco—"

Jason frowned. "No I don't. That's like saying you look Mexican."

"I'm Salvadorian, *pendejo.* Why you saying I look Mexican?" Francisco puffed out his chest.

Charnikka snickered, glancing over her book. "You do look Mexican."

"And you look like a bi—"

"Ok folks!" Ava called, waving the handouts in the air. "For those of you I haven't met yet, I'm Ms. Llewellyn."

"Cruella?" asked Paris, her face contorted.

"I can't pronounce that," Francisco said. "No hablo Englase."

"Can we call you Tiffany?" asked Sean. His earnest face aimed to please. "I saw a movie with a white girl named Tiffany."

Ava blanched. "I don't think that—"

"We could give you a black girl name," Melvin suggested. "Like LaShawnda or Concretia."

"Concretia!" a student hooted.

Paris chuckled, elbowing her neighbor. "She a heavy girl, but we love her."

The room spinning slightly, Ava put a hand on the back of a chair. In the sweltering morning heat, a trickle of sweat ran down her back. "Wow, good suggestions. Let's just stick with Ms. Llewellyn, though, or Ms. L, okay? I do have an activity for us to get to know each other…."

Sean leaned in toward Jason, probing, "Do ya'll eat a lot of rice?"

Sinking into his oversized sweatshirt, Jason groaned. "Do you eat a lot of fried chicken?"

Sean grinned. "Every chance I get. But my foster mom only makes it on Sundays. What do you like to eat, Ms. L?"

Ava thought about the book she'd read in preparation for teaching at Ida B. Wells, *Courageous Conversations About Race.* Her new school was forty percent African American, thirty percent Latino, twenty-five percent Asian and Pacific Islander. Homeroom's conversation was already well beyond the scope of her little book. Ava placed her get-to-know-your-neighbor worksheets on her desk. "Let's see. I love mac n- cheese…."

Melvin pumped his hand in the air. "Oooh, Oooh—Do ya'll eat *wine* and *cheese?*"

Another kid chuckled. "Yeah, like, what do they call those things?"

Ava waited for someone to answer, but the class was uncharacteristically silent. The students were all looking at her. She glanced around. "What things?"

Sean broke it down with the patience of a mother to a small child. "Cheese and crackers and all that other stuff white people like."

Huh. Were there things that just "white people" liked? "What stuff? You mean snacks?"

The kids shook their heads.

"Nope."

"Nuh-uh. That's not it."

From the other side of the room, Kabernay said, "With baby sandwiches and cheese."

Sandwiches. Wine. Cheese…"Hors d'œuvres?" Ava guessed.

"Hors d'œuvres!" the class cried out. Students slapped the tables, hung on each other, and doubled over.

"Do you like dinner parties too?" Sean gasped, holding his belly.

Ava nodded. He went into spasms again.

"Do you like yoga?" a girl shouted.

"And spandex?" Homeroom was now in an uproar.

"Do you shop at the GAP?" Charnikka smirked, giving Ava's wardrobe a glance. Her own tee shirt coronated her "Princess." Her Jordan tennis shoes looked new.

Ava's face burned.

"And use sunblock?" another kid shouted.

She nodded.

Homeroom roared. "White people *love* sunblock!"

When he was able to breathe, Sean wiped his eyes. "Ms. L, you're funny. How old are you?"

"Dude," another kid said, "you're not supposed to ask old people how old they are. You're like thirty-eight, right, Ms. L?"

"Actually, no—"

Ahhh. Ahhh. Ahh.

The fire alarm went off. Everyone turned to the flashing light on the wall.

Thank God. Ava felt an upsurge of relief. "Well. Looks like a fire drill, folks. Why don't you take your stuff and—"

Like smoke from a burning building, the kids blew past her.

The last student out slammed the door.

Ava picked up her get-to-know-your-neighbor worksheets. Flipping through questions that asked about favorite ice cream flavors and favorite colors, she walked the handouts over to the recycling bin. In Washington, she'd sought out alternative schools for student teaching assignments. She wanted to help teens who felt as lost as she had at their age. Moving to San Francisco, she jumped at the chance to teach at Ida B—But here, now? Despair filtered down.

"It's twenty-eight, actually," she said to the empty room. "Not thirty-eight, twenty-eight." She tossed the worksheets away.

Outside, Cheryl Wilson's homeroom students huddled a circle. While Ava's heart still beat double-time from homeroom introductions, Cheryl stood tall and calm, an island steady in turbulent waters. From Cheryl's complexion, smoky and smooth, to the sure stance of a woman in her 50s, Ava surmised that her colleague hadn't also experienced a near-miss on a race riot in her own homeroom.

Ava's homeroom students had dispersed into the street. She could see the back of Charnikka's head as the girl disappeared down the block. There was no way Ava could get her kids back. She glanced around at the students still on the sidewalk. In case the principal was watching, she pretended they were hers instead, diligently checking unfamiliar faces and making random ticks on her class list.

Most of the students stared back at the schoolhouse. Ava felt that a fire drill on the first day was a bit much, but to her surprise, the second story really did appear to be on fire. "Of course," she whispered.

The final periods she had yet to teach stretched like page 23 of *The Never Ending Story*. She hardly had the strength to persevere. If she was still at her last school, two states away, she'd come home to Dan, tell him about this unbelievable day. She didn't even want to think about returning tonight to her unfamiliar apartment.

But the day wasn't over. Dan wasn't here. Ava needed to find a way to suck it up. She breathed in deeply. It did feel good to get a little air. A little sunshine. A little second hand smoke from the wafts of pot drifting over the crowd. *Smells like college.* Finally, something familiar. All she needed was a drum circle and some protestors.

"Come *on*! Let us go back in*side*!" whined a girl. "I'm so *bored* out here!"

Protestors. Check.

Hoping for a prolonged reprieve from classes, Ava gazed at their three-story brick building. Ida B. Wells Continuation High School sat atop a hill that boasted views of half the city. Across the street were San Francisco's famous row Victorian houses, their Easter-egg hues giving rise to the nickname, the Painted Ladies. Tourists regularly traipsed over the sprawling lawn of Alamo Square Park to take pictures of the Ladies, who stood like elegant gingerbread houses, shoulder-to-shoulder, a storybook foreground to San Francisco's skyscrapers in the distance.

Smoke billowed from the school's second story window. She was touched by the grandeur of a building that granted million-dollar views. It was one of the aspects of the city that most surprised her: Since when did public schools get first dibs on prime real estate? Though most had fallen into some form of disrepair, the city's public school buildings were clearly designed with love. From the Spanish Colonial fortress of Mission High School to the modern hillside acropolis of School of the Arts, they stood as reminders of a time when everyone's kid mattered.

When Ava had asked about the city's strange habit of building schools like mansions while lowballing on maintenance, Cheryl explained that it was the great earthquake of 1906 that had served as the catalyst to rebuild the city's public schools with high quality designs. Ida B. Wells was added in 1910, boasting an unusual cream brick exterior and Roman details. The school at that time was for neighborhood kids living in stately Edwardian railroad flats—double parlors, fainting rooms.

Fainting rooms, Ava thought longingly. Yes. I'll take one, please.

She looked around students spilling off the sidewalk to study the neighborhood. Those Edwardian flats were still standing, but she'd heard they were now likely occupied by roommates who hosted keg parties or had been sold for absurdly high prices as condos to double-income couples, usually without children. Due to families fleeing the city's high rents and crime, San Francisco now claimed more resident dogs than children. The school was a quiet shadow to the photogenic Ladies' mass appeal.

Fire trucks wailed up the street.

"What happened?" she asked Cheryl.

The veteran teacher nodded toward the smoke. "Someone put lighter fluid on walls of the boys' bathroom. It happened last year too."

A student kicked at trash on the sidewalk. "Now it'll smell even nastier in there."

Ava grimaced. She pictured the tiny high school she had taught at in Washington State. The superintendent's office had been located in a trailer across the street. Unsanitary restrooms were never an issue.

Tourists riding by on an open-top, double-decker bus rubbernecked the scene. Painted Ladies forgotten, they snapped pictures of students sporting baggy jeans, tattoos, and gold teeth amid the backdrop of a smoking building.

"There'd better be some 9-11 type shit happening in there," a large kid in a Giants tee shirt growled. He'd already taken out a pack of cigarettes.

"Put those away!" Ava scolded.

The student looked her in the eye as he placed a cigarette between his lips.

Cheryl spoke from behind them. "I'll take those, thank you." She held out her hand.

"What?" The kid spat out his cigarette, shoving the pack in his pocket. "I didn't do nothing."

Cheryl raised an eyebrow. "Son, I could call your PO. I bet he'd be real interested to learn you've been suspended for having cigarettes on school grounds. Don't you have a court date coming up, James?"

James growled, "I ain't your son."

Students waved at the tourists riding by. A few kids threw up gang signs for the cameras that were uncharacteristically focused their way.

Across the street, a boy leaned in close to a tourist, items exchanging hands between them. "Don't think I didn't see that, Mark!" Cheryl yelled.

Firemen emerged from the building. Smoke from the second-story window dwindled to a thread. The principal, Ms. Sanchez, blew a whistle, indicating everyone should come in and launch into what was left of fourth period.

Ava lingered. As students rushed back into the building, she closed her eyes and filled her lungs with the pot-soaked air. If she concentrated, she could almost picture herself at a Tom Petty concert. All she needed were a couple of beach balls bouncing across the crowd and Dan singing "Last Dance with Mary Jane" out of tune.

"Hey!" Cheryl towered above her, grinning. The sunlight hit her dark, short hair like a halo. A package of cigarettes was in her hand. "We're almost done with day one."

CHAPTER 3

SECOND LIFE

Ava walked home from school in the late afternoon heat. As she approached her apartment building, two young boys were bouncing a ball against its concrete wall. One boy was about six or seven, the other a few years older. The building faced a crowded 24th Street. Cars gained speed quickly between lights only to slam on their brakes at the next intersection. Shopkeepers leaned in doorways, encouraging pedestrians to come in and try the empanadas, tamales, chille rellenos. One man stood at the intersection holding a *Bible* above his head. A megaphone blasted his message: "Jesus te ama!"

Men waiting outside the corner store raised their 40s in reverence.

Ava watched the smaller boy's ball bounce into the street, the older kid dodging cars to retrieve it. Her childhood home had been on fifty acres, backed up against forest service land. After the divorce, her mom had moved into a rental house in town. Ava remembered the shock. The yard was a patch of grass roughly twenty feet squared. Where did kids go to play?

"Andale!" the smaller boy shouted, clapping his hands for the ball. He stepped over a limp condom on the sidewalk. The apartment building was tagged with large, block writing, cryptic messages that boasted and threatened in the same broad strokes. Another language Ava didn't yet understand. She watched the boys play next to the busy street. She began to appreciate the value of twenty square feet of grass.

Opening the door to her dark apartment, she stepped into the hallway and listened. Silence. Her roommate, Pedro, wasn't home. Another business trip. The empty apartment was a constant reminder that her city-savvy roommate had a life.

In her room, she set her book bag on the floor, breathing in the silence. One measured molecule at a time, her body released the chaos of the day, time capsules of confrontation and panic. She glanced at the clock, pondering the opportunity to sit in the living room, fade out in front of the television. Or should she call it a night at 4:30 pm?

Ava took the path of least resistance, collapsing onto her bed. Then the tears came. The kids beat her today. She wasn't sure if she was going to make it, and everything was riding on making it.

From the dresser, a smiling portrait of Dan. The loneliness widened to accommodate his absence.

Dan. Ruthie. Her old hippie college town in Olympia. She had picked her college for its unknown factor. The Evergreen State College on Washington's coast promised experiences that were completely new. No sororities, no fraternities to mimic the social pressures of high school. Faculty led seminars instead of lecturing, gave written evaluations instead of grades. Ava knew she was in the right place the moment she sat in her first class. She knew her life was on the right path the day she met Ruthie.

She and Ruthie had taken the same class as undergrads, the Works of Toni Morrison. Ruthie mentioned a bipolar brother.

Ava gasped: You're my people.

Ruthie was dark-haired and decisive. She liked cowboy boots and Tom Petty. The day she and Ava met, she declared they'd be good friends. They went for a ride in Ruthie's bright yellow Beetle. A baby in his mother's arms waved as they drove by. Ruthie shrugged. "I get it all the time. It's because the Beetle looks like a cartoon."

Ava was enchanted. "*Babies* wave at your *car.*"

Four years later, they finished in different graduate programs. Ava received a Masters in Teaching while Ruthie went into science. The day after graduation, they chose a popular hipster bar to celebrate their freedom from academia. Ava's student teaching had been brutal. She had yet to find a job for that fall.

In short shorts and tank tops, they ordered Kamikazes. "To new lives ahead," Ruthie said.

Ava raised her glass high.

Then Dan walked in. Blonde curly hair and blue, blue eyes, he was a confident yang to Ava's anxiety-riddled yin. His pinstriped suit smirked salesman. He sidled up to Ava at the bar. "I'll have what she's having."

She stared. "Really?"

"No." He flagged the bartender. "Whiskey, neat." Ava felt him giving her a long, slow glance. "What are college kids drinking these days?"

Who is this guy? "I'm not a college kid. Just graduated. And you're not that much older."

Dan raised his brows. "Twenty-eight is very, very old in a college town. And Evergreen? You decide your own grades, right? Are you sure it's even a real college? Or did you get a widdle biddie degwee?"

Ruthie bristled, but Ava laughed. She liked his sharp-edged humor. This guy was clever, funny—unless he's being serious. She toasted. "It's a master's *degwee*. Now, is that a real suit, or do you have a widdle biddie job?"

He chuckled and bought her next drink.

Ruthie claimed errands, laundry. She left the rest of her Kamikaze on the bar.

Ava barely noticed. She only saw the deep blue in Dan's eyes. His witty jabs. She worked hard to keep up.

Their mutual dysfunctions clicked like a key opening a lock.

That summer was filled with make-out sessions in corners, his car, a strip tease in his bachelor's apartment, and his suggestion they move in together. Ava sat on his lap in their nearly empty living room, laughing into her glass.

He took it from her when she spilled. "Careful, wino. We can't have you hung over for your interview tomorrow."

"I'll be a model teacher who will try not to beg for the job. And I'm not a wino."

Dan nuzzled her. "You're my little wino."

Ava glowed at the word *my*. She was wanted. She was valued. She was someone's *my*.

Over the next three years, it was Dan who helped her cross the Grand Canyon separating graduate student from actual teacher. After coming home from his job at the brokerage firm, he'd try his hand grading a multiple choice test, help her brainstorm lesson plans, and rub her back when she was face-down at the kitchen table.

He also became her go-to for an outside perspective when the drama of the classroom fogged her clarity.

"They're teenage girls, Ava. You're a grown woman. You're allowed to give them the boot when they get out of line."

"Oh yeah," she mused. "I forget."

At Dan's suggestion, they went sledding at Mt. Rainier, plastic pieces flying off the sled when he took it down a "manly" slope. They made s'mores by the gas fireplace in their new apartment. He took her camping in the Ho rainforest. They listened to the patter of raindrops on the tent, nestled deep into sleeping bags, while reading aloud *The Magnificent Ambersons*, his favorite book.

When summer came, Dan suggested they try white water rafting and signed them up for vegan cooking classes at the local bookstore.

"It's for our health. And it's the right thing to do."

Ava echoed, "The right thing to do."

So they despaired over egg substitutes, learned to stomach tempeh, love spices, and stir-fries. Grocery shopping day became their favorite.

One Sunday morning, walking past a diner, the smell of bacon pulled them in the door.

"For the record, it's you who caved," Dan said over a plate of sausage and eggs.

"We'll blame me," Ava said, contented.

They had been living together almost two years when his company downsized. Dan had always coveted time for video games. Now he spent his days in front of the television playing *Call of Duty*, feverish eyes locked onto the screen. His cyber self was a hero. He kicked ass. Blew shit up. He crowed the day he brought home a new game that allowed him to step into an avatar world of his creation. The game was called *Second Life*. There was nothing *second* about it.

Ava began to have trouble sleeping. The doctor prescribed Ambien. Ava waited a month before finally downing a pill at bedtime. It did the trick, but left her less than alert during daylight hours.

At a friend's dinner party one weekend, she paused to recall an answer in a trivia game.

"She's pretending to think, but she has no idea what that is," Dan told their hosts. "You should see her at home on her computer, acting like she's typing. It's adorable."

Ava knew he was kidding—or was he? She'd taken Ambien the night before and was still groggy, uncertainty hovering under a fog that wouldn't lift. Still, she *did* know the answer. Why was he saying those things?

Then, during Pictionary, "Ava, how is anyone supposed to get a cow from that? Jesus. That's what you get for going to a college where you grade yourself."

She hauled him into the bathroom, whispering through clenched teeth. "I'm not a idiot. Telling our friends I won't know the answers in a trivia game? And Pictionary is not a graduate course. What is it with you tonight?"

"Get a sense of humor," Dan spat.

"It's not funny if no one's laughing."

She might have braved the change in Dan if school hadn't also soured at nearly the same time. That semester, after two years working with mostly sweet-tempered country kids, she encountered an anomaly in an angry girl named Sunny.

Despite CPS's reports to the contrary, most staff believed Sunny lived in an abusive home. Ava just wanted to help. In Sunny, she saw herself at that age, needing someone to step in, someone to be an advocate and not knowing how to ask.

But the student mocked her new teacher, refused to participate, and laughed in her face. Far from helping Sunny, she was hated by the girl. Ava couldn't even help herself. It was as if Sunny shone a light into Ava's most shameful secret: as a human being, she was worthless. She had gone into teaching to help kids like Sunny. By March she was leaving school each day humiliated. It made her wonder if she was meant to teach at all.

Lying in bed alone while Dan seduced sexy avatars in their living room, she felt grateful for her companion, a bottle of Ambien that rolled another day into darkness. As she waited for sleep, the projector in her mind flipped through the coming years of her life, identical slides of her days as they were at this moment. Work? *Meh.* Dan? *Ugh.* Add in some booze, wasn't that how the movie stars did it? She wondered how much it would take for her brain to shut down, organs failing.

But she didn't want to die.

That April, on her Spring Break, her college buddy, Ruthie, suggested Ava visit her in San Francisco. Dan's eyes never left the television screen when Ava told him about the trip. She said *yes.*

By that time, Ruthie had married Bill, her boyfriend from Evergreen, and together they'd made a life in the Bay Area.

Ava stepped off the plane into an alternate reality.

Ruthie and Bill took her to Fort Funston, on a bluff at the water's edge. They all stared as hang gliders took running leaps off the cliff, tucking their bodies into sleeping bags to hover over the crashing surf. Ava wanted to cry: People flew here.

They drove her through Golden Gate Park, Ruthie squeezing her shoulder when the bison came into view. Lumbering and shaggy, the huge animals lounged in a far meadow, defying the world to tell them they were out of place. Ava's mouth hung agape. Buffalo. She may as well have been on the plains in North Dakota. This place wasn't so strange. There was grass, trees, buffalo.

The ethnic array in the city was also an allure: Latino, Asian, African American. All Ava had ever known was white. It was as if she had stepped into Technicolor—cuisines, cultures, sounds, languages, attitudes, philosophies. So many people, so many ways to start over. Still, on her final days visiting Ruthie, the larger truth was that she couldn't go back to her job or her life in Washington. She couldn't go back to praying for sleep, for death. She couldn't go back to Dan. She made plans to move down while still on the shuttle back to San Francisco's airport.

At twenty-eight, she was tired. She needed a spark. So whatever came along, anything that seemed like even a halfway decent idea, she'd say *yes*. It wasn't a real plan, but what else could she do? If she didn't make it happen in this next year, in this new city, she'd know she wasn't going to make it at all. Living with Dan in Washington had been her Plan A. San Francisco would be plan B. Should that fail also, Ambien and alcohol would be plan C.

Now, lying on her bed in the apartment she shared with Pedro, a she felt slight tickle in her throat. Last week, a little Nyquil at bedtime had helped alleviate what might turn into a cold. The green liquid hit like a massage on her brain, soothing, fuzzy. It had brought on a calm that Ava hadn't felt since she was a kid, sitting on the porch. The cats, her one good thing, purring on her lap.

She reviewed the next day's lessons then got into bed. On her dresser next to the Nyquil was a note, a reminder of a dinner party Ruthie was hosting. She prayed to the gods of the socially awkward, Please let me get violently ill before the party. Ava tilted her head back and swigged the amount of Nyquil necessary to take down a mountain lion or perhaps a grizzly bear. Then she closed her eyes. The clock next to Dan's face read 5:30 pm.

CHAPTER 4

GET LOWER AND PUT YOUR SHOULDER INTO IT

On the third day of classes, the rules had all been amended. Through ruthless negotiations, the swearing rule had been further whittled down to *Try Not to Swear*. The kids' favorite words—*bitch*, *hoe*, and *nigga*, had been banned on the grounds that Ava found them offensive, though the class unanimously protested that no reasonable person could get through an entire day without at least using the word *bitch*.

She looked bitterly at the work she had done on her bulletin boards. Their primary colors created a cheery backdrop against tables set up in a U shape, a reminder that she had imagined a class in which everyone clamored to be heard, the beloved teacher stepping in between a heated debate, saying, "One at a time. Everyone will get a chance to discuss *Hamlet* throughout the quarter." Then Ava's class would laugh along with her….

The bell rang. She looked around at a room full of surly, sleepy teenagers. They glared at her through half-closed lids, daring her to ask them to do anything.

"Ok, folks," she said, her voice ringing though the deathly pall, "Today we're going to work on paragraph structure."

Several students groaned.

"Are you serious?" asked Francisco. "I don't do work." He scratched at his beard, more dense than any Ava remembered classmates growing when she was in high school.

"Well, we're here, so we're going to have to do something," she said. "Everyone have paper?"

The students shook their heads.

"Pencils?" Again, negative.

After handing out pencils to half the class, it turned out that the pencil sharpener was broken.

Ava asked Charnikka if she would mind going across the hall to borrow Ms. Wilson's. The girl seemed distracted. Ava thought a task might give her focus.

"Do I get extra credit?" Charnikka asked.

"Extra…?'" She was tired of handouts. "No. You get extra respect."

Paris snorted.

"Fuck that," Francisco said. "Don't do it, Charnikka."

Another day, another mutiny. Ava thought about her mission in teaching: to make students' lives better than hers had been. It was a dream that was so far away. She turned to Francisco. "No F's, remember?"

Charnikka finished perusing her text messages under the table. "I already have respect," she said, but she picked up her purse and left to get the sharpener.

"Let's try this again," Ava said. "Remember that a paragraph needs to start with—" A loud *Bang!* rang out from across the hall. She ignored it. "To let your audience know what the paragraph is about, you start with a—"

"Bitch!" Things were warming up in Ms. Wilson's class. Was that Charnikka's voice? She kept going, "…start with a topic sentence—"

"Fucking hoe!" Shouts and cheers sounded across the hall. Then *Slam!* Exasperated, she glanced outside her room.

Cheryl Wilson, 55-years-old, with bad knees, was in the hallway. She was braced on the outside of her own classroom door, pushing it shut.

Huh. Ava stood there, frozen. Was Cheryl holding her class hostage? Her two years in graduate school hadn't covered this situation—Damn hippie college. She looked at Cheryl, hunkered low, shoulder planted firmly against the door. Cheryl's body shook, on the wrong end of a battering ram. It looked like she could use a hand.

Turning back to her students, Ava saw they had been following her changing expressions like an audience at a silent film. "Stay. Here," she pleaded. "Pleeeeease don't hurt each other."

Across the hall, she put both hands against Cheryl's door. *Bam! Bam!* Someone lunged from the other side. She looked to her colleague.

"Ugh," Cheryl grunted. Her dark skin had a crimson undertone, sweat beading at her hairline. "Charnikka came in to borrow my pencil sharpener, saw Tasonya, and punched her."

Ava stopped breathing. She pictured her name as it would read in the police blotter.

"Tasonya hit back. I separated them and got Charnikka out, but Tasonya's still in there, mad."

Bam! Bam!

No shit. The door gave a little as Tasonya got her second wind.

Charnikka lurked at the far end of the hallway. The girl was on her cell phone. Given her sizable stature, Ava didn't want to see what reinforcements looked like when they arrived. "Where's security?"

Cheryl blinked sweat out of her eyes. "I don't know: Fifty must be patrolling a different floor. That man better show up soon or I'ma have a heart attack."

Ava's students, sensing blood, waited exactly zero seconds after she'd asked them to stay put. Like hyenas circling a dying carcass, they gathered around the teachers, overjoyed to watch the aging and the weak engaged in battle. A few kids took pictures with their phones.

She called out to the first student in her line of vision. "Francisco, run to the office. We need security up here."

Francisco tried to get both Cheryl and Ava in his camera's frame. "What's in it for me? You giving extra credit?"

Paris snorted. "Yeah, snitch credit."

Melvin said, "You need to get down lower to push, Ms. L. You aren't helping Ms. Wilson very much."

It was then that the security guard ambled up the stairs. The guard's gray, bushy hair stood up like Don King's. The kids called him Fifty, as in 5-0 for the police. It was not uncommon to hear students arguing in the hall with Fifty, and Fifty yelling right back: "Fuck me? Fuck *you*. You got four seconds to get yo triflin' ass back into class before we *both* sorry I got up this morning." Then a lower growl, "Bunch of *Bebe's Kids*...."

And still, Ava watched as the students followed Fifty's stiff, cranky figure around campus, provoking him so he'd make them behave, wanting him to tell them again he believed they could do better.

Unfortunately for Cheryl and Ava, holding a door shut in the hallway, feeling the slam of the girl on the other side, this was not Fifty's first rodeo. Years of experience had allowed him to master the art of wait-and-see. So instead of giving relief, he took his place among the kids, surveying the situation. "What's going on, ladies?"

Ava didn't appreciate the way he was smiling.

Fifty pulled out his phone, getting both women in his camera's frame before taking a picture. He noted, "You should try getting lower, Ms. Llewellyn. You're using your arms when it should be your whole weight against the door. See how Ms. Wilson's got her shoulder into it?"

"I need you to grab Tasonya when we open the door," Cheryl said. A large drop of sweat rolled down her temple.

"I'm your man," Fifty came to stand in position.

"Oooh," Melvin sang, "Fifty's warm for your form, Ms. Wilson."

Cheryl winked at him. "Story of my life." She turned to Ava. "Ready? On three: One, two…three!"

The women let go of the door. Tasonya burst out in a blur of nails and hair.

Fifty grabbed her around the waist.

"Bitch!" Tasonya screamed at Charnikka.

"Get her, Charnikka!" yelled Paris. "You show that bitch she can't beat up your sister at work!"

Tasonya clawed the air.

Fifty tightened his grip.

Paris faced Melvin. "Tasonya went into Radio Shack last night because Charnikka's sister was working there. Bitch put a lock in a sock." She turned back to Tasonya. "Hoe. You just try to come at *my* family." At roughly eighty pounds, Paris didn't look like she should be stirring up mess with anyone.

Tasonya thrashed against Fifty, who hustled her toward the opposite staircase.

Charnikka eyed the crowd, then raised her middle finger and walked calmly down the stairs to the school's main entrance. Ava figured the girl didn't want to get caught up in a suspension meeting: she had to pick up her daughter from daycare.

Cheryl wiped her forehead. "I'm getting too old for this."

Ava herded her kids back into the classroom. Ten minutes remained in the period. "Okay," she said, catching her breath. What the hell just happened? "Let's try to get something done today—"

"Ooooh," Paris said, "did you see the way Tasonya was going after Char-Char? I bet she would've clawed that bitch's eyes out." Paris sank into her chair, relishing the memory.

"No B's," Ava said. "Alright, let's all find a seat—"

"Did Tasonya's sister really beat the shit out of her in Radio Shack?" Melvin asked. He sat on top of a table, his backpack on, ready to leave.

"Bitch had a lock in a sock!" Paris proclaimed again, clearly pleased with crime's unintentional rhyme.

Ava was horrified. In a store? And she went to school today like nothing happened? "That's terrible! But now we really do need to get back to—"

Paris was on a roll. "I would've used a chain, though, 'cause you can choke 'em with it, too!"

K'Ron shook her head. "Too messy. Brass knuckles is better, but you need to put that shit over some gloves or you're gonna mess up your hands. They can catch you if you bruise up your knuckles." She looked ruefully at her own knuckles, which showed fading greenish-yellow bruises.

Ava stared. Brass Knuckles? Chains?

"You girls take shit too far," Melvin said. "Guys don't do that shit. We take it outside, right, Francisco?"

Francisco glanced at Melvin's slight frame and pink cheeks. "When you ever get in a fight?"

Melvin shook his head. "I can't fight, but I seen lots of fights, and I never seen a guy beat up another guy in a store."

Francisco nodded. "That is pretty stupid." He put his backpack on and stood up.

Ava looked around at her classroom; she had spent most of the period holding a door closed, and now the kids were milling about, swapping suggestions for public beatings. "Okay, everyone, I think that we should at least write a sentence today. So everyone needs to sit back down…"

"Oh, hell no," Francisco said. "We only have two minutes left. I ain't writing shit."

"That bitch is crazy," Paris muttered. She put her phone into her backpack and stood up.

Uh-oh. Ava felt control of the room slipping past her, a strong undercurrent going out to sea. Sitting down to write one sentence was a pretty stupid idea, but it was out of her mouth now. Fuck. What to do? She pulled out a trick she had successfully used at her previous school. Drawing herself up to full height, she said, "If you can't quiet down and get that one thing done, I'm going to look at my watch, and that is the number of seconds you will need to stay after the bell rings." She tapped her watch in case anyone doubted her seriousness.

"You can't make me stay here," Francisco scoffed.

She blanched; he was right. "I am the teacher." It was more of a question.

Paris slammed her hand on the table. "I'm not staying after the bell rings. You can't make me do that."

"I get to leave when the bell rings." Kabernay stared wistfully at the door.

Sean put on his backpack. "Ms. L, that's not a good rule," he mumbled.

The kids and Ava glared at one another, both sides fuming at the injustice of the situation.

Then the bell rang.

She stood in the doorway as students slipped past, greyhounds loosed from the gates. The last student out slammed the door. She winced. "Strike one."

CHAPTER 5
SILENT READING WITH DR. ZEUS

Strutting into class at the end of the second week, Ken was adored before he even said hello. A tall, thin student, he had a high, spiked Mohawk, purple skinny jeans, and a silver sparkle tote. In the days to come, Ken would demonstrate his love of personalized belt buckles, like one that read: "Princess" and another that deemed him *Head Bitch in Charge*, Charnikka's favorite.

That first day, Ken looked Ava up and down. "I like your style, but all you teachers need to take some time for yourselves. Take yourselves out for a little manicure sometime."

"Honey," she said, "you don't know the half of it."

Ava waited to see how students would receive Ken's sparkle bag and over-the-top demeanor. She knew that several kids were from devout Christian families. She feared they might preach a line from the *Bible*, or that boys might be so homophobic she'd have an issue with bullying. But the answer was—the kids did nothing. Francisco moved over so Ken had a place to sit. Paris noted his belt buckle matched hers that day: "Suck It."

"Nice purse," Paris said as Ken took a seat next to her.

Ken glowed, his cheeks blushing a charming pink. "I know." Then he heaved a big, devastated sigh, the kind you might exhale when you hear of yet another natural disaster in a country already hit by earthquakes and drought. "They didn't have one in purple."

Paris nodded, small face solemn. "That would've been even better."

"Ok, folks, let's get started," Ava said.

The students groaned. She thought about what she was supposed to be doing in the first few minutes of class—giving kids an overview of the day's lesson objectives. She had tried that the first few days, only to be met with increasingly louder complaints each time she told students one more activity on the agenda.

"I don't *care*!" Paris finally shouted after Ava had detailed last Thursday's lesson.

Charnikka, the class's ad hoc union representative, seconded, "All we do in here is work. I hate this class."

Ouch. Charnikka had brought her big-girl guns.

Taking the hint, Ava now wrote the day's lesson on the board for the three kids who bothered reading it. The rest of the students experienced their English test prep hour as a series of crimes against humanity, each assignment a compounded injustice, viewed as vendettas against individual students.

"It's because you hate Latinos, isn't it?" Francisco challenged after Ava asked the class to write a poem.

"But I hate reading," Paris protested daily. "Why you hatin' on black people?"

Still, many students were lacking in even basic skills, like composing a sentence or changing the word *im* they used in texting into a more appropriate *I'm*. Ava tried pointing out that even God used the full term *I am* in the *Bible*, but Melvin complained. "I'm not tryina do that much work, Ms. L."

The rest of the students revealed their own unique learning gaps. Paris had been assigned to Ida B. Wells because her love of a good fight kept her in a revolving loop of suspensions. The girl could put sentences together, but deciding where to create paragraphs made her edgy. "I'll do it my own way!" she yelled when Ava suggested that her paragraph on braiding hair not also include information on hot link sausages.

Kabernay was similarly lost. Her grandma excused her as sick several times a week. When the girl did show up, she motivated to the pace of pre-industrial age glacial melt, eyes half-closed throughout the period. On a particularly productive day, Kabernay proudly turned in a full page of writing. Unfortunately, there were no periods to break up the longest run-on sentence Ava had ever seen. She requested that Kabernay's grandma allow the girl to be tested for a learning disability. Grandma stopped taking her calls.

Overall, the students' lack of grade-level skills made them poster children for the achievement gap between minority kids and their white, often wealthier peers. This gap compounded every year with summer break. Middle and upper class kids read from book lists and traveled to new places over their summer days; Ava's students hung out with friends and watched TV. This was the primary reason she chose to take Fridays for silent reading. Nothing improved reading and writing skills like silently reading for pleasure.

"So..." she said, handing out paper, "the assignment today is to write five sentences about a favorite book that you've read." She thought about the skills involved, then added, "Like we talked about yesterday, five sentences means I should see five periods. Please count them up before you hand in your paper."

Ken took out his own purple Hello Kitty notebook paper and three light-up pens in various colors. The other students were impressed.

Paris waved away the notebook paper Ava offered, preferring a piece of Ken's special paper.

"Ken, we missed you these past two weeks," Ava said. "What happened? You look so ready to start school."

Ken sighed. "I broke up with my boyfriend. It was awful. I was soooo devastated. I just can't come to school devastated, you know?"

She felt a pinch in her chest, picturing Dan's face on her dresser. "I can relate. We're glad you made it in today."

"I know." Ken arranged his assortment of pens on the table.

"I don't have a favorite book," Francisco said loudly. The tattoo on his arm proudly declared, "ima killa."

I'm a killa, Ava begged in her head. *I'M* a killa.

"Me either," said K'Ron.

Ava tried to relate to the idea of not being a reader, but couldn't. She remembered how much she had loved reading when she was a kid, tucked away deep in the woods of rural Washington State. Evenings, her dad read aloud to her and her siblings, regaling the adventures of a horse named Smokey and the cowboy who adored him.

"I have a favorite movie," offered Tanya. This was her first day in class too. Her little sister had been sick with whooping cough. Tanya stayed home to baby-sit.

"Well, how about everyone describing a book they just liked instead? It doesn't have to be a favorite," Ava said.

Blank stares all around.

"I. Don't. Like. Books," Francisco broke it down, as though his teacher was having early dementia coupled with hearing loss.

"My sister read that book by Zane," said K'Ron. "It's about a stripper who—"

"I read a book by Dr. Zeus," interrupted Sean, his round face earnest with the memory. "There was a cat, and he played with these kids—"

Charnikka snorted. "Someone read that to you, fool." She pulled a Zane book out of her backpack: *Missionary No More: Purple*

Panties 2. The jacket cover featured a girl in violet underwear straddling her naked partner's lap.

Ava grasped for alternate solutions. Nothing. She wanted the kids to reflect on books they'd enjoyed in the past, but now she saw that horse was long dead. She gave its lifeless body one last whack. "How about five sentences on a book that you remember reading?" she said. "Any book."

The kids were quiet.

"Any book at all."

The students stared back, waiting.

Ken sighed. "Ms. L, why do we have to do work in here?"

The General raised his hand. His voice was almost a whisper. "I never read a book all the way through." Under his hoodie, he looked up at Ava.

Other kids nodded.

"I thaw a movie about a book," offered Hector, new as well. A small kid, he had a ponytail and a lisp. "It wath about a thpider."

The idea that students would ever make it to 11th or even 12th grade without reading a whole book had never occurred to Ava. When she was in elementary school, books had saved her. When her dad began spending his evenings inexplicably sobbing in the armchair, her mom, soothing him, Ava had stayed in her room. She lost herself solving murder mysteries, boarding Agatha Christie's *Orient Express* to lands far, far away. No one said the word *bipolar* then. That was before they knew. Emotional outbursts were clues left in broad daylight, but mental illness was an unacceptable suspect. Her family blamed themselves.

She tried one more tactic. "Ok, anybody remember a book that someone else read to them? Maybe in elementary school or when you were little?"

"Like how little?" asked Melvin.

"Like hopscotch little," Paris said. She pressed "send" on her phone, openly defying Amended Rule #3: Don't Text in Class *When Your Teacher Can See.*

Sean raised his hand. "My teacher read us a book in 4th grade. It was about a dog."

Kabernay looked up. She spent so much time staring into space that most classroom conversations slipped right past her. "Yeah, I remember—I was in your class." She smiled. "Ms. Anderson read it to us."

Sean nodded. "And we got to put our heads on our desks."

"I liked that book," Kabernay said, "but I didn't get to hear the ending."

"Oooh," Ava said, "maybe you could find it and—"

"The dog died," said Sean.

"Oh," said Kabernay. She resumed her catatonic expression.

A few students balled up their blank pieces of paper.

"Why don't we just write about movies?" Tanya tried again.

"I appreciate that idea," Ava said, "and movies have good stories too, but books are important to becoming better readers and writers." Following her students' lead, she gave up on the five sentences. "Why don't I show you some books I bought just for silent reading time?"

Ava didn't tell them that Cheryl Wilson had sent her to an ethnic bookstore. It was the store clerk, a woman with two teenagers of her own, who selected the urban fiction novels, books whose covers included blood, money, and gang references. The woman told Ava that teenagers would love the books no matter what their reading ability because the content was so compelling. "Urban fiction is like a gateway drug—get a non-reader hooked, they'll come back to read other kinds of books in the future," the mom said.

"*True to the Game* has everything you could possibly want in a book," Ava began. "It's got drugs, romance, violence, and a lot of stuff you probably shouldn't show your folks."

Paris held out her hand.

The next book up was entitled *The First Part Last*, a teenage boy taking care of his newborn daughter. The General raised his hand.

In her mind, Ava lay prostrate to the gods of desperation, the moms who knew back-alley deals to win kids' souls. Thank you.

The same scene played out for a book about a student pregnant by her dad, a mom who abused only one of her children, and a boy growing up Puerto Rican in Spanish Harlem. Ava assumed the role of elated auctioneer. The kids kept raising their hands.

When she got to the book, *Always Running*, Francisco said, "I already read it in Juvie," but held out his hand for it anyway. "Can I keep this?"

That's the reaction she was looking for. For Ava, a book was a portal, a glimpse of a better life–or at least a different one. Read enough, and one might just find the breadcrumbs leading out of despair.

She thought back to the years after her parents' divorce. For a while, friends and neighbors visited. They offered her dad empathy, companionship. But the stream of support dwindled to a trickle as her dad's symptoms swung between devastating depression, then volatile, scathing mania. No one, least of all his three kids, wanted to be around him. One neighbor hung in there as long as he could. And then there were none. Reading became synonymous with hiding, and her dad needed an audience. "I know you hate me," he snarled. Ava would have given anything for a quiet room and a book.

Ken picked up *The Breakup Bible.* "I don't know if I can stand to relive the pain," he said, staring at the cover. Then he straightened. "It's best to deal with bitches head-on, Ms. L. Never let them know they hurt you. I'll let you read it when I'm done."

Ava nodded. "Thanks, Ken. But let's try to keep the B's out of our vocabulary, okay?"

Ken sighed. "I'll keep them out of my vocabulary if those bitches stay out of my life."

After school on that first silent reading day, Ava discovered that three of the reading books were missing. The next Friday, two more. Noting the titles of the stolen books, she considered that her students might not become titans of the literary world while in Test Prep English. Her bank account shrinking fifteen dollars a book, they might have to make due with the goal of literary little people. Surely, even from his throne high on Mount Olympus, Dr. Zeus would say that was a good place to start.

CHAPTER 6

MY HEROES HAVE ALWAYS BEEN COWBOYS

Ava stared at the date on the email. August 31ˢᵗ—was it still only August? She scanned the message one more time. He was offering her the table. Alan, her older brother, the one who owned a home with a garage for storage, was downsizing. Somehow, thirty didn't seem old enough for downsizing. At twenty-eight, with rent prices crazy in the Bay Area, Ava had no illusions of ever upsizing. Still, she loved that he had asked: *Do you want the old table?* He also was letting go of Dad's belt buckle—something about that made her sad. He doesn't want it anymore. Ava stared at the photo of the silver buckle with its bronze bull rider. Another picture on her screen revealed the pitted oak in their family's dining room table, the faded grain. She saw them all as they had once been.

Dinner time. She was seven. Dad was in his cowboy boots, his bull rider's belt buckle straining under the overhang of belly. Though his rodeo days were long behind him, a love of western shirts and horses remained. That evening, Dad declared it time the family learned table manners.

They lived forty miles from the nearest restaurant, two miles from the nearest neighbor. They'd had to ski home that evening when the truck couldn't make it in the deep snow down the mile-long driveway. Now it was late. Ava was tired. But manners were on the menu. In the twilight of November, a coyote howled among the drifts.

Manners to Livvie, four; Ava, seven; and Alan, nine, meant putting napkins on laps and keeping elbows off the table.

"We should eat with two forks," Dad said, "All fancy dinners have two forks."

Mom smiled. "It's a casserole. I didn't have anything for a salad. Also, we only have one set, one size forks. What would the other fork be for?"

"The tater tots," nine-year-old Alan suggested.

So they ate the ground beef, the cheesy bits, the green beans with the green bean fork. The other was reserved for the tater tots.

"That's your green bean fork, Ginny," Dad said. "You're using it on the 'tots."

"Save your comments for the kids, J.W.," Mom said.

Dad farted.

Alan, Ava, and Livvie screamed in delight.

"That's what you don't do at the table," Dad said. "But if you hold it in, you'll get stomach cancer."

Alan belched his name, "AAALLLLAANNNN."

Mom laughed. "Jesus Christ! J.W., you know you set the example for them."

"Stomach cancer," Alan said, cracking up his sisters.

When Ava was young, the land her family lived on made her feel rich. A meadow splayed out before the house, miles of woods beyond that. There was no phone, no heat unless someone fired up the wood furnace. The power went out regularly. They bucked hay bales for a neighbor in the summer time. In the fall, they chopped firewood as a family. Season after season, Mom and Dad slowly built the house above them: log, by calking, by two-by-four, by plywood, by drywall. Ava fell asleep reading the lettering on the insulation above her bed.

At night, tired and dirty, Dad took off his boots, "Rub my feet for a quarter?"

Alan, Ava, and Livvie held his leathery pads like queasy beauticians. They avoided touching his thick toenails as if forty-two was contagious.

The change in Dad didn't come suddenly. No one could say that. He had always been moody. He'd shouted at Mom before, shouted at them. They walked on tiptoe until he was himself again.

But somewhere around Ava's ninth birthday, the parts of him that made him interesting, funny—Dad—those parts all drained away. His feet thumped heavy on their cedar floors. He sat in his armchair in the living room, sobbing. He snarled at Mom. She murmured soothing words while the kids played outside.

It was the marriage counselor who said *bipolar*.

Dad said, "Bullshit," and started drinking an extra beer or three in the evenings.

He and Mom fought behind their bedroom door.

"Don't yell at the kids like that, J.W.," Mom said. "Save it for me."

And he did. "You hate me." he raged. "You want me dead."

Ava looked up *bipolar* at her school's library. The book said a person might choose a member of the family on whom to focus their anger. Ava nodded: *Mom*.

Dad had been sick more than a year the spring that Ava turned ten. It was a year of crying, threats, and Mom hanging on. But that morning was different. Dawn broke into a bright June sunrise. The sun hit the meadow like a spotlight, dew glistening off showy dandelions and purple lupine in the grass. A breeze carried the faint sound of mewling from the barn. The family cat, Vester, padded over to the stacks of hay. Avoiding the wild-eyed gelding pawing the ground with his hoof, Ava felt in the rough cracks between bales, her hands touching soft fur, pin pricks for claws. One by one, she pulled them out, marveling. Cradling the kittens to her chest, she cried.

That September, Ava was in her room when her dad knocked. "It's a surprise party," Dad said.

Ava eyed him. He was manic. She was pretty sure Mom wasn't in the mood for any surprises, even for her fortieth birthday. They were all supposed to go out to dinner tonight. Mom and Dad had been fighting about money, the likelihood of Dad losing his job, his waves of depression, and that awful, angry mania.

When Dad surprised Mom at four o'clock that afternoon with a blue sequined dress, she looked dismayed. When he suggested she wear it for the party he was throwing for her in an hour, she looked ill.

That night, he set the table with both forks. Dad had invited their work friends and his friends from the community theater. He took center stage in their living room, cracking jokes and telling stories. Their guests laughed too loud, smiled too hard. They squeezed Mom's shoulder as she sat quietly on the couch. Dinner would very, very late. Her other gift, two willow trees, stood in buckets by the pond. Dad peered into the darkness, pointing. "See? Over there."

Hungry guests nodded, glancing at one another. Even they could see it wouldn't be enough.

There were in-between times throughout the next year when Dad came around again, like the evening he dressed in a fur trapper costume and took Ava and her siblings snow shoeing in the meadow. Another time, he put a chef's hat on Livvie, and together they made hamburgers the way the French did—with an accent. Ava and Alan were relegated to sous chefs, placing frozen French fries onto a baking sheet.

Unfortunately, the happy times never lasted long. The day after the French hamburgers, he was back to yelling at Mom. He called her a *bitch* in the car. Ava began to wonder if Mom was a part of what was making him sick.

The following spring, Mom's father died. By that time, Dad wasn't moving from his chair. He had taken leave from his job, but he hadn't liked Grandfather. Mom flew to Minnesota for the funeral by herself.

When she returned, the world for eleven-year-old Ava, her older brother, their younger sister, divided in two.

"Family meeting," Mom said. Only they didn't have family meetings.

Ava walked up the wooden steps, the steps hammered in place by her once energetic Dad, dreading any news from Mom's grim mouth.

"Your dad and I are getting a divorce," Mom said.

No, thought Ava.

"No," said Alan.

Livvie began to cry.

Mom would be moving to town, forty miles away. The kids would live with her during the week, go to new schools.

"You'll stay with your dad on the weekends," Mom said. "I won't take you away from him." From the way she looked at Dad, it was clear these terms had already been fought over before.

Ava felt sick. She didn't know how to be with Dad alone. She didn't want Mom to go. But she couldn't leave Dad. What would he do without them?

"This is not my decision. This is not what I want," Dad said.

"Why don't you kids go outside," Mom said. "Play. Your dad and I need to talk."

So Alan, Ava, and Livvie threw a ball around. Their silent faces projected a future too awful to talk about. But Ava knew it couldn't go on like it had been either.

That summer, Dad picked up Ava and her siblings from Mom's new, tiny house. He made small talk with Mom at the door.

Two blocks away, he peeled out from a stop sign. "Goddamn her." He sobbed behind the wheel while Alan and Ava kept a nervous eye on the road, dreading the long weekend ahead.

"I miss making love to her. I miss her smell," he said.

Alan and Livvie shifted uncomfortably. Ava held her breath, waiting for the dad she used to love to show up and save them.

Forty miles away, Mom stopped making dinners altogether. She worked two jobs and was rarely home. She developed hives all over her body that lasted a whole year.

October. Dad pulled out of Mom's driveway. "She's bleeding me dry." He jabbed his finger at Alan. "She wants me to starve. Your mother is trying to take you away from me. Will you let her do that?" Ava understood there was only one answer.

"No," said Alan.

Dad nodded. "She's trying to take my home. Will you allow that?"

"No," said Ava. What she didn't say was that he was sick; Mom was well. Maybe if Mom gave in, he would finally get better.

At her mom's tiny rental in town, Ava argued, "Why can't you just *give* him the house?"

Mom stared. "It's about what's fair. I have to survive too."

Ava had no idea what she was talking about.

November. Depression cycled quickly into mania and then back again. Waves of moods became choppy, dangerous seas. The highs, meaner. The lows, sadder. Livvie, once the family chatterbox, fell silent in the car. Dad hid all the family photo albums. He declared their family 'dead.'

Sitting the kids down at the old kitchen table, he raged. "I'll burn down the house."

They watched, silent.

"I hate your mother more than I love you."

They sobbed.

"I'll kill her." Beneath his curled lip lurked a grin.

Ava sat on the porch that evening, wrapped in blankets, the cats in her lap. The mountain air didn't feel magical anymore. The cats looked up at her with glowing eyes. She buried her fingers in their thick fur as the coyotes howled across the meadow.

In town, Mom's two jobs didn't pay enough. They went on food stamps. Ava didn't say anything about Dad's rages or his depression. If Mom knew, she'd take them away. Then Dad would hurt himself. He might even make good on his threat to kill Mom. And if anything happened to her, Ava's life was over.

When he sped away Sunday evening, Mom asked, "How was it?"

"Fine," said Alan.

"Fine," said Ava.

Livvie whispered, "Fine."

The year Ava turned 15, Alan went away to college. Ava felt relieved. Her brother was a baseball star, the serious guy amid all his jokey friends. She wanted him to be to be jokey too. She wanted him to smile.

One year later, she developed stomachaches, backaches. She started leaving school early. Often, the illness fell on Fridays, her head cloudy with thoughts about the weekend. She had always been an

A student—Now her grades were beginning to slip. She considered dropping out altogether.

Then, just a few weeks into the school year, a solution. A friend needed an escape as well. A new program in another town would allow them to complete their high school requirements at the community college for free. It was Ava's last hope. She recognized it and said *thank you.*

One week later, she moved with her friend to a much larger town an hour away. They lived in seventy-nine year-old Mrs. Bettleman's basement for a pittance in rent. Ava returned to stay at Dad's only every other weekend.

She left thirteen-year-old Livvie behind to fend for herself.

Every day, Ava and her girlfriend took the bus to the community college. She didn't mind being away from home. She didn't mind taking classes with older students. It was freedom. While listening to the professor's lectures, however, she often thought of Livvie. She pictured Dad's mood the previous weekend, whether he had been up or down, and imagined Livvie facing him alone.

Six months later, Ava got a job at a retail store on weekends. She rarely went back home at all. She pretended Dad was better when he was with her little sister. She pretended they went to the movies, spent quiet weekends at the house. She pretended one day she wouldn't hate herself quite so much.

When she returned to receive her high school diploma the following May, everything had changed.

Firstly, Dad was dead.

But Ava could only think about the reality, the finality of that, for exactly four seconds…Three…Two…One.

Livvie was a junior now. She was tall, beautiful, and close-lipped. If anything was happening with Livvie, Livvie was the last person to speak of it.

Another change in their small town was that the school district had just started an alternative high school. It was a school for students who were failing out, barely hanging on at home and in life. It was for kids who needed smaller class sizes, more personal interactions, more counseling. It's for kids like…me, Ava thought. She decided that she would become a teacher and work in alternative high schools. Be the option that she didn't have when she'd needed one herself.

Now, nine years later, in her apartment in San Francisco, Ava stared at her older brother's email. Did she want the table, the belt buckle? Our family's table. Dad's bull-riding belt buckle. Once, Ava had wanted what they had meant: laughing together, the closeness of family, her dad the cowboy. She didn't want what they stood for now.

CHAPTER 7

BRINGING A PONY TO THE PARTY

Friday at last. Ava poured a glass of wine before changing into her favorite skirt. Ruthie's dinner party would be in the Marina district of the city. Women there had earned the phrase "tits on sticks," status synonymous with size 00. Lyle Lovett sang from her computer, *See that boy with that guitar, he's got skinny legs like I always wanted.*

She frowned, tugging at her homemade skirt. *A girlfriend in his car 'cause he's got skinny legs like I always wanted.* Tits on sticks. City girls. She wasn't going to look like them. She wasn't going to feel like them.

She thought back to the writing prompt she'd given the class the day before. She'd asked her students to write a story their bodies would tell. Some students wrote about tattoos, car crashes, falling out of windows. Paris mentioned a drive by, the bullet grazing her shoulder. "See here?" the girl pulled aside the collar of her shirt to reveal a small scar. The class was silent, reverent.

Melvin told a story about running into a field post during football practice. "I was sprinting, and then, oh my God!" he pantomimed hitting the post and falling backward. The kids laughed. Even the serious General chuckled under his hoodie.

Ava told the story of that day in July when she was eleven, just after the divorce. There had been a brush pile in Dad's meadow. It was sometime after he had hidden the family photo albums. The brush pile, like hiding the albums, didn't make sense. Looking back, Ava tried to give it some reason, like he was purging the memory of the life he had before his illness. A huge pile of branches, dead grass, twigs, gathered from all over the meadow. He poured the whole can of gasoline on top of it.

"Then he gave one match to me and one to my brother," she told the class. "My brother lit his match, but it blew out in the breeze, so I went down wind to light mine. I struck the match and held it out. The flame hit the fumes. Then I was on fire."

She pantomimed stop, drop, and roll for the kids. They squealed with laughter. She told the students how Dad said she had to clean up before he'd take her to the emergency room, how her hair had come out in fistfuls in the bathroom. How the shower had torn open the blisters on her face, neck, and arms.

Paris said knowingly, "Sounds like he was trying to kill you."

Ava paused. For a second, she could smell the acrid scent of burnt hair. The unrecognizable girl in the bathroom mirror. Waves of pain. Sounds like he was trying to kill you. Then the safety valve inside her memory kicked on. The experience went fuzzy. Feelings dissipated, crawling back into cellular storage.

She told the kids about starting a new junior high school that September. Her hair hadn't grown back in. Neither had her eyebrows. The skin on her face was two-toned, as were her arms. The ER nurse said her face would scab over. Scars would be inevitable. Ava thought about how much worse it would have been if she hadn't decided to cut open an aloe plant in her dad's home, repeatedly smearing the thick gel on her skin.

K'Ron said, "I heard about that aloe shit."

A friend's father came by the house, not knowing about the fire. "Halloween come early?" he asked, mistaking her face for a mask.

Ken inhaled sharply. "That's just wrong."

Now, looking into the mirror, Ava knew the burns had left no trace on her skin. Still, she felt like the message from those years was still written on her face: Something is horribly, horribly wrong. She gave her skirt a final tug. Not a good party pep talk. This is a new start. Ruthie wants you to meet Shaun tonight. You have to try.

Stepping into her Toyota, she sang, "Sister look at me again, would you love me if I was skinny as him." She backed her truck out, inching to avoid cars and people, praying the parking gods would show her a little mercy tonight. "I'm a nice girl," she said. "Please don't make me circle 'cause I got a wide load."

The foggy skies gave way to a clear September night. The crowded Mission district sidewalks with drivers on all sides honking frustration opened into the Marina's spacious avenues. Trees. Greenery. The claustrophobia eased. Ava breathed a sigh.

She drove past mini mansions, their precisely manicured shrubs formed boundary lines, outlined rich landscaping, birds of paradise. Chandeliers sparkled luminescent light into the street. Roman columns framed floor-to-ceiling windows, stage-lit grand pianos, and made pedestrians feel like they were window shopping better lives. The message from the security signs, clear: Step back from my shit, you uncultured mother fuckers.

Ava played Realtor. Was this home worth two million? That building, five? Ruthie said that Proposition 13 kept property taxes scandalously low, explaining the effects this way: "Social services? Fuck 'em. Education? Fuck 'em. Mental health programs?"

Ava got the point.

Knocking on the apartment door, she hoped Friday Shabbat hadn't started yet.

The door opened. Ruthie, in a striped maternity dress, hugged her tight. "Oh, it's so good to see you!"

Ruthie led Ava into a muted foyer that held a rack of slippers for guests who had to part with their shoes. Ruthie's husband, Bill, took Ava's coat.

He cut as rotund a figure as Ruthie in his Giant's tee shirt. Bill listened with his whole body—Ava had liked him instantly. It didn't surprise her when he and Dan had kept up a friendship even after Bill and Ruthie had moved to San Francisco and Ava and Dan were over. Bill's robust figure, combined with a hairline that receded by the day, provided Dan with what seemed like limitless jokes, but even Dan couldn't find fault with Bill's character. Bill couldn't seem to find fault with anyone. Even Dan.

Ruthie tilted her head toward the kitchen. "Laura and Thomas are already here. Oh, and Bill's friend, Shaun, the one we told you about. We're just six for dinner. You look lovely. How was school?"

Ava groaned. "I moved here to save some kids, but it's looking like I'll need someone save me."

Bill gave her shoulder a squeeze. "Drink?"

She smiled. A drink was always in order when meeting new people. "You're my favorite, Bill."

She thought back to her last year with Dan, his lunge toward sobriety while she clung to booze as the way and the light. On a particularly unfortunate evening, she left a bar mid-swing to pick up Dan from his AA meeting. She'd begged him to let her go back on the way home: her Karaoke song would be coming up. The fight that ensued was not her finest hour. She distinctly remembered preaching the AA mantra of "Let go and let God" in a tone that was less than spiritual.

Tonight, as she walked into the light of Ruthie's yellow kitchen, a man Ava hadn't met before raised a martini glass, a red cherry floating in a pink sea of booze. This must be Bill's friend, Shaun. He had a chiseled chin and eyes that crinkled as if sharing an inside joke. He also was wearing a shiny blue shirt with flames on the collar. "I like to call this Women's Lib," he said, handing her the pink concoction.

She took the drink. It was a panty-dropper. Strong booze mixed with sugar. Any college girl knew it on sight. More than three and you might spend the next morning searching for your bra in an unfamiliar apartment, head pounding to a remorseful beat. He's friendly. Give him a chance. "I'll drink to that." She clinked her glass to his. "Ava."

"Shaun." His grin was impish. "What you have in your hand is the Susan B. Anthony. Let me know when you're ready to move on to the *Feminine Mystique*."

She smiled. "No Gloria Steinem? Oprah?"

Shaun held up a hand. "Easy, tiger. You're still four drinks away from an Oprah."

Ava disengaged and looked around, taking in the few remaining dinner guests—a couple she had met at the last party. They were confident, easily friendly. A sales executive and a stockbroker. Laura, movie star blonde, seemed to get thinner on the way up, toned calves leading to the thighs of a teenager. The diamonds on her fingers caught the light when she waved hello. Laura's husband, Thomas, wore a suit, lavender scarf draped just so. His fingernails were buffed to an exquisite shine.

Laura gave her a hug, gesturing toward Shaun. "Don't mind him."

"Poor Shaun," said her husband, shaking Ava's hand, "women's lib doesn't mean what he thinks it does."

The faces turned toward her were friendly, open. She took herself to task. These are nice people. The only one doing any judging here is you. Still, at 5'2" and in a skirt that she had sewn herself, the projector in her mind played her arriving like a Shetland pony in a room full of thoroughbreds.

Laura leaned against the kitchen counter, crossing her elegant legs. Her cashmere dress draped to reveal her hipbones, a smooth abdomen. It was like looking at a living *Vogue* cover. Laura smiled. "You're a teacher, right?"

"High school," Ava said.

"Ooh," Thomas cringed. "Sorry. Laura and I voted for the last bond. Too bad it didn't pass."

Ava raised her glass.

"Teachers," Shaun snorted. He gestured, spilling his drink on his shirt, booze to flames. "Do they ever work? I'm socially liberal and all that, but when it comes to my money, I'm fiscally conservative."

"Isn't that an oxymoron?" asked Ruthie. She tipped her head toward Ava. "And offensive."

Bill steered Shaun toward the living room. "Real smooth. Help me bring in some chairs before you alienate all of our guests."

Shaun cranked his neck. "What? That was offensive? No. C'mon—"

Bill yanked him into the other room.

Ava's expectations of a potential love connection, or just getting through the party without being too much of an outsider, floated to the bottom of her panty dropper. So this is how the evening is going to go. Shaun would not be a romantic lead in her life. What she wouldn't give for a good old-fashioned fire fighter. A real man who would put out the blaze, come to the rescue. But she had learned long ago that lusting after firefighters belonged only in fairy tales. If she was going to survive, she'd have to stop, drop, and roll. Then start looking for the aloe.

Ruthie draped an arm over Ava's shoulder. "He can be a bit of an ass."

"Oh, I don't know. I think flames are coming back, don't you?" Ava lowered her voice. "Is that the colleague Bill wanted me to meet?"

Ruthie put a hand to her belly. "I swear, he grows on you. If Shaun weren't somehow charming, I would have kicked him out after the crack about my weight."

Laura reached for a cupboard and pulled out napkins.

Ava watched her easy assurance in her friend's kitchen. Ruthie moves away for a year and this is the new best friend?

Laura motioned to Ava where to find the drawer for the silverware. "I was so glad when Ruthie said you'd be here," she said. "Maybe you can help us with an educational problem. We've had such a battle getting our kindergartener into a private school in the Marina."

Thomas explained, "That's because they don't accept the Devil into Catholic schools."

Laura frowned. "If his father disciplined him, the job wouldn't be left to a nanny."

"Have you thought about public schools?" Ava asked. She placed the silverware at each setting, two forks to show Laura she wasn't some country bumpkin. "I hear there's some great elementary schools in the city. They've got gifted classes, bilingual programs…caring parents like you could bring a lot to a school."

Gazing over Ava's head at her husband, Laura sent a look. Ava read it loud and clear: She doesn't understand. Laura said, "All we hear about is how public schools are failing. We can't take that chance."

Thomas nodded. "Atticus needs to get into a good college."

Shaun returned to the kitchen carrying a large chair. He leaned in toward Ava. "Sorry to be a douche." His eyes meant it.

Bill placed warm challah bread on the table. The room smelled of rising dough. Butter. Love.

They all sat down. Ava tried to situate herself next to Ruthie, but Laura beat her to it. She found herself sandwiched between Shaun's flames and Thomas's lavender scarf.

Bill dimmed the lights, and Ruthie placed both hands over her face. "Shabbat shalom…." Friends waited in silence.

Halfway through the salad, Thomas leaned over. "Did you see that movie *Waiting for Superman?* It was all about charter schools saving public education."

Ava grimaced. The movie had gained a lot of attention, likely because of the billionaire who funded it. That, and getting on *Oprah* never hurt. She'd watched the film with a knot in her stomach. It didn't mention charters raiding public school funding. It didn't mention a lot of things. It did blame public school teachers like her.

Shaun nodded eagerly. "I'm going to ask if my company wants to invest in a charter school in the city. It's a market that's blowing up. Everyone's making money." He poured himself a Steinem.

Oh, Shaun. The sea he swam in was so vast and ignorant, Ava couldn't be mad.

Ruthie frowned. "Doesn't the use of private funds make them private schools?"

"No," Ava said, passing the bread. "The way they kick out kids who aren't achieving makes them private schools."

Laura put a hand to her heart. "That movie was so profound."

"I cried," Thomas said.

Shaun glanced at him. "I'll bet you did."

Ruthie passed her plate to Bill for brisket. "I've heard that a lot of public schools aren't safe. I want our kid to feel safe at school, happy."

Ava felt as though she'd been slapped. *Et tu, Brute?* Had Ruthie moved down here and started drinking the Marina Kool-Aide? Or was she spending too much time with Laura?

But that wasn't fair. Ruthie wasn't in the classroom. She would be at work, and her kid would be left with someone like…me. Still, Ava had to try. "Every teacher in a school is bad? Every school in a district isn't safe? That would be amazing. *60 Minutes* would air a special: *First Graders Shoot up in Dirty Bathrooms. Teachers say, 'Fuck it,' Watch Porn in Class.*"

Ruthie and Bill chuckled.

Laura twisted her rings and glanced at her husband.

Shaun, pouring Thomas a *Feminine Mystique*, grinned. "Breaking out the porn talk at Shabbat dinner. Nice. Though I might have led up to it with—"

Ava ignored him. "Why don't you ask around about some of the elementary schools? Talk to principals, ask other parents about their kids' favorite teachers…?" She looked to Bill for help.

He shrugged. "I'm the product of public schools. I feel pretty normal. Besides, we're never having kids." He glanced at Ruthie's belly. "Oh, shit."

Ruthie smiled. "Don't worry, dear, it's not yours."

Bill turned to Thomas. "Before she was pregnant, it was like a honeymoon every day. Afterwards…"

Thomas nodded. "Bubkus. The love is gone."

Laura patted his hand. "It's just gone to another, smaller man."

Bill sighed. "Which leaves us baseball. What can I say to get you on the team?"

Thomas smoothed his lavender scarf. "Sorry, Bill. Polo's my sport."

Bill motioned to Ava's empty glass. "Drinks like a fish and swears like a sailor—any chance you play softball?"

She shook her head. "That was in high school, and I wasn't very good…"

Bill laughed. "I've got a beer ball team that needs a right fielder. We don't need good players, just good people. What do you think?"

Ava heard Dan's voice, mocking her decision to move to California. His assertion that she'd be the same frightened person in San Francisco as she was back home.

She stuck out her hand. "Then I've got a right fielder who needs a beer."

Walking into her room that evening, the clock read 1:00 am. Ava was in a good mood, though she really didn't need that last Steinem. She glanced in the mirror, put a hand to her cheek. Look, Ma, no scars….

A new message on her phone.

"Hi," Dan's voice was soft. Dan? She froze. The last time she saw him, his eyes were black. He hadn't spoken to her in a kind voice since…dating? The first year? It had been a long, long time. Then she heard that same soft tone again: "Call me."

Her mood evaporated. Loneliness crept into its place. Dan. Yes. Then, No. Then, Well…But she didn't want to think about Dan tonight. She turned off her phone and set it on the nightstand, noticing her bottle of Nyquil was empty again. It was time to put the pony to bed.

CHAPTER 8
LOVE THE ONES YOU'RE WITH

September 8th. Ava beamed at her class. After three weeks of chaos and shit-shows, the kids had spent the last few days focused on topic sentences and supporting details. Perseverance paid off.

Confident, she prompted the room, "And a conclusion sentence does what?"

Tanya waved her hand like a Lotto winner claiming her prize. "Summarizes all the important information in the paragraph!"

"Yes." Ava handed her one Starburst candy, reminding herself, It's called incentive, not bribery. "All right, folks, remember the partners that I paired you up with yesterday. I need some of you to get up and move so that you and your partner are sitting together."

The students stayed where they were.

"Come on," she prodded, "we're making new best friends today. Go sit with your partner."

K'Ron folded her arms across her chest. "I ain't moving."

Francisco jerked his head toward his partner, the General. "He can move to me."

Under his hoodie, the General shook his head.

Students glared at each other across the room.

Ava felt her confidence evaporate. Seriously? A power struggle over who moves to whom? She bet her last chip. "In my experience, it's usually the better looking people who move. I don't know why, but that's the way it generally turns out."

The kids laughed, then glanced around.

"That's not true," Sean said, but it was more of a question.

Ava shrugged. "That's what I've observed."

Tanya, Sean, and the General got up.

Melvin strutted over to his partner. "You like what you see?" he asked Charnikka. She hit him on the shoulder. Melvin lost his balance. More students made their migrations.

Ava grinned. She turned to get some pencils.

And that is when a homeless white man walked into the classroom.

What the hell?

The man was in his early twenties, blonde hair hanging in matted dreads to his shoulders. His tee shirt showed Jesus taking a toke from a blunt. The man's eyes had an unfocused, fevered gleam. Weaving his way into the classroom, the visitor grinned broadly, revealing a missing front tooth.

"Oh my God!" Melvin snickered, "Look at that dude's hair."

Ava positioned herself between the unexpected guest and her students. "Good morning."

He stared at the kids, a grin fixed on his face.

Oh, no.... Her breakfast rose into her throat. She could hold her own with blow-ups and blowouts, but crazy hit too close to home.

"I'm a madman," Dad loved to say. On Sunday afternoons, he'd line up Ava and her siblings at the kitchen table, describing the order in which he would shoot their mother and stepfather. Then he'd muse about his inevitable jail time, the misery that would follow his children the rest of their lives. His doctor had determined that he posed no danger to himself or others, but in light of Ava's experience, as well as periodic killing sprees by the mentally ill, she knew that logic was fucking insane.

"He'th wearing a weed shirt." Hector was delighted.

"Quiet," Ava said. Did he have a knife? A gun? "Can I help you?"

Behind her, a kid said loudly, "Do ya'll smell that?"

"Shut. Up!" Ava hissed. She smiled at the visitor.

Francisco half-stood, "You can't tell us to—"

"I said, Sit. Down. And. Shut. Up." She pointed to his seat.

Francisco sat down.

"I just wanted the children to have this," the man said. His skin stretched taught on his unlined face.

He's so young, Ava thought. Just a few years younger than me. It was sad. And frightening. And sad.

He put his hand into his pocket and pulled out a greeting card. "This is the truth, darlin.' Be sure to hold it near your heart."

"Thanks." Ava took the card with two fingers. It smelled of piss and alcohol, proclaiming Jesus as the way and the light. "Did you come in the main doors?"

The visitor smiled. "I'll just stand here and watch the beautiful children."

"You know, I'd love you to stay, myself," she said. "But school rules say you need to go check in with the office." She pushed the air with her hands, as if herding a lost duckling. "Just out that door."

"Office?"

"Down stairs, past the dangerously unsupervised main en-trance. That's where security should have told you where to go."

He ran a hand over his matted hair. "Well, I guess I done my piece." He nodded to the class. "See you later, children!"

"Bye!" Tanya waved.

Ava grabbed the phone on her desk, misdialing twice before reaching the secretary. Fuckfuckfuckfuck. "Get Fifty to sweep the second floor for a white man," she spoke into the receiver. "I need to talk to the principal as soon as possible."

The kids looked on silently as she tried not to cry, their somber faces disapproving. Then Ava remembered: She'd told them to shut up. Shit. She wasn't here to yell at them. She wasn't here to be her dad. She slumped down in a chair. "I said *shut up*, didn't I? I'm sorry."

The students thought about it. Some nodded, rolling her apology onto their all-important judicial scales.

"Ms. L?" Charnikka finally said.

"Yes?"

"Can I ask you a question?"

Ava was touched. Charnikka always just blurted stuff out. "Of course. I suppose everyone is kind of freaked out—"

"Was that your boyfriend?" Charnikka looked at her expectantly.

"My boyfriend?" Hurt, she waited for the kids' laughter. They were quiet though, puzzling.

"He was white," Tanya reasoned. Other students nodded in agreement.

"Yeah, was he your boyfriend?" asked Sean.

Francisco snorted. "Naw, fool, he's not her boyfriend."

"Thank you," Ava said. Finally, some sanity in the room. A man who looked homeless, wearing a blunt-smoking Jesus tee shirt….

"How do you know?" Charnikka challenged.

Francisco tapped his temple. "Duh," he said, "he's too young to be Ms. L's boyfriend."

"Oooohhhhh," Sean nodded, thinking it over.

Ava didn't know whether to laugh or cry. She settled for resting her forehead against the table. "You're killing me," she said.

"Awwww, Ms. L," said Melvin, "you know you love us. Can I have a Starburst?"

That evening, she called Dan.

He picked up on the first ring. "Ave! I was just talking to Bill about you. He says Ruthie's pregnant. I guess it was just a matter of time. How's it going in the big city? How much do you miss this handsome mug?"

She glanced at his photograph on her dresser, his dark eyes and blonde curls. She remembered the camping trip they had taken to the rainforest, the feeling of freedom as he drove them deeper and deeper through the towering trees. They'd had so much fun. "I might miss you a bit. I'm barely hanging on here."

"That's not the teacher I know. I'll bet you're doing much better than that." And that was Dan. Even when he cut her down daily over little things, he'd always supported her too.

"Probably not much better. Tell me the news from Washington."

"Lost the last fantasy football round to Bill—bad luck on the injuries list."

She nodded into the phone, as if she'd ever understood what a fantasy league meant. "And the garden? Are you still harvesting?"

"Not so great since you left. I show the tomatoes your picture, but they don't believe you're coming back. I think the lavender bush has given up the will to live."

"Are you remembering to water her regularly?"

"There is that."

Ava smiled. "Don't let me know who else withers away."

"Well I am, without you. What do you say to a visit in a month or so?"

Bad idea. Breaking up was hard. Don't go back, don't go back—But then... Dan was fun: rafting, biking, hiking. She thought of the long hours now she spent at school and at home—grading, planning...She missed fun. "Maybe. It's a whole new world down here, though. They don't even have a country station."

He gasped. "I had no idea it was that bad. Let me bring the sunshine that is myself down to brighten your world."

And, of course, that was exactly what she had been hoping someone would do. Even Dan.

CHAPTER 9
PEOPLE WHO NEED PEOPLE

Ava sat on her bed, laptop propped up on a pillow. Outside, brilliant blue September skies offered opportunities she was too exhausted to entertain. Her roommate, Pedro, was home again from his latest business trip, but she hadn't seen him.

She prayed to the computer gods, Please, I just need a little connection. Adult interaction. Anything. A funny pet video would work. Amen. She typed "tired teacher" into Google, hoping for stories of failure, exhaustion. Nothing. Fucking Internet.

Okay then, Hotmail. When she was a child, she'd read about Donald Duck's nephews, Huey, Dewey, and Louie. For a while, they had a Magic Mailbox. Wonderful surprises arrived every day. As an adult, Ava couldn't stop hoping that was how Hotmail worked: an email delivered from the cosmic void that just might change her life. C'mon, Hotmail. Mama wants a million bucks. Or a smokin' hot boyfriend. Or a reason to go on.

Hmm…no new life today. Just an Evite from Bill: "Beer Ball Game #3—Be There or Be Sober."

Ava groaned, then clicked on: *Yes.* Maybe Ruthie would join them, support her husband and good friend by being the knocked-up cheerleader every ball team needed.

She scrolled past spam to a message from her mom:

Hi sweetie!

How goes it in the big city? Kids still calling you Concretia? Ha! Your stepdad and I had a good laugh over that one. Say, I don't want to be a butt-insky, but you mentioned that you're talking to Dan again? It's your business, but you just never seemed that happy with him. By the way, what are you doing for fun? Drinking doesn't count, Sweetheart.
Love you,
Mom

Ava saved the email into the folder entitled "Love." She didn't want to think about what she should and shouldn't be doing about Dan right now. What she should be doing at this moment included going for a jog. Getting fresh air. Forgetting about how she was going to get through tomorrow. What she should not be doing was finishing the beer in the kitchen or taking Nyquil.

She reached for the Nyquil on her nightstand, took a swig, then logged onto Facebook. C'mon, connection.

Photos of families. The college diaspora complete, her friends were having kids now. Ava trolled her sister, Livvie's page, savoring her two-year-old nephew's photos like a celebrity stalker. Mechanically-inclined, serious little Leo had learned to walk well before he acknowledged any human interaction. He was a man, and he was going to do manly things: conquer, walk upright. Unlike many children his age, Leo really was perfection, no need for Livvie to embellish there. But other parents? They posted daily, chronicling their toddler's achievements as if Mensa had cyberscouts.

Ava thought about Leo, how much she loved that little boy. But that wasn't her life, not now. She wasn't ready to come home to little people who needed something from her, like, say, a balanced meal. She didn't know if she was capable of getting out markers or Legos or blocks or Bob the Builder and spending some quality time on the floor. Faking it at school was one thing: a little face at home would look to her to model confidence, love, compassion. Riiiiight.

She really should turn the computer off, but…. She wanted some connection. People who would understand what these days were like. She looked up Francisco's name on Facebook. He didn't have any locks to block strangers from viewing his page.

Her student's latest post dated just twenty minutes ago. *Snitches end up in ditches. RIP MANNY Bros before Hoes.*

Startled, Ava clicked off his page. She typed *Paris Love.* The girl had started her day with typing the upbeat: *I don't have friends. I have associates. Bitches be back-stabbin.*

Ava felt sad. She read Paris's next thread of comments with someone named UWantDis.

Paris began the exchange: *Triflin ass hoe!*
Fuck you!
Ima mess you up, bitch!
Aint my fault ur nigga like this betta!
Gutta hoe. Ima slap yo mouth off yo face!

Ava exited Paris's page shaken, a voyeur who'd seen more than she should.

She thought about when she was little, growing up in the basement of the home built log-by-log above them. No Facebook, cell phones, phones for the Llewellyns then. Dad would drive them to the local tavern, ten miles away, to make the weekly phone calls to the grandparents. Above the din of honkey-tonk, truckers, and loggers, they'd relay the week's news. Her sister, Livvie, not understanding the concept, nodded into the phone.

"She's saying yes!" Mom shouted toward the receiver while Dad started bundling the kids into the truck for the drive back home.

Clicking on her cyber photo album, Ava chose a picture taken in Hawaii three years ago when she went with Dan. She looked thin, tall—an illusion of water and shadows. She uploaded it, posting, *California is everything I dreamed it would be.*

A key in the lock. "Hello?" Pedro knocked, popping his head into her room. One arm clutched a bag of groceries. "Dude, I'm making dinner."

She felt familiar gratitude at the sight of her roommate, the perfect combination of Latino surfer and hipster techie. At 5'10" he cut a slim figure in his black tee shirt and black jeans. "What are you making?" she asked.

"Mexican." He gave a lopsided grin. "Wanna join me?"

Connection. "I'll get the beer." Pedro made the differences, the total strangeness of her new city, this new life, more manageable.

She thought back to last summer, staying with her mom in Eastern Washington to save money for her move. She'd cruised Craigslist, made calls. San Francisco rents were very high and her salary would be very low. The Mission was close enough to walk to school. When she called Ruthie, her college buddy said it was a Latino neighborhood. Ava was ready. After all, she had wanted diversity, right? She was excited about a multiethnic city…right?

She drove twenty hours to interview with her only prospective roommate. Pedro had offered the gold standard: a space to park her truck, her own bathroom, and a contract ready to sign. His easy manner and surfer's grin were bonuses. Ava said the word "teacher" and she was in. Pedro worked for one of the many tech companies in the city. He would be out of town a lot. He wanted someone stable to sublet the place. *Teacher* equaled *stable.*

It wasn't until she was finally walking down the crowded Mission sidewalks as a resident that diversity felt different than she expected. She might as well be in a foreign country. Skin tones didn't resemble hers. Spicy, complex aromas wafting out of tiny restaurants weren't the scents she knew. She felt noticed on the street, like a neon sign flashing: "Miran amigos! Una gringa! Quien se cree que es?" Who does she think she is? Or maybe it was Ava's string of racial gaffes that made her feel so out of place.

Yesterday, she'd strode into the local Walgreens. She needed magazines for the kids to use in an art project and had seen a Spanish version of *People* magazine on display only days before. Ava flipped through the selection on the shelves, looking for the faces of her students on the glossy pages. What she saw were skeletal white women posing in thousand dollar dresses, hunched from hunger. White couples hiking, backpacking. White celebrities grocery shopping (*they're just like us!*). In one magazine, a black woman in a dress barely covering her lady bits leaned against an Escalade. A rapper, posturing on the hood of the vehicle, bared his gold grill teeth and stared at her tits. White homemaking. White sex tips. Any Asians in magazines these days? An issue of *Ebony*. Black professionals. Yes.

Not seeing the Latino edition of *People* she was looking for, Ava approached the sales clerk. His dark skin gleamed. She smiled. The variety of ethnicities in the stack she held felt like an admittance ticket into the wider world of race. She asked, "Do you have Latino *People*?"

The clerk stared at her before he broke it down straight-faced. "Ma'am," he said, "we're in California."

She froze. "*People* magazine. I meant, Latino *People* mag—never mind." She paid for her magazines, deciding not to ask the man about Asian *People*. It was also not the time to inquire about black *People*.

Ava went to the kitchen, reaching into the fridge for two beers. She opened one for Pedro. He held a spatula over dough sizzling in a pan.

"I think I'm too white for my job," she said.

Pedro glanced over. His dark, shaggy hair hung over his eyes. "Oh yeah?"

"These kids need to have teachers who look like them, understand their lives. They need me to be a large black man, or a Latino woman, or an Asian man. They don't need another blonde teacher telling them how to live."

She swigged her beer. It mixed nicely with the buzz from the Nyquil. She noticed the label. "Oops. This was one of yours."

"No worries," Pedro said. "I went for your trail mix the other day. The bag was full, but I couldn't find any chocolate chips. The bag said there were chocolate chips."

Ava shrugged. She set two plates on the table. "I'm thorough."

Oil crackled in the pan. Pedro flipped the dough. "The kids see people who look like them at home. Didn't you come from a mostly-white community?"

"Yeah, and I wanted out."

"Exactly. Dude, it's good to be around people who don't look like you. You'll get it. We Latinos aren't so strange." Pedro smiled a goofy grin. "We're a different culture, not a different species." He slid a perfectly round, fried disc onto her plate. It steamed hot and greasy.

"What is this?" she asked.

"A pupusa."

So that's what they look like. She groaned.

"What? No good?"

"No. It's just…pupusas." She put her head in her hands, the memory hitting a pause button on her ability to breathe normally. "Last week, I thought Hector said a bad word."

"A great start to a story. Is this a student? What did he say?"

She shook her head. "First period. He was leaning back in his chair, licking his lips. Then he said real slow, 'I want me some pu-puuuuusasssss.'" She cringed. "It was the way he said it. I thought he was saying *pussy*." She took a deep breath. "I sent him out of the room. Told him he wasn't allowed back until he could speak like a gentleman."

Pedro laughed. "Dude, you didn't!"

Ava put a hand over her face. "The vice principal brought him back up and described what pupusas were. I had to apologize to Hector." She whispered, "Then I had to explain my dirty mind to the vice principal."

That evening, she took a break from the grading and lesson planning that filled most evenings. Since her students' eyes glazed when they opened textbooks, she created most lessons from scratch. If one day included reading and questions, the next would need to involve moving around, groups, hands-on activities. Slacking at night meant winging it tomorrow. And winging it was bad. She lay back on her bed anyway. The Nyquil buzz hummed while she reviewed her Walgreens purchases. Bathing in a sense of the familiar, her body relaxed as she opened up an issue of white *People.*

CHAPTER 10
TEACH FOR AMERICA

Mark Jeffries, the new math teacher, had been having a bad day. He sat in the faculty room, dark hair stuck to the sweat on his face. "It's that fucking third period," he said. "Today I just left them there. Ingrates. Told them I'd come back when they were ready to learn."

Cheryl and Stella looked at each other. A smile tugged at Cheryl's mouth. "How'd that turn out for you, Mark?"

"They applauded my leaving. Then they cranked up the radio."

Ava felt for her fellow newbie. Mark had been hired that year from a program called Teach for America. Twenty-one years old and without a teaching credential, five weeks training in the summer was all the preparation he'd had before signing a two-year teaching contract. His Harvard diploma in applied mathematics hung prominent behind his desk. Her homeroom students talked about his energy, his unconventional lessons.

She rooted for her young colleague, someone even more green than she was. She saw him trying. She saw he had the best intentions. But under the strain of learning how to teach on the fly, his unconventional lessons fell apart. He suffered as students played him. Then he yelled at them, sometimes calling them names as he stormed out of the classroom.

Ava had been that frustrated once. She saw her classroom in Washington State, the shiny vinyl flooring and Sunny's look of hatred—but, *no*. Ava shook her head. She couldn't think about Sunny. She would do better this time around. She would get it right. She would help these kids—their academic abilities, their lives. She knew more now than she knew with Sunny. She was starting over.

Waiting for the faculty meeting to begin, Mark combed his fingers through his hair. Dark circles sagged under eyes that were too young to look so tired. "I don't understand why they aren't grateful for the opportunity to learn."

Principal Sanchez walked up, young hands smoothing the front of her polyester slacks. "You hang in there, Mark. Are the night classes helping? Do your professors have suggestions?"

"I can't even think straight after school gets out. The professors try, but I'm too tired after days like these."

The principal grimaced in sympathy, turning to the room. "All right, people, I'd like to see a bit more support for Mr. Jeffries from his colleagues. We're lucky to have some fresh ideas for the classroom."

Ava felt slapped. Fresh ideas? What are my ideas? The energy in the room deflated.

Cheryl leaned in. "Oh, please. Wipe off that sour face. She likes him cause he's cheap. A lot less than a credentialed teacher. Poor guy. He's gonna leave next year like the last one did when his contract was up."

"No," Ava whispered.

Cheryl shrugged. "Eighty percent leave by year five."

Principal Sanchez glared. "Let us all hear it, Cheryl, if you're going to use this time for coffee talk."

Cheryl smiled, turned to Mark. "Of course you're having a tough time, honey. Five weeks isn't long enough to learn any profession. Shoot, that's just common sense. I'll come in tomorrow on my prep hour and give you a hand. I'ma bring my lion-taming gear. Don't you worry—we'll get that class saying 'Yes, sir' in no time."

Mark grimaced. "Thanks. At this point, there's not much of me left for them to tear apart."

Ava thought about the hours she'd spent volunteering at alternative school sites, her year of student teaching, the Masters Degree in Education. And each day was still hard. She raised her hand. "I've got some Starbursts you can have."

CHAPTER 11
WELLNESS

September 19.th Principal Sanchez popped her head into the classroom to introduce Emmett. A slight kid with striking features, Emmett wore a purple lollipop tucked into his visor cap. It matched the color of his shirt and shoes.

From inside the room, Ken gasped appreciation.

Ava smiled at Emmett and indicated he should take a seat. She noticed he wore violet contacts. Turning back to the principal, she kept her voice low. "Really? He's a month behind. What am I supposed to give him for a grade?"

The principal shrugged. "I'm sure you'll figure out something."

But it wasn't long before Emmett's love of intense eye contact, as well as his career ambitions, raised Ava's warning flags.

"We've been working on paragraph structure," Ava said. "I'll get you the handouts."

Emmett looked bored. "I'll probably make it big soon," he said. "I won't need to write my own paragraphs."

"Oh? What are you doing to make it big?"

"Nothing. But that's how most celebrities are discovered, you know. I'll probably be discovered as a rapper."

"Do you rap?"

"Naw."

The other kids stared.

Ken grimaced. "What a waste."

But then Emmett was absent for five days, and a fight between Paris and a boy from the Special Ed. class absorbed Ava's focus. The vice principal later described the scene, "Tore into him like a rabid Chihuahua latching onto a pit bull."

So it wasn't until the following week, when her new student took a practice spelling test, that Ava began to get a larger understanding of Emmett's mental state. "Make sure you don't get the same wrong answers as your neighbor," she said as students' eyes darted to other's papers. But Emmett was shifting strangely in his seat. When he dipped his hand into his waistband a third time, she saw that he was looking at a small piece of paper, a cheat-sheet stuffed down his pants.

Ava took a moment to decide if what she was seeing was a product of her morning shot of Nyquil: Hand in pants. Paper cheat sheet. It was real. Shit.

She whispered, "Emmett, will you please come here?"

Emmett dutifully got out of his seat and shuffled over, pants making a crinkling sound. It was sad, and Ava couldn't help feeling for a kid who didn't know any better.

When Emmett had slowly, noisily, completed his odyssey, she leaned in close. "Do you have a cheat sheet down your pants?"

He shook his head, "Nuh-uh." His purple pupils locked onto her gaze.

"Are you sure?"

He didn't even look down. "Nope."

She rubbed a hand over her eyes, as much an attempt to break-up the staring contest as to relieve a headache that was coming on. *I am out of my league here, kid.* "Well, then, could you go downstairs and ask the vice principal what I should do if I suspect that a student has a cheat sheet stuffed down his pants?"

Emmett nodded. "Sure." He shuffled out the door.

After school, she reviewed Emmett's file. His prior school record was punctuated with psychotic breaks. The Wellness Center, the school's counseling program, had put a call in to Emmett's parents. The number was disconnected.

Ava remembered when her dad had been discharged from the psychiatric wing of the local hospital, no longer a threat to himself or others. That weekend, Ava and her siblings watched him at his play rehearsal. The man running the lights had missed Dad's cue. Dad stormed the light booth, stopping his fist just before it made contact, yelling long after the director demanded he calm the fuck down.

The vice principal sent a certified letter to Emmett's home, requesting a parent conference.

Emmett was gone the next five days. Ava worried what had happened to him, but her focus was on the field trip she was planning, a poetry workshop across town at the library. As usual, Francisco balked when she announced the field trip to the class.

"I can't go through that part of town on that bus! That's a *Sureño* bus!" He tapped his head, a harried parent explaining basic safety to a small child.

Ava waved away his concerns. "I'll protect you." The school district assigned kids to schools based on addresses that didn't conflict with gang or turf affiliations. She was vaguely aware that they were a red, *Norteño* school. It couldn't be that big a deal, though, really.

Of course, Emmett showed up on the day of the field trip. Ava kept an eye on him as she marched her fifteen students down the street, the smokers straggling behind. At the bus stop, she begged kids to board the front of the bus, using the student passes. They needed to be legit. She watched as Francisco, K'Ron, and Melvin slipped in the rear doors.

The bus was packed. "Move to the back," the driver called. They all pushed and squeezed as far as they could go.

Ava found herself crowded next to Emmett. When the bus pulled forward, she lost her balance, lunging toward a homeless man curled up on a seat.

Emmett leaned close. "Did I tell you that everything is green?" he asked.

Her stomach lurched with the bus. "What do you mean, green?" Teenagers wearing blue hats, belts, and shirts got on the front.

In the back of the bus, Francisco slumped down in his seat like a five-year-old. His tattooed neck and red tee shirt let everyone know which gang he claimed.

"Like the walls are green and these seats are green and my hands are green," Emmett explained, smiling.

At the moment, Ava was seeing everything in terms of red and blue. She had only seen gang fights on TV. What was this? East LA? *The Wire?*

She peered through the crowd at her students. Hector, his clothing and shoes edged in red, was slumped down in his seat now as well. Shit.

K'Ron wore a tight-fitting red tee shirt over black jeans and knee-high boots, attitude in her painted-on eyebrows. Despite this tough affect, she molded her body into her seat, slouching low so that the top of her head barely skimmed the bottom of the window.

Tanya sprayed the homeless man with perfume.

"Stop that," Ava hissed. "I'm sorry," she told the man. He didn't move from his fragrant fetal position on an adjacent seat.

For the remainder of the bus ride, Francisco and other Latino kids looked wary. Ava's heart stopped every time a teenager wearing blue got on the bus.

Finally, they arrived at the library. Ava hustled the kids up into the teen section. The children's librarian, an older woman with short gray hair, wasted no time telling Francisco and Melvin that either they took their hats off in the building or they could just leave her Teen Corner, thank you very much.

Then Ava realized that Emmett had disappeared.

"I'll be right back," she told the librarian.

Francisco and Melvin held their hats in their hands as Ava left the room.

She combed the hallways and racks of books in each of the library's three floors. Finally, she spied Emmett hiding behind a fichus tree near the main entrance. People walking past stared at his violet pupils glowing as he stood there in plain sight, crouched behind the plant's thin leaves.

"I'm blending in." Emmett said as she approached.

She motioned for him to come out. "You did a good job. Now it's time to come with me."

Two security guards ambled over.

"It's all right," Ava said. "I'm his teacher." She imagined his grin like that of Alice's Cheshire cat, white teeth against a background of green. She put a hand on his shoulder. "I need you to blend in with the class for the rest of this trip, ok?"

When they returned to the Teen Corner, Ava's students were hard at work writing poetry. Francisco wrote a poem about surviving the streets. K'Ron wrote a poem about her mom, the repeating stanza being, "You don't give up on me." Ava thanked the librarian. She wondered how to add poetry into more classroom units.

Unwilling to drag her Norteño kids through the same dangerous route, she gave students the option of calling parents and being dismissed from the library. Hector, K'Ron, and Francisco left together. Ava didn't allow Emmett out of her sight. On the ride back to school, he explained that everyone was the color of money. "You're like a green $20.00 bill," he said. She took it as a compliment.

When they got back to the school, she called down to the Wellness Center coordinator, Mary Kline, to see what could be done for Emmett.

"Why haven't you been answering your phone?" Mary asked. Her normally cheerful tone contained an edge. "Come down to Wellness and we'll have a chat."

Ava looked down at her cell phone. She had turned it off, trying to model for students what it looked like to not compulsively check your phone every twenty seconds. She had missed ten calls.

She dialed voicemail. The security guard, Fifty, was first. "Ms. Llewellyn," Fifty panted, "when you got on the bus, I saw a bulge in Francisco's waistband. I need you to turn around and come back to school."

The second message was Principal Sanchez. "Ms. Llewellyn, when you get this message, I need you to bring your class back to the schoolhouse. Fifty thought he saw a gun when Francisco got on the bus."

The third message was the principal again. "Ms. Llewellyn, I need to be able to contact you while on a field trip. It is imperative that you give me a call."

Ava pictured Francisco pulling out the gun on his way home. She found his permission slip and called his house.

He answered on the second ring. "'Sup?"

"Francisco?"

"Yeah, who's this?"

Ava thanked the gods of curiosity that her students picked up for every unknown caller. "Ms. L—I'm calling because Fifty thought he saw a gun in your waistband."

"Ms. L, we're not allowed to have guns at school," Francisco said.

"I know, but security said—"

"Fifty didn't see shit."

Ava saw she wasn't going to get anywhere. "You left with K'Ron. Do you know if she got home ok?"

"Yeah, K'Ron made it home." Francisco grunted good-bye.

Ava approached Principal Sanchez before leaving for the day. "He's seeing green, you know. Were you aware of that when you enrolled him?"

"Who?"

"Emmett."

The principal frowned, smoothed out the front of her polyester pants. "Oh, well, send him down to Wellness."

"I did, but Mary said we don't have any services for mentally ill kids. He also doesn't qualify for Special Ed services. What am I supposed to do with a kid who is out of his mind? I can't teach him like that."

"Well, I expect you to treat him the same as you would any other student. Access and equity."

Ava burned. *And. Fuck. You. Too.* "And when he's seeing green? What should I do?"

Principal Sanchez sighed, looking suddenly as young as she was. Young and…sad. "I don't know." She spread her hands. "I'm sorry."

Ava walked home that evening, passing the usual cast of street people. Two blocks from her apartment, a man shouted obscenities into the air, one shoe off, his foot a crusted mess. She wondered whom he was yelling at. She thought about what the world must look like to Emmett when everything was green. With no supports beyond a once-a-week psychologist, it was likely that Emmett would one day see everything as homeless.

CHAPTER 12

A BALLPLAYER

Late September. Walking onto the beer ball field, cans of Bud in the hands of every player, Ava felt an unexpected rush. She had forgotten how much she loved the feeling of a rough glove on her hand, kneading the hard leather to make it softer, more pliable. The evening had cooled, and there were tiny droplets of dew on the grass. She kicked. The droplets sprayed prisms onto the field.

Bill's team was hanging out by the dugout. They all wore yellow and white jerseys declaring them the *Sitting Ducks*. From the middle of the group, Bill waved. She looked to see if Ruthie had come to root him on, another familiar face. Nope.

Ava steeled herself and plunged in, avoiding eye contact with his teammates. They were laughing with one another, slapping each other on the back and taking beers from a massive cooler. She quietly groaned. This was a bad idea. She would be an outsider. A placeholder on the field for a position that everyone knew was no position at all. She heard her dad's voice: You've got to buck up, Buttercup. She gave Bill a hug. "I brought your right fielder, where's the beer?"

He handed her a can of Bud Light. "Time to warm up."

Ava clinked her can to his. "Warmer already." She took a deep breath and picked up a softball from the pile. "Throw me a couple balls, Coach?"

There had been a time in her childhood when Ava was a ballplayer. Coach John, a local in his early twenties, had made it his mission to grow the small town hardball league into a nurturing, positive environment. Beaming behind his logger's beard, he'd declare each kid was destined for the Major Leagues. His job was to lovingly prepare them for the day they were called up. Every kid in the league adored Coach John. Coach John adored them back. "Everyone matters," he'd say, looking into the eyes of his ballplayers. Ava understood he wasn't talking about their usefulness on the field.

She felt anointed when she was randomly selected to be the girl allotted to his little league team. She tried out for pitcher and made third on the list, her throw accurate but slow. She played a happy second base instead.

When Coach John's mom got sick mid-season, another kid's father took over the team. The rules changed. Ava was sent to right field. The new coach didn't look at her when giving the team instructions.

Late in the season, during a particularly frustrating game, the pitching went to hell. The starting pitcher got hit with a line drive to his throwing hand. The number two man took his place, walking the next three batters. Ava waited to be called to the mound. But the coach chose the third baseman. His pitches, too high. Then the left fielder. Then the catcher.

Finally, from the stands, her dad protested. "C'mon Mike, don't be an ass. Let Ava pitch."

She flinched, as did her older brother, Alan, and their younger sister, Livvie, who sat beside her dad on the bleachers.

Defeated, the coach waved in his right fielder.

Ava trotted to the mound, her body pulsing adrenaline, apprehension.

The next batter stepped up. The kid smirked. Pointed to center field.

Ava glowered. Jerk. She clutched the ball to her chest, squeezed out the fear. Her arm revolved in a fluid arc, fingers releasing, hard laces rough against her skin. Then she waited.

The ball moved through the air as though shot through atmospheric gel. Graceful. Patient. The batter swung hard. His legs twisted as the bat hit the ground behind him.

"Strike!"

The batter swore.

Floating over home, the ball made a small *pft!* when it hit the catcher's mitt.

Yes! Ava smiled behind her glove.

Dad put both fingers in his mouth, whistling loudly.

Mothers in the stands looked up from their books. Fathers elbowed each other and grinned.

"Hey, batta, batta, batta!" the infield chanted. Their words, bellows to Ava's confidence.

She wound up again, released. The ball hung in the air like a well-constructed glider. Easy. Sure.

The batter swung, slicing the air, connecting with nothing.

"Strike two!"

Someone's mom yelled, "Atta girl!"

"You can do it!" the outfield encouraged.

A few women in the stands crossed their fingers. Dads leaned forward in their seats.

Alan and Livvie stood up.

The third pitch wrote a message in its arc: Something about risking a try and how everyone, everyone matters.

The batter, conflicted now about when to swing, watched the ball float in over the plate like a sailboat coming home to port. *Pft!*

"Strike three! You're out!"

The crowd was yelling, clapping. "Hey, Mike," the coach's wife hooted, "looks like you've got a new pitcher!"

The other team mocked the batter as he slunk off the field. "Oohh, is that your girlfriend? Did your girlfriend strike you out?"

The next batter stepped forward.

"Strike one!"

Moms rose to their feet.

"Foul ball!"

Dads hung off the backstop, giving Ava advice. "Put some grease on this one, darlin'; he can't hit!" They mocked their own sons. "What's wrong, Willy? She got you all red in the face! Look at your boy, Mama--I think Willy's in love!"

Again and again, the boys swung hard, anticipating a ball that was still seconds away. One kid tipped three fouls but couldn't catch a solid hit.

The crowd loved it. It was like watching the Kentucky Derby in slow motion or a hundred yard sprint in freeze frame. They placed bets on how long it would take for the ball to cross the plate. "Whoohoo! Three seconds that time, J.W.! Pay up!"

Her teammates hollered, laughed like they had thrown the slow strikes themselves.

Ava didn't mind. She was there to do a job. She drew her arm back again, prepared to give this one her all. The ball left her fingers, hung in the air.

The batter lined himself up, hesitated, hesitated….He swung the bat around to connect with the sweet spot, smacking the center of a bulls-eye.

"Ahhhhhh!" The crowd let out a sound of wonder, watched as the tiny rocket launched over the infield, kept going.

The outfield backed up, backed up. It looked like the center fielder was on a collision course with the fence—he's going to hit it now—He's gonna—He hit the fence! The tiny guy slammed into the chain-link, stretching his gloved hand toward the ball.

Thump! The ball landed solidly in his mitt.

Joy rose up in Ava's chest. A lens of tears turned the ball field blurry.

The spectators for both teams were stomping, clapping. Teammates slapped each other on the back as they ran off the field. Ava's heart soared. *Remember this feeling* her eleven-year-old self reminded.

In the dugout, she high-fived until her hand stung. The coach kept his gaze on the ground. He mumbled that Wayne would pitch next. Ava went back to right field grinning.

Four years later, she played fast-pitch Varsity softball on a talented team full of seniors. Her freshman year, she'd been named MVP as second baseman on her Junior Varsity team. The entire team, with the exception of Ava, had voted for her. Now a senior played second base. Ava took left field.

By then, weekends were unbearable. Without her mom, her dad went unchecked. He lined up his children at the kitchen table. "I have nothing to live for," he spat. "My family is gone. I want to die." This vein in his temple bulged contempt.

Ava went back to school on Mondays unsure. Once among the fastest on the team, she stopped stealing bases, afraid she'd get thrown out. In the field, her hands began to shake.

One Saturday, at Alan's ballgame, Ava sat next to Dad and Livvie in the stands. Her brother was on the mound, a rising star on the varsity team. Even though he often arrived in a mood, Dad never missed a chance to watch one of his kids play ball.

Then Ava saw her mom and stepdad arrive, an unexpected move. The game transferred off the field. Dad was in checkmate. No one said anything as they took their seats well away from him and the girls.

Dad gritted his teeth. "Be right back."

Ava and Livvie held hands, waited.

It didn't take long. "Stay the fuck away from my kids!" he shouted.

Everyone in the stands turned to look.

Ava's stepdad, Randy, spoke softly.

"Why don't you come with me and we can settle this right now?" Dad screamed. "I will rip your fucking throat out!" His face pulsed purple as he raged. The two men stood nose-to-nose.

Minutes later, a black-and-white pulled up. The officer who handcuffed Dad apologized. "Hate to do this, J.W."

Ava's stomach churned as she watched the officer eased him into the patrol car.

Parents, classmates gawked.

The inning over, Alan ran into the dugout, his eyes finding Ava's in the stands. When he took the mound again, he walked four batters in a row. The coach sat him the rest of the game.

Toward the middle of the softball season, on a Friday when her dad would be picking her up, Ava walked to her mom's house from practice. She'd been thinking about the weekend ahead, the interminable hours stacked one on top of another—She stopped mid-stride. Ooooooh, no. She had to pee. Right NOW. The burning sensation came on so strong, she whimpered. Get home! Get home! But it was already too late. Warm urine streamed down her legs.

Looking around the empty street, she wanted to die. Face burning with embarrassment, she shuffled past homes belonging to classmates, the Safeway clerk, the town's doctor. Her sweatpants clung to her body. An acrid smell emanated with every step. She washed out her pants in the bathtub when she got home, hung them up in the basement, telling no one.

That weekend, Dad gave Ava, Livvie, and Alan a tutorial on how to use the new lawn mower. "See here? That's the blower valve. Don't touch it. Ever. Ava? Goddammit, don't you look away when I'm talking to you."

He slammed his fist on the blower, breaking off a piece. "You're just like your Goddamn mother, all of you." He narrowed his eyes. " You hate your old man. Well I'll tell you, I'm going kill that bitch and her bitch husband. Then I'm going to burn down this house. I'll give away your pets."

Livvie sobbed openly.

Ava saw Mom as a bullet ripped through her. The family home in flames. The cats, their loving eyes. Gone.

Alan squeezed her shoulder.

"Oh, that got your attention now, didn't it?" he gloated. "I'm going to give away your cats. You'll never see them again."

The lawn mower tutorial lasted six hours.

The next Friday, Ava made it to the back porch before hot urine burned down her legs. Nononono! What is wrong with me? She left the ball field just fine. The walk home was only fifteen minutes. But the closer she got to Mom' house, the worse the feeling became. She stood on her back porch, clammy. Stinking of urine.

The following Friday, Dad coming early to pick them up, she peed herself once more while walking home. Washing out her sweatpants, shame ran over her hands, the horror of what she had done only outweighed by the unbearable thought of anyone finding out.

By the end of the season, she couldn't catch any ball hit her way. The coach moved her to right field. The older girls taunted. Ava wanted to disappear.

"Go talk to your teammates," Dad admonished, embarrassed to see her standing against the fence instead of sitting with the girls in the dugout. "What's wrong with you?"

Ava looked at him through dead eyes.

Now, on the beer ball field, she thought about those softball years. She glanced around at her team, a mix of men and women, cans of Bud set down next to some of the fielders. She felt the shame of being in right field, where she would do the least amount of damage.

Panic rose in her throat. She was a liability. What was I thinking, coming here?

The first baseman encouraged the pitcher, "C'mon, Bill, strike him out!"

"Hey, batta, batta, batta!"

In the fifth inning, a pop fly to right field startled her out of a reverie. Ava allowed the center fielder, a man who had already caught plenty of pop flies, to run up in front of her and catch the ball. As he approached, she considered waving him off, but she couldn't bear the thought of dropping the only ball to come her way that evening.

Thump! The ball hit his glove, solid. Familiar. She knew the satisfaction in that sound. She dredged a feeling back from storage, nostalgia hitting as if looking at a black and white photo. That sound. She could have caught that ball.

Her body remembered the adrenaline-soaked anticipation of waiting for a ball to emerge in the night air, a star falling from the sky. You put a foot back, ready to zigzag a retreat, slightly dizzy from looking up. Bend your knees, ready to bolt forward if it falls short. Steady, steady…Reach. Grasp. Yes! Bring the weight of the ball to your chest, then release--power it off to the cut-off man. She knew this. She watched Jimmie trot back to center field. How had it all gone so wrong?

At her second at-bat, she hit a hard grounder to shortstop, just beating the throw to first. Yes! She high-fived the first base coach.

"Good hustle," he said. "Now, when the ball leaves the pitcher's hand, I want you ready to run."

She nodded. Like a sprinter, she crouched, weight on the ball of her right foot, sweet anticipation rising.

The batter smacked the ball.

Ava flew.

Later, at the bar, the center fielder walked up. Jimmie's jersey was filthy from sliding into bases. It stretched across his large frame, a billboard of his evening. He clinked her glass, "Looked good out there, rookie."

Ava shook her head. "I didn't touch the ball once. Right field doesn't really count as a position."

Jimmie wagged a finger. "That's not true--everyone on the field matters. And everyone here has their own version of tonight's game." He jerked his thumb toward the second baseman, staring morosely at her beer amid teammates who were talking, laughing. "Alison's thinking about the grounder that went through her legs." Jimmie tipped his head toward Bill, loudly gesturing in the center of a group of guys. "Bill will spend the next few months talking about his homerun, which in my version of tonight doesn't count since that fence line is way too close." He looked her up and down. "And in my version, you still looked good out there."

She smiled, glanced up. Made eye contact. "Next time, let me catch my own balls."

Jimmie scooted his seat closer, green eyes shining under matted red hair. "Yes ma'am. But you want the ball, you better speak up. Start playing like you matter." He asked if she'd be at the next game, said he was looking forward to being ordered around in the outfield. "Maybe I could even take you out sometime?" he asked.

Ava thought about Dan's visit in a few weeks. He's not the boss of me. She grinned into her beer. "Maybe."

CHAPTER 13

A BLUEPRINT FOR JOY

O ctober 1st. Brilliant sunny days made the Painted Ladies gleam. By now, Ava had developed a better understanding about her Homeroom duties. Student tiffs were becoming easier to mediate. She had a much better grasp on how to evaluate kids' transcripts and, every once in a while, she felt like she knew what she was doing. She was also willing to admit that that confidence might be a byproduct of the Nyquil shot she'd begun downing most mornings.

What Ava still dreaded were the calls she made to students' homes. Part of her duties as a homeroom teacher included regular calls about truancy and behavior. Ava found that positive phone calls about good attendance were as appreciated as the ones announcing that a student had been skipping class again. If she was lucky, she would get through to apologetic moms or grandmas. More often, she would leave a succession of messages on answering machines, ask emergency contacts to relay messages, or wait twenty rings for the voice mail to announce it was full. Often, numbers that worked one week were disconnected the next.

The only calls Ava regularly received regarding her students were from coaches. "Ms. Llewellyn? Coach Green from Balboa High School here. I've got a player on my team named General? I need to get his attendance and current grades. Only students with 2.0 GPAs are allowed to play, you know."

Ava was confused. "Balboa? I thought General was kicked out of Balboa?"

"Well, as a student, yes, but we still take back kids as players…."

She thought about the General wanting to play ball. She was here to help her students, find a way to improve their lives. General said that basketball was his ticket to college. She resisted the urge to hang up on Coach Green.

That Friday, the magic genie of calm disappeared back into the bottle. It started with an early-morning faculty meeting. The principal was coming from a briefing with the assistant superintendent, who was none to pleased with SFUSD's data. In addition to raising test scores, this year the superintendent had added an additional mandate, calling for teachers to create "joyful learners." Sadly, the superintendent did not provide a blueprint for how teachers might develop said joy. Perhaps he assumed joy was included with the standardized tests that kept kids grasping at ever-moving benchmarks and threatened their diplomas. Yes, there was a lot of joy to cover.

Ms. Sanchez glared at the faculty, handing out thick packets of charts. The twelve teachers, vice principal, Wellness coordinator, and security guard sat in the cafeteria, faces prepped for bad news.

"It's about rigor, people. Do more. Teach more. Set a higher standard! When I walk by your rooms, I have a checklist, and let me tell you, most of you aren't making the cut."

In her mind, Ava saw all the times she had looked up to see Principal Sanchez's face in the doorway of her classroom. The principal's eyes were usually narrowed, busily scratching something on a clipboard while Ava tried to get Charnikka back on track, or Ken, or K'Ron. Whatever was written down on that clipboard wasn't supposed to be part of Ava's formal evaluation, but it couldn't help either. If the principal gave her a poor evaluation as a first year teacher in the district, this would be her last year.

The Wellness coordinator, Mary Kline protested, "But the kids are so much more than those test scores show. There's too much going on outside of school. Maybe we should do more than curricul—"

Ms. Sanchez pointed her finger at a page in the thick packet she clutched in her fist. "Page thirty-four. Our scores are abysmal. Look at this number for Japanese-American kids. What are we not doing for these students? We need to step it up."

Everyone was silent, flipping through pages, thinking, staring at the stats.

Cheryl raised her hand. "I think, statistically—"

"We are failing our students, yes."

"Well, statistically, Ma'am, the number of Japanese-American kids on this chart adds up to one kid."

Ms. Sanchez's mouth set into a hard line. "Well, what are we doing wrong to fail this kid, then?"

Stella, the art teacher, raised her hand. "Maybe we should ask him."

Mary Kline frowned. "Is it Ken Oshiro?"

"He's the only Japanese kid I have," another teacher said.

"Me too."

"You mean the kid with the sparkle bag? Mohawk?"

"I wonder what's up with Ken?"

Ava raised her hand. "He got dumped at the beginning of the semester."

"Ohhhhh."

"He was devastated," Ava said.

"That explains it."

Stella shook her head. "Poor Ken."

Principal Sanchez narrowed her eyes, closing her packet. "We'll talk about this more at our next meeting. The assistant superintendent is visiting later today. I have to prepare. I'd like to have Ms. Brill see a little rigor today, people." She jabbed her pencil at the faculty. "And joy."

Unfortunately, the day didn't get much better from there. First period didn't want to work at all. There had been a shooting over the weekend and several students knew the victim. Second period was interrupted with an earthquake drill. Third period, a girl informed Ava she was pregnant.

By the time the bell rang, announcing the start of Ava's fifteen-minute homeroom, she was done. She held up a sheet of announcements. "Ok, folks, I need you to quiet down so I can read these—"

Paris shouted, "Ms. L, I need you to sign me up for night school!" Back in class following a week's suspension for fighting, Paris had renewed her dedication to finishing school this year.

Ava scanned the table for the folder that held night school information, lost in a stack of similar requests.

Sean raised his hand. "I don't like my science class. Do I have to have a science class next quarter?"

She made a mental note to deal with Paris during her prep hour and searched for Sean's transcript. "I imagine that you will need another science class sometime—twenty credits is the minimum." She had referred him to Wellness last week because he was arriving at school in wrinkled, dirty clothes, often hungry. Sean's foster mom wasn't returning her calls. Sean didn't want to talk about it.

Charnikka raised her hand. "Can you move me from first period English to fourth period English? I hate my English class."

Son of a— "That's my class! No, you cannot switch out." She found Sean and Paris's folders and opened Sean's.

The General called out, "Ms. L, do you know how I can find me a job?"

Ava pointed to the bulletin that she had yet to read. "I thought I saw something in today's announcements. You need to ask the vice principal for more information."

Tanya gripped her head. "Do they have aspirin in Wellness?"

She picked up the classroom phone and called Wellness. "Are you allowed to hand out aspirin?"

On the other end of the line, the part-time nurse sighed, "No, but the art teacher usually has some in her drawer. Send the student to me for some hot tea, but tell them that they should see Stella if they want any drugs."

Kabernay, finally present after another week of excused absences, chose this moment to come alive. "Ms. L, my granny needs you to call her. She says I don't need testing for special education."

Then the bell rang, and like a crowd fleeing a gas leak, they were gone.

Ava surveyed the aftermath of her homeroom tsunami, the front table covered in stacks of blue folders holding kids' transcripts, class-change forms, and night school applications. Finally her prep hour, Ava put her head down on the table, using Stella's suggestion of breathing in troubles and breathing out pink sparkle dust. In breath: troubles; out breath: sparkles. In breath—

"Hi there!" Principal Sanchez called, startling Ava mid-breath. The principal stood in the doorway with her boss, Ms. Brill, one of the school district's three assistant superintendents. The principal's mouth smiled. Her eyes didn't. "We were just touring the school. I thought I'd show my boss one of our Exit Exam classes." She glanced around. "Looks like we caught you on your prep hour, though."

Ava stood up, shoving blue folders into messy piles. "I'd be happy to talk to you about the curriculum," she said, shaking Brill's hand. "I'm Ms. Llewellyn." Contrasting the principal's young, eager face, Ms. Brill was a heavy woman in her late forties. She wore a gray suit and sensible shoes.

Ideas for improvements pushed aside the chaos of the day. "I've been wanting to talk to someone about the Exit Exam books," Ava said. "I'd like to request some different texts, maybe more focus on conquering discrete skills?"

Ms. Brill glanced at the bookshelf, containing rows of Exit Exam workbooks. "Looks like you have enough materials," she said. "That's good to see. Some schools I've visited haven't been following the letter of the law about maintaining enough district-adopted texts in the classroom."

Ava shook her head. "I don't think I'm making my point. Actually, these are pretty worthless. They're almost all practice tests—they don't give kids much support. The stories are boring and—"

"These are the books the district has adopted. Access and equity, you know." Brill eyed the messy stack of blue folders.

Disappointment filled Ava's body. "I'd be happy to draft a propos—"

"I can't stand that man's voice!" Ken burst through the doorway, pushing past the principal and assistant superintendent. He was out of breath but still impressively shrill. "Ms. L, you need to take me out of that art class, 'cause I'ma kill that bitch!" In addition to his silver glitter bag, Ken had on a Day-Glo tee shirt that read *Your Boyfriend Likes Me Better*. His Mohawk was slightly askew.

Brill and Sanchez glared.

Ava put a hand on his shoulder. "Ken, this is the assistant superintendent, Ms. Brill."

Ken eyed Brill's sensible attire. He wrinkled his nose. "Mm hmmm." He turned back to Ava. "Ms. L, if I have to go back into that drumming class with that man, I'ma scream." It seemed a real threat.

Principal Sanchez cleared her throat, displeased about the direction her boss's visit was taking. "Why don't you and Ms. Llewellyn talk it through, Ken? I think you'll find some ways to cope." She turned to leave.

Ava felt desperate. "I'd love to talk to you both later, especially about some ideas I had for different test-prep curriculum…."

Ken took a seat at the nearest table, pulling out a chair for his teacher. He tapped his foot and eyed the three adults impatiently.

Brill gave him a dismissive glance. "I don't think further conversation is necessary, Ms. Luella." She pointed to the shelf full of workbooks. "Looks like you're covered here."

As Brill disappeared down the hall with Principal Sanchez, Ava could hear the women speaking in disapproving tones—something about teachers not making effective use of their prep hour….

Ava sat down next to Ken, "Really?" she rubbed her temple. "You want to drop a class because the drumming teacher, whom you only see once a week, has an annoying voice?"

Ken stuck out his chin, exasperated by the roadblock of her ignorance. "Really annoying voice," he said.

She sighed. "We pay for that man to come in—you deserve some kind of music classes. Some people might see drumming as a privilege."

"Not when some screechy-voiced man teaches it."

This was not an argument she would win. She tried anyway. "You need that art class to graduate, you know."

Ken waved his hand wearily. "Just sign me up for a night school class," he said, as if his homeroom teacher was a concierge at some cheap-ass affair on his world tour.

"That's not on the list as a night school option."

"Well, I'm not staying in that class."

Ava held up her hands. "What do you think should happen, then?"

Ken eyed the blue folders and transcripts littering the table. "It looks like a dump in here."

"Thanks."

Ken smiled, batting his lashes. "I could be your teacher's aide instead."

She looked at him. He was one of the few students who brought his own school supplies, organized his pens by color. Having him help keep the paperwork tidy would—but, no. Teacher's aide was an elective. "Good idea, but not gonna happen while you still need art credit, mister; now get back down there and beat on some drums."

Ken let out one last sigh at the injustice of it all, then picked up his sparkle bag and waved good-bye. "I told them I was going to get some water," he said. "I don't need a pass. Bye, Ms. L!"

"Bye, hon."

Ava watched him saunter out of the room, swinging his sparkle tote. Then his gait slowed. Ken paused in the doorway, "Ms. L?"

"Yes?"

He kicked at the fraying carpet. "I'm sorry I wasted your time." Self-doubt hung on him like an ill-fitting jacket.

Ava shook her head, making eye contact. "You're never a waste of time."

Ken smiled. Then he was gone.

She dug for Ken's folder. His transcript showed him failing all but three classes his first two years of high school. Notes from his last school counselor indicated outbursts, conflicts with teachers and students. His mom never answered her phone.

Ava thought about Ken's Mohawk, Day-Glo tee shirt, sparkle bag, yelling in front of the assistant superintendent…He was trying all her could to be heard. And Ava didn't have the slightest clue how to help him with that.

At the second faculty meeting later that day, the principal echoed Brill's disappointment in Ida B's rigor, joy. Ms. Sanchez frowned. "I'm not seeing it, people," she said. "We can't afford to be labeled a failing school."

Mr. Brennan, the history teacher, raised his hand, "Our kids were kicked out of schools labeled as successful. How successful can those schools be?"

The principal continued as though she hadn't heard. "And on a final note, a new policy will go into effect soon that places Special Day Class kids into regular ed. classrooms."

Ava was confused, then afraid. The Special Ed. Department made up twenty percent of the school. The kids in Special Day Classes had significant disabilities that required an eight-to-one student-to-teacher ratio. The laws were totally different for them. Even Emmett, seeing green, didn't make the cut to get into one of those classes. You had to really have issues. She looked to Cheryl.

"Saving money," her colleague whispered.

Principal Sanchez glared. Her young cheeks burned the color of her mauve pants. "Test scores in Special Ed. classes are down. Kids aren't getting the subject content they need. We're lacking rigor, people."

"Is she shitting me?" Stella mumbled. Still wearing her apron from ceramics class, her white hair was dyed purple at the ends. She raised her hand. "Do you mean the kids with severe learning disabilities, or the kids who are emotionally disturbed? Because giving them less attention in larger classes doesn't seem fair either."

The principal put her hands on her hips. "All Special Ed test scores."

"Gotcha. And those kids will be placed in my classes now?"

"Through a well-thought-out transition program, yes."

Mr. Brennan spoke up. "And that transition program is?"

Principal Sanchez shrugged. "That hasn't been decided on yet."

Cheryl collected her things. "Well, I hope it's joyful."

Stella snorted. "I was going to say rigorous."

CHAPTER 14
HELP ME—I'M WHITE.

October 7th. Ava shook her head, incredulous. The kids were purring like kittens for her guest speaker, a law student named Tolliver Anderson, lecturing to them in a blue sports coat and tie. Tolliver was part of a program out of Hastings Law School called "Street Law." The program promised to use real-world scenarios to teach kids about their rights. Over the next several months, Tolliver Anderson would prepare the students for a mock trial in a real courtroom.

Ava hoped Street Law would spark interest, get her kids reading and writing. A number of students already knew how it felt to be frisked, searched, and arrested. Street Law could give them a chance to experience the law from the other side of the bench.

When she first introduced her speaker, the students homed in on the most important question surrounding the guest: "What kind of a name is Tolliver?"

Tolliver laughed, unbuttoning his blazer. "Well, it's a long story, really. See, my parents—"

"Can we call you *T*?" Sean asked.

He frowned. "No. But my friends call me Tolly."

Ava held her breath. A kiss of death was sure to follow.

The kids were silent.

Are you kidding me? Just last week, she had said, "Okie dokie, artichokie," and her students were still mocking the phrase in falsetto. But a grown man calling himself *Tolly*? Apparently, that had dignity.

And now Tolly was lecturing on the specifics of Good Samaritan laws. And students were paying attention. Ava studied her guest. Who is this guy?

Tolly smoothed his tie, "Designed to make the average citizen take responsibility for his or her neighbor's well-being. Let's look at a scenario—"

Hector burst into class. "Thnappleth for everyone!" His long hair was in a disheveled ponytail, cheeks flushed.

The room erupted in shouts, Samaritan laws forgotten.

That's my boy. Ava leaned in to the morning's Nyquil buzz, trying not to smirk. Welcome to my world, Tolly.

Snapple iced tea bottles rattled from a box in Hector's arms.

"Here!" Sean yelled.

Hector threw a bottle.

Ava lunged for it, attempting an interception. Too late.

Sean held the bottle above his head.

"That's enough," Ava hissed. "Everyone, Knock it off. Sit down. We have a guest."

Hector found a seat and opened a bottle. The kids reluctantly settled back into their chairs.

Tolly seemed frozen.

"Please. Continue," Ava said, moderator now between academia and Bill Hickok's Wild West Show.

Tolly resumed his lecture, his voice wavering, "So…if you were walking past someone who was being beaten, the current law says that you don't—"

Hector took a final gulp of the drink in his hand. "I'm done," he announced. The bottle was still half-full. "Who wantth thith Thnapple?"

"Here!"

"No, me!"

"Throw it!" yelled Francisco.

Oh, for the love of God. Ava glared. She strode across the room, took the whole box of drinks from Hector, and set it crashing down on her desk. "We'll decide that later. We're going to be a good audience now for…" she took a deep breath… "Tolly."

Tolliver nodded, flushed. "…past someone who was being beaten, you don't have to call the police, but wouldn't that be the right thing to do?"

"Hell, no," Francisco said. "It's none of my business."

"Someone getting beaten," Tolly said, "in front of you. Is none of your business?"

"Fuck no," Charnikka said. "You'll get yo ass whooped for snitchin' like that."

K'Ron shook her head. "I ain't gonna get my ass whooped for no stranger."

Tolly and Ava stared at one another. "But what if it wasn't a stranger?" Ava asked. "What if it was me getting beaten on the street? You'd call the police then, right?" She looked around.

The students avoided her gaze.

Ava felt a knot in her chest. She asked again, softer, "Right?"

Francisco thought about it. "I might when I get home," he said, "but you'd be dead then, so what's the point?"

She glanced at his cell phone lying on her desk. "You wouldn't call on your cell phone?"

"Hell, naw. Someone would be coming after me then, and that's your business." He paused. "Maybe if *you* made the call…"

"But I'm the one getting beaten to death."

Francisco shook his head. "But you're white."

"That's for sure!" the kids chimed in.

"I've never seen someone so white."

Francisco raised his hand.

"Thanks for raising your hand," Ava said. She looked pointedly at the rest of her students. "What's your comment or question?"

"Can I call you *honkey*?"

Ava stared.

"You could call me *nigger*," Francisco suggested.

Tolliver turned red.

"That's not even—no," Ava sputtered. "We're not doing racial slurs."

Melvin waved his arm, a banner in a windstorm.

"Yes?"

"Can we call you 'cracker'?"

Ava put a hand to her temple. "No. Now can we please get back to the subject?"

"But that is the subject," said Francisco. "You see someone getting attacked, and you just call the number and say, "Help! I'm white!" and the police will come. We call for help and we get our asses whooped for snitchin' 'cause no one will bother with Latinos."

The students nodded their heads.

"That's for sure."

"Try livin' in a black neighborhood. Ain't no one gonna help your ass."

"My cousin waited for three hours when he got shot."

Under his hoodie, the General said, "Ambulance don't go into my neighborhood either."

Hector spoke up. "We gotta all thart calling for help and thaying, "I'm white! Help me—I'm white!"

The students agreed. "Betcha Ms. L's fingers are always on 9-1-"

"Yeah, she makes five calls on her way home."

Melvin shouted in falsetto, "Help! This is Ms. L! Yes—I'm white!"

Thirty minutes later, Ava gave Tolliver an apologetic smile as he left for his law class. "You're doing a good job," she said. "Some days are like that."

Tolliver shook his head as he left the room. She wondered if tomorrow, while within the confines of law school, he'd debrief the day's lesson. She saw how days like this would encourage his cohort to join a growing number of middle class parents who sent their children to private schools.

On her way out, K'Ron touched Ava's arm. "You know those Snapples?"

She nodded, frowning. The Snapple incident seemed like a long time ago.

"You figured out they were stolen, right?"

Ava covered her face.

"Off the back of a Walgreens' truck. Hector and Francisco were talking about it in Spanish all period."

She thought back. "I heard Francisco talking, but all I could make out was 'puta' every once in a while. I thought they were talking about me." She grimaced. "Puta means "bitch," right?"

"Actually," K'Ron stared at the carpet, "they were saying whore."

Ava's face fell. *Bitch* was a general term; *whore* was personal. All this time. They hate me. She glanced at the clock. 9:45 a.m. Way too early for committing crimes and calling your teacher a whore. As K'Ron closed the door, Ava wiped her cheek. Fuck it. Fuck all of this. Maybe next week Tolly could lecture the class on the consequences of larceny. If she was still here, she would study up on the difference between how to say "bitch" and "whore" in Spanish. And "Fuck it." That should probably be on the list as well.

CHAPTER 15

SHITTING GREEN

It was after school that day when Ava realized she was shitting green.

In the faculty bathroom, the lighting was always off. The lavatory was a former closet in the copy room, lit by one bare bulb. The bleak light turned one's business into more of an interrogation seat. She looked down. Yep, green. She put her head in her hands. Shit.

The day seeped down. When she got home, she called Ruthie. "Did you ever call your teacher a whore in high school?" She didn't feel wrong for hoping the answer would be *yes*.

Ruthie chuckled. "No they didn't! That's really funny."

The balloon in Ava's chest deflated all the way. "Not really."

"Oh, hon, I wouldn't worry about it too much. In high school, I was too high to notice we even had teachers." Ruthie groaned. "Now I'm too pregnant to remember I ever had feet. Do you know what cankles are? My legs go straight down. No calves, no ankles. Textbook cankles."

Ava pictured Ruthie's ankles, thick as telephone poles. "Anything I can do?"

"Naw. I sent Bill out for ice cream and a Whopper. It calms the demon voices. How are you? Besides the kids calling you a whore." Ruthie snorted back a laugh. "Sorry." She snorted again. "A whore?"

"I can call back."

Ruthie took a deep breath. "Okay, okay—I'm done. Why the hell would they say that?"

Ava sighed. "I'm pretty much a failure."

"Now you knew going in this would be tough—"

"And I'm shitting green."

Ruthie coughed. "Beg pardon?"

"Green." Ava spoke clearly into the phone. "I think it's from taking Nyquil every night."

"Oh, God—"

"And some mornings—for the past six weeks."

"Shit!"

"That's what I said."

"Well, stop taking the damn stuff!"

"See, now that's the problem. I'll stop, but I know I'll just start right back up again. It calms the demon voices." She heard Dan's voice, the kids'. "There's a lot of voices."

"Honey, you've got to get some help."

"I'm not going to AA or NA," Ava groaned. "I'd never hear the end of it from Dan. And I'm not giving up drinking either. Complete sobriety is for sad, sad people." She thought about it and added, "Alcoholics at least are fun at a party."

There was silence on the other end. Then Ruthie said, "Well, I'm with you—who doesn't love a good fall-down drunk? But, Ava, you need to do something. A colleague goes to ACA—Adult Children of Alcoholics—and dysfunctional families. Doesn't that sound fun?"

Ava considered. "I'm not sure how much the alcohol part applies. Is there an Adult Children of Motherfucking Crazy?"

Ruthie laughed. "I don't think so, but you could look it up. They have meeting days and times listed. Do you want me to come with you?"

Ruthie's kindness reminded Ava of when she started junior high in a new town. Ava's arms were still wrapped in bandages, bangs spikey from the fire. She sat in the car outside of school.

"I can't go in," she told her mom. Her reflection in the passenger's side window reminded her that other kids' faces were not two-toned. Monsters were not welcomed in junior high.

"I could go in with you," Mom offered, describing the only scenario worse than going into the school building alone.

"No thanks," Ava said. She opened the car door.

That first week, the kids were welcoming. A girl with long curly hair showed her to her math class. In social studies, a large boy chatted up Ava before dragging her, desk and all, closer to his seat. "You're too far away!" he declared.

Ava shrank in her chair. She didn't want to be noticed. She didn't want him to see the scars.

A redheaded girl put him straight. "Leave her alone, Alex, you're embarrassing her."

"But I want the new girl to sit near me."

Ava sat still, cheeks crimson, confused. Did they not see her face? Her hair?

She didn't understand why these kids were being so kind. Just like she didn't understand why Ruthie was kind to her now. Obviously, her friend didn't have the good sense to run.

She pictured Ruthie on the other end of the line, eager to help. "No, thanks," she said. "I'm embarrassed enough to have to go. I'd rather just do it alone."

That evening, she looked up meeting dates online, finding one on Friday she could commit to trying. This was Tuesday. She reluctantly poured out the rest of the Nyquil knowing if she threw it away, she'd just find an excuse to take it out of the garbage. It was for the best. So why do I feel like shit?

The rest of the evening stretched into infinity. She had papers to grade, lessons to plan, but all she wanted to do was climb into bed and try to forget she had been called a whore by kids she wanted so badly to like her. Then Ava thought of Dan telling her he'd wasted years of his life checked out on pot and alcohol. She knew that making a new start didn't mean numbing out. She hoped ACA had some answers. Shitting green wasn't exactly the future she'd dreamed of as a little girl.

She looked at the clock by Dan's face. It was only six. A whole evening yet to fill. She left the ungraded papers in her school bag. Digging in her closet for her photo album, she lied down on her bed, flipping to the first few pages. She needed to see the cats. She wanted to feel that deep, dull ache of loss that made it seem like being near them hadn't been so long ago.

The cats. Always, it came back to the cats. She remembered how she felt when she found them in the haystack when she was ten, lifting their tiny bodies up into the light, her love for them immediate, consuming, maternal. Eyes half closed, they'd communicated adoration and followed her around like puppies. Ava gazed back at them through lowered lids. I love you. Love you. Love you.

In the photograph, Pumpkin, appropriately round, burrowed under her arm, his thick orange fur was therapy on her fingers, heart. Ava had named the long-haired black kitten after a character in a children's book, Sambo. The book's protagonist was a young, black child. He chased tigers around a tree until they melted into butter for his pancakes. Ava adored him. It would be years before she learned the name was racist, cringe-worthy, and hateful. She would cry, but that was later. She spent the evenings of her childhood sitting cross-legged on the porch with the cats piled onto her lap. The cats' raspy, rhythmic breathing conveyed contentment. Matching her breath to theirs—in, out—she'd watch the sun drift softly below the mountains.

Holding tight to the album, without the comforting promise of Nyquil, Ava kissed her fingertips and pressed them against the furry heads in the photograph. Tears turned the pictures blurry. She closed her eyes and saw them trailing behind her through the stands of cedar, tamarack, spruce. Like an expedition of naturalists, they wound deep into the foothills, careful to avoid the delicate white trillium and tiny wild strawberries wafting a sweet scent into the mountain air.

CHAPTER 16
CAREER DAY

On Thursday, a box of new textbooks sat outside Ava's door. In response to the pressure of keeping test scores up, the district supplied all schools with textbooks dictating day-by-day not only what should be taught, but highlighting in bold what teachers should say to their students when teaching that material.

Cheryl Wilson passed her in the hallway. She nodded toward the box of books. "Burn them," Cheryl said.

Ava looked doubtfully at the shiny new covers. "The old ones are pretty useless. I can't imagine these are much better."

Cheryl smiled. "The school district would like to think those books are teacher-proof."

"And that means?"

"They'd like to think that whether it's me up there teaching or a trained horse tapping out metaphors with its hooves, no one should be able to mess it up." Cheryl snorted, her dark complexion giving way to cheeks that bloomed pink. "Teacher-proof texts are supposed create joyful test-takers. The kids hate them."

Noting that her students went into comas when asked to open the older versions, Ava decided to ignore the new teacher-proof books altogether. The thought of bringing kids from fifth grade literacy levels to that of tenth graders gave her a stomachache. Still, if Ava could get them to pass the Exit Exam, her students would have a chance of passing college classes, finding better jobs, living better, happier lives. She wanted them to be happy. That's why she was here.

So Ava spent her evenings and weekends creating lessons that would get her students to the appropriate grade level. Today, her kids were set to share "how-to" speeches. Tomorrow, they'd write essays from that information.

With thanks for it being a Thursday—students often didn't come Mondays or Fridays; sunny, but not *too* sunny—attendance dropped on rainy days and those that were brilliant and warm; and not a national holiday like April twentieth, most of the class was present. Ida B. Wells was home to 250 students on the books. On any luke-warm mid-week day, 180 showed up.

That morning, students taught Ava how to pierce her own tongue, make Top Ramen, pick out the best pair of Jordan sneakers, and do the "Stanky Leg" move on a dance floor.

"Ok, Tanya," she said. "Your turn." Without Nyquil, the room was more in focus, her emotions hanging on the edge. She surveyed the rest of the class. "I really want everyone to concentrate on getting your audience points. That means if you aren't presenting, I shouldn't hear you rapping." She glanced at Emmett.

Despite his glowing purple pupils, the kid was still seeing green. "I gotta practice my art," Emmett said. "I'ma lay down another track this week. Anyone wanna buy my album?"

The class groaned. They were over it, over him.

Tanya refused to get up. "Charnikka already took mine."

"Really?" Ava reviewed her list of presenters. "How to make Top Ramen?"

Tanya nodded.

"I'm sure you have a lot of talents." Ava looked at Tanya's long hair, braided into a neon rainbow of greens and yellows. "How about how to put in a weave?"

Charnikka snickered.

Ken shook his head, patient father to slow learner. "Everyone already knows how to do that."

Ava didn't point out that boiling water for Ramen wasn't exactly groundbreaking information.

"How about how to make a sandwich?" suggested Sean.

"How about how to be a dumb-ass?" said Francisco, slouched low in his seat.

"Be nice." Ava warned.

"What about how to not get a job at Macys?" suggested K'Ron.

The class looked up, interested.

K'Ron glanced around. "They wouldn't even let my sister have an interview."

"Why not?" Ava frowned. The school had just lost funding for its half-time college and career counselor. Many students spent a lot of time looking for jobs without a clue how to start.

K'Ron sighed. "Because my sister is darker than me. She sounds white, though, so she was called in for an interview. But when the lady saw her, she said, 'We're not looking for more of you here.'" K'Ron twisted her large hoop earring. She had drawn her eyeliner into Cleopatra-like cat's eyes. Ava wondered how she'd feel seeing K'Ron for the first time in an interview.

Melvin chuckled. "That's 'cause they know Cholas are gonna steal."

K'Ron stuck out her chin. "Not if I'm getting paid to work there."

"She's Salvadorian, fucktard," Francisco said, half-rising in his seat. "Cholas are Mexican."

Melvin stood all the way up, nostrils flaring.

"Stop! Stop!" Ava said. She held her hands out, adrenaline rising.

Melvin eased into his seat.

Niesha, sporting pink lace-up stilettos, turned to K'Ron. Niesha had joined the class a week ago. She made the 33rd student enrolled in Ava's Test Prep English, though Principal

111

Sanchez was quick to point out that no more than twenty-four had ever shown up on the same day. "They wouldn't give me or my cousin an interview either," Niesha said. "The lady made us wait for thirty minutes, then she comes out and says, "I don't think our store is a good fit for you." I told her, "Bitch, what you know about me?"

The class stared open-mouthed, Niesha the new favorite.

"Then what happened?" Ava breathed.

The girl shrugged. "The lady called security and now we aren't allowed in there." She laughed. "So last weekend I helped myself to these jeans."

"And girl, you're looking fiiinnne," Charnikka air-high-fived across the room.

"I'ma be a make-up artist," K-Ron said. Her arched brows challenged any nay-sayers.

"Girl, you could work for my clients," Ken said. He hugged his sparkle tote. "I'ma be a Gucci buyer and personal shopper." Ken's tee shirt read: *Blink if You Want Me*. He looked Ava up and down. "First thing I would do is give Ms. L a makeover."

"That's for sure," a kid muttered.

Ava stopped breathing. Oh, no. New topic.

Ken sat back, hand to chin. "Maybe a pencil skirt. You're either working with those hip or against them."

"Big hoop earrings," said K'Ron.

"A military jacket."

"A military jacket?" Ava thought about it. It wasn't a bad idea. "What about the shoes?" She looked doubtfully at her sensible, comfortable clogs. "I can't wear these with a skirt."

Ken muttered, "You can't wear those with anything."

"Some knee-high boots," Niesha weighed in.

Ava smiled. "I like it."

Tanya perked up. "I know what I can do for my speech, Ms. L."

"That's great," Ava said, shaking herself out of the makeover reverie. "Are you ready now? Do you want time to prepare?"

Tanya was already out of her seat. "You have tin foil in the art supplies, right?"

"On the big table in the corner."

Tanya pulled out a roll of tin foil that Ava's senior English class had used in making statues of Nike, in preparation for studying *The Odyssey.* "Do you have a paper bag?" she asked.

Ava found a bag behind her overflowing desk. "I'm so glad you thought of something." She was really working on getting students to be more solutions oriented, rather than telling their teacher all the reasons they couldn't do an assignment.

Tanya stood in the front of the room, showing off her materials. "I'ma show you how to make a beeper bag," she said.

Trickles of laughter filled the room, then morphed into an eruption.

"You are so ghetto," Charnikka hooted, wiping a tear from the corner over her eye. Her usually rosy cheeks glowed bright red.

Sean pounded on the table.

Francisco chuckled, leaning back in his chair.

"Preach it, girl!" yelled Niesha, thrusting her fist into the air.

Tanya held up the bag. "First you need a shopping bag. This one's a little big, but I'ma make it work." Tanya's brow furrowed as she concentrated on lining the bag with tin foil. "If you don't put the tin foil all the way around the inside of the bag, the beeper will go off," she informed the group.

Ava glanced around, confused. "What beeper?" she asked, breaking her own rule about not interrupting during presentations.

Charnikka chortled. "The store beeper."

Tanya nodded, explaining to Ava as if helping a child, "You put the clothes into the bag," she said, pantomiming, "then when you go through the doors, the sensors don't go off."

Ava wasn't following.

Tanya broke it down. She pointed inside the bag. "The tin foil prevents the beepers from going off when you boost clothes." She looked at her teacher. "Get it?"

"You mean…when you steal?" Ava's stomach hurt. She imagined the kids talking to their folks tonight about what they'd learned in class today. "Tanya! You can't give a how-to speech on stealing!"

Tanya looked confused. "Why not? You didn't say we couldn't talk about boosting."

Francisco chimed in, Tanya's legal representation. "That's true. You can't change the rules halfway through. That's not fair."

Emmett, who had most recently been pissing off the class with claims of a million-dollar record deal, got up to leave the room.

"Emmett!" Ava called, "You need to ask first. And take the pass."

Emmett kept going through the door.

Exasperated, Ava hustled after him, grabbing the large bathroom pass on the way.

"You need to give clearer directions!" Paris yelled at her back.

Ava soon saw that Emmett had no intention of going to the bathroom. He stopped at the classroom door, handing a plastic baggie to a kid Ava hadn't seen before. The kid gave Emmett a twenty.

She stared in horror. "You've got to be kidding me." She grabbed the cash out of Emmett's hand.

Emmett stared back, purple pupils glowing in disbelief. Their mutual outrage had them both in slow motion. "Who you think you is?" he demanded. His chest puffed up.

"Get back in the room," Ava said, shaking. Makes a drug deal right in front of me? Asshole. She would nail his disrespectful ass to the wall.

Emmett walked back to his seat.

Ava marched over to the phone.

"Oooohhhh, Emmett." laughed Hector. "You'th in trouuuuble!"

"C'mon, Ms. L.," said Francisco, "he's just trying to make some bones."

"Yeah," pleaded Paris. "Don't be a snitch." She turned to Emmett. "You sure is dumb."

Emmett leaned back in his chair, unconcerned. "Wanna buy my album?" he asked Ken.

Ava used her shaking snitch finger to dial the office. "I caught Emmett making a drug deal," she told the vice principal.

"What was he selling?"

Powder? Weed? She tried to remember..."I don't know. Something in a baggie."

"Snitch!" yelled Francisco.

"I'll send Fifty up to get him," said the vice principal.

"Don't tell them anything," Francisco advised Emmett.

"Dumb-ass," Melvin mused. "You need to do that in the park across from the school, or at least in the bathroom."

Charnikka agreed. "You do that in front of a teacher, you know they're gonna call the cops."

Ava put down the phone and walked Emmett to a corner of the room. To her surprise, he didn't look upset, angry, sad—anything really. She leaned in. This was it. Neither one could undo what had been done. "I'm so sorry," she said. "I can't have students making drug deals at my door."

"I gotta have bones for studio time," Emmett said, matter-of-fact.

Ava watched his eyes not register the situation. The weight of his impending suspension, or, worse, expulsion, pulled at her conscience. She'd made things worse for him. He needed therapy, medication, a job. Snitching wasn't going to make any of that happen. She shook her head.

Fifty arrived to escort Emmett away.

"We'll continue tomorrow," Ava told the class. Without Nyquil to look forward to this evening, she had had enough sober how-to's for one day.

CHAPTER 17
BUNDLES

Friday. In the waning October evening, she walked slowly into the church—Russian Orthodox, regal, worn. Loved. There were a few people already seated around a foldout table. Professionals and those dressed in jeans and sweaters. Tired. Worn. In between the silence, they spoke in whispers. Everyone clutched mugs with both hands as if clinging to life rafts, hot comfort steaming into the air.

Mug. Got it. Ava made a note of what to bring next time—if there was a next time. She smiled and forced eye contact, regretting not downing a glass of wine before she came.

A large woman in a teal sweat suit smiled back. "Welcome. This your first time at this meeting?"

Ava nodded.

"We're glad you're here," said another woman at the head of the table. She had presence, a quiet assurance. "I'm Georgia."

"Hi," Ava said.

The door opened. More people came in. A man in his mid-sixties, a woman in a business suit.

"Well, it's almost time," Georgia said. "Good to see you Jerry, Angela."

Everyone opened up thick red books, their names written on the edges of the pages. The woman in the sweat suit pushed a book over to Ava. "I'm Lydia."

At seven o'clock, Georgia, the secretary, read off a welcome. Then everyone monotoned a prayer. Something about wisdom and what we can't control. Ava felt that if she had enough wisdom, she would have more control. Maybe this wasn't the group for her. Everyone said their names. It felt a bit like camp, or how one might become indoctrinated into a cult.

When it was her turn to speak, she forgot her own name. *Breathe. Just breathe.* Still, a church, chants, a format that everyone else knew…She was already way out of her league.

Georgia read off the Laundry List, fourteen dysfunctional traits common among adult children of alcoholics.

Awesome. Fourteen habits of highly ineffective people. Ava zoned out. There was something about controlling behaviors, being reactive rather than proactive….

Georgia read out, "We will do anything to hold onto a relationship, avoiding painful abandonment feelings."

Ava snapped to attention. She saw Dan's photograph on her dresser. That's a whole trait by itself?

Georgia read, "Number Ten: We have stuffed our feelings from our traumatic childhoods and have lost the ability to feel or express our feelings because it hurts so much—denial.'"

Ava flipped through her catalogue of feelings. The selections were limited. School terrified her. She was afraid that Dan would be gone from her life forever. What made her happy? Most often, the kids. Ruthie. Bill. What did she need? She felt only a dead emptiness, the absence of feeling.

She glanced around at the group of mostly middle-aged San Franciscans. They were nodding, Georgia reading out their dysfunctional lives. No one was mocking the process. Then it dawned on her: Twenty-eight years old and these are my people. No wonder I'm fucked.

After the recital of the Laundry List, Georgia read out the numbered list of Promises, as in what ACA promised if you stuck it out. "Number seven: We will feel stable, peaceful, and financially secure."

Ava thought about her love life, her career, her credit card debt. Throw in a pony and I'm sold.

The meeting format called for reading from the large red book and then sharing. About feelings. Shit.

Georgia admonished the group against cross talk. "Cross talk means interrupting, referring to, or commenting on another person's share. We don't cross talk because, as children, we were not listened to. What we say here is true for us."

Ava's family didn't talk about the past, each person wanting to move forward, avoid acknowledging that anything bad had happened. It was eerie, like a crime scene throngs of people walked through everyday and never mentioned. But what was it Georgia had read? *What we say here is true for us.* It didn't have to ring true for anyone else. Ava felt a space clear in her chest.

The group read a section of the text that focused on bundles, as in, adult children carry bundles that were passed on to them from their parents: messages of worth, personal safety. Childhood coping skills morphed into dysfunctional behaviors in adulthood—and all of this, the messages, behaviors, one's parents had received from *their* parents.

For the first time in her life, Ava contemplated the impact of her grandparents' behaviors on her parents' self worth. No wonder.

Lydia, fiftyish, barely fitting into her size-sixteen tracksuit, shared out first. "It's those housewives." Lydia rubbed her face with both palms. "I tell myself, 'Lydia, get it together, woman. You are not watching the *Real Housewives* tonight, and you will not, under any circumstances, eat that whole carton of ice cream in the freezer.' Then it becomes, 'Lydia, don't you dare finish that episode, and there better be at least two bites of ice cream to put back in that freezer.'" Lydia groaned. "I just get so *nervous*. Growing up, I had to be wary all the time. Would Mom be drunk? Would Dad come home? Who knew I'd still be on edge, even now?" She sighed. "So I'm off the booze. I'm in the Other Program. But now I play whack-a-mole with other addictions. Shopping. Eating. My mother was like that too. Her bundle became mine. Or maybe I just want some effing ice cream. Thank you."

"Thank you," the group responded.

Ava tried not to stare in horror. She wondered who went next, if they talking in a circle or—

Across the table, Jerry spoke, "Like I've shared before, my dad was a miner. When he first went into the mines, he was twelve. He worked miles underground. Started drinking then, too, from when I hear. By the time I came along, he didn't see me. Maybe because I didn't have anything in common with him, like he had with his dad—mining, drinking. Now I can see the ways that I was just like him—I used silence and moodiness to get what I wanted from my own family.

When I first came here, I didn't see how I was manipulating. I see that now with my last two wives. I would get this loop in my head. I started thinking that my ex wanted to leave me three years ago. I accused her of hating me, of wanting a divorce. I think I talked her into it."

Ava pictured Dan sitting a the bar their first meeting. She remembered the thrill of him taking jabs at her. She was beginning to see her own role in her apocalyptic love life.

Jerry stared at his coffee mug. "But now I'm not sure what I'm doing here. I think it's helped my relationship with my sons. We talk now. I listen. I never drank, but I don't suppose it's a coincidence they're both married to alcoholics anyway." He shrugged. "I'm sixty-four years old. How much am I really going

119

to change? Mostly, digging up this old stuff just hurts. Anyway. Thank you."

"Thank you, Jerry," the group intoned. They waited for the next person to volunteer to share.

Ava took a deep breath. This is stupid. I don't need to share on the first—"I'm Ava," she said.

"Hi Ava."

She was surprised at how good their acknowledgement felt. "I guess I'm here because I can't seem to make anything work."

People nodded their heads.

"I used to live in Washington." Ava took a breath. "One day my boyfriend and I were at a Seahawks game. I was talking about a play, about the players. Then it hit me that I was talking too much. And I panicked, you know? I held my breath and stayed still. It felt like I had been caught doing something awful. Sure enough, my boyfriend snapped. Just like my dad used to do."

Ava picked at her cuticles. That was enough. She didn't need to say any—"I'm a teacher—am I allowed to share that?" She looked around for an okay. "I tried to help kids in Washington, but I couldn't even help myself."

A woman handed her a tissue.

Ava continued, "Anyway, I thought about taking a bunch of pills, just ending the cycle that way."

Ava died a slow death of mortification until Jerry leaned in, his eyes kind.

"But I'm not a quitter. I dumped the boyfriend, said I'd give a new city a try—a new life. Maybe I could save other kids. I wouldn't choose those kinds of guys. But here I am—new city, same life. I took the bundle. Now I don't know what to do. So I came here."

The group nodded. "Thank you."

Georgia read out a prayer. Ava heard, "Let go and let God." What the prayer didn't do is specify *how*.

When the meeting concluded, Lydia walked over. "Thanks for your share," she said. Her smile was warm.

What an odd thing to say, Ava thought. She found Lydia less of a caricature in her tracksuit, standing there like that, face open.

"I hope you'll come back next week. It gets better."

Ava willed a smile. Had Lydia not heard her own share about the ice cream? *That* was better? But something in her really liked Lydia. Hearing the other people's stories of failure and fucking up was like having a warm blanket tucked around her shoulders in the cold. She didn't feel as out there, alone as she had when she'd walked in that night.

"I'll be back," Ava said.

Later, at home, she called Dan. He picked up on the first ring.

"Hey, you'll never guess. I went to a meeting."

"AA?"

She ignored his tone. "No, ACA."

"That's a start."

She switched gears. "I miss you. What time are you driving down on Friday?"

CHAPTER 18

BUBKUS

A cool, gray morning. Halloween was a day away, and many students had already announced they'd be taking today as an unpaid holiday. Ava glanced around the room. Though her class was making steady progress, they still had a long way to go in order to pass the Exit Exam. Kids' grades were looking as abysmal as the weather.

At least Tolly was proving a big hit. The students were already brainstorming situations for their mock trial, and Ava got a lot of mileage out of having students write from real-life scenarios, such as the ever popular: "Let's review all the situations in which you could shoot someone and call it self defense."

On this day, drab and dark over the Painted Ladies, students only wanted to chat and play around instead of revising their essays. Ken was showing Paris how she should braid her hair with a side part instead of down the middle. Charnikka kept pulling out her novel, *Deep Throat Diva.* Francisco was swapping information with another student that seemed to include the words "dime bag" and "supply." Ava couldn't wait for the day to be over, Dan driving up to her apartment.

Watching her squirrelly crew get busy on everything other than their assigned task, she finally lost patience. "Ok folks, I want to see you all get going on your ess—"

Hector burst into the room. His 49ers jacket reeked of weed. He triumphantly waved a late pass at Ava's face.

She stepped backwards as an involuntary reaction to the fumes. Losing balance, she bumped the closet door ajar, which held the cleaning supplies she'd brought for the room. A broom clattered to the floor.

"So that's where you keep it," Melvin observed.

K'Ron snickered. "Bruja," she whispered to Francisco.

Witch. They're calling me a witch.

Francisco chuckled.

The other kids turned to watch their teacher unravel.

"Hector," Ava said, her face flaming, "you smell like weed."

Hector looked at her blankly. "I don't thmell anything."

"You've been smoking pot!"

"No, I haven't."

"Ms. L, you can't accuse a student of smoking weed," Paris said. "You can't prove that he smoked anything."

Ava glared at Paris, then back at Hector. "Well, then, did you *eat* something that smells like weed?"

Hector shook his head, eyes wide with innocence.

Charnikka opened a window, "I can't be smelling like that when I pick up my daughter."

Ava could see that accusations weren't getting her anywhere. She took a deep breath, inhaling a strong, skunky scent reminiscent of her dorm years. "Ok, Hector, were you riding in a car with someone *else* who was smoking? And maybe that smoke got into your jacket accidentally?"

Paris laughed, which turned into a cough.

Hector tilted his head to the side. "Maybe."

"Well, then, I suggest that you take your jacket down to the vice principal and leave it in his office. Then you can come back up. We'll see if that alleviates the majority of the problem."

Hector nodded.

Ava took his late pass. "Tomorrow, if you *once again* ride in a car with someone who is smoking, I'm going to send you home."

Taking another hit off her student's smoky aura, she marched him into the hallway, writing on the other side of his late pass that he needed to leave his jacket in the office or go home.

Returning to the room, Ava addressed the class. "Ok, folks, " she barked, "if you don't turn in your final drafts, I'm not giving you any credit; you'll get *bubkus.*"

That got their attention. Students sat up, alarmed.

"What she say?" asked Sean. His usually cheerful demeanor was at high alert.

Francisco stared at her. "I'll get what kissed?"

K'Ron made a face. "Ewwwww!"

Ken turned pale.

Other kids shifted uncomfortably in their seats. The room grew quiet. Students looked down at the tables in front of them.

Melvin whispered, "Ms. L, I don't think you're supposed to say stuff like that."

Stuff like what? Bubkus? Bub-kiss, Butt-k—They thought I said I was going to kiss their... "Oh my God," Ava put a hand to her face. "*Bubkus* is a Yiddish word meaning *nothing*. That's all I was saying—if you don't turn in final drafts, you'll get nothing."

A slow smile spread across Melvin's face. He sat straight in his chair and began to sing, "I got a feeling..."

Sean set a beat with his fingers on the table. Both boys began bouncing up and down.

Ava stared. What the hell was going on?

The General, in an uncharacteristic bout of showmanship, picked up the song. "That tonight's gonna be a good night..." He put his shoulders into a Temptations-like groove.

Tanya shook her neon braids, chiming in. "I know that we'll have a baaaaall…"

K'Ron tapped her long nails on the table. "If we go down, get out, and just lose it aaaaall…"

The rest of the class took up the cause. Even the usually quiet Kabernay bounced up and down while singing, "I feel stressed out, I wanna let it go, let's go way out, spaced out, and losing all control…"

"Ok, folks," Ava held up her hands. She knew the song, but had no idea what the kids were getting at. The sing-along had gone on long enough.

But the students were hitting their stride. "Fill up my cup, MAZEL TOV!" they all pantomimed lifting glasses high in a rousing toast.

Everyone laughed. Ava put a hand to her mouth. Ida B. Wells didn't have any Jewish students. They must have seen the toast on the Black Eyed Peas music video, but how did Melvin know that *mazel tov* was a Yiddish word?

She gazed at the ragtag bunch of kids in front of her. Stoned, under-educated, and over-brilliant. She may be a bruja, but even this witch had to give them credit. She thought about ACA, feelings, what made her happy. *They make me happy.* She raised her own imaginary goblet. "Mazel tov." She would make it through this day. Then she would see Dan.

CHAPTER 19

DAN

Ava walked home in the bright afternoon light, expecting at every corner to see the glare of Dan's cherry red convertible. It was the car they had taken on so many adventures, wind against their faces. It was the car whose top refused to close during an April thunderstorm when they were still in Seattle traffic, an hour from home. They arrived in Olympia soaked though and laughing. It was the car and the man she had left behind. The last time she had seen that car, she never wanted to see it again.

When she turned the corner onto her street, he was standing outside her apartment building, tossing a ball against the concrete wall with the neighborhood boys. Tall, blonde, sure—Dan. When he wrapped her in a hug, she smelled spearmint gum, the scent of the past three years. She knew the width of his shoulders, his laugh, the look in his eyes when he was planning a new adventures for them.

He suggested a restaurant his guidebook recommended, a Cuban place two blocks from her apartment. Over a plate of spicy pork, he told her about their mutual friends, filling her in on his life since she'd left. "I'm volunteering at the animal rescue on weekends."

Ava sat back in her chair. "I didn't know you even liked animals. You won't go near your brother's dog."

"I didn't like eating animals."

Ava pointed to the last few bites of pork on his plate. "Until you did."

Dan smiled that old smile. "I'm trying to balance out my karma."

Ava talked about Stella and Cheryl and the beer ball team. Happy and stuffed, she suggested an evening in, but he insisted she go to her game tonight; he wanted to see her new scene.

They took his car. Ava had always thought the convertible was cool, but now, driving through the city, it seemed too much. A moving target, a display of money.

"So you're Ms. Social Butterfly now that I'm not around to hold you back," Dan said.

She hoped they'd make it to the game without being carjacked at a light. She locked her door. "I don't really know them. We all just went out for beers after the last game. Bill's the only person I'm friends with."

Dan ran a hand over his abdomen, taut under a navy button-down. "Well, I hope Bill's lost some weight since he and Ruthie were up last year to visit. Or have they both gained weight?"

Ava felt the high she had been riding on begin to ebb. Four hours here and he's back to making jabs. "It's called pregnancy, Dan. Lay off. Say something nice, ok?"

He placed a hand on her knee. "Something nice." He put in a Lyle Lovett CD.

The twang of a slide guitar hit Ava's ears like salve.

"Sounds like you've been doing a great job here, Ave. I'm impressed." Dan turned right into heavy traffic. He flung an arm when he hit the breaks fast. "Every time I call up Bill about our fantasy league, he says you're fitting right in."

"Mmmm." Ava relaxed, releasing control of the traffic, Dan, the classroom. She had forgotten how comforting it was to let someone else drive. Maybe he'd have a fun idea for the weekend. On the phone, they'd talked about driving down the coast, going to the aquarium in Monterey. Dan was back. Fun was back. Life felt good.

Lights were on over the ball field. Warming up in the outfield, Ava inhaled the salty breeze flowing up from the ocean. The scent of fresh cut grass lingered in the air. She looked over at Jimmie, his uniform still clean. His red hair stuck out under a Sitting Ducks ball cap. He was a friendly wall of a man. His big size gave him the look of being slightly overweight and goofy. Amid the coiffed and buff Marina kings and queens, it was a nice change. He waved.

Ava lifted her glove.

I hope he's your brother," Jimmie called, nodding toward the dugout where Dan was laughing with Bill. Jimmie threw the ball high in the air.

Ava positioned herself, staring into the night sky, gauging where that spinning sphere would fall.

The ball hit solidly in her mitt. She threw the practice pop fly as high as she could. Jimmie ran towards her. "An old friend," she said, wishing for the 11th time that she'd just skipped beer ball altogether.

But the game was off to a good start. A grounder to right field startled her. She bounded toward it, nerves jumpy. The ball bounced along the uneven grass, and Ava panicked that a funny hop would have her looking foolish if it flew past. But it didn't. The weight of it hit her mitt, a satisfying *thump!* She threw it to the cutoff man, exhilarated. Damn, I'm good. Ava pictured herself catching a game-winning out, being carried off the field. Could happen.

"Whoohoo!" Jimmie cheered from center field.

She grinned, heat rising up her face. She looked to Dan. He waved, cell phone to his ear.

In the third inning, the action was all left field. Ava took the time to review her day; Hector defying pot accusations, The sing-along ending in *mozel tov*, laughing with Dan over their Cuban dinner. Would she ever—

Crack! A grounder, hard to right field. Adrenaline jolted her out of the reverie. "Got it!" Ava yelled, waving Jimmie back. But this one had speed. It hit a divot in the grass and flew toward her face. Fear flooded her system right before the ball smashed her lip against her skull.

Dazed, she fell to her knees. Her hand flew up, tasting iron before her fingers felt the blood. Shit.

Jimmie's hand was on her back. "Ava? Are you okay? Where did it hit?"

She blinked back tears.

Jimmie winced. "That must really hurt. Let's get you—"

Dan ran toward them. Shit. She waved him off. Shit.

"I've got it," Dan said, kneeling down.

Jimmie backed up.

Dan tilted her chin to get a better view. "It looks like you've cut yourself. Next time, try using your mitt instead of your face."

Ava's lip went from throbbing to stinging. Kill, kill….

Then Bill was there. "Oooh, ouch! You need to have that checked out. Dan, you got her?"

Dan put a gentle hand to her cheek. "Let's get you stitched up. Then we'll make up a story about what happened to the other guy."

Mortified, Ava wanted to get off the field before she made an even bigger spectacle. Her lip was blown up to grotesque proportions, bleeding. On Dan's arm, she walked past her teammates, waving good-bye. Ladies and gentlemen, your right fielder.

Dan drove to the emergency room. "Maybe you just aren't athletic," he said, leaning back in his seat. He waved his hand leisurely. "I'm sure you have other talents, like…hmmm."

Ava hit him on the shoulder.

"No time like the present to develop a talent," Dan said. "I could always let you have some of mine. Let's see, there's my communication skills, my ability to make money effortlessly, my charming sense of humor…"

"Very funny," Ava said, trying not to move her mouth.

"What's that?"

"I said—"

Dan started laughing, then patted her leg as she bristled. "Settle down, settle down."

Ava smiled involuntarily. It hurt.

He tuned into a country station. This was how they used to be. Teasing. Joking. Comforting.

Two stitches later, Dan tucked her into bed with some Advil. He stroked her back. "You'll feel better in the morning."

The way Ava's face felt now, she doubted that, but it was soothing to have Dan there. He took the loneliness out of the room. Maybe she'd ask him to join her in visiting her mom over Christmas.

Sometime in the night, she felt Dan's hands. Soft, familiar.

She opened one eye. Leave it to Dan to think two in the morning was a good time for sex.

"C'mon, Ava," he whispered.

"C'mon?" This is romance? Are you kidding me? She pulled the blankets up, pushed his hand away. "Enough, Don Juan. You're rewriting the *Kama Sutra* to be two sentences long. First sentence: 'Wake her up.'"

Dan chuckled. "I don't think I want to hear the second sentence." He brushed his hand across her cheek.

"And you're trying to retitle the book, *You're Welcome!*" She winced as his fingertip bumped her lip. "My mouth isn't exactly primed for love here, buddy."

But Dan's fingers were making their way over her breast. "Your mouth doesn't need to be primed for love," he whispered. "Mine is." His mouth followed his hand down her body, a trail of skin-on-skin, lips on soft flesh.

She moaned. Never gonna happen. Three years together, you should know that. What am I doing? Why is he here? Oh...that feels good.

"Is this the second sentence?' Dan whispered.

Just go with it, she willed. He's here. This is nice, Let go of control. What would ACA say? Let go. Let God. "This is better than the second sentence." She breathed. Let go and let God. Let go and let God. Ava pried her grasp off the cosmic steering wheel, allowed herself just to feel. No thinking. Let go. Let go.

Let go and let—Oh. My. God. Ava felt waves of pleasure roll through her body, Dan a lovely memory to this moment. And this one. And this one.

A voice in her head whispered, "That's not the appropriate way to use that phrase."

She smiled, sighing. Oh, I think I used it exactly right.

Sometime in the night, she turned over. Dan was still sleeping. His blond hair fell over his face. A curl formed an upside-down question mark on his forehead. That familiar face. What was she going to do?

After the beer ball debacle, Dan suggested a drive down the coast. He booked a bed and breakfast in Monterey, the kind of place that had lace pillow shams and homemade cookies. Dan produced bubble bath and a bottle of champagne. They spent Halloween evening in the oversized tub, slick with bubble detergent. They alternated between giving each other foam Mohawks and beards, catching up, laughing, and making love.

Sunday morning, they walked along the boardwalk and Dan named the sea otters bobbing on their backs in the bay. "That one over there is manly. His name is Thor. Or Dan." Further down the boardwalk he took her arm, pointed. "See that one? It's got a scar on its head. Possibly demented." He nodded, his face serious. "Clearly an Ava."

On Monday morning, she waved as he drove off in that too-bright convertible. They would talk on the phone, and she'd made the suggestion he come home with her at Christmas. But he must have packed up all the light and humor of the weekend into his bright red car. She watched the last of his taillights turn the corner and then looked overhead: even the weather had changed. The blue skies of October had turned cloudy and cold. Leaves scattered the sidewalk like remnants of a party now over.

CHAPTER 20

JOHNTAY

The days stayed chilly. Dan's calls were infrequent as November slogged on at Ida B. One morning, Ava got a new student into her Test Prep English class: Johntay. He was a tall, stocky kid with a tee shirt that read: *Don't Shoot This Man*. Long, twisty braids hung down to his shoulders. His usual look was one of either disinterest or disdain. When he smiled though, Johntay had a grin that filled his entire face. In his eyes, Ava could see a seven-year-old boy still waiting for it to be safe to come out and play.

Johntay attended school just a few days a week—not so unusual, since the school's collective attendance record hovered around sixty-five percent. When Ava became dejected about the large number of absences, Cheryl reminded her that Ida B.'s abysmal average showed positive growth from the zero percent attendance most of the students exhibited at their previous schools.

On the days he did deign to show, Johntay arrived late, demanding his teacher give him the work "to go."

"This isn't a McDonald's drive through!" Ava raged. "You have to be in class to get your work. I'm not giving you anything!"

Johntay shrugged, happily leaving school after attending for only three minutes.

After several rounds of denying him work, Ava finally brokered a deal. "I'll give you a few assignments," she said, "but you need to stay in class at least thirty minutes first."

He grunted agreement, thirty minutes soon becoming a whole hour, the whole day. Not one to admit defeat, Johntay demanded Ava give him a few pages of work at the thirty-minute mark anyway. He'd clutch the papers in his oversized hand the remainder of the period, ready in case he needed to bolt.

Finally, after Johntay had been at the school two weeks, Ava took a seat next to him. The other kids were reading to themselves, punishment for no one following along with the story as their teacher read aloud.

Ava turned to face Jontay's hulking frame.

He punched a hole in his paper with a pencil. "I don't need no help."

And good to see you too. "I wouldn't dream of giving you help. Just wanted to see how you're getting on. You like the school okay?"

Johntay shrugged.

"Ms. L," Melvin whined, "I can't find the answer to number three."

"What's the question?"

"I don't know. I didn't read it."

You have got to be kidding. Ava looked to the ceiling. "You're killing me, folks. Really. Years off my life." She took a breath, turned back to Johntay. "So what brought you to Ida B?"

He looked at his teacher sideways. "I been told that lady in Wellness, but she must've not talked to you yet."

She shook her head.

He stuck out his chin. "I ain't no snitch."

"Not asking you to be." Ava was intrigued. This wasn't the usual, 'I was ditching school so the counselor sent me here,' or even

Paris's 'I kicked the principal in the shins and called him a bitch' reason for school reassignment.

"Well…" Johntay glanced around. His classmates were listening to their ipods, bubbling in answers to questions they hadn't bothered to read. No one cared about Johntay's business. He spoke low. "It was 'cause of that shooting, Lakeview, outside Drake's Funeral Home. Big G's service. Niggas from Sunnydale pulled a drive-by."

Ava cringed. A drive-by at a funeral? What the hell is wrong with people? But as awful as it sounded, there was something familiar about the story too….But where? *The news.* The story had made the evening news last August, just as school was starting. It had shocked her at the time—someone killed at a bus stop, in the middle of the day.

"Me, Trey, and Silas, we was at Balboa High School when it all went down at Drake's, but Trey's cousin, Gutta, he been dropped out. Trey and Silas and me went to the bus stop after school that day. We didn't know Sunnydale was looking for revenge. Gutta's name was in they mouths."

Ava was silent, trying to follow. Trey's cousin shot someone outside a funeral home. Johntay was with Trey and Silas at the bus stop. They didn't know about the shooting? She felt sick.

Johntay said, "The bus was late, so we was hanging out, chopping it up. Trey be geekin in some new stunnas."

"Stunnas?"

"Sunglasses. Think he the boss. Say he gone get some fine honeys with those." Johntay gestured conversationally, as if he and Ava had been there together. "Silas put him in check. He say, "You ain't gone get no pussy with that shit, and you really ain't getting no pussy working at Safeway." Johntay smiled, his first in three weeks. "Silas stayed clownin' on Trey. He say, "Let me bag your groceries, ma'am? That ain't no kind of game!"

Ava nodded. No pussy at Safeway. Where's he going with this?

"Trey told Silas that Gutta could get him a job too, but Silas, he know how Gutta is. Gutta got him a deal on a Buick few months back. Straight-ass bucket." Johntay turned to Ava, explaining, "Gutta racket."

He chuckled at the memory. "Gutta so racket, he'd try to shine on hisself. Sell hisself a raggedy-ass bucket and think he got one over."

Ava shook her head. "That sounds racket. Then what happened?"

"Trey called us haters. He say, 'Ya gotta feel the love, mayne!' Then Trey closed his eyes, Wonder style, sang, "I just called, to say, I loooooove youuuuuu!"

Johntay ducked his head, a sad smile lingering. "Freak. We was friends since first grade, called ourselves the Lil' Homies. Trey was gonna teach me to drive." The smile faded. "He was still singing when that that Lexus rolled up. The backseat window lowered. It felt like time stuck. I saw the gun and hit the ground."

"I yelled to him when I dropped, 'Get low!'" Johntay looked like he was still trying to puzzle it out. "Trey's eyes musta still been closed behind them stunnas. That fool was still singing, 'I just called, to sayyy how much I—"

"That's when I heard a *Pop!* That nigga in the Lexus yelled, "Who on top now, son?" Johntay's face turned hard. "*Pop!* 'Who on top now?' *Pop!* 'Who on top…'"

"Ten times. That nigga shot him ten times. Trey leakin' everywhere."

Leaking? Ava thought a moment. Bleeding. Oh, honey.

"I didn't feel like going to school no more after that, without Trey. Kept hearing those shots, seeing his blood on my arms, on my white tee. Ms. L, I just want to graduate and get out of here."

Ava watched her new student's face. She didn't know what to say. Real people weren't supposed to get shot. That was for movies, the news, crime shows. Ruthie hadn't mentioned this kind of violence, not when Ava was thinking of moving down to San Francisco or after.

She asked about Johntay in Wellness. The school had only one full-time counselor. Mary Kline had a full caseload already. An intern had been assigned to help put the young man back together again. Unfortunately, the interns weren't permanent. Ava worried this one would leave while Johntay was still in pieces.

Along with the latest Jordan shoes and a large white tee shirt, Johntay wore a placard around his neck with the words "RIP Trey." That's when Ava started counting all the kids wearing RIP placards or tee shirts at Ida B. Wells. On any given day, she tallied no fewer than five. She had seen them before, of course, but it only now dawned on her that those killed were kids' friends, relatives. Who was I thinking they were? Dead rappers?

Then she noticed the RIP tattoos, grief so palpable it needed to be permanently etched into DNA. The General sported one of those.

Cheryl shook her head. "That was a sad one for the community. Trey has friends at Ida B. too, kids who went to Balboa before being sent here."

"Why don't their families move?" Ava asked. What kind of parents would put their kids in danger like that?

"Where would you suggest these families move to?" Cheryl's voice was quiet. "Do they move their extended family as well? Generations? Away from friends they've known their whole lives? And where does the money come from to do that?"

"But kids are dying."

"That's for sure. And wouldn't you think the city would care enough for its children to do something about it?"

Ava was silent, thinking.

"Anyway," Cheryl's tone softened, "Stella and I are going hiking this weekend in Marin. You should join us, get away from death and concrete for a while."

Ava didn't really want a hike. She wanted to curl up in bed and sleep for a long, long time. She forced a smile. "Yes."

CHAPTER 21

WILD HORSES

Walking home that evening, the November rain pelted her jacket. Thanksgiving was just a few days away. She'd spend it with Ruthie and Bill. And Laura and Thomas and their son, Atticus, a child who would never see the inside of a public school.

She pulled her hood further over her head to brace against the rain that came down harder now. Glancing at teenagers huddled under the bus shelter, she thought about Johntay, how much he held the reins in their relationship and how much she wanted to help him, make his world safe. He reminded her of what had happened in Washington.

She shook her head, wanting to erase the memory of all that had gone down with her former student. It's over. You don't need to drag that back up. Until now, each day's classroom chaos, beer ball games, missing Dan, had successfully shoved aside thoughts about Sunny. But not forever.

Ava had had difficult students before Sunny—she'd even sought them out. Her volunteer and student teaching placements were at tiny alternative schools: angry, tired, sad white kids who battled their parents, drug addictions, life. She liked those kids. They reminded her of herself as a teenager, more like the unbroken horse her dad brought home than the confident classmates she saw every day. When she looked at students in these alternative schools, they had the same warning in their eyes as that skittish horse: *I spook easily.* She learned to make her movements clear, slow. Be patient, kind, firm, and they'd tolerate her enough to let her near.

Of course, that same unbroken horse bucked her off so hard her skull shook. Bone slammed against the dirt. Her dad said a horse has to know who's boss. He often quoted his hero, Buck Brannaman: "Your horse is a mirror to your soul. Sometimes you may not like what you see. Sometimes, you will." It was no surprise when that unbroken horse, Ava, and much later, Sunny, all arrived at the same conclusion: None of them respected Ava.

Alternative schools not hiring, she applied for her first teaching position at a tiny comprehensive high school miles from the nearest large town. In the following two and a half years, she grew used to classrooms filled with farm kids sitting forward in their seats, earnest faces wanting to do their best. A few mean girls and fewer mean boys added spice every now and then, but nothing a stern glance, a serious tone, or a trip to detention couldn't fix.

Small-town parents responded immediately to her phone calls home. Neighbors looked after each other's kids. When Mrs. Remy, an aide who had worked at the school for fifteen years, saw one of Ava's male students come in with hands raw from chemicals used in milking, she called the farmer, threatened with information only a small-town neighbor knows. The boy was given gloves from then on.

And so it went. Cows wandering onto the baseball field during games, the superintendent's office in a trailer across the street, Ava looking at her watch and telling unruly students, "I'm just keeping track of the number of seconds you'll have to stay after class." And they stayed. Ten extra seconds, thirty. Two and a half years humming by. Then Sunny was assigned to third period world history.

Her first day in class, the girl surveyed the room, the bright colors, the posters. "What is this bullshit?" she said. "Kindergarten?" She looked her new teacher in the eyes and sneered. There was nothing immediate to which Ava could attribute her student's anger. It didn't help that Sunny was overweight, face dotted with acne, her dark stringy hair hanging over her eyes—those things couldn't have been good for her self-esteem, but there was something cold and hard in her gaze that went beyond normal teenage insecurities. Among all the other students waiting quietly for class to begin, her voice, her glare, her contempt made a statement. She might as well have pissed on the floor.

Ava felt apprehension mix with compassion when she looked at the girl in front of her, something akin to approaching an animal that has been abused. This is how Ava could have turned out. This is how her sister, Livvie, whom Ava had abandoned, or her brother, Alan, could have turned out. No student was beyond redemption. She would bring Sunny around. This was why she became a teacher.

But working with sweet-tempered kids had softened her. She made the one mistake that was a death knell for teachers: She wanted Sunny to like her.

It began the first time Ava saw Sunny smile. The class assignment was to act out a dramatic incident from the life of a famous woman in history. Sunny chose the role of Cleopatra. She got a kid to drag her in a sleeping bag into the cardboard palace of Julius Caesar. The research must have taken Sunny hours. The time to make the palace, at least a week. Sunny beamed throughout her performance, revealing herself in tinfoil jewels to an underwhelmed Caesar and bored classmates. Ava wanted to cry. She clapped so hard her hands stung. I knew you were in there.

But one success does not a transformation make. Ava lived for the days her surly student smiled.

Sunny creating an oversized newspaper on the Roman Empire—Smile.

Sunny glaring at Ava through silent reading—Fail.

"Eyes on the text please. Eyes on the text. That means everyone. Sunny? At least pretend like you're reading."

Sunny mumbling, "Fuck you," loud enough for the class to hear. Ava pretending not to notice—Fail.

Acting out the French Revolution—Smile.

Refusing to write about the French Revolution, Sunny flipping her the bird. Ava acting as though she hadn't seen—Fail.

She inwardly beat her head against the wall the day Sunny again refused to pick up her pencil. "Well, maybe you could just sit there an think about what you might write."

"Yeah, that's a great idea." A few kids tittered at Sunny's defiance.

Ava turned away, trying to hide her embarrassment, but she was too slow. Sunny's tongue, red and vulgar, stuck out from puckered lips. Ava realized: It isn't going to stop. You can't le this go on. Resolve knit itself together like a backbone forming. She walked over to her student, placing a hand on the girl's shoulder. "That wasn't necessary."

Sunny jerked away. "Get away from me! You can't touch me. Get the fuck away from me." Then she was on her feet, nose-to-nose with Ava.

The rest of the class sat open-mouthed. Danger. Someone should go find a safe adult.

Ava's thoughts caught in a loop. *I shouldn't have touched her. Why did I touch her? I shouldn't have touched her….* Then, slowly, the class, all those shocked faces, came into focus. Her words spilled out, "Detention. Go. That disrespect isn't allowed in here."

Everyone turned when they heard the principal's voice boom in the hall.

Shoulders squared against her teacher, Sunny transformed. A slow smile spread across her face. "*Your* disrespect isn't allowed in here. Ask Principal Hansen. You can't send me out because you did something wrong."

And for a moment, God help her, Ava stood there confused. The girl's conviction seemed to make her right. Following Sunny's orders, she ran into the hallway, tattling like a first grader, "Sunny says I can't send her out for talking back."

The principal stared. "If you feel the need to send her out, send her out."

Shame spread through her body. She went back into the room.

Sunny looked at her triumphantly.

Ava called security.

"Liar!" Sunny screamed. "Fucking whore!" After ten minutes, security finally convinced the girl to leave.

A horse is a mirror of your soul. In front of the stunned faces of third period world history, Ava sobbed.

The next day, Mrs. Remy, in charge of the detention room, came by to have a word. Her motherly face bore the lines of resignation. "I've known Sunny since she was in kindergarten," she said, "and I've watched her change over the years. Since her mom died and she started living with her uncle, I've called CPS more than a dozen times. I'm almost positive he's molesting her. I don't have proof, but I've seen it with other kids, and that's usually the case when they turn mean. But every time a social worker visits that rotted-out shack, the girl denies, denies, denies." Mrs. Remy almost sounded apologetic. "You can't take it personally."

But under Mrs. Remy's watch in detention, Sunny performed like a show pony. It was totally personal.

The day after the debacle, one of those third period students, a quiet girl with long red hair, brought her teacher a vase of yellow roses, and a card:

Dear Ms. L, I hope you have a better day today.

And the world breathed out. Ava placed the card in her wallet behind her driver's license. It was the thread that kept her tethered to humanity. She'd keep the card until it turned to dust. And then she'd keep the dust.

In the months after sending Sunny out, the girl spent more time in detention than in class. Ava felt herself unable to help, as though Sunny were herself, or her sister, and she just stood by and let her circle the drain. The girl was failing most of her classes. When Sunny did show up, there was no sign of the smile that had once graced the classroom.

Then one Tuesday in March, her uncle entered the room in the middle of the period, dirty ball cap over his haggard face, teeth rotting out. "Moving to Oregon," he said. "Sunny, let's go."

Ava's stomach churned. *Not with you. She can't go with you.* But the principal stood in the doorway holding the paperwork.

When Sunny handed back her silent reading book, she leaned in toward her teacher.

"I'm sorry," Ava said. *I'm so very, very sorry.*

Sunny's dark eyes projected dread, fear, as if she already saw what awaited her in Oregon. She nodded, whispering, "Fucking cunt."

The night Sunny left, Dan played video games in the living room all night. Ava looked at the Ambien beside her bed. She thought about how much alcohol it would take to shut down completely. Thought about how she wasn't able to do the only thing that mattered—save other lost kids. Then it came to her: *Here. I can't save them here.* Maybe she needed to try someplace new, completely different from the small rural towns she had known, far away from her failure with Sunny. By that time, her college buddy, Ruthie, had moved to San Francisco. Ava would visit.

Now, walking home from Ida B, it hit her: Johntay was the new Sunny. This time, she told herself, *I'm going to get it right.*

CHAPTER 22
CHASING WATERFALLS

Saturday morning, Cheryl picked up Ava in a Subaru Outback that had clearly passed the 200,000-mile mark. Cheryl was wearing a UCLA sweatshirt. A yellow scarf covered her short hair. "Morning!" she chirped. "Get your butt in the car, girlfriend. Stella's been blowing up my phone since six this morning. Hasn't that woman ever heard of a weekend?" She turned a smile toward Ava. "Glad you could make it."

Ava tucked herself into the front seat. "Happy to be invited. It'll be nice to get out of the city. I haven't been to Marin yet."

Cheryl turned into traffic. "That's what I thought. I told Stella, 'You know, Ava's not doing well. We need to get that girl out into nature. Get her out of that school and away from Pants.'" She accelerated through an orange light.

Ava held on to the door. "Pants?"

"Principal Sanchez. You ever notice how she's always wearing those God-awful polyester pants? She sat next to me at a conference last year. When her pants brushed my hand, it felt like sandpaper. I told her, "Emilia, you better back away me with those pants.""

"Huh," Ava mused. "I guess I haven't seen her ever wear a skirt. How long has Pants been at the school?"

"Two years. Came in like she owned the place. Can you believe she started telling me how to run my classroom in the first week? 'More homework. Put the desks in rows' She looked the fool." Cheryl sighed. "I've been in this district twenty-three years. I've never been worried about losing my job. Pants gave me an "unsatisfactory" on last year's evaluation. This year I have a teaching coach with only five years' experience—and that was in a sixth grade classroom."

Understanding dawned as Ava thought back to the woman she'd seen in Cheryl's room on a weekly basis. She'd assumed the young woman was from one of the various community-based organizations Cheryl invited regularly to provide expertise in poetry, writing, or other language arts areas. Ava felt ashamed of her ignorance. *A teaching coach.* How humiliating. And unnecessary. Cheryl was a great teacher. Pants had never even *taught.* How was this even possible?

Cheryl sighed. "Four bad evaluations this year and I'll be fired. I think Pants doesn't like me speaking up at faculty meetings."

Ava stared. "She can't do that." She thought about Pants coming up to her yesterday, asking to sit in on the mock trial Ava and Tolly were putting together. "I'm not sure if a law student is the best fit for a Test Prep English class," Pants said, frowning. Ava couldn't afford a bad evaluation her first year. But it was set: in two months, Pants would observe.

"She can get rid of me," Cheryl said, "if she wants to badly enough, though the teaching coach can't seem to catch me doing anything other than teaching the kids English. I don't know. It might be time to hang up my hat. I'm eight years away from retirement, but my bullshit meter's about worn out."

Cheryl gunned her Subaru past a Mercedes, vying for positioning at a light. "So what was the principal like where you left?"

Ava loosened her grip on the door handle. The image of Principal Hanson appeared; she saw his kindness, his faith in her abilities. "He was really good man. He'd been a principal a long time. The kids and staff respected him."

Cheryl nodded. "I miss those days." She laughed. "You should have seen the day Pants said we were supposed to start singing to our kids."

"Singing?"

"Woman had the nerve to tell me that black kids need you to sing to them. I told her, 'Ma'am, I raised four young black men. We sing in church, we sing in the car, but we do not need to be singing to each other in the classroom.' It was awful. No one would do it except for Stella, but she already sings to her kids."

"What does she sing?"

"Mostly instructions. Sometimes just nonsense. I was in the office the other day with students who'd been kicked out of their classes." Cheryl raised her brows. "The kids were discussing which drugs Stella might be on."

"Did they come to a conclusion?"

"Cocaine."

Ava nodded.

Nearing the end of the Golden Gate Bridge, the fog dissipated, revealing the green hills of the Marin Headlands. Dirty city streets widened into open space, sky. Pale blue-green eucalyptus and tall, golden grasses replaced the hard concrete. These weren't the cottonwoods or tamaracks she grew up with, but there was green. As a girl, Ava had helped her family get firewood for the winter, spending autumn weekends bouncing across the meadow in the back of the red pickup. Her family drove deep into the woods, following a trail from old logging camps. Under the canopy of trees, Ava and her siblings explored mossy nooks while Dad felled giants and Mom hefted an axe. Ava, Alan, and Livvie stacked firewood onto the truck, restacking it back at the house. At the day's end, their small bodies were filthy and tired, lumberjacks ready for a bath.

Ava relaxed against her seat. She took in the trees, shrubs, grasses. *Home.*

After a while, she turned to Cheryl. "It's another world over here."

Her driver snorted. "I'll say. There are schools on this side of the bridge that would make you cry. Take a look at some of the houses we pass today—starter castles. It's those property taxes that Ida B will never get, and as long as school funding is tied to property taxes, wealthy areas have wealthy schools and poor areas have poor schools. Show me one wealthy area with poor test scores—then we can start talking about teacher effectiveness."

"And we can't get a PE teacher because there's no money." Ava remembered how hard she had tried to get the job in San Francisco Unified, with Ida B. Wells in particular.

June. Four hundred dollars for a plane ticket to the city. For the past three months, Ava had sent out twenty resumes, called Bay Area schools on a weekly basis. What she didn't know is that principals played a shell game with openings—they wouldn't admit to an open position until it had already been filled with a teacher recommended by someone on the inside. Ida B. was the only school that had even requested an interview.

By that time, Ava had already broken up with Dan and given notice at her school. Summer break was about to start across the country. She had no other job prospects.

Halfway through the interview, Ava felt she was doing well, impressing the panel, including Cheryl and Stella, with her student teaching experience in alternative education. She talked about challenges with behavior and filling in achievement gaps. Oh, she was on a roll.

Then it happened.

"So," said Principal Sanchez, "Tell us about a difficult student you've encountered your last three years teaching."

And, instead of thinking of some kid who'd talked back, or the boy who'd refused to stop talking and made the whole class stay late, Ava thought of Sunny. Living in a rotted-out trailer with her uncle, and there was nothing Ava could do. Sunny's last words, *Fucking cunt.* That's all it took for the waterworks to get started. Ava was too choked up to even explain to the committee why she was crying.

Panel, meet your applicant. She may as well have flashed her boobs. Tears formed rivers down her face. She wanted to disappear. Four hundred dollars. Her only interview. Fuuuuuuuck.

It was then that the eccentric woman in her fifties, Stella, white hair flying about her face, had reached across the table. She handed Ava a tissue.

Cheryl, tall and motherly, closed her eyes. "We've all been there." She turned to Principal Sanchez. "C'mon, Emilia. You remember how the staff all bawled when DeShaun was killed? I think we've found a keeper."

Cheryl and Ava drove miles, higher and higher through winding forest, the road finally opening to reveal a view of the bay, sparkling waters. The sharp scent of pine mingled with eucalyptus. The city's dead concrete was long gone. Ava rolled down her window, wanting to breathe and breathe and breathe.

Halfway up Mount Tamalpais, Cheryl eased into a shaded parking lot. "That's our girl," she said, pointing to Stella, who was waiting next to a bicycle.

Stella wore a ponytail on top of her head, her white hair tinted pink today. Like Cheryl, Stella was in her mid-fifties, but already had more energy than Ava could remember ever having in her entire life.

Stella bounded to the car. "Finally. I already rode my bike thirty miles this morning. We're not getting any younger, ladies. Let's move."

"Girlfriend, please." Cheryl said. She got out of the car slowly, stiffly. "We're here, we're hiking, and you can just move on ahead with that kind of energy. I plan to enjoy my day."

It took Stella one continuous motion to separate the bike into two parts and place it in Cheryl's car.

The hike began at a rigorous pace, and Ava regretted letting jogging go to the wayside these last few months. A hike with Stella was proving a task one should train for.

Her pink-haired colleague huffed ahead, toned thighs working under durable spandex. "So what have you been doing for fun?"

Ava thought about it. "I play on a beer ball league. Right field."

Stella's head bobbed. "Good. What else?"

"Well, I visit with my friend Ruthie, and her husband, Bill. They have Shabbat dinner some Fridays."

"Good. What else?"

"I used to love karaoke."

"It's worse than I thought." Stella shuddered. Her death march slowed.

Ava sighed. "Most nights I just want to sleep or drink."

Cheryl overtook them.

Ava was startled to see both colleagues frowning at her. "That's what I thought," Cheryl said. "Bags under your eyes. You need activities that don't involve drinking."

Hmmmm. That sounded bad. "Like what?"

Stella rolled her eyes, "Mountain biking, hiking, kayaking, surfing."

Ava nodded. No, no, no, and no.

Cheryl ticked off on her fingers, "Quilting, poetry groups, knitting groups, writing classes…"

Oh, God. Ava couldn't imagine anything worse.

Stella said, "There's a triathlon coming up, why don't you join my team?"

"And for God's sake, go on a few dates." Cheryl said. "Stella met her boyfriend online. There has to be one more good one out there."

Married peoples' favorite lie. "How'd you meet your husband, Cheryl?"

"In the army. I was his commanding officer."

Of course you were. Ava gauged her heavy breathing, aware that the uphill portion of their hike was yet to come. "Maybe I'll see how this hiking thing turns out first."

They came to a fork in the road. "This is a shortcut," Stella said, pointing to the right, a bare hillside straight up.

"You sure about this?" Cheryl asked.

Ava's stomach turned. There were few trees up above, not much to keep her from sliding back down. "I don't see where it meets up with the trail," she worried.

Stella was already climbing.

Ten feet up, Ava realized that the hill was even more steep than it appeared. Had there been shrubs or even grass, she could have braced herself, held on to roots. She felt with her hands for something to grab. Her toes slid in the loose gravel. She dug in her knees for traction. Sweat rolled down her back.

"I'm too old for this shit, Stella!" Cheryl called from below.

"Shortcut!" Stella repeated.

Thirty minutes later, panic set in. They were up too far; the only way back to where they had started involved a quick downward slide ending in a life-altering free-fall. She scanned the cliff above. Where the fuck is that trail? They had to keep climbing. Panic rose in her throat. Her breathing became shallow. Goddamn it, Stella.

Below her, Cheryl grunted. "Stella, I've killed men using only my hands. I'm willing to go back on my pledge never to do it again."

Ava edged herself an inch closer to a small rock, her fingers digging into the loose dirt. Her right toehold gave way. Oh, God. Fear and adrenaline surged as she felt herself falling. Her fingernails clawed the dirt. She flattened herself against the hillside, her belly the only surface providing enough traction to keep her from plunging to a certain death. She prayed to the gods of spare tires, Thank you.

Far above, Stella shouted, "I see the trail!"

Ava looked up. Stella clung to a small shrub, her body plastered to the nearly bare hillside as well.

"You better be right," Cheryl growled.

Ava concentrated on not sliding farther down the cliff.

Ages later, Ava swung her leg onto the trail above. She felt a rush of exhilaration and accomplishment. I did it. Looking down the mountain at the sheer wall she had just scaled, she was oddly sad that the life-threatening adventure was over. The sun shone over Marin county, hills of reddish manzanitas, bright green madrones, yellow alders—it was like a page from a fairy tale. Sailboats dotted the deep-blue bay. Ava often forgot, living in the Mission, that the city was surrounded by water.

"It's beautiful," she said. It was a truly different world, away from city streets, noises, hurts. She'd missed the sturdy peace of trees and newly-minted oxygen. Space.

Stella took a few misshapen snack bars from her backpack. "Time to celebrate!"

They sat on rocks along the trail, turtles basking in the midday sun.

Stella closed her eyes. They all breathed in and out with the warm breeze. And in. And out. "Same time next week?" Stella asked.

Cheryl sighed. "I'll bring lunch."

That evening, Ava called up Dan, "Guess what?" she said, "I climbed a mountain—or really, it was like rock-climbing without the—"

"I'm finishing up a report, Ave," he said. "Some of us have real jobs. Shit. I can't remember the figure I just entered. Shit."

"I can call back later," Ava mumbled. What does he mean, 'real jobs?'

"No— I've already lost my concentration. Thanks a lot."

She closed her eyes. He's already being a dick again. "I'm sorry," she whispered.

"Oh, I'm over it," Dan said. "Let's talk about something else. Hmmmm," his voice took on a playful tone, "I sure loved Vagtastic time the other weekend."

Ava went from sad to furious. "You know I hate it when you call it that. It sounds like a disease. Other people say they had sex or made love. They don't call a tender moment with their girlfriend 'Vagtastic.'

"It's a good thing you're not my girlfriend then. We still on for Christmas?"

It was out before she could think. "Yes." And then she didn't know how to take it back, or why she had invited him in the first place. Something about knowing he was there, even this dickhead version of him, made her less lonely. And for that, she hated herself.

CHAPTER 23
SEARCH AND SEIZURE

Ava surveyed the two law students, Tolly and Mina, ready for discussion, standing cheerfully against the backdrop of her overflowing desk. Tolly wore a suit each time, though it seemed overkill in a classroom with paint peeling off of the walls and faded carpet coming up at the seams.

This morning, the kids were sleepy. A few displayed their usual breakfasts of Arizona iced tea and hot Cheetos on the tables in front of them.

Ava already opened a window, warning Johntay that tomorrow she expected he not be in a car with someone who'd been smoking weed.

"Remember," she told the class, "a guest speaker means that you need to be extra polite."

The kids grunted. Only a few bothered to look up.

Tolly cleared his throat. "Mina Hernandez is in the same law program as I am. She's done a lot of research around students' rights in schools. She's here to talk to you about that."

"Good morning!" Mina chirped, a tiny woman with short, dark hair. Her skinny jeans tucked into orange sneakers. "How is everybody today?"

The students slumped, catatonic.

Really? A hello is going to break you? "We're good," Ava said. "Glad you're here."

"I'm not," mumbled Francisco. The vice principal had walked him to class late this morning, explaining his mom locked him out of the house two days ago. He'd been spending his nights on the streets.

Ava rubbed her temple. "Be nice."

Mina continued, "Well, as Tolly said, I'm here to talk to you about your rights on campus. I hear you're going to have a mock trial in January that involves a search-and-seizure case. I thought I could give some background about when you can be—"

"Are you married?" Ken interrupted.

Ava winced, but Mina did have a rock on her finger that demanded attention. Ain't nobody in rural Washington wearing a ring like that.

Mina was puzzled. "W-Well…since you asked, I got engaged last month—"

The class, in a collective stupor until that moment, sat up en masse and broke into applause. Had they been in a hospital setting, it would have been studied as a miracle.

"When are you getting married?" K'Ron breathed, eyes wide in anticipation.

Mina blushed. "This summer."

"Ith he Latin?" Hector asked.

"Is he Filipino?" shouted Melvin.

"Is he black?" asked Johntay, punching his first into the air. He was wearing an oversized sweatshirt with block letters that read: *I AM a Man.*

Mina twisted her engagement ring. "Actually, he's Filipino."

"I knew it!" yelled Melvin, He turned in his seat. "See K'Ron? Once you go Filipino, you never go Latino."

K'Ron flipped him off.

Mina scowled. She whispered something to Tolly.

"Ok, everyone," Ava pleaded. "Let's get back to search-and-seizure."

Tolly looked relieved. The kids settled into their seats.

Mina took a deep breath. "So a school official is supposed to have good reason to suspect a student is carrying a weapon or illegal substance in order to search them or their belongings. Now, can anyone tell me what size knife is allowed?"

"Three inches!" yelled Sean. He took out a pocketknife and showed the class.

"Ath big ath your hand," said Hector. The knife he held against his outstretched palm was clearly breaking that rule. Also, his eyes were red and unfocused—drinking? Pot? It deserved a call to Wellness.

Francisco produced a switchblade, opening it to reveal a six-inch, serrated knife.

Ava inhaled. Oh, God.

K'Ron took brass knuckles out of her purse and placed them on her table, "Are you allowed to have these?" she asked.

Mina went pale.

Ava's breakfast rose in her stomach as her mind went back to her own teenage years. She remembered her dad firing his shotgun into the night air, making a point to the universe while she sat in the kitchen and her sister hid. She remembered talking Dad into coming back inside, giving her the gun. Putting the car keys down. Talking about the hurt he felt and could do nothing about.

She covered her face with her hands. "Put those away!" she hissed. "I'm not supposed to see that stuff...and you're not supposed to have that at school!"

The students stared blankly back at her.

"But I need it to get home," said Sean.

"You don't know my neighborhood, Ms. L," said Johntay.

Francisco pointed his knife in Ava's direction, "What if you had to walk through two Surreno blocks to get home?"

"Put. It. Away. The rule is, you can't have any weapons on campus, and I'm supposed to tell someone if you're carrying something." Ava looked at the class. Against the background of primary-colored posters and student drawings, the artistry hovering somewhere around fourth grade, two-thirds of her students now had their weapons on display. "Everyone understand?" Ava pictured knives being stashed around campus after class was over. She would be using that time to do her mandatory snitching.

The kids put their knives away and waited for Mina to continue.

The guest wasn't looking so good. "Well," she said, "if there is reason to suspect you're carrying a weapon, and it looks like there might be here, then the school has a right to…"

Niesha raised her hand.

Mina sighed. "I'm almost through my first point. Can I just get this out?" Ava would have to talk to their guest about tone of voice.

Niesha persevered. "Where did you get your shoes?" She pointed to Mina's orange sneakers. Niesha's own hot pink stilettos laced up her ankles.

"Those are great shoes," K'Ron seconded.

Mina looked down at her footwear. "My shoes?"

"Yeah," said Paris, "are those Adidas?"

"Do they have those in purple?" Ken asked. He had been wearing purple exclusively for the past few weeks. He said he needed to brand himself, let fans know purple was his signature color.

Johntay, always in a new pair of Nikes, threw Paris a look. "Adidas don't look like that. Those are Eccos or some shit."

"Ok, folks, that's nice that you like Mina's shoes, but let's try not to interrupt when she's—" Ava said, but Mina had left the room.

The kids and Ava looked to one another. Two weeks ago, Francisco had exited the classroom by flipping them all off with both hands, then slamming the door. The class accepted his apology when he slunk back in a day later. But Mina just leaving the room without a word? That was hurtful. A few students slumped down in their seats.

"She doesn't like us," Sean said quietly. Ava saw sadness creeping into his little billiard-ball face.

Oh, hell, no—no guest speaker is going to walk out on my kids. Ava turned to Tolly. "I need you to watch them for a minute."

Tolly took a step backward. "I don't think…" he said, shaking his head.

Ava left the room.

She caught up to Mina at the end of the hallway.

"They're just so rude," Mina sobbed.

Some students lingered nearby, tagging up Ms. Wilson's bulletin boards. They paused to stare at Mina. Ava waved them on to class. She wanted to feel sympathy for the woman, but she just didn't have time for an adult crying like a kindergartener while kids with 5th grade reading levels wielded brass knuckles in her classroom. "I'm sorry they keep interrupting," she said. "That just means they like you—they want to know you as a person before they hear what you have to present."

Mina sniffed. "I can't go back in there."

"You're going back in."

Mina shook her head.

Ava sighed. "If you don't go back into that room, they'll think you're giving up on them. Not only does their behavior get reinforced, but the idea that they're worthless gets more ingrained."

Mina sobbed.

And I've had quite enough. "Listen," Ava whispered, "you made a promise to those kids just by walking into that room. Now I need you to be a fucking adult, got it?"

Mina stared. "Got it."

"Okay." Ava found a Kleenex in her pocket. She gave Mina a moment to get herself together. Then she took her guest's arm and walked her back down the hallway. "Now, tell me about your fiancé," Ava said. "Where did you two meet? I'll bet that's a great story."

CHAPTER 24

WHACK-A-MOLE AND LETTING GO

Ava eased her car into the church's parking lot. She felt in her pocket for her dollar donation. Check. She looked in the rearview mirror: Pathetic, desperate woman: Check. "We're good to go," she whispered.

Inside, only a few people were sitting around the folding tables. The room was eerily silent for being just minutes away from the start of the meeting. From the open, adjoining kitchen, Jerry stood next to a boiling kettle. "Want some?" he called, holding up a mug.

Ava gave a thumbs-up. She cursed herself for being more than five minutes early. She'd have to attempt small talk. Shit. Next time, she'd come late, sneak in while Georgia read off the greeting.

Amid the silence, Jerry offered her a steaming mug. The tea was chamomile. The warmth, soothing. It reminded her of when she was very young, playing board games with her family and drinking tea. The cats sat outside, looking in, her love for them mirrored in their half-closed eyes.

Lydia pulled up a chair beside Ava. She was wearing a black wrap-around dress today. Gray showed at the roots of her curly blonde hair. Leaning in, Lydia whispered, "Glad you made it back."

A young woman with blue hair walked through the door. Her boots hit the ground with a reverberating *Thud!* Everyone flinched, glancing up. She didn't return the tentative smiles sent her way.

Georgia watched the clock. Ava noted that she was picking at her cuticles. Even Georgia gets nervous.

"Well, I think we should start," Georgia said. "Welcome to the Tuesday night meeting of ACA…"

"Step one: We admitted we were powerless. That our lives had become unmanageable."

Unmanageable. Ava felt her shoulders collapse. She thought back to her last conversation with Dan. "Some of us have real jobs." She didn't know who else was out there, if there was any man who would treat her differently. But what would she do if she let him go? It was as if she had imprinted on him, like an orphaned gosling to a Rottweiler. It was inappropriate, but without him, she would be so alone.

Powerless. Emmett making the drug deal at school. "Who you think you is?" He had a point.

Jerry started reading from where they had left off in the official red book: "Step Two: We came to believe that a power greater than ourselves could restore us to sanity."

The reading asked Ava to imagine a personalized higher power, one to whom she could relinquish control, one that didn't judge. Ava shook her head. Everyone judges. Especially God. Isn't that the job description?

When it came time for sharing, the blue-haired woman went first. "Fuck," she said.

Georgia prompted, "And your name?"

"Britt."

"Hi Britt," the group parroted, a class of first graders learning names.

"Yeah," Britt said. "So, I'm in this Other Program, you know, and a woman there is all up in my shit, really laying it down about how I'm not working the steps, and I'm like, 'Bitch, I got three kids at home and three weeks sober. What the fuck do you have?'" Britt looked around. "I said it just like that, 'What the fuck do you have?'" She put a hand to her cheek. "The woman says, "I have twenty years' sobriety, and I'm telling you, if you want to make it to week four, you have to work the program. Do you need a sponsor to help you do that?" Britt blinked back tears. "I said what the fuck do you have?" She shook her head.

Ava was confused. Program? Does ACA have a program? And sponsors? Oh God. There's more to it than this? She glanced at Britt. This woman's got a program. What the fuck do I have?

Britt continued, "So I think about my kids and how I was so out of control. My oldest boy is seven. He flinches when I hug him. My life has become unmanageable. I don't know about a higher power yet, but I'm looking for a sponsor in ACA now. The Other Program is helping me with my drinking problem. I think this program can help me with the reasons why I started drinking in the first place. I called people on the ACA phone list, but no one's been in the program long enough to sponsor."

Ava glanced around the table, willing someone to raise their hand.

Georgia said, "That's something you're welcome to ask folks at the end of the meeting."

Britt deflated. "Oh. Okay. I didn't know how it worked here. I wasn't looking to cross talk."

Lydia shared next, "I think this step is just asking me to be open to the idea that a higher power could provide me with more clarity than I've had so far. Really, my five-year-old niece has more clarity than I do. The other day she said, 'Don't eat that cake or you'll be sad.' It's not rocket science. I'm just afraid of what feelings will come without the cake. What if God doesn't have anything in place for me then?"

Jerry picked up the theme. "Give me a microphone and I'll speak to a room of thousands. Put me at a social event with five people I don't know, and I'll cower in the corner." He laughed. "Let go and let God. I wish it was just that easy. Is God going to step in if I stop over-performing at work? If I approach someone at a party and they reject me? I want to let go. I want to let God. I just haven't seen God for such a long time."

Jerry. Ava saw her own confusion and hurt mirrored in his pale-blue eyes. Then she realized she was one of the few people who hadn't spoken yet. *You could just keep your mouth shut. No one is making you*—But no. This was a place where people told the truth. Ava took a breath. "I'm Ava."

"Hi, Ava."

Again, the forced acknowledgement felt good. "What happens when you can't believe that there is any higher power looking out for you? I need to decide about my ex-boyfriend, but I can't even think about letting him go, being all alone. He might be a kind of addiction. The last time I remember having fun—real fun—it was with him. Fun is hard. He makes it seem easy. Is there really a higher power who will step in if I break it off? ACA says Laundry List behaviors helped me to survive childhood. Now they're holding me back."

She paused, the faces around the table coming into focus. *Why are you saying this to these people?* "The Laundry List reads like my resume: people pleasing." Dan's face appeared in her mind. "Fear of abandonment." Dan's face. "Dating alcoholics." Dan's face. "I don't know what it means to work the steps. But if that's what it takes to be done with this, I'm in."

Georgia nodded.

Ava took a breath. "I guess the best I can do is say, 'I give up' and hope that God shows up anyway. God or a sponsor. I'm not picky."

After the meeting, Lydia touched Ava's arm. "I've only been coming to these meetings for four months," Lydia said. "I really hoped I'd find a sponsor by now."

Uh-oh. Ava didn't like where this conversation was going.

Lydia continued, "I was thinking we could form a little group to help each other work the steps, like a co-journeyers. Meet Monday nights. Use the workbook. I thought we could ask Britt to join us."

Oh, God. Nonononono. There were so many other ways Ava would rather spend Monday nights than in the company of Adult Children of Alcoholics. Drinking was high on that list. Sonavabitch. "Yes," Ava said. "Where do I get the workbook?"

That evening, Ava stopped by Safeway for some cake. She had a better understanding now about what Lydia called playing whack-a-mole with addictions: first Nyquil, then wine, then Dan—always Dan. She'd bop one on the head only to have another surface immediately. Trusting a higher power to step in? She thought about Cheryl's request that she give Internet dating a try. See who else was out there. It couldn't hurt. She sat in the car and ate the gooey piece of cake from the box, frosting sticking to her chin. She sighed, looked heavenward. "I *am* trying," she said, but her mouth was full.

CHAPTER 25

BOYS

December 7th. Ava surveyed the baby's room, taking in the greens and blues and monkeys swinging from palm trees. "Is it a hard and fast rule that little boys like monkeys?"

Ruthie shrugged. She looked tired today, dark hair in a ponytail, slippers on her swollen feet. "It was either a jungle theme or trains. Shaun said that monkeys didn't sound manly." She grinned. "Bill and I took that as a green light."

Ava glanced around the shelves holding plastic nipples, bibs, and tiny tee shirts. "So what do I get a baby boy?"

"Oh, I don't know. A set of free weights, some guns?"

Ava pointed to her friend's bulging belly. "You ever think this was a terrible idea?"

Ruthie swatted her arm.

"Sorry." Ava rubbed her fingers on fringe of a fuzzy blanket. "Yours is going to be awesome. I'll take him for the day, we'll drink pints of Mountain Dew. I'll suggest he needs a pony, drop him off at home."

Ruthie put an arm around Ava's waist. "I know. That's why these will be our last few months as friends."

"Then you'll ditch me?"

"Let's just enjoy the time we have left."

Bill stuck his head in the room. "What's up, slugger? Going to make our next game?"

Ava touched her lip, now completely healed. "Still a little gun-shy. I'll think about coming back after Christmas."

Bill picked up a stuffed elephant. "The sooner the better. Shaun's been filling in, and it's not pretty. Jimmie wouldn't mind having your mug to look at instead of that cretin."

"No fair!" Shaun said, lugging in a rocking chair, "I look better in spandex than Ava." In a tee shirt today rather than his flaming button-down, Shaun was less like a slick salesman than an annoying older brother.

Ava thought about Jimmie, his green eyes, how intently he listened. She liked him. She liked his size, his smile, his thoughtful conversation. But that was the problem. Better to not ruin something with a great guy. Better to take her chances with strangers on the Internet. In junior high, she'd been asked out by Alex, the boy who'd pulled her desk over to his. He had motioned her to him, his friends hovering just a few feet away.

"Want to go out?" he asked.

Ava had wanted to date him. Really, she did. She just had no idea what that meant. Would it involve telling her dad? Alex was a great guy—funny and smart. But in that moment, she thought about the previous weekend. Ava's friend had spent the night. The sump pump went out again. Dad came undone.

"Fucking motherfucker!" His voice sent Ava and her friend hiding with Livvie in the trees, cats curled up next to them, waiting hours for Dad's mania to subside. What did dating look like when going out with someone who spent her weekends hiding in the woods?

"No thank you," Ava said, and quickly walked away.

Behind her, Alex's friends consoled, incredulous. "No thank you? Who says that? That's something you say when you're asked if you want fries with that."

And that was it. For junior high, high school, dating was over. Ava was the girl who didn't want fries with that.

"Enough with sports and baby boys." Ruthie pushed the drawer shut. "It's girl time." She pointed to Ava. "I promised you an Internet dating profile, missy, and that is what you will get."

Ava died a little, mortified that Shaun was listening. "Well, it didn't really have to be today," she mumbled.

"What's that?" Shaun said. "Internet dating? Ava? Let's see this thing."

She waved him off. "I don't have a profile yet. Ruthie was going to help me, but now I'm embarrassed." She turned to Ruthie, pleading, "We should just forget it."

Shaun sat down in the rocker. "You may not know it, but I am the king of Internet dating."

Ava looked him over. Shaun's tee shirt was from Hooters. "You get a lot of dates, do you?"

Ruthie frowned. "Yes, and it would be nice if he called anyone back for a second date. Be a gentleman, Shaun."

"Ah, but that would mean that they had been ladies, and let me tell you, the things I've done with some of these girls…."

Ruthie held up her hand. "That's enough. There's a child present. Bill, reign in your friend. Ava and I will be in the back bedroom."

"Call if you need any help!" Shaun called. "Nude pictures get more hits!"

In the cool back room, Ruthie opened up her laptop. "Now, what are you looking for?"

Ava put her head in her hands. "I can't believe it's come to this."

One hour and a package of peanut M&M's later, Ava submitted a profile that she hoped would attract more than the stereotypical desperate man. Coming from a stereotypical desperate woman, however, she wasn't sure how successful her efforts had been.

I'm a 28-year-old high school teacher with a sarcastic sense of humor (survival mechanism). I love my job, but on the days that I'd like to forget that it took a master's degree for teenagers to make fun of me, a beer with friends is a good remedy. (Much beer was needed after singing "For What It's Worth" to my students in lieu of buying the actual CD by people who could actually sing). I'm a closet karaoke fan, but my friends kindly try to overlook it. I moved to the city last summer and am always looking for someone interested in hiking, beginner rock climbing, or helping me improve my skills as a right fielder on a beer ball team.

Ruthie shook her head. "I still think you should take out the karaoke part."

"Why? It's fun."

"Debatable. You need to be more generic—open up the pool."

"It's a shallow pool anyway."

"My point exactly."

Shaun knocked. "Chick time is over," he yelled. "Time for a little broom ball." He pushed the door open, grinning a salesman's smile, broom and whiffle ball in his hand. "Physical therapy," he said, pointing to Ava's lip.

"I need all right fielders across the street in the park in five minutes!" Bill called.

Ava smiled broadly. "Show me what you've got, Shaun."

CHAPTER 26
IS YOUR DAY WORSE THAN MINE?

I t was a clear, quiet December morning. Ava pulled up to the school district Health offices for a training on running a Gay Straight Alliance club, a mandated program at every school in the district. The Health offices were located in the Sunset district of the city, across the street from Lincoln High School, one of the city's highest achieving schools, largely populated by Asian and white students from the surrounding neighborhoods.

She easily found parking on the extra wide streets. Ava took in the view—baby blue skies emerging from the fog rolling over the ocean. She looked forward to a day in which she wouldn't be reacting to students first thing in the morning. She'd be sitting in a small room with a cup of coffee, surrounded by reasonable adults. They would exchange pleasant words, thoughtful conversation. No one would flip her the bird or call her a bitch. Heaven.

The phone rang. Ava looked at the screen. *Pants.* She panicked. Don't answer. Just go inside. There's coffee and quiet and reasonable people—The phone went to voicemail. She sighed. It rang again. Fuuuuuuck. "Hello?"

"Ava," the principal chirped. "Glad I caught you. We need you to come back to the school."

"No," Ava breathed. She saw other teachers walk into the School Heath building. They were talking to each other, laughing, having adult conversations. She glanced at her watch. "I mean, it's 7:45 already. My training starts in fifteen minutes." Her heart sank. "I put in for a sub weeks ago."

"Yeah, but no sub showed, so we need you to come back and teach your classes."

Ava's day drinking coffee with grown-ups slipped past her like a warm breeze now gone. "But this training is mandatory. We're expected to get a GSA up and running. They're paying me eight hundred dollars," she pleaded.

"What can I say?" Pants was firm. "We don't have anyone to cover your classes. You need to come back to school."

Ava arrived at Ida B. thirty minutes late for first period, out of breath, and fuming. She barreled up the stairs just as Johntay flew down, twisty dreads flying. His Jordan tennis shoes took the steps two at a time, as if fleeing a collapsing building.

She stepped into his path. "What are you doing? You need to be in class." Her tone was angry. She was aware that it wasn't Johntay's fault.

He shook his long braids. "You're llllllaaaate," he said.

Ava ignored both the judgment in his tone and the hypocrisy of his statement. "Back to class. Now."

He raised an eyebrow. "I don't feel like being in class today." Johntay glanced at his teacher's flushed expression and then down at the worn jeans and Lyle Lovett tee shirt she had put together for her "adult day." He poked her gut with one finger. "You're getting a belly on you, Ms. L."

Kill, Kill, Kill. Ava's vision blurred. "I lost eight hundred dollars today. Is your day worse than that?"

"No." Johntay looked interested.

She pointed to the top of the stairs. "Then get back up to class!"

He turned around and started to climb. "That sucks, Ms. L."

"Yes, it does."

"My uncle was jacked for his iPod the other night."

"That so?"

Johntay continued up the stairs. "They put a gun in his face."

She slowed down, then stopped, looking up at her student. "I'm sorry. That must have been really scary for him."

Johntay grunted.

"Ooohhh, you're late, Ms. L!" Sean yelled when she walked into the room.

Ava gritted her teeth, nodded.

"Ms. L lost eight hundred dollars," Johntay announced.

Francisco eyed her. "What you doing with eight hundred bones?"

"I'll help you find it," K'Ron said.

"Wow, Ms. L—you need to be more careful," Melvin warned. "Put it in a clip or some shit."

Ava closed her eyes. "Noted."

CHAPTER 27

A TEACHER AND A BANKER WALK INTO A BAR

That night, Ava waited nervously at the bar. It was decorated to look like the 1940s—dark, polished wood, dim lighting, paneling and mirrors. The bartender slid her a beer without looking at her, eyes locked onto his next customer, a woman who must have been a Greek goddess in her past life. Why had Ava agreed to meet John 323 in the Marina? Would he recognize her from Ruthie's photo-shopped picture? She thought back to that afternoon, in Ruthie's bedroom, doctoring up photographs to get a date.

"Just take out the wrinkles by my eyes," Ava had begged.

Ruthie erased the wrinkles. "You know, these are supposed to represent you, not the fake version. People can tell." She rattled the empty M&M's bag. "I should have bought the big bag."

Ava peered at the screen. "And add a little shading under my chin—I promise, I'll try not to show a double chin in person, but c'mon, don't take the picture if I have the profile of a toad!"

"Watch it, diva," Ruthie said, a weary hand to her dark hair.

Ava rubbed her shoulders, "I've got more M&Ms in my purse."
"Well, that changes things."
"That's my girl."

And now, sitting at the bar, Ava tried not to feel like a wrinkled toad. She glanced around. Men in suits lounged against tall mahogany tables. Women leaned in, flirting from stools, swathed in leggings and cashmere, the kind of blonde only found in movies or the Marina District.

But no. You are not going down that path. Ava smoothed out her favorite skirt. Not thin, but not heavy either. You look fine. She glanced at the mirror behind the bar to check her lipstick. Still where it should be. Since Mina's unfortunate Eccos, Ava was more concerned about her footwear. Tonight, she had opted for cowboy boots. See? All good. She checked her hair. The natural blonde highlights were fading a bit to show all-too natural dishwater roots. Still—not awful. She checked her turquoise blouse. Good. She checked her moral standards. …And still cheating on Dan. Shit. She picked up her beer, a silent prayer. Let go and let God, right? Just got to let go and let—The beer somehow missed her lips, fell like a waterfall down her front.

Ava froze. This is what I get for not staying home. She brushed at her skirt with a tiny napkin, a dark stain spreading, the air around her thick and hoppy. Who was she kidding? Dan was still flying from Olympia to see her family over Christmas. Tomorrow she was meeting up with Lydia and the gang for a rockin' evening of ACA. Step one: My life has become unmanageable. Check.

Then she saw him. John 323 in a sweater vest making his way past the suits, the cashmere. A man walks into a bar…Oh please, let this not be one big joke…

"Ava?" He peered at her through Clark Kent glasses. John's dark hair lay in short curls around his head, a sexy banker who'd written that she sounded intriguing.

"Yes." She leaned from her perch, held out a hand.

John's grip was solid. He settled onto a stool, smile wary. His gaze took her in, lingering at the dark stain spreading across her skirt. His smile faded. He nodded at her half-empty glass. "You need another?"

She shook her head, heat rising like lava up her temples. "No, I managed to spill most of this one down my front. I'm going to work on my fine motor skills before having any more. Maybe take classes at a community college, Drinking From a Glass 101…"

John frowned. "So, no?"

"No."

He turned to the bartender while Ava dabbed at her shirt. She wanted to go home. She wanted to become invisible, or at the very least, die.

Beer in hand, John relaxed. He took a drink, leaned back. "So what do you do again?"

Ava ignored the fact that they had already emailed about their jobs. I'm a high school teacher."

"That's interesting," John said. "If unions weren't destroying public education, I'd vote for a lot more bonds."

Ava forced a smile. And we're done here, Mr. 323.

"I'm just a boring bank manager."

"Oh? Any robberies recently?" Ava didn't feel bad for hoping the answer would be *yes*.

He smiled, his first real one of the evening. "I get asked that a lot. Actually, yes. We had one two months ago—a guy who comes in regularly."

"What? You knew who he was?"

John laughed. "Amanda, the teller at the time, tried to talk him out of it. 'You sure, Phil?' she said. 'You sure you want to do this?' Phil didn't have a gun. Just demanded she hand over two hundred dollars. We all felt bad that we had to call the cops."

"That's awful." Ava's love of a good story fought her better judgment about men. "Tell me more."

"Well," John turned in his seat so his knees were almost touching hers. "There was this other guy, not a regular, who came in with a runny nose."

"Bank robber?'

"Just wait for it—he comes in and demands money. I tell him no, I'm not going to give him anything. So then he asks for a tissue."

"No way!"

"I told him to get out. I wasn't going to give him a tissue either."

Ava gasped. "That's so harsh."

John shrugged. "I was pissed."

"What did he do then?" She tried to memorize the story in her mind so that she could tell it again, twist it to make it her own. I could listen all night long.

"He asked where he could buy tissue. I directed him to a Walgreens down the street. When the guy left, I called the cops. Ten minutes later, he came back carrying a box of Kleenex and they cuffed him."

Ava closed her eyes. "I love that story."

John's whole body leaned in toward hers. "Now, tell me a story about your job."

Ava was doubtful. "There isn't a whole lot to say. I guess there was the time I took drug money away from a kid."

John flagged the bartender. "Lady needs another beer. Drug money? No way—how does that happen? Don't you teach kindergarten or something?"

Great storyteller, shitty listener. Good thing he was buying the next round.

CHAPTER 28
A TOAST FOR THE SCUMBAG

Two weeks before Christmas, Santa Claus came to Ida B Wells. Big Moe had just transferred into the school. He must have weighed over 300 pounds and didn't know any students or teachers, but that didn't stop this one-man welcome-wagon from creating a meet and greet line down the hallway. "Good morning!" he waved to the special ed. teacher. He pointed to his massive chest. "Big Moe. It's my first day. I'm looking forward to it!" He held out his knuckles to a kid in a Giant's tee shirt and dreads. "Nice jersey, dude!"

The kid stared, then slowly held out his fist for Moe to bump.

Moe continued down the hall, still fairly empty fifteen minutes before the start of the day. He turned in Ava's direction. "Yo teach! Have a good day!"

Ava looked behind her: No one. Back to Moe: Still waving. You're talking to me? You're wanting me to have a good day? Months of students not responding when she greeted them good morning. The entire class becoming enraged when she forgot to say, "God Bless you," to a sneeze.

Big Moe. Day one.

"You have a great day too, Moe." Sweet Jesus, bless you. In fact—fuck it—God bless us, every one.

174

All day that day and everyday thereafter, Moe high-fived his new peers in the hallway, goodwill toward man following in his stride. Students, stunned by a disposition in clear contrast to an awkward physique, high-fived him right back. It was a Christmas miracle.

Wellness put out a memo that Big Moe suffered from a myriad of health issues. He wheezed with the effort of walking down hallways. He remained winded ten minutes after taking the stairs. Lung problems had kept him out of school often, creating gaps in his learning that were as massive as the student himself.

Ava watched him assume an uncharacteristically dejected attitude on his fifth day at Ida B, the day that he had to take the Exit Exam. "I already failed it twice," he whispered as she handed him his test.

"Third time's a charm, haven't you heard that?" Ava patted his arm, trying to quell the rage she felt with a quarter of her class missing on test day. Ken wasn't there. Neither was K'Ron. Are you kidding me? Students had known about this day months in advance. She'd reminded them, prepped them, begged them to be here, on time, not high, and now….

Johntay's head was down. She tapped him on his arm, prayed to the gods of teachers everywhere about to hand out a test, Please, if you're out there, if you care about me at all—please, get them here and make them give a shit. She had worked so hard to get them ready to pass. This was their ticket to graduation. College. A better life. Ava finally achieving her goal for them. She put a hand on Moe's shoulder, speaking to the group, "You're all going to do great today, just try your best. I'm going to read out the directions now…."

Time ticked by. She watched as students alternated between sweating over, then skimming through pages of reading. K'Ron crept in late. Overslept. Then Ken. Couldn't find a bag to match his shoes. The latecomers sped through the first few sections.

"Slow down, take breaks," Ava begged. Please read it. Any of it. Please don't be high.

The length of the readings created a collective depression. Students used strategies for test taking that had been drilled since elementary: Look at the questions first, then go back and read. Except that Ava's students had only absorbed the idea that the reading wasn't as important as the questions. Some never went back to the text, guessing answers and moving on. All kids paused at the essay directions.

Big Moe was the first to identify the problem. He raised his hand, pointing to the phrase "keys to the city." "I don't know what this means," he whispered.

Ava glanced at the prompt. Shit. The essay asked kids to write a letter to the mayor, telling him why someone they knew deserved the keys to the city. She'd worked with students on essays for the past few months. They'd gone over and over how to construct a paragraph. She hammered in the idea that essays had a pattern, that each paragraph had its own function, and how to use transitional words and phrases to string the paragraphs together. All of this went out the window when kids didn't have a background understanding of the topic they were to address.

Last year's topic had asked students to imagine that they were in charge of an advertising campaign for a local museum. They were supposed to design a poster in their heads, advertising an exhibit on California's history and scenery, then write a proposal describing that poster. When Cheryl Wilson recounted that prompt, Ava had laughed at its absurd complexity.

Cheryl said some kids had cried. "Only the special ed. kids get a break on the test. Our students are held to the same standard as kids from schools all over the state, like kids who've actually been to a museum."

Ava glanced around at her sleepy testers. Another hand went up. She walked over to Ken, who pointed to the words *keys to the city*.

The General raised his hand, "What's this mean?" he asked, ignoring the rule about talking during the test. Ava saw he was looking at the essay prompt as well.

"I don't understand what I'm supposed to write," said Kabernay, back in school after three weeks out for "personal reasons." Her grandmother's hip surgery required Kabernay help her with tasks around the house.

Testing rules dictated that teachers couldn't give any hints on any of the test content. Ava glanced at Sean's face. Really? I can't say anything? "Sometime in my life," she said loudly, "I really hope to get an AWARD for being a good citizen. If the MAYOR thinks I deserve it, he might give me the KEYS TO THE CITY."

The students looked at her, puzzled.

"But what's it mean?" asked Big Moe, still pointing to the phrase.

"Honey," Ava said, "I'm not allowed to tell you—I just gave you a hint." But she knew that hint was pathetically ineffectual, because, at its core, receiving the keys to the city is a complex concept if you'd never heard of it before. It wasn't just an award. It was recognition of your status in the greater society, or of a helpful act you'd done for your community: it represented the whole city being 'open' to you. Some of Ida B's students could not safely cross whole blocks in the city—how could she possibly explain the concept of having a key that made the entire city 'yours'?

She wanted to cry when Johntay fell asleep midway through the test. She woke him up, suggested a glass of water, urged him to take walk around the school. Johntay's head stayed down, too tired to care.

After the students handed in their tests that day, she glanced at their essays. While many students wrote at least four paragraphs, some still wrote entire pages without a paragraph break. Sean's paper had two paragraph breaks, but instead of writing his letter to the mayor of the city, as per the directions, Sean had written, "Dear Major."

Breaking the rules again, Ava stopped him on the way out of the room. She held the directions next to his letter. "Do you see any difference between these two words?"

Sean shook his head. "I'm tired, Ms. L. Can I go to lunch now?"

She tried one more time. "I've always pronounced this word," she pointed to the test, "as *mayor*. But this word," she pointed to his paper, "I pronounce as *major*."

Sean looked at her blankly.

"No difference?"

He shook his head. "Can I go get lunch now?"

"Of course." Ava put his test back on the pile with the others. This mistake could cost Sean a lot of points. Students didn't get to review their answers the following day when they were fresh or make up sections they missed. This test was supposed to make the playing field fair for kids like Sean. However, that playing field was sloped like a ski hill, and the test was a teaspoon rather than a bulldozer. She added "basic spelling" to the enormous list of skills she still needed to teach.

Throughout the next day, during which time students took the math portion of the test, Ava kept hearing from kids who popped their heads into her room while on bathroom breaks. They were elated to inform her that their math teacher, the young, white guy from the Teach for America program, was coaching his students through questions as he proctored the math test.

"I was worried," Big Moe said, stopping by Ava's room on her prep hour. A bathroom pass dangled from his large hand. "But then Mr. Jeffries showed me on the test that only one answer could be right."

Uh-oh. Ava didn't want to dampen Moe's enthusiasm, but giving out answers shouldn't have been on Mr. Jeffries' agenda today. Moe must be mistaken.

But another knock revealed Paris in the hallway, beaming. "How's the test going?" Ava asked. Paris had been kicked out of math class repeatedly this semester. As her Homeroom counselor, Ava called Paris's house a number of times to let her family know about her failing grade.

"It's easy!" Paris whispered. "I just raise my hand when I don't know an answer, and Mr. Jeffries comes over and tells me which answer is right."

Oh, God. Ava went into a full-body rage. Her newbie colleague was handing out answers. Sonofabitch. She thought about all her hard work this quarter, the kids' dogged efforts learning language arts skills. And he's telling them what to bubble. Should she call Pants? If the principal asked students about cheating, they wouldn't admit to it. Ava would look like a jealous snitch, especially when the math test results came back so much better than hers. She turned to Paris. "He's not supposed to do that, you know," she said. "I want you to try your best on your own. You can do it."

Paris gave a withering look. "I'ma pass. That's what I'ma do. Mr. Jeffries wants me to pass." She added pointedly, "He cares about us."

The afternoon of the math test, Mark Jeffries came to Ava because he had had, in his words, "an incident" with Melvin. He admitted to calling Melvin a *faggot* during testing.

"I snapped," he explained, shrugging.

Melvin? Ava thought. Sweet Melvin, her Filipino joker? Jeffries had called Melvin a what? Ava concentrated on the acne dotting Mr. Jeffries' hairline. He was young. She was young. Murder would ruin both their lives.

"I have a temper."

Think about the acne.

"I don't know how anyone can teach these kids."

Zits all over his forehead.

"I'll be glad when my two years are up. I'm thinking about graduate school. Maybe become a professor for new teachers."

Ava took a breath, a lack of courage all that prevented her from calling him a fucking scumbag and shoving Harvard up some dark and lonely place. "You need to make this right with Melvin."

To her young colleague's credit, Melvin later did inform Ava about the name calling and Jeffries' apology. "I shouldn't have kept asking to use the restroom," he said. His eyes stayed on the floor. "It's okay though. Mr. Jeffries said he didn't mean it."

Ava shook her head. She didn't trust her words.

That night, she brought a bottle of wine over to Ruthie's apartment.

"Apparently, I am not in a real profession." she said. "Anyone with a BA in bullshit can get a classroom of their own." She pointed to an invisible audience, Oprah-style. "You get a classroom, and you get a classroom and you get a classroom!"

Ruthie nodded. She topped off Ava's glass.

"Nice resume boost if you can get it. Working with poor kids 'cause their parents won't complain. Calling them *faggots*."

"Do you want me to call the principal?" Ruthie asked. "Rat him out?"

Ava shook her head. "She would just replace him with another TFA."

"Why would Pants do that?"

Ava moaned. "TFAs are cheaper than real teachers. And I'm the one who's going to look like an ineffective asshole when the test scores come out."

"Seriously, I could write a letter to the newspaper or something."

"Yeah? Well, maybe." Ava sighed. "Enough. New topic. This one's making me mad. How's the baby? Ready for college yet?"

Ruthie put a hand on her belly. "Just about. We're planning a tour of universities this spring." She blew on her tea. "Oh, yeah—how did your date go the other night?"

Ava shook her head, heat spreading over her face.

"You didn't give it up to him, did you?"

Ava died a little. "No," she whispered, "I didn't give it up."

"Why are you whispering?"

"Because, while I know all dating catastrophes are entertainment, sometimes I feel like shit about mine and prefer to remember them in a whisper."

"Aww, I'm sorry. What happened?'

"Well, he was kind of a dick, but he had good stories."

Ruthie put a hand to her forehead. "Uh oh. Can we just say that if someone is 'kind of a dick' on the first date, they're eliminated immediately?"

"…So I let him take charge on the end-of-date hug. I was giving up control. Being a lady."

"That would be great, except for the 'kind of a dick' thing. I don't think you're getting the game plan here, woman."

"Well, that was where it all went to hell anyway."

"Oh no."

"He went in to kiss me, only really slowly."

"You didn't want him to?"

"I don't know. Probably not. But I got nervous. Before I know it, I'm thinking, Fuck this. I took control and end up going for it— you know, a real kiss."

"Oh, shit."

"Yeah. It turns out that what he was going for was a closed-mouth, chaste, 1700s kind of kiss. I added tongue."

Ruthie snorted. "Jesus. This is what you do when you're nervous?"

"Yeah, it was awkward. I ended up feeling like a whore, which is strange because I really was a hoe with Dan, who was a real dick the last time we talked, even though he's still planning to visit my family for Christmas."

"Ouch."

"Yeah. I won't be holding my breath for anyone's call. Dating isn't my thing. I need to give up now."

"Honey, you've got to change your attitude."

Ava laid her head on the table. "You think?"

"No one puts a doormat on a pedestal."

6:00 am. A harsh alarm tore Ava out of oblivion. She had fallen asleep on Ruthie's couch and could feel makeup and sweat congealing on her face. "Ohhh, God," she moaned.

"Call in," Ruthie yelled from the bedroom.

Ava glanced at her watch, disappointed in a fact she already knew. "I can't."

"Why not?"

"I'm a moron."

"And?"

"It's after six."

"What does that matter?" Ruthie strolled into the living room, surveying her rumpled clothes and smeared makeup. "You look like hell."

"Yeah, pretty much. I feel like shit too."

"So call in."

"Yeah. That was my thought, but now it's too late."

"You don't have a sick day you can use?"

Ava got up and put a hand to her head. "I have a ton of sick days, but it's after six. You can't call in if you don't call by six. Besides, I don't have a lesson plan ready for a sub." She wanted to cry.

"Aren't subs supposed to come prepared with those?"

"Yeah, and the school district's supposed to pay them a living wage." Ava didn't mention that the pool of substitutes varied wildly: from three very professional men under fifty to a bunch of retired teachers so old they kept falling asleep during class. The last time Ava was out with the flu, her radio and several silent reading books had walked right out of the classroom.

She washed the eye makeup off her face. The knees of her dress slacks were stretched to deformed bubbles. She tried to wipe the wrinkles out her shirt and had to call it good enough. Fuck it. The students could care less about what she wore. Last week, Stella woke up late and taught in Christmas pajamas. "Not one kid mentioned it," she told Ava when the day was over.

CHAPTER 29
PANTS' CHRISMAS CARD

December 17th. Ava opened her school email.

Staff,

This is a reminder that this week is still considered school (instructional time) this must be taking place. Ms. Brill will be here touring the school fasilites.

Important: NO music, chrismas or otherwise should be heard in your rooms. NONE! We need to uphold all norms. Remember, all parent conferences should already be scheduled for the end of the week. If you have questions or concerns please see me.

Cheryl printed out the email. "It's like a little poem," she said. "I'ma send this out in my *chrismas* cards. I wonder if Pants knows that *fasilites* is not a word."

CHAPTER 30
PARENT CONFERENCES

Two days until Christmas break. Parent conferences were the last hurdles before Ava stepped into freedom. Cheryl Wilson warned her: In the entire school year, parent conference days were the hardest. Once before Christmas and once in late May, homeroom teachers used conference time to talk to kids and parents about grades and future academic goals. Ava just had to make it these last two days.

"I'm looking forward to talking with Sean's foster mom," Ava said. "I can't seem to get her on the phone, but Sean is a great kid. It sounds like he might need someone to remind his foster mom of that."

"Sean's a sweetheart," Cheryl agreed, "but don't get your hopes up. We can only do so much. You can't fix what's wrong for them outside these walls, you know."

Ava was shocked. "Of course we can. That's why we're here, isn't it? I don't know how, exactly, but I'm thinking that parent conferences are a good start at helping them at home."

Cheryl observed her a moment. "I didn't pick you out to be a fool, so let me just give you a word of advice. You're their teacher, not their mother. You weren't there when they were born, and you're not going to be there when they die." Cheryl's face turned hard. "Some much sooner than others. We can try to help in small ways in the classroom, and we can make suggestions to parents, but I'm worried you're setting yourself up for failure."

"That sounds cold, Cheryl. I came into this to help kids. Pants was just saying yesterday that we need to do more to counsel students, to—"

"Pants is holding to the party line: Hold us accountable for graduation rates and no one has to address the bigger issues— Poverty. Segregation." Cheryl paused, her lips a hard line. "You want to help? Use this time to observe. You can learn a lot about students on conference days. Look for the kids who sit two chairs away from their parents. Parents can't hit as hard when they have to reach across a chair."

When Sean came in, Ava thought about the conversation she'd had with Mary Kline in Wellness. Mary had revealed that Sean's foster mom, Ms. Collins, wasn't feeding him if he wasn't home by six. Ms. Collins was also not washing his clothes. Sean didn't want Child Protective Services to get involved, dreading the idea of being sent to a group home, a modern-day orphanage.

Sean walked in behind Ms. Collins. His young, eager face, a beautiful dark hue, contrasted with the older woman's light cocoa complexion.

Was she his grandma? Ava made a mental note to ask.

Sean waited for Ms. Collins to pick a chair, then sat two seats away from her.

Uh-oh. "He's a really good kid," she said, spreading the contents of his blue folder on the table between them. "Such an upbeat addition to the classroom."

Ms. Collins placed her purse in her lap and sniffed. "Well, I'm glad he shows that here. He's been nothing but trouble at home."

"Really? What's going on? I heard there's some confusion about meal times?"

Ms. Collins reached across the empty chair, whacking Sean's arm with her purse. "What you been telling people?"

Ava flinched. She thought about objecting to the whack, then realized it was Ms. Collins, not her, whom Sean would face later, alone, at home. Tread lightly. "I just heard something about not making it home in time for meals."

"Well, I put dinner on the table at six. I got three other kids I'm looking after in my home, and if he thinks I'm going to serve him whenever he feels like walking in that door, he's got another damn think coming." Ms. Collins stuck out her chin.

Sean shrank into his seat.

Ava felt like shrinking too. Ms. Collins had a point. Already, this conversation was beyond Ava's capabilities. But she wasn't ready for Cheryl to be right. It *was* her job to try to smooth things out for students outside of school. It was her job to make sure she helped them in the ways she had needed help at their age. She took a breath. "Sean? Why aren't you making it home by six?"

The student mumbled at his feet.

"What's that?"

"There's kids from Sunnydale who hang out near my house. Sometimes they're there until late at night."

Ava leaned in. "What do you mean? You can't walk past them? What do they do?"

His foster mom sighed. "A few weeks ago, them boys beat up Sean when he was walking home. I been talked to the police about it, but there's not much anyone can do. Sean needs to hustle home immediately after school. But he doesn't do that—so he should just handle his business with the boys. Either way, I'm not running a restaurant here."

"Why don't you go right home after school?" Ava pleaded.

Sean whispered, "Then I'm there all night, from four to bedtime."

"See there?" said Ms. Collins. "You can't get a straight answer from this kid."

Ava sat, mute. She wasn't his guardian. Staying with Ms. Collins was his choice. She'd talk with Sean privately when they came back from Christmas break and ask him how she could help. Maybe Wellness? But he was already seeing someone in Wellness. Could Pants talk with local law enforcement? She was grasping. Her first conference. Sweet Sean. There had to be something she could do.

But other parents were already in the hallway waiting for a meeting. Ava shook Ms. Collins' hand and tried to make eye contact with Sean, silently promising them both she'd do better.

Stella had a saying, 'The longer the nails, the bigger the personality.' Charnikka's mom, Janice, had very long nails. Janice had also had both legs cut off at her knees, the result of complications from diabetes. Charnikka wheeled her mother into the room, the student's gangly three-year-old daughter, Iyanla, trailing behind.

Ava was hoping to talk about the need for Charnikka to have more reliable childcare for her daughter. Charnikka's grades had suffered from little Iyanla not having someone to take her when she was sick. As soon as Ava saw the wheelchair, though, she knew that Janice wouldn't be spending more time running after a little girl. As it turned out, Charnikka's mom had other concerns.

"Nikka's always been smart," Janice said. "It's that smart mouth I worry about. That and her health. You know we have two liquor stores on our block, but I gotta take the bus forty minutes to get to the grocery store." She gestured at the wheelchair. "I'd complain, but I don't know who to complain to….and I'm tired."

Ava nodded.

Charnikka put an arm around her mother.

Janice teared up. "I'm afraid this same thing is going to happen to her. We've always been big-boned in my family."

Charnikka snorted. "Since when you get big-boned eating Popeye's chicken? We fat."

"Fat," Iyanla echoed. She poked her tiny belly with a finger.

Janice bristled. "Charnikka, don't you dare talk to me like that. I gave life to you—"

"And then I gave life to Iyanla. And if she lucky, she won't be giving birth to any babies before she graduates like you did, or I did." Charnikka shook her head. "Look at us, Ms. L."

Ava opened her mouth, closed it. All she could tell them is what they already knew. "You know, if you fill out the school lunch form with your income, Charnikka could be eligible for free breakfasts and lunches. It's not a real solution, but—"

"I won't eat that," Charnikka said. "That shit is nasty."

Ava couldn't argue. Many students didn't like the small portions and poor quality of school lunches, so they didn't fill out lunch forms. Since these lunch forms also dictated how much money Ida B. received to run the school, everyone lost out. Mary Kline had recently asked the Food Bank for donations to help feed hungry students. Stella called the Food Bank's daily deliveries of old fruit and packaged crackers 'homeless food.' Sean filled his pockets with homeless food every day.

"And I'm tired of putting my business out there," Janice sighed. "No one needs to know my financials but me. We just gone do us, even if that means Popeye's Chicken. We'll make it by, won't we, baby?"

"I'm hungry," Iyanla said. Her tiny purple jeans were loose around her little waist.

Ava added to her list as she watched them leave: Talk to Charnikka after the break. Get Wellness involved. Ask if the city had any childcare options. Ask Pants to see if the Food Bank had anything extra for families of students. She felt how wishful her ideas were even as she wrote them down.

Francisco's mom, Ms. DeLeon, was already crying when she walked into the classroom. "You're going to end up dead or in jail, mijo!" she said.

Francisco sat two chairs away from her. He stared out the window.

Ava glanced at the clock. Ten a.m. Fuuuuuuck. She wasn't looking forward to talking about Francisco's behavior, though his grades were pretty good overall.

His mom slapped his arm.

Ava winced.

Ms. DeLeon wailed, "Listen to me! I am your mama! I care about you!" She turned to Ava. "Francisco and me had a hard time when he was younger. I was working all the time," she said, "but now I'm here for you, aren't I, mijo?"

Francisco took out his phone.

His mom explained, "Now I try to be home on weekends. I don't take more jobs." She looked at Ava, pleading. "Can you tell him that he should love his mama? That I'm trying the best I can? Francisco has two younger brothers who look up to him, but now they're starting to get into trouble at school."

Ava had rarely felt this inadequate. "Francisco, can you see how this is hurting your mom?"

He glared, eyes hard. "She didn't care about me when I was their age."

"Your brothers' ages?"

Silence.

Ava saw his hurt. His mom was years too late. Still—conferences should be an opportunity to mend what was broken outside the school. She asked, "But you want better for them, right?"

Francisco shrugged.

"He's very smart," Ava said. "He turned in one of the best essays in class." She tried to reason with him. "You are obviously tough. And bright. Your mom just wants you to be safe, and from what you've said about gangs, you aren't really safe on the streets…" Ava trailed off. She didn't even sound convincing to herself.

Francisco puffed up his chest, "My gang is mi familia," he said. "They protect me."

She referred him to Mary Kline for counseling, but there weren't any services to get students out of gangs—even if kids wanted to leave, which Francisco didn't. The gang had been there when his mom wasn't. Ava made a note to talk with him privately after break. Or maybe Pants could use her authority and talk to his probation officer—but, no. Pants spent the last faculty meeting telling Ava and her colleagues it was teachers' jobs to raise kids out of their situations through rigorous curricula. The principal wasn't taking on anything.

Mrs. DeLeon, still crying, thanked Ava as she left the meeting.

"Have a good holiday," Ava said, miserable.

Francisco grunted.

Kabernay's grandma came in with her. This was the conference Ava had been dreading. What could she say about a student who'd missed so much class that she earned zero credits? Ava still remembered the beginning of the school year when Grandma called during fourth period, asking if Kabernay was present.

Ava forgot for a moment that the girl was in her first period class. "I don't see her," she reported.

The next day, Grandma called again during fourth to say Kabernay insisted she did attend class the previous day.

"I'm so sorry," Ava said, mortified. "'I got the periods mixed up when you called. Of course she was here yesterday."

"Well, this is why you teachers get yourselves shot!" Grandma shouted. "I done yelled at Kabernay yesterday. Now you gone' have to tell her you messed up." Then the phone went dead.

Ava stared at the receiver.

"I know she ain't earned nothing this quarter," Grandma said before Ava could even show her Kabernay's grades. "What with whooping cough and I don't know what, Kabernay already told me she flunked out."

Ava decided not to mention Grandma keeping Kabernay out for a month after Grandma's hip surgery. "Well, it is too late for this quarter, but I think that with Kabernay in better health and a little more monitoring of her attendance—"

Grandma held up a hand. "I appreciate what you're doing," she said, "but I'm gonna put Kabernay into a charter school near my house."

Ava grimaced. She knew the school Grandma was talking about. Charters operated on school district dollars but outside of public school regulations. They were supposed to be centers for innovation, sharing expertise with the public schools when a new strategy was working. Instead, they siphoned off funds, then students, from the public schools. Charters got to pick and choose from committed parents who wanted a more exclusive atmosphere. Because the money the school district provided wasn't enough to run a school, most charters had backers—corporate, private, and hedge funds. Many charter schools turned a profit, money that never went back into the school districts' depleted coffers.

Charters also had a reputation for only retaining students who excelled, raising their public image. Low-achieving students were sent back to their home schools, public facilities now poorer for having to supplement the charter's corporate funding. Despite this, one in five charters did not do as well as their public school counterparts, but that didn't stop the country's educational secretary from mandating the expansion of charter schools in his national agenda.

Kabernay was not a stellar student. She must have been accepted by the one charter school in the city with a reputation for using its special exempt status to become a diploma mill. It required fifty fewer credits to graduate. Students worked exclusively from packets.

"Students who've gone to that school come back to tell me that they aren't really learning," Ava said. "They just go there to get an easy diploma—"

"That's exactly what I'm looking for," Grandma said. "I'm too old to be doing this shit." She jerked her head at Kabernay. "I need her to get out of high school as soon as possible. This new place says that they can graduate her before June."

Ava glanced at Kabernay's credits; graduating that early should have been impossible. "Kabernay, is this what you really want?"

The girl stared into space. Ava wondered what had happened to the animated student who'd sung along with the Black-Eyed Peas. She remembered Kabernay's description of hor d'oeuvres, 'baby sandwiches,' her joy at the distant memory of a teacher reading a book about a dog—a story to which she'd never heard the ending.

Grandma clutched the girl's transcripts. "This is what we need right now." She shook Ava's hand. "Thank you for your time. Kabernay? Let's go."

Kabernay gave a weak smile as she followed Grandma out the door.

Ava watched them leave. She suddenly wished she had found out which book it was, what dog. It wouldn't have been a difficult to get a copy. Unable to help her student in any real way, she could at least have read Kabernay the ending.

The General's mom was a slight young woman with large, tired eyes. "What is it this time?" She sat her little self down heavily. The General slumped into a chair next to her.

"I think you'll be proud of General," Ava said, pulling out his report card. Her only goal for this conference was to share the General's progress. General's mom had called often during the quarter to check up on her son, and Ava hoped there wouldn't be any surprises now. "See?" She pointed to his grades and credits. "He earned an A, a B, two C's."

The General's mom started crying.

Ava handed her a Kleenex from the almost used-up box. She dreaded what new information might come next about one of her favorite kids.

"But I did good," the General pleaded.

"I know, baby." His mom blew her nose. "I've just never seen a good report card for you."

Ava took a breath. Thank you. "He's worked really hard."

The General beamed. "I've been coming to school almost every day, haven't I, Ms. L?"

"You sure have." Ava noted that the General's transcripts showed him failing out of three comprehensive high schools in the city. "Can you tell me what's working for you here that wasn't working at your last schools?" A part of her hoped it might be a newfound love of English class, their hard work.

His mom looked up. "General's brother was shot two years ago outside our house. When that happened, General stopped caring about school. He's always been a quiet kid. Those schools have such big classes...I think he kind of disappeared for a while."

"What's your brother's name?" Ava asked.

The General whispered, "Lil' Eddy." The boy pulled down the neck of his oversized hoodie, *RIP Lil' Eddy* tattooed across his chest.

As General left with his mom, Ava stared at her notepad, full of promises she knew were bullshit. She added a reminder to ask The General more about his brother when he came back in January, placing a box to check off next to the line item. That one she could do. No helping students into better relationships, into better life circumstances. Ask The General about his dead brother. Check.

During a break, Ava caught a glimpse of one of Cheryl's meetings across the hall. She watched a father stumble into her colleague's room.

Cheryl's voice rang clear. "Mr. Johnson, have you been drinking? Where is your son?....Oh no, he's not getting out of this that easy. Dial his number for me." A long pause, then, "Ian? Where are you?...At a *bar*? What are you doing at a bar? You're not twenty-one! Your father's here for your parent conference. You need to get over here now!...Well, of course...Yes...Of course... Of course I don't want you to drive drunk, but what about taking the bus?"

Ava shook her head. Ian had already gone to jail once this semester—arrested for pimping in his neighborhood. During the time Ian was locked up, he sent a young woman in a mini skirt, pockmarks all over her face, to pick up his missing schoolwork.

"That is not his sister." Cheryl frowned.

Ava stared. It wasn't his girlfriend either. She felt disgusted, full despair and rage. Pimps were real. Prostitutes were real. And there was nothing she could do.

4:30 pm. Four no-shows for parents and kids, including Ken and his mom, a disappointment since Ken was one of Ava's favorites. She left a message to reschedule in the new year.

Conferences over, Ava met up with Cheryl in the hall. Her veteran colleague was on her way home. Ava still had to finish the paperwork on her last five meetings. "I don't think I can do another one of these in the spring, too," Ava said.

Cheryl nodded. "Honey, no one gets out of parent conferences without feeling low. Go home and give a lot of love to your pets."

The thought made Ava instantly, inconsolably sad. She saw herself on that icy day in January, the shocked haze of her dad's funeral. Later, she had held the cats close, said good-bye, and gave them away to a neighbor. Eleven years later, the hurt still felt new. "I don't have a pet."

Cheryl wrapped her in a hug. "Then go home and get one," she said. "We have half a year to go still. Dan's joining you in Washington for Christmas, right?" Her look turned stern. "Everyone goes insane around the holidays, girlfriend. Keep your head straight with that one."

CHAPTER 31

DOMINOES

Dan called her as his flight took off for Spokane. In two hours, she would pick him up from the airport and drive to her mom's house. It really was a small request, but she read *victim* into his tone—a worldly man forced into backcountry ways: "Please, I don't want to be riding in cars without seatbelts."

The visit flashed like a movie of other trips they'd made to her home over their three years together. Dan whining throughout, making small, cutting comments about her family, about her. No more. Rage boiled up. "*One time* we get a Christmas tree and there are too many people for seat belts. Going twenty miles an hour on backcountry roads isn't exactly dangerous freeway driving."

She chose not to mention the years before open container laws came into effect in Washington. "One for the road, J.W.?" The neighbor handing her dad a beer. Ava and her siblings climbing on top of the pickup load of hay. A sweet, dusty smell, then air rushing by as J.W. pulled onto the highway. Three kids riding high atop hay bales at forty miles an hour, her dad enjoying a cold one behind the wheel—now those had been good times.

Ava sighed into the phone. "I can't believe you'd bring that up. Of course we'll all be wearing seatbelts, you wuss."

And then, of course, the following afternoon, they all piled in to her mom's car. Mom was taking them to lunch at the local tavern. There were not enough seatbelts for everyone. Dan remarked, "You sure the friendly folks in law enforcement won't mind?"

Ava's spirits sank. "You can say we forced you to lunch at gunpoint."

That evening, Ava's mom and stepfather stayed up late, after her brother, Alan, and his wife had left, after her sister, Livvie, and her husband had taken little Leo to bed downstairs. The living room was appropriately trashed, wrapping paper and bows strewn across the carpet. Baby carrots lined the fireplace mantle, three-year-old Leo concerned Santa's reindeer might be hungry too. "Reindeer," he scowled at Livvie, "don't eat cookies."

Ava was enjoying some extra time with her mom and stepdad, Randy. Her stepdad pulled out a box of dominoes, brewed tea. It felt comfortable. Maybe the ACA promise of creating better relationships with family actually meant something.

As the evening wore on, Ava came to understand the game a bit better. Dan was winning, as usual.

"So tell me about your students," her stepdad asked.

"Here we go," said Dan. "You got an hour or twelve?"

Ava beamed. "They're such cool people. Lots of personality and…"

Ava glanced at the clock. 1:00 am. When had that happened? She stifled a yawn. "Excuse me. I think I'm done for the night."

Mom picked up the yawn. "I'm tired too."

Dan glared at Ava, his face reddening. "Just because you're losing," he said. He turned to her mom. "Ginny, don't let her fool you. She does this all the time."

Ava stared at him, nonplussed.

Randy put up his hands. "Now, I think we're all tired," he said. "We can play again tomorrow." Ava saw the darkening spots on the back of his hands, was surprised to see how much he had aged in one year.

Dan stood up and left his dominoes where they lay on the table. He mumbled, "Thanks for ruining the game." Then he headed downstairs to the bedroom.

Ava stared at the tiles spread out on the table. A game of Dominoes. She should let it go. But no. Last spring, it was the Seahawk's game. Now seatbelts, then Dominoes. She didn't know what Dan was mad at, but it wasn't her, not anymore. She stayed up on the couch after her parents had gone to bed.

Ava thought about the night, last March, when she and Dan had broken up. She'd thrown a glass of merlot across the room, watched it shatter against the brick fireplace, spraying onto the furniture, carpet. Glass shards and wine stains everywhere. Fuck it. Ava wouldn't be around to clean it up. "Because there will be nothing left of me left if I stay with you!" she yelled.

"Don't blame me for your problems!" Dan raged. "You're the one who's a drunk. You're the one without a sense of humor!"

"For the last time, it's not funny if no one's laughing! If you want to criticize, say what you've got to say. Don't put me down and call it a joke." Ava grabbed her suitcase and started throwing clothes in.

"Leave, then. Run away. You'll be the same crazy, fucked-up person wherever you live."

"Well, then, at least I won't be crazy for still living with you." Ava wrestled her suitcase shut. She took one last look at the wine-stained room before grabbing her keys, slamming the door so hard the windows rattled.

Now, at her mom's house, Ava could still feel the emotional tsunami of that day, the months of angry phone calls, the slow reconciliation. To be now back where she had began—She had become a cliché. She had to let go of Dan for good.

She looked through her mom's big picture window at a light shining across the river. That would be Mrs. Branson's house. Her husband had left her last year—shacked up with a waitress the next town over. Everyone knew. No one spoke of it. Mrs. Branson never brought up Mr. Branson's absence. Ava wondered what kind of courage it took to go on alone. To face those who know you and know your shame. To hold yourself up, keep the lights on.

Thirty minutes later, she made her way slowly down the stairs to the basement guest room. Dan woke when she opened the bedroom door.

"Jesus, where've you been?" he asked.

She felt in the closet for an extra pillow and blanket. "I'm calling this what it is—my fault. I shouldn't have invited you here. You and me together is never going to work. One of us has to end this for good." Ava was glad for the darkness, to not see his face. "I booked you a plane ticket for the morning," she said. "We're done. I need you to go home. Your taxi comes at six."

Dan snarled in the darkness. "You're kicking me out in four hours? I'm not going anywhere! This is some fucked up shit, even for you."

She felt the truth in his words. "It *is* fucked up," she said. "And I'm sorry. But you will take that taxi, and then I don't care where you go, but you can't stay here because it's motherfucking Christmas and I intend to enjoy some part of it, finally, without you."

It was a little after six the next morning when the taxi pulled away from the house. Ava turned from the kitchen window to find Mom sitting on the couch, a book in her lap, looking out across the water.

"I'm sorry," Mom said. She wore the lavender fleece robe Ava had gotten her eight years ago for Christmas. Her hair, still dark until this year, was starting to show wiry curls of gray.

Ava plopped down next to her. "Yeah."

"Feel like talking about it?"

"It should have been over last spring." Ava shook her head. She was tired of being a mess. She was tired of herself. "Sorry about all the drama. Let's talk about something else." She motioned to Mom's book. "What do you have there?"

Her mom ran a hand over the plain blue jacket cover. "It's a book of poetry. My mother's poem is in it."

"Grandmother wrote poetry?"

"No, not my step-mother. My real mother wrote poetry. She was an English teacher at the university before she married my dad."

"I didn't know that," Ava mused. And for the first time in twenty-eight years, Ava paused to piece together her mom's bundle.

CHAPTER 32

SUG

Ginny's mother was fat. Not plump, not big-boned, but honestly, cozily, fat. She wore a housecoat most days, a gingham pattern of pinks and blues. On icy Minnesota days, she liked the heat on a little too warm. She loved poetry read in the lamplight on November afternoons. She served her children white bread with thick coats of butter and sugar. She spread out crafts on the dining room table, adding glitter to pipe cleaners they would make into chains, put on the Christmas tree.

She was the kind of woman no one wanted to be and everyone wanted to be near. She gave the gift of allowing others to feel thinner, neater, better. Her voice was warm, her house, sweltering, and all of it—all of it—was Sug.

When Ginny's father was away at sea, Sug would sit her children down with pie, telling them to wish on the point, "So that daddy's ship will have boiler trouble and come home." And the ship did. It turned around, came back home. Because Sug told it to.

Doctors diagnosed Sug's brain tumor when Ginny was ten. Ginny and her two brothers, one older, one just three, were sent from their home in Minnesota to stay with an aunt New York. It was

1954. The brain tumor was inoperable. The children left, Sug was sick. When they returned two months later, Sug was gone. Ginny was charged with the care of her three-year-old brother.

Her father, Roy, was not the nurturing type. He was a businessman. After Sug's death, he quit the Navy and went back to advertising. He met Gloria, a colleague at the office, a month after Sug's funeral. He married Gloria five months later.

"Ginny!" Roy called. He rattled the ice in his glass, scotch and soda. Gloria was drinking bourbon on the rocks.

It was cocktail hour, and Ginny, now eleven, wasn't used to being called into adult presence until dinner. She set down the book she was reading to John, a tubby four-year-old who still wouldn't sleep through the night without calling out for Ginny. She would come and tuck him in again, smooth his baby-fine hair and tell him, "Hush little baby, don't say a word."

Ginny walked cautiously into the living room, orange and yellow the new color scheme.

Gloria swallowed her drink, a hand to her dark curls. She and Roy sat side-by-side in matching armchairs.

"Come here," Roy motioned Ginny closer. "Give your mother a kiss."

Gloria gave a little smile and leaned to one side, allowing Ginny to put her lips to Gloria's cool, dry cheek.

"That's good," Roy said. "Now, Gloria is a wonderful mother, isn't she?"

Ginny nodded.

"And you love her as much as you loved your first mother, don't you?" It was not a question.

Ginny nodded.

Roy turned to Gloria. "See that? I told you the children accept you. Enough of that. You may go now, Ginny."

When Ginny returned to John, he was crying for her to finish reading his book.

"You read it." She pushed him aside. "I'm not your mother." Locking his door so he wouldn't come out, she went to her own room, where she picked up Sug's picture. "I hate you, I hate you, I hate you," she whispered. Then the tears came.

When Ginny turned seventeen, she filled out an application for Cornell University, her father's alma mater, the school her brother extolled before beginning his studies abroad. Ginny waited on the college's response.

And waited. And waited.

Giving up, she attended the University of Minnesota.

Upon completion of her degree, she began teaching elementary school, where she met Ava's father, J.W. She called up her parents to tell them she was engaged. "That's nice," her father said, speaking from the phone in his living room, "but we're on vacation. We'll talk to you about this later."

Before the wedding, Ginny and J.W. had dinner with his parents. His father sat Ginny down after dessert. "When my son says 'jump' you say, 'how high?' the old man grunted. "He says, 'shit,' you shit. Got it?"

The ceremony was held in J.W.'s parents' backyard. No one said the word *bipolar.* No one knew.

Ginny and her groom, full-time firefighter and part-time bull rider, moved to Washington State. J.W. wanted to be a part of the back-to-the-land movement. Ginny wanted to rejoin humanity.

When Roy died, two years after Gloria's death, Ginny and the brother she'd raised cleaned out her father's home. They found, along with the urn containing Sug's ashes, a letter from Cornell University.

Dear Sir,

Thank you for your letter regarding Ginny Low. We have withdrawn her application as per your request.

Ginny stared at the letter a long time, unable to breathe, the life she might have lived projected in her mind. She balled the letter in her fist. "Cheap bastard," she whispered. "I hate you. " The next whisper came from a ten-year-old. "I hate you. I hate you."

When Ginny arrived back to her home in Washington, she filed for divorce from the man she no longer recognized. J.W. was often insane.

Ginny knew her children—nine, twelve, and fourteen, would take his side, be manipulated by their father to hate her for it. They did. She knew that shared custody would be the only solution her kids would accept. It was. She knew that J.W. would call her up late at night, threaten her. He did. All that no longer mattered: Ginny had finally had enough.

CHAPTER 33
BILLY-JO IS TEACHER-PROOF

Arriving back at school after Christmas break, Ava felt the therapeutic effects of two weeks away from kids and chaos. She walked into the office fresh, ready for the new semester, ready for life without Dan.

The secretary, Mrs. Letoa, greeted her with a smile. "You've gained weight!"

This was not the welcome Ava expected. "No, I don't think so—"

"But your face is fatter!" said Mrs. Letoa. She stood up to get a better assessment. "Yes!" she said. "You have definitely gained weight!"

Deflated, Ava made her copies and slunk her heavy self up to her room. The new semester was on.

That afternoon, following up on the list of promises she had made to kids during conferences, she hit more than a few dead-ends: The school had no way to help Sean with the neighborhood boys. Charnikka would need to fill out a lunch form for hot lunch, no more Food Bank food was available beyond apples and crackers for the girl to take home. Wellness would try once again to talk to Francisco about his involvement in gangs.

In the office, she heard that Johntay had also started his semester with a hefty dose of self-efficacy. Like a world-weary sophisticate, he had arrived at school late, marched into the counseling center, and demanded to know, "Where's my therapist?"

The Wellness coordinator, Mary Kline, explained that his counselor, Jessica, had been an intern. Jessica had finished her requisite hours of volunteering at the school. She would be moving forward with her own studies now.

Johntay refused to leave. He shouted, threw a chair, and was sent home suspended. As he left that day, he clutched Jessica's home phone number in his oversized hand. Ava figured he was tired of describing how it felt to watch a friend die. Ten shots in all. The smell of blood on his clothes. Johntay didn't have more retellings in him.

Jessica refused his calls. Mary referred him to another counselor, but Johntay declined services: The new counselor was an intern as well.

Later in the week, Ava attended an all day professional development on the latest editions of teacher-proof curriculum. At her previous school in Washington, she used to walk across the street to the superintendent's trailer to request funds for professional development workshops. This year, Ava put in a request with Pants to attend a workshop reviewing the effects of PTSD on students' classroom behaviors. Denied.

Instead, Ava sat in Mission High School's library with other English teachers from San Francisco's high schools at the district's training, sponsored by the megalith publisher, McDougal-Littell. A sales representative, a woman in her early twenties in a smart black suit, explained what Ava and her peers would be teaching for the next several years. The new English Language Arts textbooks weighed approximately ten pounds and cost schools fifty dollars each. Like the previous editions, these were filled with stories, poetry, and excerpts from novels. All 9th through 12th grade students in SFUSD were to learn from the same books, regardless of skill levels or backgrounds. The young representative took the entire day to explain that students should read the text and answer questions at the end of each chapter. Revolutionary.

Ava had little hope for these new editions. Students balked at the sight of the older textbooks sitting on Ida B.'s bookshelves. In August, the first day Ava had tried to assign a story to her senior English class, she was met with a reality check.

"Ms. L, I'm not going to do any more work from that book," a kid had said.

"Why not?"

"Because every year, we have to read from a book that looks just like that, only a different color, and every year I fail."

Ava seldom used the textbooks since. Instead, she purchased various paperbacks and supplemental videos. She created lessons from scratch, as did the rest of the staff, focusing on skills her students lacked. She mourned for the days of real professional development. It was painful to imagine the kind of teacher she might have been with help beyond McDougal Littell's spoon-fed bullshit. *I could've been a contender.*

On a Tuesday, during her prep hour, Pants came into Ava's room to review the textbook situation.

"Silent-reading books?" Ava suggested.

Pants shook her head, pointing to the McDougal-Littell texts lining the bookshelf, "The school's only allowed to purchase these. It doesn't look like you have thirty here, and you have thirty kids in your senior English class."

"They don't all show up on the same day," Ava said. "And besides, we don't use them."

Pants looked shocked, then disapproving. "My expectation is for you to be teaching from adopted texts. Besides, the district got sued last year. Not having enough textbooks for every kid. It's a legal issue now, which means we need to buy…" Pants made a tally, "seven more."

It being a new semester, Ava gave one more shot at trying out the test-prep workbooks, but they were as confusing and monotonous as they had seemed at the beginning of the year. She soon had a mutiny.

"Ok, folks, what did everybody get for the answer to the first reading question?" she asked.

The test-prep reading was about a girl named BillyJo who lived on a farm. BillyJo's big problem was getting the heifers to go into the barn at night. After Ava tried to read the story to the class and no one paid attention, she asked students to read the story to themselves. But, since this was not the actual test and the plotline held no interest for them, only the General and Tanya read the story. The others just bubbled in guesses to questions on the answer sheet.

"I don't know what this word is on number three," said Paris. She pointed to the word *heifer* on her answer document.

"It's a big woman," Melvin explained patiently. He was making the bubbles on his answer document spell out his name.

"That's heffa," Ken corrected.

"No!" Ava said. "We talked about this: A heifer's a female cow. Remember, you can use clues from your text, like how they're talking about BillyJo being on a ranch? And the story uses the word *cow*?"

"They don't have a bubble here for when you don't give a fuck," complained Francisco.

"No F's," Charnikka said. "Ms. L, why do we have to read this shit?"

"No S's," Tanya said. "Yeah, why can't we just watch a movie?"

Ava thought about what her students could read that might at least get their attention long enough to practice some reading skills. They liked to hear about injustice. They also liked it when

people double-crossed each other, or when they heard about family drama. For this reason, Ava had chosen *The Odyssey* and then
Hamlet for her senior English classes, for kids whose skills were
more advanced. Her seniors howled over Odysseus's luckless trav-
els. They sat breathless as one student shouted out updates on
Hamlet's ending, the kid racing ahead in the text so he could be
the first one to know the hero's fate. "The sword is poisoned!"

"No way!" The class sat agape.

"Read it!" Ava begged.

"Hamlet's been hit! Gertrude drank the wine!'

The students' eyes were riveted on the reader.

"Nuh-uh!"

"You're a liar!"

Ava smacked her forehead. "It's true! Read it!"

"Gertrude died!" the student yelled, eyes fevered. Other kids
hurriedly flipped through their scripts.

Yes, Ava thought.

But what to choose for kids who'd failed an English Language
Arts test, some of them many times, because they'd given up on
their abilities to read and write?

Francisco shoved a progress report at Ava. "Can you sign this? I
have a court date tomorrow."

Ava filled in his attendance and grade, lingering over the section to describe his attitude. "Tolly comes tomorrow," she said.
"He's going to be talking to you about the trial we're going to have
in three weeks."

"Don't make me a public defender," said Francisco. "My public
defender don't do shit for me."

Ava thought about what Francisco and other students knew
about the judicial system. Her students could read about Billy Jo
and her heifers, or they could read stories that other students,
kids not relegated to test prep, were reading. With emotions high
around injustice, she decided that her class would read the play

The Crucible, which focused on teenagers, injustice, snitching, and witchcraft.

Reading about the play's allusions to McCarthyism, the kids fully grasped the concept of persecution.

"That's like gang injunctions, or when they charge you with gang enhancement," said K'Ron glumly.

"It's like security following me around when I go into Macy's," said Niesha.

"It's like Ms. L calling home when you don't come to school," said Johntay.

Another bonus in reading *The Crucible* included the numerous opportunities to use the more tricky reading strategy of inference to understand character motivations. Ava's students struggled with the idea that there wasn't really witchcraft in Salem Village.

"My auntie says she feels evil spirits around the 41 bus," Tanya informed the class. "She also told me that you shouldn't spit after it rains." The kids looked at her wide-eyed.

"But how do we know Abigail is lying about seeing witches?" Ava asked.

"She isn't lying; she's telling the truth," asserted Paris.

"Naw," said Ken. "She just wants to get it on with John Proctor."

"And how do we know that?" Ava prompted.

"'Cause she was fired for being a hoe!" Melvin yelled gleefully.

"No H's," Ava warned, "but you're right."

The kids loved the injustice in the play. When Ava showed the movie, students voiced their enthusiasm by yelling, "Bitch!" every time Abigail appeared on screen.

Still, Ida B. looked anything but great on standardized tests. The *Los Angeles Times* had started printing classroom test scores next to teachers' names. A beloved teacher at a low-income school saw his name in print in the bottom percentile. Two days later, he committed suicide. It gave Ava pause. She was no different from that teacher. Those could have been her students' scores in the paper.

CHAPTER 34
EN POINTE

The faculty meeting had already gone on too long. Stella had been openly texting for the past half hour. Cheryl gathered her things and left, stating the time and looking pointedly at Pants. But the principal's list wasn't over just yet.

"In addition to the change in evaluation procedures, I also have some good news," she stated.

Ava was still mulling over the edict that Pants could ask to formally observe any of her lessons during a week-long window. Ava doubted the kids could go a whole week without someone's melt down. She knew she'd be a wreck by Friday.

"Ballet tickets!" Pants held up the agenda triumphantly, pointing to the last item. "It's a student matinee. And they're free."

The faculty stood up en mass, gathering their belongings, coffee cups, and wrappers from candy that Stella dug out of storage.

"Hell, no," Stella said.

"You've got to be kidding. No way," said the Spanish teacher.

"Only when I'm dead," said Mr. Brannon.

Ava had never been to a ballet. She pictured lots of action, tutus whirling, loud music drowning out her students' never-ending string of commentary. Why shouldn't her students get to experience a bit of high-society? Why shouldn't she? She raised her hand for tickets.

Of course, not all students dreamed of seeing a ballet. Johntay responded her announcement of the field trip in this way: "Niggas don't go to no ballet!"

Ava shook her head, thinking, Just because you don't see ballet images in black *People* doesn't mean black people don't go to the ballet.

A week later, with fifteen students along under protest, she rode the city bus to a dress-rehearsal, matinee performance of a ballet, performed by the SF Ballet Company.

They were only halfway there when Johntay casually walked off the bus to get a burger at McDonalds. Ava's stomach lurched and she scrambled off the buss after him. The rest of the students trailed her like ducklings. Then all the kids felt they needed food. The class ended up getting on another bus forty minutes later, reeking of onions.

Naturally, Ava's students entered the theater with only minutes to spare, the smokers whining that they be allowed a cigarette before the performance. But stepping inside the War Memorial Opera House, everyone fell silent. More than tutus and orchestras, this was an event that demanded respect. The lobby was gilt-trimmed, marble columns flanking grand marble entrances, elegant marble hallways. Inside, lush red draperies hung everywhere. The sweeping staircases to the box seats brought to mind ladies making dramatic entrances in voluminous ball gowns. A colossal chandelier hung from a sky-blue ceiling. Red velvet covered the floors and chairs.

She hustled the students down the isles, glancing around to see how much her fifteen students would stand out, whether she should turn around now. She was not prepared for this, and more to the point, she hadn't prepared the kids.

But, as promised, Ava noted it was an audience of students and their teachers. A lot of short kids. In fact, most students attending this performance looked like middle-schoolers. Nice. Middle schoolers were loud people. They liked to say inappropriate things and talk back. She nodded. We got this.

Ava followed an usher down rows of middle school kids squirming in their seats, swatting each other....Then, mid-way down the isle, she paused, noticing a trend. Besides being short, these kids didn't really look like Ida B students. They were mostly white, with a few Asian and Latino students as accent colors. These kids had starched, preppy collars. Their shirts were button-down. Girls were wearing dresses.

Ava's breathing stopped, veins suddenly pumping ice. Son of a bitch. These kids had been taken to the ballet before, maybe even several times—maybe even by their parents.

She gazed at her students, lovable and loud in their sneakers and puffy jackets. These were the same people who had to be reminded while watching *The Crucible* not to yell out "bitch" or "snitch" or "hoe" when the femme fatale, Abigail, took the screen. And that was just their movie behavior.

An usher finally stopped at their seats, which turned out to be in the front row.

You've got to be kidding me. Ava asked, "Isn't there anyplace else you can seat us?"

The usher looked at her pointedly. "You were supposed to be here thirty minutes early. We're filled up. It's important that you try to be on time."

Ava couldn't imagine what being so close to the action on stage would bring out in her students. The orchestra warmed up, a prelude to Armageddon. Ava sent a plea to the heavens, Don't let me go down like this.

The lights dimmed.

"Aaaaahhhhhhh!" Paris, Hector, and Tanya screamed as if in a haunted house.

"Shhhhhhh!" Ava whispered. She slid down a little in her seat, clutching the armrests. She prayed for a dancer to twist an ankle in the first few minutes, cancelling the performance. The kids knew that she had little authority over them in public. Fuuuuuck.

The middle schoolers waited quietly.

The orchestra played the first sweet notes. Three ballerinas took the stage.

"That girl is fiiiiine!" sang out Melvin.

"Shhhhhh!" said the middle schoolers behind him.

A male dancer floated onto the stage, pirouetting, twisting high in the air, an Adonis among mortals. The dancer's taut legs flexed beneath his tights.

"Ewwwwww!" yelled Paris. "Look at his pants!"

The dancer caught a ballerina by the waist, lifting her above his head, an angel being offered up to heaven.

The middle schoolers took a collective breath, enthralled by the symphony of movement. Ava was aware her students were focused solely on the dancer's package.

"Oh, gross!" yelled Johntay. "Ms. L, WHY are you SHOWING us this?"

The dancer frowned. He could hear their every word just as Ava and her students could see his every...muscle.

"Shhhhhhhh!" scolded the middle schoolers.

The ballerinas lifted their legs high, long graceful limbs extending like reeds in the wind.

"Why they so skinny?" asked K'Ron.

Johntay agreed. "That girl needs to eat."

Ava leaned over in her seat to address her row. "If you can't be quiet," she hissed, "I'll take you home."

"I'm ready to go," announced Francisco.

"WHAT is he DOING? Oh, MY GOD!" Melvin yelled, enthralled and horrified by the contortions of the elegant dancer. He elbowed Paris, who was texting.

The jostle made Paris's phone clatter to the floor, where it came apart. "Watch it, bitch," Paris said. She was testy after a week-long suspension for beating a girl with a chain outside the school. In Paris's defense, she hadn't brought the chain; as a van of girls from a rival neighborhood gang pulled up to the school and began harassing her, Paris's friend, a special education student, pulled the chain out of her bag and handed it to the girl. Ava's eighty-pound student got quite a few whacks in before the van sped off.

"I swear to God…" Ava warned in the loudest whisper she dared.

Tanya leaned across two people. "Did you see how high he jumped, Ms. L?"

Paris gave Ava a reproachful glance from under her shiny pink puffy jacket. "You shouldn't swear to God," she said.

"Wow," the General breathed. "How do they do that?"

Ken was riveted. He clutched his silver sparkle tote to his chest. His eyes held the light of heaven. "I love this place," he said.

Ava loved him.

When the last note sounded and the dancers took a final bow, Ava got real with herself. This is when the question-and-answer sessions happened. She didn't have enough courage left to make it though whatever questions her students might have for the dancers. She hustled her kids out of the theater.

As she hurried them out, an usher touched her arm. "You really should educate your students on proper theater etiquette."

"You think?" Ava muttered.

Outside at the bus stop, she spelled it out for the kids. "Gather round," she said. "Johntay, get out of traffic. Get. Back. Over. Here."

The intersection light turned green. A car honked at Tanya who was standing in the middle of the street, talking to a boy Ava didn't know.

"I have two points to make, and you will be quiet until I have made them," Ava said.

"Yeth thir," said Hector.

Ava held up one finger. "Point one—it was entirely my fault that I didn't tell you how to behave at a ballet."

"Yeah," said Francisco, "I didn't—"

"I said you will be quiet until I'm finished." Ava was aware that she had, as the kids liked to describe it, "crazy eyes."

"Second," she said, "even though you didn't know ballet behavior, you *did* know that I asked you to be quiet while the ballet was going on, and you ignored what I had to say. Also—"

"That's three points," said Tanya helpfully.

"Also," Ava continued, "you needed to be aware of other people in the theater. *They* weren't yelling out comments at the dancers!"

Johntay laughed.

"Funny?" she asked.

"No," he said, his face serious.

"The respect you give is the respect you get," Francisco muttered.

Ava's mouth filled with anger. "What? I respect you every day!"

K'Ron scraped her boot along the sidewalk. "Actually, Ms. L…"

Ava froze. "What do I do to disrespect you?"

"You don't tell us what we're doing right," Melvin whispered.

"What you're doing right?"

"Yeah, you just tell us what we're doing wrong."

"Give me an example."

"I sat in my seat quietly," the General said.

Ava's felt sick.

"I wore new slacks," said Paris.

"I got to school on time," said Johntay.

Sean nodded. "You never tell us what we do right."

Ava paused, stuck. She saw herself getting off the bus that morning. She had been following Johntay, but the rest of her students had been following her. She thought about the red marks she help-fully placed all over their papers.

"Tell us what we're doing right, then tell us what we need to do better," K'Ron instructed.

Ava felt like crying. *That's all I want too.* She saw herself yelling at the kids on the street. *What a dick.*

At home, she discovered that the etiquette page on the SF Ballet website spelled out what she hadn't bothered to check before taking students to a performance. The website advised parents to ask themselves the following questions before taking a child to the ballet:

1. Has your child already enjoyed a two-hour movie without talking or asking for explanations about what is happening? Thinking about that poor snitch, Abigail, in *The Crucible*, Ava had to admit a definite *no.*
2. Is your child happy sitting in her or his own seat without kicking adjacent seats and without getting up and down? No.
3. Has your child demonstrated the ability to hold a question for later? *Shit.* It really wasn't their fault.

Field trips were one area in which Cheryl often fought the rest of the faculty. "You have to give them opportunities," Cheryl argued. She maintained that field trips got kids out of the classroom and exposed them to positive community experiences.

Ava shook her head, the ballet too fresh. "It's too overwhelming."

"That's because we ask them to feel uncomfortable in order to have a new experience." Cheryl explained. "It's not something you know to say thank you for until much later."

Ava thought about that. During her last year of high school, she'd had an opportunity to join a teacher and twelve classmates on a ten-day trip to France and Italy. Social security money from her dad's death helped pay her way. The group had landed in Paris, and, with the exception of this year in San Francisco, Ava had never felt so out of place. Like a refugee, she arrived that first evening hungry and unable to negotiate the unfamiliar enough to do anything more than fall all over herself at the sight of a Pizza Hut.

CHAPTER 35

ADMITTED WE WERE POWERLESS

Ava walked into Lincoln High School's huge auditorium. A man in a wrinkled, oversized suit stood at the podium on stage. Every few seconds, he punctuated his speech with a fist in the air. A new contract was in negotiations. The union's bargaining team—teachers, substitutes, paraprofessionals, sat in folding chairs behind him.

"I was hoping there would be more young people here," Cheryl said. Today, the lines around her eyes were particularly prominent. Cheryl was looking her age.

Ava glanced out over the crowd assembled in the faded auditorium. There was a lot of gray hair.

"Goddamn ingrates!" Stella sputtered. "We work to get them decent class sizes, keep wages above the poverty line, and they don't even show up at a contract rally." She turned to Ava. "I'm worried about your generation."

Cheryl nodded. "Don't I know it. When we retire, there'll be no one left to fight. All our rights will be bargained away. Damn shame."

Sometimes It Looks Like That

Ava didn't understand. "But Mark Jeffries says there's no money to stop the layoffs. He says there's no reason to fight. Shouldn't we made a bigger fuss at a later time? "

Cheryl put a hand on her shoulder, a shell bracelet jangling from her wrist. "Honey, I'ma break this down so you can pass it on when I'm gone: it's not our job to worry about whether the district has money. The district has lawyers looking after their interests. The superintendent can pressure the mayor, legislators who are supposed to be funding education instead of making us fight each other over crumbs. Look around you—right now, these gray-haired old biddies are the only power our profession has. That's how the game is played. It ain't pretty, but since when is politics pretty?"

The man on stage boomed, "Eighty administrators are set to be given pink slips, but just like past years, we know all of those will rescinded. Two hundred and forty teachers are slated for pink slips. The district tells us that none can be rescinded!"

Ava blinked. Could that be her?

"Booooo!" The crowd yelled.

"And can you tell me that every administrator is effective?"

"No!"

"Who's looking over their shoulders? Holding them accountable? The superintendent, who has increased the number of administrators every year he's been in office?"

"Booo!"

"While class sizes increase."

"Booo!"

"So we're going to march into that school board meeting on Thursday, and we're going to tell them: You're hurting the people who are doing your work!"

"Yes!"

"You're hurting the people who care for your children!"

"Yes!"

"You are overcrowding classrooms, gutting support staff, and gouging their paychecks!"

"Yes!"

"You're chipping away the rights of veteran teachers, and you're telling us we have to take this?"

"Booooo!" Cheryl and Stella raised their fists in the air.

Ava scanned the crowd. She hadn't understood that layoffs were looming. She hadn't understood that her job might be on the chopping block. *What will I do then?* Fear poured into her like water filling a pitcher. She watched the man on the podium, the teachers in the crowd. Everyone there had had a long day. But they hadn't gone home, let someone else fight, as Ava had wanted to do. They had left school, driven to Lincoln, and lent their voices to the idea that teachers mattered, kids mattered.

It occurred to her, looking around, that superheroes may not, in fact, wear capes and latex body suits. In this moment, caped crusaders had gray hair, sported wrinkled, ill-fitting suit jackets. They taught in their pajamas, sang to their students, and protected other people's children.

After the rally, Cheryl and Stella gave Ava a lift to a bar near Ava's house.

"Remember, you're the queen," Cheryl said. She leaned over for a hug.

Stella boomed from the backseat, "Aw hell, get a little, you'll feel better."

Ava groaned. "Am I really doing this? I should go home."

Stella put a hand on Ava's shoulder. "My mother always said the best way to get over a man is to get under one."

Ava gave her hand a squeeze. "I'm sure it will make a great story tomorrow."

The bar was packed. Jerseys from various sports teams hung above the taps. There were no empty stools or seating of any kind as far as Ava could see. She really wanted a seat. Her feet hurt.

Ava glanced around for the man she'd been emailing for the past few weeks. It had been two months since she'd kicked Dan out of her mom's house. Cheryl and Stella had urged her to get back on the horse. Ava maintained you couldn't ride a horse after it was this long dead, picked over by scavengers, maggots gnawing on a rotted carcass. Still, she said she'd say *yes*. Trey worked for the tech industry. He said he'd be coming after work. She scanned the room. No Trey.

"Ava," a man with a ruddy face called. "Over here!" He was standing near the bar's only window, talking to a leggy brunette.

Ava walked over, noting Trey didn't seem to match his photos. They must have been taken a few years ago, before the spare tire. This is bad. But she thought of Cheryl and Stella's hopeful faces. Give him a chance.

"It's crowded in here," she said.

Trey ushered her to sit on a stool someone just vacated. "Here take this. I'll stand."

Ava sighed. "It's been a long day on my feet."

They talked about his car, his politics, his career ambitions.

She thought about her students, Dan, whether her feet would survive the long walk home later. She smiled politely and glanced at her watch. What happened to the fun, funny guy I emailed? Online, he had been interesting, made witty jabs. Still, she appreciated being able to rest her feet while he stood. The second glass of wine had helped. It seemed a bit early to bail—she didn't want to hurt Trey's feelings.

"…And that's when I told my boss to shove it," he finished his story.

"Mm?" Ava leaned into her buzz, the one blocking out the news that she may soon be laid off. What was that number? Two hundred and forty teachers on the chopping block. Shit. She took another drink.

Trey looked her up and down. "You dress like a social worker."

She stared at him, upset for herself and for social workers. Then, realization dawning…faded Goodwill blouse, sensible shoes…Fucker's right. The evening over, she pushed her glass aside. I should leave, but…. The urge to save his feelings fought the urge to save herself.

She sighed. "I guess I do."

"Huh. Anyone ever tell you, you talk funny?"

"Nope."

"Like you're from the south, only Washington isn't in the south."

"Very true." And we're done here, Trey.

Her date took another drink and looked around the room like a talent scout hoping for better candidates.

Ava collected her purse.

Try sighed. "I guess I could do this."

She frowned. What the hell is he talking about?

Trey leaned in. Then he was kissing her.

His lips were big, all over her mouth. Ugh. No. Nonononono. How had this happened? She tried to gently push Trey back.

He held on.

She pushed harder, turned her face away. "No," she said. The shame of being here with this man, in this situation, flooded her senses.

Trey's grip tightened.

The bartender leaned over the counter "Do you want this to be happening?"

Ava shook her head, mortified at how far she let the evening progress, and sick over her own poor judgment.

"Okay, buddy," the bartender said, "I think it's time to pay up and go home."

"Hey!" Trey protested, "I don't—"

"I'm leaving," she whispered. She couldn't look at Trey. She couldn't look at the bartender. She fished out a twenty and laid it on the counter. Shaking, she tried not to run until she got to the street.

The cool air hit her like a slap. Ava sprinted past couples, shouts, scents of the Mission. Get home. Get home. But as awful, awful as Trey had been, she knew she wasn't running from Trey; she was running from the person who allowed herself to be put in that position.

At the door to her apartment, she dialed Ruthie's number.

"Ava! You're home early! How'd it go?"

"I'm done," Ava said.

"Tell me about it."

"I can't. I'm ashamed. I just want to—" Ava started to cry.

"Nothing you could do would ever be that terrible."

"He gave me his chair, was super self-absorbed, then he was kissing me. I felt bad for him when the bartender stepped in, saved me—"

"You felt bad for him?"

"And…and then I paid for the drinks, the food, and left."

"You paid for the creep? He gave up a *chair*. You don't owe him anything. Oh, honey." Ruthie was silent a moment. "My therapist will call you tomorrow. You're going to book an appointment."

Ava said, "Yes."

CHAPTER 36

ON THE COUCH

Rain pelted from dreary January skies. The therapist's office was near the Giants' ballpark. She groaned as she pulled her car into a mercifully close parking spot.

Gary's MFT certificate hung on the wall. Ava appreciated this, since the tie-dyed tee shirt and leather pouch hanging from his neck did nothing to enhance his professional credibility.

"Ava. Glad to see you found my office okay." Gary had a way of ducking his head when he spoke.

She smiled, shaking his hand. Jesus God, look at all that hippie shit.

"Please, lie down on the couch. I'll put that blanket over you. Just get comfortable."

Hold on there, tie-dye. She edged slowly to the couch. She wasn't a therapy virgin—she knew this wasn't how it was supposed to go. "You don't need to hear about my family history first? You don't want to know what brought me here?"

"Nope. This is hypnotherapy. You're going to tell me everything I need to know while you're under."

Ruthie hadn't mentioned hypnotherapy. But then, if she had, Ava wouldn't have come. She lay down on the couch, a sway-back pleather that was yard sale material before it ever made it out of the factory.

Above her, Gary said, "Pay attention to the heart on the ceiling."

She stared up at a heart sticker on the popcorn ceiling. Shouldn't a real therapist be able to afford an office with a real ceiling?

Gary monotoned from somewhere above her—close. Too close. "Just focus on the heart. Take a deep breath in…..hold it…..hold it….now slowly let it out. Imagine that you've been lying here for a very long time. You are relaxed and your eyes are getting heavy. Now they're closing."

Ava did as Gary asked, imagining herself lying on a blanket on warm sand. Waves lapped at her feet, hanging off a towel. There was a light breeze. Gary explained that earlier she had gone for a walk, and now she was happy to be lying there, feeling the breeze, feeling the sand. Ava relaxed. This isn't so bad.

Gary said, "You're going to stand up now. Stretch. Feel the sun as you reach toward it. Just to your right there's a path, do you see it?"

Ava made her way up the short path, lined with small bushes and daisies, to a cabin flanked by fragrant cedars. She climbed the stairs into a bare room, a mirror its only furnishing. She stood in front of the mirror.

"Now, what do you see and what do you feel?" Gary asked.

Ava looked around, uncomfortable. "I see me. It's an empty room, and I'm just standing here. I liked it better at the beach."

Gary persisted. "Let's stay here a minute. Take your time. Let me know when something changes."

Ava waited, then, "Still the same, only…" Aww, you're not going to say that out loud are you? "There's something that hurts inside my chest."

"What is it?"

Ava visualized pulling back her ribs like a gate. "I see darkness, something rotting." Ava wanted to leave the cabin and go back to the beach. She exhaled the breath she was holding.

"And what does this represent?"

"I'm worthless. I'm failing these kids just like I failed myself."

"You feel worthless. Stay with that," Gary said.

You betcha, Ava thought. Great plan there, hippie.

"Our core beliefs as adults come from events in our childhoods. We're now going to go back to a time in your childhood when you felt worthless."

Oh, let's not....

"When I finish counting, you're going to be very young. I will count back from eight and your subconscious will know exactly where to go."

Fear rose in Ava's chest. What? My subconscious doesn't know where to go. What's your job here, Tie-dye?

"Eight: going back now; seven: getting younger...

Ava's mind was blank.

"Six: smaller and smaller..."

Think, Ava willed, think of something.

"Five: younger and younger; Four: really going back now; Three: younger and younger...."

Projected images of Ava's childhood flashed by too quickly to grab.

"Two: smaller and smaller...One! You're there. What do you see and what do you feel?"

The projector stopped, like placing a finger on a spinning globe. The scene came to Ava clearly. "I'm twelve years old, kneeling by my dad. We're fixing the neighbor's fence. Dad's been on a rampage. It is only Saturday morning. We've still got the whole weekend to go. He's yelling at me. I'm kneeling behind him, holding the tools, praying."

"What are you praying *for*?" Gary prompted.

This is stupid and—Let go and let God. "I'm praying that he'll stop yelling." Ava sighed. "For someone to finally come and rescue me."

"But no one comes?"

"Of course not. It was stupid to think anyone would."

"Can you see the twelve-year-old now, kneeling behind her father?"

"Yes."

"Would you like to go rescue her?"

"Me?"

"Yes. Go take her from the yelling. She's not wrong. The situation she's in is wrong. So go back there and take her hand. Take her away. Do you think you can keep her safe?"

Oh, for heaven's sake, this is the strangest— "I guess so," Ava said.

"Then go on."

The sun beat down warm, Dad frozen mid-hammer. Ava walked up to the girl, holding out a tentative hand. "I'm here to get you. Take you someplace safe."

The girl looked up, frowning. "I thought no one was coming."

A guilt trip now too? "Well, I'm a little late." Ava tried a smile. "Sorry?"

The girl's lip quivered. "You came back for me." Warmth flooded Ava's body. She felt the girl's wonder, the years that had passed. Relief. The hand that grabbled hers was soft, small, familiar. They both turned away from the man at the fence.

Ava cried out of both eyes. Fucking therapy.

Gary's voice rang clear. "I want you to thank the mirror. I'm going to put the headphones on you. The music will be the medicine you need. When the first notes begin, your spirit guides will come."

Of course my spirit guides will come.

When she opened her eyes ten minutes later, Gary asked, "So, how do you feel?"

She inhaled deeply, her shoulders relaxing. From a cavernous place where her heart should have been, she felt a tiny spark. "Like a superhero."

CHAPTER 37
PLEASE DON'T COME HIGH

January 22nd. Ava worked hard to acknowledge small triumphs in the classroom, let students know she saw what they were doing right. "Thank you for asking," she told Melvin when he raised his hand to use the restroom.

"You indented!" she told Paris before critiquing the rest of the student's error-filled essay.

Paris beamed.

And then there were the small triumphs and setbacks for the mock trial that took everyone's attention.

Preparation for Tolly's mock trial had been on-going for the past few months, every other Monday spent preparing students to be attorneys, witnesses, judges. There were understudies for the understudies since students were never all present on the same day.

It didn't calm Ava's nerves that Pants had requested to sit in. The trial would be regarded as a formal observation. Along with the potential for a poor evaluation, Ava feared the unknown configuration of students who might show up on the date of the trial. "Please come on time," she begged the class. "Please don't come high—but please come—on time—not high."

After much debate, the students had outvoted Tolly about having a trial focus on a search and seizure case. They wanted a murder trial with nothing less than the death penalty at stake. Ava was beginning to understand why: A few weeks ago, Melvin had mentioned a drive-by in his neighborhood, how he hit the ground while bullets snapped the air around him.

Shocked, Ava asked the students how many of them had ever dodged a drive-by. Over half of the class raised their hands. Many of them came to school after long weekends with placards around their necks featuring cousins or friends who'd been shot, many for being in the wrong place at the wrong time. Death was something the kids stared down on a regular basis. Why not have a trial with the highest stakes?

The kids' new, negotiated mock trial involved a lover's quarrel at a local club between the defendant, Johntay, and his girlfriend. The girlfriend left the club with a male friend and rode the bus home. She was later found shot in front of her apartment. Her friend and the bus driver were the last two people to see her alive.

After the trial scenario was decided, another problem arose: No one wanted to be the public defender.

"C'mon, folks," Ava pleaded, "it's a really important role—someone has to defend Johntay!"

"My last public defender was a bitch," said Francisco. "He didn't have enough time to look over my case. The judge gave me gang enhancement."

"No B's," Ava warned. She didn't point out that the tattoo across his neck was the only evidence of gang enhancement a judge needed.

"My public defender was cool, but she dressed like she be broke!" Niesha complained.

"Public defenders don't make any money," said Johntay. "I want to be a lawyer who makes money."

Tolly suggested, "How about you be a lawyer from a private law firm?" It was, after all, a made-up scenario.

Ken lit up. "Oooh, you could hire an exclusive lawyer from the firm of Ken, Ken, and Ken! I usually don't take on murder cases," he looked disdainfully at Johntay, "but this time I might. I would wear a gray suit with a silver tie and—"

"I ain't paying for no private lawyer!" protested Johntay, shaking his twisty dreads. He waved his hand, diva-weary. "Just give me the free shit."

Melvin finally volunteered for the role. "I got your back, bra," he said. "I'm down for the brown."

"I'm gonna die," Johntay lamented.

That afternoon, Ava told Cheryl Wilson about their new mock trial case and the kids' insistence it involve a shooting, death.

Cheryl nodded. She handed Ava a newspaper article about a former student who was on trial for murder. "I was really hoping it would be attempted murder," Cheryl said, "but the man died two days after he was shot."

The crime was being prosecuted as a capital offense because it involved gang members who had been shooting each other, apparently in excess, over the past year. Most murders in the kids' neighborhoods went unsolved. No one would snitch on those doing the shooting, even though the murders Ava's students' referenced occurred in broad daylight and involved several witnesses. As Johntay informed Ava one day, "Snitches end up in ditches."

"So what do families do?" Ava asked Cheryl.

"Do?" Cheryl said. "They keep their mouths shut. No one wants to place parents and younger siblings in danger."

"How is it okay with city officials to have murderers go free? What's being done to stop this cycle?"

Cheryl dug in a pile on her desk, retrieving the printout of an email. "He's the supervisor for this district," she explained. "This is the city's response to the violence."

Dear Supervisor M___,

I am a teacher at Ida B. Wells High School, and a former teacher of Jamal

Little who was recently murdered at 10:30 am on the corner of Laguna and Eddy. Yours is the district in which I both work and live. The deadly violence (and the fear it creates) in the Western Addition affects my students and me on a daily basis.

At the time of Jamal's death, according to the news, the security camera installed on that corner was not operational and therefore did not capture the crime on video. This is a corner where, as I understand, several other people have also been shot this year. My question is this: Is this camera now functioning? And if not, why?

Thank you,

Cheryl Wilson

And the supervisor's reply:

Dear Cheryl,

Please excuse the delay of my response.

The violence crisis goes unabated in San Francisco. This is not a resource issue as much as it a leadership and an accountability issue. This starts with the Mayor and his appointed SFPD Chief and on down the command chain to district captains. The DA is part of the calculation as well as the Housing Authority.

I doubt that the camera does work as it is up to the Mayor and the Housing Authority to require that Public Housing/Housing Authority replace ineffective security operations with decent on-site protocols. In addition, the community needs to apply greater pressure on the Mayor, Police and District Attorney to step up the arrests and prosecutions of those who commit these violent crimes since a large majority have gone unsolved over the last 3 years.

Since the Housing Authority does not have to subscribe to local law it's incumbent upon all to apply pressure - maybe Ida B. Wells' students can help?

I'll keep pushing for sensible reform.
Best regards,
Supervisor M___.

"Students?" Ava asked.

Cheryl smiled. "That's what the man suggests."

CHAPTER 38

STEP 5

Ava lit a candle and sat in the quiet of her room, ACA workbook spread out on her bed. Evening light filtered through the window that overlooked the street. Britt would arrive in a few minutes. Then Ava would share out her 5th Step: *Admitted to God, to ourselves, and to another human being the exact nature of our wrongs.* Awesome.

She flipped through the workbook pages, a "searching and fearless moral inventory" in which she'd penciled harms she'd suffered and harms she'd delivered. It was a crime scene. This felt like a forced confession.

A knock on the door. Ava thought about canceling, not going through with this step. Quitting ACA altogether. "Coming," she muttered.

Britt, blue hair turned green under the hallway light, held up a package of herbal tea. "Vodka for sober people. So glad I'm not going first. Lydia and I are still firming up a time for her to hear my 5th step." She sighed. "It was hard enough doing this in AA. I am not looking forward to a second time around."

From the living room, the sounds of the television. Minor tones—a tuba, or was it a cello? Da…dah. Da…dah. Pedro was watching *Jaws*. How appropriate. Ava managed a smile. I am trying.

Ten minutes later, she rethought the process. The reality of sharing what was written in her workbook felt as exposed as attending a high school reunion buck-naked.

Britt kicked off her boots and nestled against the pillows on the bed. She opened up a notebook.

Ava blanched. "Do you really have to write down the stuff I say?"

Britt made a face. "The process sucks. But it does help to get the monsters out of the closet. I think I opened the door to Medusa when I did this step, but my AA sponsor helped to put her into perspective. That's something I tend to lose first. That, and compassion." She looked tired. "The point is," she said as she put her cell phone on silent, "I'm here for you, bitch."

Ava sat cross-legged on the edge of her bed. The process was pretty straightforward: Read from her workbook while Britt listened and asked questions. She'd get Britt's notes at the end. Then, on her own, Ava would read through her shame all over again through someone else's interpretation. At her group's last meeting, it had seemed a reasonable process. Now the process seemed as rational as asking her inner critic to babysit her inner child.

She glanced at the first items on her chart: Three instances in which she'd felt harmed. This was going to suck so bad. She started with the first one. "My dad was a cowboy. I was nine. Prince was just a year old, a gelding, and small. My dad worked with him until he tolerated a saddle, but Prince needed someone to break him for riding. Dad was too heavy. Alan, my older brother, refused. I wanted Dad to see me as a cowgirl."

Britt raised an eyebrow. "That's one way to get love and attention."

Ava stiffened. It seemed a little early for judgment. "We'd begged for the horse, Alan, Livvie, and I. Dad loved horses, and we loved him. We thought asking for a horse was a harmless way to make him happy." She added, "My parents even played a rodeo song at their wedding, *Strawberry Roan*." Ava recited a few lines:

> *"A feller steps up and he says, "I suppose*
> *You're a bronc fighter from looks of your clothes."*
> *"You figures me right, I'm a good one," I claim.*
> *"Do you happen to have any bad ones to tame?"*
> *Said he's got one, a bad one to buck*
> *At throwin' good riders, he's had lots of luck."*

Britt cocked her head. "They played that song at their wedding?"

Ava nodded. "I guess it says a lot. Still, we loved it. We'd belt out the song in the car, beg my dad to sing it when he started to fall apart." She felt the bravado of the lyrics deflate. "But sitting on Prince—that wasn't a song. My dad was a bull rider. I was a nine-year old girl. I didn't know what to expect when I gripped the saddle horn with both hands." She thought about the next lines:

> *He's about the worst bucker I've seen on the range*
> *He'll turn on a nickel and give you some change*
> *He hits on all fours and goes up on high*
> *Leaves me a-spinnin' up there in the sky.*

Ava saw the wooden rail fence, the large corral, the broad expanse of Prince's back. "He bucked. My face smashed into his neck. Then he reared up. My shoulder hit the hard ground while his hooves were still coming down." She felt the bruises, the adrenaline, and the dirt in her mouth as she scrambled to her feet.

"Dad put me back on again. I was terrified. He said to roll away from the hooves when I got bucked off. I don't know how many times Prince threw me off that day, or in the days that followed. I kept getting back on until Dad gave up." When she'd written down the harm, it was because of the terror of being bucked off, the feeling that Dad shouldn't have put a small girl on an unbroken horse in the first place. But every time she thought about it, it was the disappointment in Prince's unbroken status that lingered long after the anger. Ava couldn't shake the thought that if she had ridden the horse, Dad might have had something to smile about, a reason to get better.

She glanced across the bed at Britt. Her co-journeyer was writing. What would she be writing? She felt buck-ass naked. "That's it."

Britt didn't even look up from her notebook. "And did he force you to get on the horse?"

"No." The question bugged. "Of course he didn't." Was this going to be an inquisition too? But Ava sat a moment while the woman wrote, thinking about what it meant if Dad didn't force her. He wanted her to. Was that the same thing?

Britt's face was friendly when she finally looked up. "Got it. And the next one?"

"Well…." She ran her finger down the list. "That would be the gun." She really didn't want to talk about this one. Like the story about Prince, she'd never mentioned it to anyone. But this one was worse than the horse.

"I was fourteen, Livvie—eleven. We were alone with Dad. It was nighttime. Dark. Not another neighbor for miles. He'd been on the phone, raging at my stepdad. When he slammed the phone in it's cradle, I knew it was going to be bad. Then he beat the receiver against the wall. He kept beating it after it was in pieces."

"He grabbed his shotgun from the hallway closet, and Livvie ran and hid. Then he picked up the keys to the truck and said, "I'll kill that bitch.""

Britt's eyes mirrored the alarm she had felt.

Ava looked at her hands. "He opened the front door to leave. I was too afraid to move. I could see him barging into her house, killing them both. But then he just stood there, outside. That's when he started shooting off the deck. I was frozen in the living room, watching him through the glass doors. Each shot made me flinch. When he finally came back in, he was crying."

Britt shook her head. "And how'd that feel, watching him cry?"

Ava saw his tears, his hand wiping at his face. She felt the terror of watching him crumble. "Like I'd rather he was still shooting."

Britt's pen was finally still on the paper. "What was your mom's reaction?"

The answer seemed so obvious, Ava was surprised anyone would ask. "I never told her."

"Shit," Britt breathed, "why not?"

She was fast becoming Ava's least favorite person in the world. Ever. "He'd never have forgiven us."

Britt's face didn't change.

Ava tried to keep her patience as she broke it down. "He didn't mean it. He didn't go through with it." But in her chest, a sense of unease lurked. Then why was she so scared? Why did the screams she didn't let out that night still press against her throat? He could have. What if he had left in his truck? Would she have called Mom? Called the cops? She wanted to say *yes*, but... "I was afraid he'd hate me." And there it was.

Britt nodded.

Ava could only imagine what the other woman was thinking. She knew what she thought of herself. For a while, Britt's pen on paper was the only sound in the room.

Finally, Ava lost patience. Britt didn't need that much time to judge. She glanced down at her last entry—time to be done with this. "We did leave him—once. My brother, Alan, had had enough. It was a Sunday morning. We'd cleaned the whole house. Dad came in furious because we weren't outside helping him in the garden.

Alan was seventeen and had a car. He told Livvie and me to get our things."

"Dad watched us with our backpacks. We didn't say anything on the way to Alan's old beater." But after they got in…Ava could see him running after the car, yelling as Alan pulled away. "He called us *traitors*."

"Harsh," Britt said.

Ava nodded. "Leaving Dad felt so much worse than staying." Tears threatened. "And I've never loved Alan so much."

Britt glanced at her watch.

I'm boring her, Ava thought, wiping her eyes. Maybe we should just end it now. This was too much. Clearly, no one wanted to be here.

Britt took out her phone. "Sorry, Ava. I need to check in on the sitter. Break time?"

Babysitter. Britt wasn't bored—she was a mom. Ava stood up. "I'll make us some tea."

In the living room, Pedro lay on the couch, watching a program about sharks. His short dark hair stuck up every which way. "Dude," he said, "this is some scary stuff. I don't think I can go in the water again." He stared at the television. "I can't leave. It's like seeing a car accident. Dude, what's wrong with me?"

That was exactly what Ava had been wondering her whole life. She waited for the kettle to boil.

Three minutes later, she poured the tea, the rising steam reminded her of the comforting camaraderie in her regular ACA meetings. Sharing out without having hearing others share too was lonely. She placed Pedro's mug on the coffee table. "Here," she said. "I've heard a hot drink makes the scary stuff easier."

Pedro nodded, his eyes locked onto the image of a Great White tearing a seal to bloody shreds.

When Ava returned to her room, Britt was turning off her phone. "All right, bitch, let's do this." She laced her fingers around the steaming mug Ava offered. "One last section to go. So…harms you've done to others?"

Ugh. This would take a while. Ava saw all her ex-boyfriends flash by, a museum of men. It wasn't a popular exhibit. "I guess I'll start with the last few guys I dated." She saw their faces, felt the guilt. "I thought they were being funny, that I was being funny, until, inevitably, I'd realize what they said hurt. More than one has said the same thing: 'Get a sense of humor.'" She looked over at her dresser, where the photo of Dan still lay face down after she'd ended things at Christmas. She couldn't yet bring herself to put him in a drawer. "Then I'd dump them. It could be that I don't have a sense of humor. Maybe I am crazy. More than one said that too."

Britt stopped writing. "Going for guys who put you down. Sounds like it felt familiar."

Ava pictured that day, picking up—no—auditioning Dan at the bar. Her 'widdle biddy degwee.' His "widdle biddy job.' Maybe that did feel safer than dating someone who'd be kind. That type of person couldn't possibly find much reason to stay with her. So it was Ava who'd been unkind in the end. Dan was so confused when she'd broken up with him. He'd had a lot of great qualities, but those weren't the main reasons she'd chosen to date him.

She sighed, running her finger down the worksheet. "My remaining harms are to my family." She loosened her grip on the one door she'd tried so long to keep shut: Medusa. It was time. "I'll start with my sister. I left her behind when I went to college. I didn't come back for her." Ava paused, waiting for Britt's inevitable gasp, but Britt was writing. "Livvie was all alone with Dad. I left her." She couldn't even bring herself to imagine what it must have been like. It was enough to make the breath freeze in her throat.

Britt looked up, puzzled. "What else could you have done?"

"Not gone away." Explaining herself was getting old.

"Really?"

No. Leaving Livvie hadn't been the right move. But staying with Dad wasn't either. Ava remembered the walks home from softball practice, wetting her pants. The shame. The fear of those long weekends in the woods. "No, but I still shouldn't have left her. I should've told Mom how bad he got and why Livvie couldn't stay with him. I should've made him get help. I should have helped them both."

"Why didn't you?" Britt's blue hair, charming at the ACA meetings, now seemed too much to Ava. Everything about Britt at this moment was too much.

"I was afraid I'd make it even worse—him worse. Nothing would change except weekends would be even more horrible for Livvie." But that wasn't it, not really. She made sure she looked Britt in the eye when she told the truth. "I was afraid he'd hate me." For that, she'd sacrificed Livvie. Enter Medusa.

Britt said. "Have you talked to Livvie about it?"

Again. This bitch was as dense as they came. "Of course not. None of us talk about any of this."

"How's that working out for you?"

Ava felt like throwing her tea in the woman's face. "I can tell you that this is feeling pretty shitty right now."

Britt's laugh rang ugly. "Then you're doing it right. It's also going to feel like shit to finally talk about it with Livvie and with your family. But that's what you'll have to do when you get to the steps on making amends."

Amends. Good God. Ava looked at the remaining two harms. Let's just get this over with and this woman out of my house. She planned on quitting ACA before getting to any amends step. "The next person I wrote down that I harmed was my Dad."

Britt shifted on the bed. "You've mentioned in meetings that he died. What happened to him?"

What happened to him? Depression. Rage. Mania. Everything terrible and unfair. "Hit by a car. He was going to get an award. Crossing the street after dinner."

Ava picked at her cuticles. "The night Dad told me about the award, he hadn't slept in days. I was drying the dinner dishes. He broke in his story, looked at me a moment, and said: 'Jesus Christ, Ava, use a dishtowel, not a hand towel!'"

Ava looked at Britt. "There was no difference between the towels."

"Yikes. He was like that a lot?"

"At the end?" The remembrance made Ava sad. "All the time. Then he tells me, 'So the boss shows up and says, 'J.W., I hope you can take some time off. You're going on a trip.''"

Ava shrugged. "I didn't know if it was a real trip or not, if it had to do with his job as a trail boss with the Forest Service. He was manic, probably delusional, so I just said, "Umm hmm. Are we done, Dad? I should go to bed.'"

"I spent the next day with a friend. She dropped me off at my mom's house. Later, Dad pulled into the driveway. He and Livvie had had a good time at the movies, just the two of them. I knew I should run down to say hello. He would want to see me. Instead, I hid, listening to his car drive away. That was Sunday."

Britt remained silent. Ava had to finish the story. "On Tuesday, I was sitting in my history class when the counselor came and asked me to gather my things. He said my mom was waiting." She looked at Britt. "I knew it had to be about Dad. I wondered what he had done. I wondered how bad it was."

"When she said there'd been an accident, I pictured a hospital bed. He was resting comfortably. I saw him with monitors. We would get through it. Then I saw it on Mom's face. She said he'd been killed instantly."

Ava waited out the deep freeze that the truth, that finality, had on her body. Three, two, one. Breathe. "We had a long drive to tell Alan—Silence the whole way. When we got to his college, inside his dorm room, my brother kept shaking his head. 'He got a shitty deal.'"

Britt had stopped taking notes.

Ava paused, the silence in the room palpable, another witness to her confession. "Mostly, I remember how strange it felt to be free."

Britt nodded.

"I'd wished for so long for a way out. It almost felt like I'd killed him."

They both were quiet for a moment. Then Britt said, "You didn't wish for him to die."

"No." That was true enough. Never that.

They both let silence take a turn. Outside, darkness sighed.

Finally, Britt spoke. "So, now you've shared it all. The last question I have is, what would you like to make amends for?"

Ava stared at her worksheet. The words blurred, her perceived harms suffered merging with the harms she'd doled out. "All of it, I guess." She nodded. "You were right. I did choose to get on that unbroken horse. He didn't make me. I also chose to keep the secret all those years that he was falling apart. I didn't ask anyone to help him, stop him from slipping so far. I left my sister behind. I didn't speak up to anyone about anything." She felt the shame. "I was relieved when he died."

Medusa.

"Anyone else on the amends list?"

Ava didn't want to say it. She'd written down the name, but not the why. "My mom. I made her feel like the divorce was all her fault. I was awful."

Britt grimaced. "That's kind of the way it goes with mothers and daughters."

Ava shook her head. "No. Her leaving was the worst thing that happened to all of us. I made that clear. And still, I knew that the only way any of us was making it out of there was if she got out first. She left so that Alan, Livvie, and I could have at least one parent who kept us safe." Ava paused. She picked at the hole in her comforter. Say it. "I never told her about any of it, how bad it was when we were alone with him, about the gun. And I've spent most of my life blaming her for what she didn't know."

Medusa.

Concluding Step Five, Britt handed Ava her list—patterns of behavior she'd observed from Ava's share. "I'm leaving the tea with you," she said. "It's a nice alternative to getting fall-down drunk after this step."

She held out her arms, and Ava walked stiffly into a hug. To her surprise, it felt good.

"The worst is over. I'm sorry it sucks so bad, but breaking patterns and making amends is where the good stuff is." Britt let her go and stood in the hallway a moment. Her shoulders slumped. "My amends involve my children. Be glad you're clearing out your demons before you can hurt your kids." She gave a grim smile. "Just stick to the program. At this point, it's all some of us have left."

Ten minutes later, Ava sat on her bed, still frozen. Her mind was stuck in a loop: The share, how scary it had been, and what was she supposed to do with that information now? Dan, the horse, Dad, the gun. Alan, Livvie, Mom. A siren wailed on the street. She shook her head, glancing at Britt's list. She couldn't bring herself to read it right now. Right now, she wanted to erase the whole experience.

She went to the refrigerator. Pedro's beer. "Pedro!"

He was still in front of the television.

"Mind if I have a beer?"

Pedro gave an almost imperceptible nod. "Dude! Did you see how far that one shot out of the water? By the time you see the teeth, it's already *over!*"

Ava held the bottle a moment, then let it sit unopened on the counter. She wanted some Nyquil to go with it, but she hadn't had any in the house for months.

She went back to her room for her car keys. Her phone rang. "Hello?"

"Hi, slugger, how goes it?"

"Bill!" Ava felt soothed by the sound of his voice. "How's fatherhood?"

Bill sighed. "Well, they say the third trimester is the hardest time in a father's life, and I have to admit, I've put on a lot of weight. Don't judge me, Ava."

She looked at the keys in her hand, poised for a Nyquil run. "No judgment here, my friend. Everything all right on the home front?"

"Yeah, but there's a problem with the team."

"The beer ball team? What's wrong?"

"You're not on it. When you coming back?"

"Bill, you're better off without me."

"Try telling that to Jimmie. Hey, by the way, he wants to give you a call. Is it okay if I give him your number? I'll have the missus punch him out if he tries to get fresh."

Ava felt a surge of elation, hope, then…no. She wasn't ready for fries with that. "You know, I really like Jimmie, and I'm flattered, but Bill—I'm a fucking mess. Maybe I'll give the team and Jimmie a try in a month or so. I'm just not feeling that brave right now."

"No worries. Hey, we love you. You know that, right?"

Ava felt his sincerity. He was going to be such a good dad. It gave her pause. There were moments when her dad had been a good dad too. When he wasn't sick. She pictured Bill, listening to his baby, his child, his teenager with his whole body. What would her Dad have been like if he hadn't been sick? A canyon of grief gaped between the possibility and the reality.

"I know you do, Bill. You take care. I'll come visit soon."

She felt the jagged edges of the keys in her hand. Nyquil wasn't the direction she wanted to go tonight. A beer wasn't either. She put the unopened bottle in the fridge, went back into her bedroom, and shut the door. Britt's notes still lay on her bed. She put down her purse and took in the room full of lingering Medusas. "All right, bitches," she said, picking up the notes, "let's do this."

CHAPTER 39
MOCK TRIAL

Ava was nervous about taking her students to the mock trial courtroom at Hastings Law School. Coming so soon after her Step Five share, she started to dream of Nyquil. The ballet on her mind, she addressed the class, "I appreciate how hard all of you have worked to get ready. I need you to understand that this is a nice event in a really nice college. That means I shouldn't hear a peep from you when we have to walk past classrooms, even if you see someone cute you'd like to holler at." She raised an eyebrow at Hector.

He twisted his ponytail around a finger. "What if girlth want to holler at me?"

Ava looked at him, appreciating his optimism. She wanted college for him, wanted him to break the pot habit that still made his lids droop on too many mornings. "Girls hollering at you is a cross you'll have to bear in silence."

Last week, she told her students she'd give extra credit for dressing up for the courtroom. They wanted to know what that included.

"Button-down shirts, dresses, slacks…what you'd wear to church? Oh, and if you can, no white sneakers."

"I only have white sneakers," the General said.

"Me too," said Sean, looking down at his scuffed Adidas. He reached for an apple from the Food Bank bin.

"I'm not wearing any other shoes," said Johntay. He recently missed school to stand in line for hours to buy the latest pair of Jordans. As the defendant in the trial, it somehow seemed fitting he wouldn't take more effort on his own behalf.

When a student got suspended for fighting, Ava had to change Hector's role from Juror Number Eleven to a witness from the club, Patricia Thompson. "You can make the character into a male witness," Ava said. "You could call him "Patrick" instead."

Hector thought about it. "Can I call him Paco?"

"If you like."

His eyes lit up. "Can I call him Paco *Taco*?"

She smiled. "Really? You think a witness named Paco Taco would sound believable?"

Hector nodded. "Yeth."

Ava took the bus to Macy's that evening. She asked the woman behind the counter about a pencil skirt, knee-high boots, military jacket, and—what had K'Ron suggested? Hoop earrings.

Trying it all on, Ava felt a new confidence in the cut of the jacket, boots solidly hitting the floor. She glanced at her clogs kicked aside on the floor of the dressing room.

The saleswoman nodded. "I wasn't sure," she said, "but that's a sharp outfit you've got there."

"I know, right?" Goodbye khakis and sensible shoes. Hellooo to working with these hips. "I have the best stylists. Got any applications?"

The morning of the trial, on the first of February, Tolly and Ava met the students outside the entrance of Hasting's Law School. With students coming from all over the city, it didn't make sense to meet up early at the school, wait around for the stragglers, and then leave late. Tolly's navy suit transformed him into an attorney, making him appear even taller, in charge. Standing next to Tolly's suit in her new outfit, Ava felt like they were two parents awaiting their kids' graduations. All nineteen of them.

Then Pants walked up. While her mauve slacks didn't denote the importance of the day, her briefcase reminded Ava that this was an evaluation that would go into her record.

Ava prayed to the gods of those-who-know-what-they-are-getting-into-and-proceed-anyway, Please may they show up. Please may they not show up high. But please may they show up. Not high.

A bus pulled up in front of Hastings, then another. She watched a fashion parade alight. Niesha and K'Ron wore dresses. Charnikka, dress slacks. Ava's heart pumped maternal pride. Ken, as promised, strutted down the street in a suit. Sean had traded his usual striped polo shirt for a white button-down. Johntay informed Tolly that the neon green and purple Nikes on his feet were brand-new. His large tee shirt read: *Innocent Black Man.*

Ava got it: They are trying.

When Paris alighted from the bus, she stared at her teacher. "Ms. L, you look beautiful," she breathed, a non-believer witnessing a true miracle.

The kids were remarkably reverent as they entered the building. Ava and her students silently gathered in the lobby, awed by the quiet college atmosphere. Marbleized floors. Hushed hallways. Freshly vacuumed carpet. The sharp scent of cleanser in the bathroom. This was a school.

They walked down hallways, glimpsing classes through window panels. Hector waved as he passed the co-eds.

Entering the mock-trial courtroom, students let out a collective "Aaahhhhh." In the front of the room stood a real judge's bench, a witness stand complete with microphone, attorney's tables, and a jury box. The students were going to get a true courtroom experience, and this time, they would be the ones holding the gavel and making the arguments.

Pants took a seat in the back row, pulling her clipboard from her briefcase.

The General and Paris, the trial's two judges, walked cautiously up to the leather chairs behind the stately oak bench. They ran their hands over the smooth wood, picking up the gavels.

"What do you think?" Ava asked. She dug in her large bag for two black graduation gowns. Paris and the General reverently zipped them up, Paris's ten sizes too big.

"I could get used to this," said the General. He sat down in one of the heavy chairs, puffing out his chest as he leaned back. "I'm a real judge, Ms. L."

She smiled. He had been coming out of his shell lately. She wanted to see him grow to fit his name. "Looks good on you."

"I'ma be Judge Dansforth," asserted Paris, rocking in her chair.

Ava was impressed by her reference to the main judge in *The Crucible*. "I hope you'll be more open-minded than he was," she said. "Remind me what your job is today?"

"I'ma listen to all the evidence and keep order in the court," Paris said. Spying Johntay sitting in the defendant's chair, she leaned over the bar. "Hey, Johntay—you gonna hang!"

Melvin donned a tie Ava had bought at the Salvation Army. The prosecuting attorney adjusted the knot for him. "I had to do this for my boo when he had his court dates," Charnikka explained.

After a couple of false starts, the trial got under way. Ava stood next to the jury box. Tolly positioned himself behind the judges.

Tanya, as bailiff, made Paco Taco swear to tell the truth over Charnikka's copy of the Zane novel, *Daddy Long Stroke*.

The prosecution then had a chance at her first witness. "Isn't it true," Charnikka asked Hector-turned-Paco Taco, "that you saw the argument between the defendant and his girlfriend get worse during the time that they were in the club?"

The witness wiped his hands on his jeans, lisping, "Worth? Hmmmm…"

Charnikka reviewed her notes. "Your statement says that they were yelling louder and louder before the defendant's girlfriend left crying like a—" She glanced at Ava. "Like a B-word."

Paco looked at Johntay.

The defendant made a slashing movement across his throat.

"Objection!" Charnikka yelled.

Johntay smacked his lawyer, Melvin, who had been staring at his tie. "Defend me, bitch."

"Objection!" Melvin yelped.

Tolly leaned in to conference with the judges.

Pants frowned, but Ava was thrilled to see them so engaged.

Gathering himself, the General pointed to Charnikka. "You have to say why you object."

Charnikka puzzled for a moment. "He," she motioned to Johntay, "threatened my witness." She thought about it. "I didn't like that, so I objected."

The General looked down at Johntay. "Is this true?" Ava hadn't seen him looking so authoritative before.

Johntay shrugged.

The General motioned to the attorneys. "I need you both to approach the bench."

The courtroom erupted into shouts, jurors leaving their seats to slap the railing, howling with laughter.

"Ooohh!" chortled Hector from the stand, "You in trouble!"

Niesha fell to the floor in the jury box.

"Watch out Joe Brown!" hooted Paris, swinging in her chair. "General's gonna have his own show!"

Tolly turned pale.

Ava guess what he was thinking: Five minutes in, the trial was so off-script, there'd be no recovery. She opened her mouth to reassure him this could be a good thing, but—

"Order!" The General pounded the bar. "Order, ya'll!" He pointed his gavel at the jurors. "Ya'll need to shut up! This is a murder case!" He peered down at Melvin. "You need to get a handle on your client," he said. "I don't want to see him doing that shit again." He pointed his gavel at Melvin's face. "And you need to start paying attention!" He turned to Charnikka, "You. Good job."

Ava closed her mouth. It didn't matter what Pants was furiously scribbling on her clipboard. The day was an unequivocal success: They've got this.

The attorneys walked back to their tables. "Kiss-ass" Melvin said.

"Your client's going down," Charnikka said.

When it was Melvin's turn to question Hector, he got right to the point. "Mr. Taco," he said, pacing in front of the witness, "isn't it true that you had had quite a bit to drink that night yourself?"

Paco Taco thought about it. "Yeth," he said, "I had a fifth of withkey under my shirt."

Ava eyed Paco's bulky sweatshirt. Knowing his penchant for being a bit glassy-eyed in the mornings, she hoped he did not have a fifth of whiskey on him now.

Melvin glanced pointedly at the jury. "Hmmm…" he said, raising his eyebrows, "so would you say that you were drunk?"

Paco Taco nodded. "Yeth."

The jury came to life. "Ooooh, get him, Melvin!" yelled Niesha.

"Order!" shouted Paris, beating the bar with her gavel.

Melvin broke into a broad smile. "So if you were DRUNK, how could you remember how bad the argument was between my client and his girlfriend? Maybe you didn't even hear their argument; it could have been another couple arguing." He looked at the jury, disgust all over his face. Then he turned to Paco. "You make me sick," he said. "No further questions."

CHAPTER 40
MOCK TRIAL PART II

Next, the bailiff called Big Moe, AKA the bus driver. "What were you doing the night of December 22nd?" Charnikka asked after Tanya had sworn Moe in.

Moe's eyes shone. "Well, you see, the peoples—" He turned to the jury, "That's what we like to call the polices. The peoples was heavy up in that club that night, and I had a couple of ladies around me. We was sipping Hennessy, just gettin' friendly-like…."

Ava started to regret having part of the scenario take place in a club.

"Objection!" yelled Niesha from the juror's box.

"You have to say why," the General said.

The juror's objecting, Ava thought. God bless us, every one.

Tolly put his head in his hands.

Niesha broke it down for the court. "No girls are gonna be drinking Hennessy: Girls like that fruity shit!"

"Ooohhh! Good one!" Melvin pointed to Moe. "You're a liar."

"That must've been the night before," Charnikka said pointedly. "On the night of December 22nd you were driving a bus, right?"

254

"Oh, yeah," Moe said, stroking his chin. His other hand rested against his substantial belly. "I guess I musta been drinking with the ladies the night before."

Ken and K'Ron, as the owners of the nightclub, insisted on taking on taking the witness stand together in the manner of rock stars entering the stage on a reunion tour. Ken wore a shiny, light gray suit with a silver tie. K'Ron had wedged herself into a stretchy, hot pink dress. She stood wobbly on bubblegum-colored stilettos. Judging from Ken's last-minute fussing over her hair, which was in loose waves rather than shellacked to her head, she had employed a stylist for this event. They both practically sang their oaths to Tanya before taking their seats on the witness stand.

Ken reapplied K'Ron's lipstick, then took some paperwork out of his briefcase, notes written on purple Hello Kitty notebook paper. He leaned into their microphone. "All right, bitches," he said, "Ken's in the house."

Ava expected disco lighting to begin pulsating to a techno beat.

Paris banged a gavel on the bar. "No "B"s," she reminded the courtroom.

Charnikka walked up to Ken, her dress slacks no match for the witness's sparkle. "Mr. and Mrs. Cabbot—"

"Cabbo," Ken corrected. He turned to the jurors. "It's French."

K'Ron affirmed. "It's Cabbo."

Charnikka rolled her eyes. "Mr. and Mrs. Cabbo, you were both at the club on the night of the 22nd, right?"

"Yes," Ken said.

"And on that night, it became apparent that the defendant and his girlfriend were involved in a heated disagreement?"

Ken reviewed his notes. "I had been noticing their argument escalating for…" he looked at K'Ron, "about an hour, wouldn't you say?"

She nodded. "Escalating for an hour."

"But weren't there other people in the club? Wasn't it noisy?" Charnikka probed.

Mr. Cabbo shook his head. "We have a surveillance camera that pans the club. The defendant and his girlfriend were sitting near the camera the whole night, until she got up and left with that other guy."

"Isn't that illegal? You can't videotape someone without them knowing it."

K'Ron read a statement from the Hello Kitty paper, "California is a two-party state, which means that everyone needs to be aware when you're recording them, but that only applies to conversations you can reasonably expect to be private. The defendant and his girlfriend happened to be seated near the camera, but that camera looked over the whole—establishment. It was a public place. They had no reason to expect privacy, especially under the camera."

The jury, Tolly, and Ava hung on K'Ron's every word. Ava smiled. Keep your Grishams and your Turows, I'll take a Cabbo testimony any day. A tiny spark within her breathed.

When it was Melvin's turn, he got right to the point. "You say there's a tape with evidence of a fight between my client and his girlfriend. Do you have this tape?"

Ken looked down. "We erase it every night."

Melvin pounced. "Oh! You erased it!" He looked pointedly at the jury. "Mr. and Mrs. Cabbo, even if you had the tape, it only shows they were arguing, not that my client killed his girlfriend."

Ken stuck out his chin. "The defendant got upset when his girl-friend left with that other guy. He started going crazy."

Melvin put a hand on the witness stand, leaned in toward the couple. "I'm gonna need you to define *crazy*."

Ken was unfazed. "He grabbed my arm when I told him to calm down."

"Ah hah!" Melvin looked back toward the jury. "How do we know this when there is no video to prove it?"

Ken, smiling, pulled back the sleeve of his silver suit, revealing three purple bruises.

The jury gasped.

"Aren't we doing so good?" Niesha whispered to Ava from her seat in the jury box.

Ava wasn't sure how to respond. It wasn't the trial she and Tolly had mapped out. It wasn't going to be favorably regarded by Pants, who demanded rigor and rigid adherence to rules. *Fuck rigor. This is real.* "Yes, hon, you sure are."

It looked like Sean, the last man to see Johntay's girlfriend alive, might just be too anxious to testify. He clutched his wadded-up witness statement in his hand, billiard-ball head sweating as he took the stand.

"You seem nervous, Mr. Phantastic," Charnikka observed.

Sean signaled for water. "I think I'm just thirsty. It's hot sitting up here."

After Sean had downed an entire bottle of water, Charnikka got down to business. "Mr. Phantastic, you were a childhood friend of the deceased?"

Sean furrowed his brow. "Who?"

Charnikka looked toward the ceiling. She took a breath. "The defendant's girlfriend."

A light went on behind Sean's eyes. He spread out his crumpled witness notes and peered at the smeared lettering. "Oh, yeah. I knew her from when we was kids. We'd play on the swings together and sometimes she'd pretend that we was husband and wife. I'd be a DJ and—"

Charnikka cut him off. "So you were friends from way back, you're saying?"

"Yeah." Sean wiped his forehead with his sleeve. Sweat stains appeared under his arms.

"And you left with her the night the defendant and his girlfriend had an argument at the club?"

Sean nodded. "Yeah. She was sad, so I said I'd ride the bus home with her."

Charnikka walked back and forth in front of the witness stand before coming to a stop, asking Sean pointedly, "Did you ever get with the defendant's girlfriend?"

Sean leaned back in his chair, a smile on his face. "I hit that a few times, yeah."

Johntay's eyes bulged. He smacked his lawyer.

"Objection!" Melvin yelped.

"You have to say WHY!" Tanya called impatiently from her post as bailiff.

"Oh, please!" Charnikka said. She pointed to the witness. "Ladies and gentlemen, does this look like someone who could steal any girl away from her boo?"

Sean looked around, wide-eyed as a kitten.

The jury shook their heads, embarrassed by his innocence.

"That's just sad," Tanya said under her breath.

"No further questions," Charnikka said.

Judge General asked Melvin if he'd like the question the witness.

Melvin shook his head.

Amid complete silence, the witness was allowed to step down.

Johntay's only testimony entailed yelling, "I'm innocent! I plead the fifth!" and "She shouldn't have been messing with them other dudes!" into the microphone.

"Get off the stand, murderer!" Francisco heckled from the jury box, rising.

The General pounded his gavel. "Quiet in the courtroom!" He addressed Francisco. "The next time you say something, I'm going to have the bailiff take you out of here."

Tanya waved *Daddy Long Stroke* threateningly.

"I'm not afraid," Francisco said, but he sat down, remained quiet.

"I need to have a word with my client," Melvin begged, but a side conference did little to enhance the defense's case.

Given Johntay's testimony, it was no surprise to anyone when the jury pronounced him guilty.

Ava suggested that Paris thank the jury members for their service. "Let's also appreciate everyone's participation."

"Thank you to the jury and the murderer," Paris said, standing tall behind the bar. "We all did a very good job. Ms. L, can we do another trial soon?"

Tolly's program paid for him to bring pizza into the courtroom after the trial, a celebration of the end of his time with the class. His work at Ida B had earned him three credits.

Pants left immediately for the school. She pointed toward her clipboard. "We'll talk about your evaluation next week."

Ava didn't care what was written on Pants' clipboard. Today had been a win. Her students could stand their own in a courtroom. They were job-ready. They were amazing.

Ava stood next to Tolly, watching the kids eat. "You did a great thing here," she said. "You ever need prep for a trial, I have some uncooperative witnesses with great fashion sense at the ready."

"I think I might want to be a lawyer someday," Charnikka told Paris.

Paris, still in her judge's robe, nodded. "I was scared of you!"

Tolly smiled. "It's hard not to love them, isn't it?"

Ava nodded. "I find it impossible."

CHAPTER 41
STEP 7: FIND THE EFFING DOOR

February 7th. **Step 6:** Willing to let God remove all defects of character. Ava pulled into the church parking lot. She had made the decision the day before to go. Step Seven in ACA required she humbly ask God to remove all her shortcomings. Having lost faith a long time ago, she felt stuck. How to put trust in a God she didn't believe was there? She sat in her apartment, head in her hands. She had come this far. It was time to say *yes* to church. Shit.

Of course, no one was dictating which church. Ava chose her first house of worship because she'd heard that Anne Lamott belonged to the congregation. She loved Lamott's novels, and was harboring the hope that even if she didn't find God there, she might see the author.

But now, at the correct address, she sat in her car a moment. She had expected the church would be one big building with a large door and maybe a cross. But this place was a series of low buildings, with one, slightly larger dome structure. This shouldn't be so difficult. Watch where the people go in. Ava observed women in flowered dresses, African fabrics. They carried casserole pans into a room near the center of the cluster of buildings.

`With only minutes until the service began, Ava was still frozen in her seat. Would they know that she was a celebrity stalker, not a true believer? What if they sensed the only religious education she'd had was the Easter that Mom had shown *Ben Hur*?

Ok, that must be the door. Ava got out, smoothing the dress that had taken two hours to settle on. She tried to inconspicuously walk toward the door. With each step, she realized that only women with food bundles were entering the building. Ava glanced around.

A woman in a red scarf smiled. "If you're looking for the service, it's over there." She motioned to the dome-like structure on Ava's right.

Of course. She hurried toward the larger building. This makes sense. But there didn't appear to be a doorway, so she walked around the building, her trek finally blocked by a large bush. Her cheeks flamed red. Well, you're not going to find God if you can't first find the effing door.

But of course, there it was. A young couple held it open for her. Ava took a seat inside.

Throughout the service, she mouthed the words to songs that had elusive page numbers. She closed her eyes when the pastor told her to pray. She felt a peaceful energy in the room, lulling her into thinking it might be a place to come back to and then—

The pastor raised her arms. "Rise up, now. Greet your neighbor. Peace be with you."

Ava started as everyone around her stood up. Was it over already?

A woman, bent with age, held out a wrinkled hand. "Peace be with you."

"Peace be with you," Ava mouthed, her stomach tightening. She hadn't planned on this being a social event. She already felt like a party crasher. All she wanted to do was sit in her pew and wait for God. A social hour was too much.

Nearby, two women hugged. "How's your daughter, Evelyn?"

A child came up to Ava, holding out her tiny hand. "Peace be with you."

Ava wanted this all to be over. "Peace be with you." Again and again the ritual repeated itself. She cringed inside each time, an outsider among all of these kind people who knew each other and must be wondering why the hell she was there.

Across the room, Anne Lamott shone in a lavender tee shirt. Short dreads embraced her head like a halo. She laughed and hugged a teenager. "Peace be with you."

After an interminable ten minutes, everyone had had enough peace, and the service began again. When children came around with baskets, Ava gave too much money to a penny drive. She didn't have any cash left when the women took the baskets around for the fellowship. Oh, God, she would be the cheap outsider.

Step Seven: Humbly asked God to remove our shortcomings. She bowed her head.

On the way home, she felt she had earned a burger. I came, I saw, I got real uncomfortable and really, really hungry. Eh, it was a tall order to find God the first time she went searching.

Pulling up to the drive-though window, she was surprised to see a familiar face looking down at her. She squinted. "Johntay?"

He laughed, shaking his twisty braids. "Ms. L!" He turned to the other people in the little room. "This my teacher!"

She felt a peace that had eluded her in church. "How long have you worked here?"

He puffed out his chest. "About three months. My mom needed some help with the bills." He leaned out the window. "I'ma throw in some extra fries, but don't tell anyone, ya feel me?"

She took the oath. "It was great seeing you."

Driving away with a second bag of fries, she smiled. Anne Lamott, Johntay. It had been a good day. God or no God. It had been a very, very good day.

CHAPTER 42

ADEQUATE

February 15th. Pants conferenced with Ava about her Mock trial evaluation—"More rigor!" At the end of a long write-up about creating a college mentality, Ava received a *Satisfactory* ranking, the lowest without requiring dismissal or intervention: *Needs Improvement*. Fortunately, the conference was short. Pants was in a good mood because the Exit Exam test scores had finally arrived.

Later, at the faculty meeting, the principal crowed, "We haven't had this number of kids pass the math test ever!"

Mr. Jeffries took a bow.

Cheryl lifted an eyebrow. "I've found those scores to be very unreliable. No telling what conditions kids find themselves in on test day."

Ava ducked her head. English test scores were still noticeably low. Fortunately, with the math coup, no one was mentioning those. She thought about talking to Mr. Jeffries about giving kids the answers— maybe he had simply misunderstood the purpose of the test?

But it was that fucking test that bothered her too. A one day, one chance, all-or-nothing assessment. She had to ask herself: Under these conditions, do I understand the purpose of the test? She wanted the kids to have academic goals, for graduation to mean something. But not this test, not this way. She didn't know how she'd break it to Moe.

Telling students who passed and who didn't was a delicate endeavor. Charnikka passed the test with flying colors, as did Francisco, Niesha, and six other kids from Test Prep English. The rest of the class did not. Ken scored 349, 350 required to pass. Most students were dejected about failing.

Big Moe was beside himself. "I can't take it again!" He threw himself across his desk. "This is worst day of my life! I can't do work today, Ms. L. I'm too depressed."

Watching Paris's lip quiver and Sean slump in his seat, Ava had to agree—she had been counting on the test to be her kids' gateway to graduation, better lives. The happiness that had eluded her when she was their age. Moving on right now was just too hard. So they did a little art therapy instead. She handed out a list Stella had given her of positive and negative feelings. Stella said that tapping into emotions was key to art, but these students weren't versed in identifying feelings. They only knew *angry* or *tired*, so Stella had them choose from a wider range of options.

Ava asked students to draw and share what they were feeling.

Francisco chose *tenacious*, a bull charging.

Ken talked about *diminished*, his drawing a tiny dot on the opportunity of paper.

Paris picked *ashamed*. The picture, she explained, was a self-portrait. A small person on a big cot: the last time she'd been locked up in juvenile hall.

Moe perused the list, asked questions, then chose *doomed*. He drew a stick figure, a large circle belly, reaching toward a diploma too far away for his five stick fingers to grasp.

Charnikka's drawing showed her receiving a diploma onstage, her daughter right beside her. *Adequate*.

Ava paused at the word. *Adequate*. She remembered the looming threat of *Needs improvement*. "Now *adequate* a great word," she told the class. She talked about *adequate* and George Herbert's poem entitled "Love." In it, Love invited the narrator to dinner. "The narrator felt too inadequate to be there. He talked about what a mess he was, how he didn't deserve to look at Love, but Love said, 'Who made the eyes but I?' It means we're born already adequate," she explained. "We're always adequate, no matter if we fail or pass. There's no test that can make us more or less adequate." She thought a moment. *That would mean I'm adequate too.*

"So what did the narrator do?" asked Paris.

"The poem ends, 'You must sit down,' Love says, 'and taste my meat/ So I did sit and eat.'"

Francisco chuckled. "She said, 'taste my meat.'"

CHAPTER 43

BEER BALL REDUX: THE POWER OF NOW

Ava drummed her fingers on the steering wheel. Ekhart Tolle monotoned over the speakers, an audio book reading out *The Power of Now*. Ekhart reminded her to live in the spaces between thought, quiet her mind. Find the God state within. Time was an illusion. All we ever had was now. Ava thought about getting a treat after tonight's game. Some No Pudge Fudge, the brownie mix with a pig on the box. The ball field emerged on her left. What to say to Jimmie? Maybe he won't be here tonight. Her mind wandered back to the brownies. What time did Trader Joe's close?

Boom!

Ava's truck smashed into the small Nissan pickup in front of her. Her backseat came unhooked from its moorings. Items scattered throughout the vehicle flew into the front seat. The morning's coffee, sitting in the hot sun all day, spilled everywhere.

The driver motioned for her to pull over into the ball field's parking lot.

She got out of her truck as the other driver alighted from his.

Oh, no…Ava prayed to the gods of the perpetually fucked. It can't be….

Jimmie walked toward her, jersey stretched across that solid wall of chest.

Fuuuuuuuck. "I hit you so *hard*!" Ava cringed. "I am so sorry! It was all my fault!"

Jimmie laughed, his smile widening with recognition. "Well, at least you're not a lawyer. Great to have you back!"

Ava fumbled in her purse for her insurance information. "Are you okay? I can't believe how fast I was going when I hit you. How much damage did I do?"

Jimmie didn't bother to glance at his truck. He sidled up, leaning against her Toyota. "I'm sure you didn't hurt anything. I put that bar around my bumper last year. I'll take your information though."

Ava wrote her number on the back of a receipt, digging in her overstuffed purse for her insurance card.

"The car in front of me stopped short," Jimmie explained. "I saw you coming up quick behind me. I thought you'd have time to stop. What happened?"

She was not about to go into the No Pudge Fudge. "I was listening to a book on CD."

"Oh? Which one?"

His interest unnerved her. "Eckhart Tolle."

"I love him! *A New Earth?*"

Ava shook her head. "*The Power of Now.*"

The corners of Jimmie's mouth twitched. "How's that working out for ya?"

She grimaced. "I seem to be living a little too much in the moment right this second."

"Hey, I'm happy this happened," Jimmie said.

"That's Zen of you."

Jimmie waved his slip of paper. "I got your number didn't I?"

Bill and Shaun walked towards them through the parking lot.

Shaun grinned. "Thank God! Relief's come!" He tossed her a ball.

Bill put an arm around her. "He's been bitching about taking the field these past few months. Glad to see you, Slugger. You're just in time for the playoffs!"

"You told me to show up for some beer, " Shaun said. "You didn't mention I'd have to play for it." He gestured grandly toward the field. "It's all yours, Ava. I kept 'er warm for ya." He pulled a flask from his back pocket. "Time for the big leagues."

Back in right field, adrenaline pushed Ava onto her toes, ready. She bent her knees, prepared to dash forward or turn around and bolt if someone stabbed one deep behind her. The team had been on a roll while she was gone, the *Sitting Ducks* climbing their way up to the division playoffs. This game determined who would play in the championships. She shook her head. No pressure.

From center field, Jimmie threw her a warm-up toss. She ran in. "So how long have you and Bill been playing together?"

Jimmie moved closer, stood in position for the pop fly she tossed back. "We were in a Berkeley class together. Both of us coached little league teams at the time."

Ava nodded. She thought back to her little league years with Coach John, how he'd look his players in the eyes, telling them that everyone matters. Of course you did.

Two outs, bases loaded. Bottom of the ninth. Shit. She reviewed the last play: the ball speeding past the first baseman, Ava running in too fast. The ball took a hop and missed her outstretched glove by a few feet, Jimmie cleaning up her mess behind her. *Shit.* The runners advanced.

A big lefty stepped up to the plate, took a couple of powerful practice swings. He had already smashed a line drive to center field in the fifth inning. The infield took three unified steps backward.

Bill turned on the mound, waving her back, "Lefty! He's hitting to you, Ava!"

She jogged back, deeper. No shit, Bill. She could tell a right-handed batter from one who was left-handed. Let me do my jo—

Crack!

The ball smashed the night air, careened high above the infield, a rocket headed straight out into the Milky Way.

"Got it!" Ava yelled, unsure. The ball was moon-high, nearly invisible. She zigzagged a retreat. Looked up. Glanced down at her path. Looked up. Got dizzy.

"You want help?" Jimmie yelled.

Ava zeroed in on a tiny globe among the lights, waving him off.

The ball slowed, drew out its trajectory into a graceful arc. But where was it coming down? Here? Ava moved to her left. Here? She zigzagged back, back, back, reached up to grab the sky.

Thump! A meteor landed in her mitt.

"You're out!" yelled the ump.

Startled, Ava gazed at the ball. No way. It was as if she had really caught a star as it fell. The third out—there it was, hiding, cradled in the webbing of her mitt. No way. They had won.

The team roared, storming the outfield.

Jimmie lumbered over, skipping every other step. "Whoohooo!" He picked her up, hiked her higher to hold below her knees and lifted her above his head.

"Aaaaaahhhhh!" Bill came barreling toward them. He bear-hugged Jimmie, squeezing Ava's knees. "Ducky victory! What a catch! Best right fielder bar none!" Bill threw his head back and howled, "This is the best day of my life!" He glanced back at Ruthie, standing by the dugout. "Except for the day I got married!"

The rest of the team formed a circle around them, bumping chests, slapping backs.

Ava reached down, high-fiving her teammates until her hand stung. She knew she looked ridiculous, sitting atop Jimmie's shoulders. But allowing accolades in anyway…She had to admit, it felt really, really good.

Bill led the team to the dugout to drink what was supposed to have been drowning-our-sorrows champagne.

Jimmie let Ava down slowly, pulling her tight against his body until she was nose-to-nose, feet not yet touching the ground. "Go out with me," he said. His solemn expression didn't leave room for negotiation.

Bad idea. Bad idea. Bad— "Yes," Ava grinned.

CHAPTER 44
TRIBES

February 28th. Ava lay on the couch, the blanket over her. She glanced doubtfully at the popcorn ceiling above. "If you're taking requests, I'd like to go to Fiji this time. With the huts."

Gary raised an eyebrow. He had on the same tie-dyed shirt as last time. "Fiji? Really? Well, let's see what we can do. Stare up at the heart on the ceiling. Breathe in. More, more…."

Leaving the lapping waves behind, she walked up the path into the cabin. No Fijian hut today. Her feet on bare planks. Dust kicked up as she walked to the mirror.

Gary prompted, "Today we're going to see who's a part of your tribe."

Ava sighed. She had had a long day—two referrals, one kid called her a bitch, and the faculty meeting ran forty-five minutes late. She wasn't quite ready to join her therapist in Hippieville yet. "My people come from the whitest part of Europe, Gary. I'd love a Navajo in the mix, but I'm pretty much stuck with being a paleface."

"Thank you for that commentary. Now, I want you to look around for the parts of yourself who make up the facets of your personality. Sometimes we act out of younger selves, sometimes out of parts of ourselves that are deeply angry. I'd like you to know who's a part of your tribe. And then, most importantly, where's your healer?"

Healer? In this empty room? "I don't understand. You told me to leave the beach and walk up to the cabin. There's no one here. You want me to go back outside?"

"No, stay where you are. I'm asking you: Where's your healer?"

Uh, I think that's why I'm here, Gary. She gave up. "I look inside my heart—I've got nothing. I look around this room and it's empty. I want to live. I just don't know why."

"Be patient. She's there…Look around. Who do you see?"

"No one."

"Get still. Breathe. It's okay. Who's with you?"

Then Ava saw them, lined up on cots: a baby, crying for attention; a spunky nine-year-old in a cowboy hat, a glaring teenager, a twenty-six-year-old curled into a fetal position, already exhausted with the business of living. "Okay, I see them now. All ages. It's like a hospital ward in here."

"And who is the healer?"

Ava glanced around. "Nope. Must've taken a smoke break."

"Who else do you see?"

Think. Think. Ava saw herself, wisecracking. "I guess there's a member who tries to be funny. Like a comic. In a terminal ward."

"Yes. A comic isn't supposed to be a healer, is she?"

"No." The thought made Ava very sad. "But she makes it bearable in here."

"Who else do you see?"

"There really isn't a whole lot more room. I don't think you realize how crowded—"

"Who else is there? It's okay. Take your time. Take a breath."

Ava waited, glanced around. There they are. In the shadows. "I see another little girl."

"How old is she?"

"Seven."

"And what does she want?"

Ava thought about it. The answer didn't make sense. "To ride a bike? Swim in the lake? Sing? Play? That sounds like such a strange word, *Play.*"

"Yes, I'll bet there are some of your wounded who tell her why she shouldn't. Who else?"

Ava peered again into the shadows. "I think there's a writer."

"Do you write?"

"I used to. In third grade, high school, college."

"Why did you stop?"

"I needed to work. I needed to save kids. I needed to find a purpose."

"Do you really need those things? Or are those just stories from your wounded?"

"I don't know."

"That's what we will find out. I'd like you to thank the mirror now. I'd like you to go outside, but take your tribe with you. Open your heart to the tribal members you've met today."

Ava looked around the room at her motley tribe. She sighed. I could have been in Fiji right now. But no. These are my people. There was nothing left to do but let them in. She picked up the baby. The wailing subsided, its small body molding onto hers. She opened up her heart, a gatekeeper. Her tribe marched in. The little ones moved in a pathetic lockstep.

"Now I'm going to put the headphones on. When the music floods your ears, your spirit guides will come. They will help you find your healer. This will be very important. You're in charge. Not the comic."

Ava waited, tribal members huddled on the porch, silent, waiting for the spirit guides.

Drums beating in the distance marked their arrival. The rhythmic *thump thump* a soft heartbeat at first. Then, as they crested the hill, it became a call: resolute, strong.

The twenty-six-year-old lifted her head, opened her eyes, sat up.

Over the hillside now, a procession. The majestic animals lumbered silently. They marked the solemnity with their size, the etched lines in their hardened skin, wizened gaze.

Ava stared. They brought elephants. Through her disbelief, hope inexplicably crested with those plodding, quiet missionaries.

The seven-year-old grabbed the hand of the girl in the cowboy hat. Her eyes took it all in, mouth agape. "They're gonna let me ride."

CHAPTER 45

FIRE

When those seniors who didn't pass the Exit Exam took another shot at it the beginning of March, they meant business.

The General brought large, studious eyeglasses with him on the day of the test. There were no lenses in the glasses, but he assured Ava they made him feel smart.

Sean kicked off his shoes.

Paris brought a year's supply of pixie sticks. "I'm ready to GOOOOO!' she roared as Ava handed her a test booklet.

"Take it easy on the pixies," Ava said, pouring her a cup of water.

Moe hung his head. "I can't fail another time."

"You only missed it by ten points. We've worked hard on these skills. I feel good about this one."

Moe gave a wary thumbs-up. He opened his test booklet.

Ava remembered the kid he was when he first came to the school, high-fiving students he didn't even know in the hallways, giving his new teacher a big grin, telling her to have a good day. She didn't want a test to dampen Moe's enthusiasm for life.

At the end of the day, against the rules, she glanced through the students' essays. When she got to Moe's, she groaned. The essay topic this time had been refreshingly clear: students were to write about someone they admired and would like to emulate when they got older. While Moe's essay was technically correct, four paragraphs each performing their functions admirably, there was one glaring flaw evident in his first sentence. Moe had chosen to write about the musical artist, Mac Dre. His essay began:

I've always been a big fan of rapers. Mac Dre is the best raper in the Bay Area. He's been raping around here for a long time. I'd like to be a famous raper when I grow up too.

Ava held her breath. She hoped that the person grading Moe's test wouldn't dock him. The omission of another "p" shouldn't cost a diploma.

When Ava got home that afternoon, a slender letter, addressed from the school district, sat in her mailbox. Amid the bills, she didn't put a priority on the flat envelope, only opening it as an afterthought.

Dear Ms. Llewellyn,
    "Due to budget cuts, we may not be requiring your services for the coming school year...." was as far as Ava read before she started crying.

She walked up the stairs to her apartment, shock clouding real thought. Afraid to look at the letter again, she went through the rest of her bills: She needed to stop buying snacks for students, charging materials for her classroom.

She called up Ruthie. "I'm coming over, and I'm bringing bottle of wine," she said. "Something cheap."

Ava's next call was to the union. The representative was sympathetic and tried to explain the process. State and city officials would wrangle over the budget for the next few months. If parents got involved, far more layoffs would be rescinded. There was a chance Ava might not receive an official lay-off notice in May. However, the rep noted, it was equally likely that she would.

An angry soundtrack played in Ava's head. She blinked back tears. Fucking San Francisco. Why did she want to teach here anyway?

Miraculously, parking opened up and she marched down the spacious Marina streets in her pajamas, a bottle of wine tucked under each arm. Fuck it. She already wasn't a size 00. She already wasn't tits on sticks. Might as well show 'em how the rest of the world lives.

She pushed the door with her hip, bursting into Ruthie's kitchen. The sound track in her head stopped. Ava froze. Oh, shit. "Ruthie, you didn't tell me you had company."

Ruthie gave her a hug, took the wine. "You remember Laura?"

Laura held out a lovely, willow-branch arm, a Chanel model. "Ava. So good to see you again. I just stopped by to drop off Atticus' old baby clothes. I was glad to hear you were coming over too."

Ava squelched the embers that wanted to burn. And I'm wearing pajamas. Ava wanted to hate her, but Laura was just too damn nice. And how did she get her hair all shiny like that? "Hi Laura. Just got my lay-off notice. Came to drown some sorrows."

Laura slumped a little in her suit. "It must be the day for bad news. My mom was just diagnosed with early onset Alzheimer's. I'm trying to pretend like it isn't happening. My husband's already cracking jokes about forgetfulness." Laura gave a small smile. "He wouldn't be joking if it was his mom."

Ava looked at Laura and saw more than shiny hair. Laura's eyes were red. She held a wadded up tissue in her hand. Ava chided herself, It ain't all about you all the time.

Bill, big and loving in sweatpants himself, entered the room. "Ave!" He grimaced. "I heard. That's just bullshit."

Laura nodded. "I know you really love that job. I was just saying that Atticus is so fond of his teacher—I help out in his classroom once a week. I wish I were a kid—it's more like going to camp every day than school. We'd be devastated if his teacher were pink slipped."

Camp. Ava saw Sean's foster mom whacking his arm, Tanya showing the class how to boost clothes, Johntay's frightened voice describing what it felt like to watch a friend die. She forced a smile. None of this was Laura's problem—she had her own. And Ava was glad for little Atticus. But…who was looking out for the Johntays, the Seans, the Tanyas? Ava's campers.

Ruthie was at her elbow. "Oh, you're going down, aren't you? Come on, honey, let's get you a drink."

But, for the first time in her adult life, Ava didn't want a drink. She wanted her job. She wanted these kids. She needed her life to matter, this part of it at least. "I think I'd like some water."

Bill poured a glass. "Don't give up yet, Slugger. The team needs you."

Ava shook her head. "I'm a right fielder, Bill. No one needs me." Don't cry in front of Laura. Don't cry. The members of her tribe beat their drums. The gods of self-respect felt the tears well up, hauled out the sandbags.

Ruthie rubbed her belly. "You matter to me."

Laura held out her arms and Ava allowed herself to be hugged, be pathetic in front of physical perfection. It was like hugging a tall, fragile fairy. Let go. Let God.

Ava wiped her eyes. "Thanks," she said to "Sorry I'm such a mess. Don't mind me." She glanced up. The kitchen was warm. Her friends, inexplicably compassionate. "Of course, Ruthie, you're right. I didn't mean to throw a pity party."

"It's a kind world," Ruthie said. "I didn't used to think so, but now I do."

Ava thought about that, mulling over the incredulousness of such a statement. But her friend wasn't a fool. Ruthie had also lain on Gary's couch, looked in that mirror in the cabin in the woods. Gone back and back in time to when she first felt....

Yesterday. On the couch. The elephants. If Bill and Laura weren't here, she'd tell Ruthie about them. How it felt to swing her leg across that endless prickly back, feeling her body rise when it did, surging into the air on borrowed muscle. Ava had sat tall, drums still beating, startled to realize she was at the front of the procession.

"Just keep going until it gets better," Ruthie suggested. "It always does."

Ava nodded. "I'm trying."

CHAPTER 46
FREAKIN' WEEKEND

It was an early March morning, still cold, but the birds were out. The sky was a pale, sleepy blue. Ava's first period was not ready to get started on grammar that day.

"C'mon, folks—just a little comma rule practice, then we'll start silent reading," she coaxed.

"I wanna be on summer break!" Johntay whined.

Ava had to admit, since opening her pink slip, her enthusiasm for grammar had also waned.

It didn't help her spirits to remember that Cheryl said apathy was a natural reaction to the threat of being fired. "These last few months are the most dangerous. Demoralized teachers don't feel like donating their own time to hallway supervision. Instead, they hold to the contract, stay in their classrooms tending to students during passing time. Fights break out."

Ava observed her students, slumped in their seats. They needed some good news as much as she did. "Next week we have a three day weekend," she encouraged. "Does anyone have anything fun planned?"

Sean groaned, likely imagining a long weekend with his foster mom.

"C'mon," Ava said, "You must have something you're looking forward to?"

Ken mused, "I might do me a little *Remix*."

Francisco snorted.

From the depths of apathy, students suddenly came alive. "Yeah!"

Ava glanced around. "What?"

Ken sang, "It's the *Remix* to *Ignition*."

K'Ron chimed in, "Hot and fresh out the kitchen."

"Mama rolling that body, got every man in here wishin'," Johntay rolled his shoulders.

Francisco grinned at the look of horror on Ava's face.

"Ok," she said, "that's probably not the kind of song we should be—"

The General sang loudly, "Sippin' on coke and rum!"

"I'm like tho what I'm drunk," sang Hector. He did look a bit glassy-eyed that morning.

All the kids chimed in, "It's the FREAKIN' WEEKEND, baby, I'm about to have me some FUN!"

"I got fellas on my left," Tanya sang. "Honeys on my right!"

"Wooop! Woooop!" yelled K'Ron and Paris, singing back-up.

"Bring 'em both together we got jukin' all night." Tanya made a thrusting motion with her hips. The crowd went wild.

Ava held up her hands, not wanting to contribute to teenage pregnancy. She'd heard the song on the radio, but the relevance eluded her.

The General stood up, a preacher to his flock. "Can I get a—"

The choir resounded, "TOOOT! TOOOT!"

"I said, can I get a—"

"BEEEP! BEEEP!" Even Francisco laid on the horn.

Tanya pointed to her teacher.

Ava panicked. Me? Oh, God. But the kids were looking to her to keep the party going. She took a deep breath. "It's the freakin' weekend, baby, I'm about to have me some fun!"

Tanya nodded. "You got—

Ava looked around. "Students on my left!"

Ken waved his arm back and forth, singing, "Ken is on your right!"

The kids looked at their teacher.

More? She shrugged. "Bring them both together we got essays done right!"

The class groaned.

Tanya sang into her pencil, "And after the essays?"

"It's a grammar party!"

"And after the party?"

"You'll all go to bed early!" Ava was on roll, so she finished the stanza, "And round about six you're gonna wake up for school and put some food in your body!"

Melvin buried his face in his hands. "Ooohhhh, Ms. L!"

"You ruined it!" Sean groaned.

Tanya shook her head. "You need to learn how to have fun, Ms. L."

Ava paused. That's what Gary said too. But she was used to being the Grinch Who Stole Fun. "I was thinking that we all should probably get on with our assignment today."

Paris appealed to her teacher. "But we have to have some fun, Ms. L—the world's gonna end next year!"

Big Moe nodded. "That's true."

"Next year," Hector echoed.

Ava stared her students. Half of them were living under the certainty of imminent annihilation. "Where did you hear that?"

Tanya tapped her florescent-color braids. "Duh, Ms. L—everyone knows that!"

Paris seconded, "My granny said it was written down by some man who predicted everything right in history!"

Sean snorted. "That ain't true!"

"It is too true!" Paris held her backpack to her chest, outraged.

Melvin looked at Paris, "Why you want the world to end?"

Paris sighed, Melvin's ignorance just too, too much. "You watch. The world's gonna end, and Jesus is gonna come pick me up. Then I'ma lean over his plane and I'ma say, 'Byyyye, Melvin!'"

"Jesus isn't gone come get you in a *plane!*" Melvin retorted. "Jesus is gonna have a spaceship or some shit!"

Tanya turned to Ava. "Don't worry, Ms. L—I'ma tell Jesus to come back and get you."

Paris smirked at Melvin. "Yeah, and we gonna have Ms. L tied to the plane and we gone say, 'Byyyye, Melvin!'"

Ava nodded, accepting as a compliment the idea that, though Jesus may not think to include her on his Lear jet, her students weren't about to let her go down like that. Yet another reason for holding out hope that she might get to spend at least one more year at Ida B. Who besides these kids would send a reluctant Jesus back for her?

CHAPTER 47
FRIES WITH THAT

The restaurant was hushed, a golden Buddha smiling silently near the Hostess station. Lotus flowers floated in small bowls on each table.

Jimmie pulled out her chair. "I'm not a huge sushi fan, but this place got the best Yelp reviews."

"So what are you a fan of?"

"Pizza. I grew up in Chicago."

Ahhh. A legendary Midwestern boy. Ava had seen how the Bay Area redefined metrosexual men, stepping up the definition to include designer clothing, buffed nails. In a seven-mile by seven-mile city, it was slim pickings for women desperate to attract the relatively few number of straight men. Third date sex was the goal for many heterosexual guys who had no need to settle down before the last hair on their heads turned gray. For this reason, family-minded Midwestern boys were the crumbs God sprinkled into the waters to feed the starving fish, keep women from fleeing San Francisco altogether. "Not much sushi in the Midwest?"

"There's a little bit of everything there. My dad was a pretty good cook, so he'd make his own rolls for my siblings and me."

Siblings and ME. See that, kids? Grammar. Maybe Jimmie would be willing to come to her classes. Tell them she wasn't making this shit up. She perused the menu. "I suppose now is not the time that I tell you I'm not a fan of raw fish."

He laughed, hailed the waiter.

Don't tell him that story— "The first time I ordered tuna in the city, I thought it was a fluke it came uncooked," Ava said. "The second time, my friend refused to let me send it back—I guess it's supposed to be raw." Yes, lead with stupidity. A great date tactic. She glanced through the menu. Keep it positive. "There's plenty of other stuff to eat here, though."

Jimmie gave the menus back to their server. He held out a hand to his date. "Let's try something else. How do you feel about well-cooked Italian?"

Ava took his arm. "I love it."

"Next time, will you tell me what you don't like before we're at the restaurant?"

"I'll try."

"That's all anyone can ask."

In the pizza parlor, Ava ran her hands over the plastic tablecloth. Oldies cranked above the din of kids shouting to their friends, parents shushing. It was the kind of restaurant she and Dan would have frequented. Ava sighed, contented. Their pizza was thick crust. She couldn't remember the last time she allowed herself to have thick crust. Or bacon and pepperoni. The oils in the cheese combined with spicy sauce on her tongue. Good-bye waistline, hel-looo happiness.

Jimmie leaned in. "Good?"

Ava found his wool jacket and Dockers comforting, like he was going to dinner back home in Spokane, not San Francisco. She groaned. "In heaven."

"So I have a question for you."

"Bacon was definitely the way to go. Never going to regret that decision."

"Excellent, but not my question. I've been wondering: Why'd you take so long to come back to the team?"

Ava paused. She didn't like the question. Keep it light. She pointed to her lip. "It seemed appropriate to admit defeat when I tried to catch the ball with my face."

Jimmie shook his head. "Not buying it."

"I'm not athletic. Right field? The team can do better."

But Jimmie just looked at her, a small frown on his face.

She felt the magic of the evening begin to fall away. Who is this guy, putting me on the spot? Maybe Jimmie was a mistake. Her mood deflated. The date all but over, she admitted, "I was embarrassed."

"Why?"

"You were kind. I didn't feel like I deserved it. You didn't know me." Ava waited for Jimmie to respond, but he just sat there for a moment, thinking. He wants to leave and needs an out. She looked at her watch. "Well—"

"I'm a pretty nice guy," Jimmie interrupted. "Or, at least that's what my grandma claims, but she also voted for Bush Junior twice." His face was serious. "I like you. Can you handle that?"

Ava looked at the greasy slice of pizza in her hand, bacon sliding off the extra cheese. The date wasn't over. Amid the relief, it occurred to her then that she most definitely, desperately wanted fries with that. "I'll try."

By the time they reached the door to her apartment, she was sweating through her dress. Would he kiss her? What if he didn't want to? Would she take over, kiss him? Shit. Then, another voice, her own. Ava? No tongue.

Jimmie leaned in and kissed her cheek. "Can I take you out again?"

Thank God. "Yes."

CHAPTER 48

JOURNEY

March 9th. She struggled with the code to her therapist's office building. Goddamn hippie bullshit. No coffee before a journey? No breakfast? This man was going to pay.

Opening the door, she stepped into a space transformed. Gary sat on the floor in front of an altar, a thick mat laid out behind him. The incense and hippie music told the story: Some freaky shit is going down in here today. Still, Ruthie said it would be OK.

He waved her over. "Come in. Put your pictures down. Sit next to me."

She placed the photos she had chosen for this journey by the framed picture of a tribal elder on the altar. The woman in the photograph had long, gray hair, the lines on her face deep and worried, like she had been pondering the same question for a long time.

Gary handed Ava a smudge stick. "Go ahead. Take this around the room. Make it yours."

Smoke billowed from the dried bundle of plants. She gagged a little at the scent. In college, her roommate loved smudge sticks. Ava hadn't known where the smell was coming from, didn't know sage. For months, she assumed her roommate had an issue with body odor.

She took the B.O. stick around the room, wafts of smoke billowing behind her. Then she returned to the altar.

Gary tamped out the burning sage. "Okay. Why don't you take the medicine and say a little prayer?"

Ava took the small box, remembering the conversations she'd had with Ruthie, about the mushrooms as therapeutic medicine.

"You'll be tripping your balls off," Ruthie said, "but it's the most healing experience I've ever had."

Gary had mentioned the journey a month after Ava started seeing him weekly. He explained that the healing would happen on a cellular level, that her spirit guides would be with her, reading her light, providing the experience she most needed.

Ava thought about this as put the medicine into her mouth, chewing the way Gary instructed: slowly, thoroughly. It was nasty, chalky. Anxiety rose. She closed her eyes searching for a friendly, familiar image. Her student, Johntay, leaning out of the drive-through window, offering an extra bag of fries. Please let God, Johntay, and Anne Lamott look over me during my journey.

"Now," Gary said, "It'll take twenty minutes to kick in. Tell me what you've brought."

She pulled out her photographs. "This one," she pointed, "is me as a teenager." She felt something dead, lifeless in her chest. "I don't know how to love her."

He put the picture on the altar.

She pointed to the next two photos. "This one is me when I was about two years old. I was fearless. I'm in footie pajamas, and I've got a huge grin."

Gary chuckled. "Let's give the teenager some company." He set the second picture in the center.

"This one," she said, "this I got from a magazine. I like the simplicity of the huge hand opening a box of light. I feel like the box represents the reason I'm here."

He nodded.

"Only I don't know what that reason is. I need God to help me open that box. I need to feel that there even is a God."

Gary took the picture. "You will do good work today. Now go ahead and lie down. When you feel the medicine tingle, let me know. That's when I'll put on your headphones. Then your spirit guides will read your light and know exactly what you need. They will take you on a journey."

Ava did as she was told. But what if her spirit guides didn't come? She didn't know what to do. What would ACA tell her? Ahhhh--Let go. Let God.

Gary lifted her head, put the sleep mask over her eyes. His voice, soothing. "I'm going to read to your from "A Hopi Elder Speaks.""

She inhaled deeply. I hope that Hopi elder knows a lot more about what's going on here than I do.

Gary began:

"You have been telling the people that this is the Eleventh Hour, now you must go back and tell the people that this is THE HOUR. And there are things to be considered...

"Where are you living?
"What are you doing?
"What are your relationships?
"Are you in right relation?
"Where is your water?
"Know your garden.
"It is time to speak your Truth.
"Create your community.
"Be good to each other.
"And do not look outside yourself for the leader.

"Then the elder clasped his hands together, smiled, and said, 'This could be a good time! There is a river flowing now very fast. It is so great and swift that there are those who will be afraid. They will try to hold on to the shore. They will feel they are being torn apart and will suffer greatly. Know the river has its destination. The elders say we must let go of the shore, push off into the middle of the river, keep our eyes open, and our heads above the water. And I say, see who is in there with you and celebrate.

"At this time in history, we are to take nothing personally. Least of all, ourselves. For the moment that we do, our spiritual growth and journey comes to a halt. The time of the lone wolf is over. Gather yourselves! Banish the word 'struggle' from your attitude and your vocabulary. All that we do now must be done in a sacred manner and in celebration.

We are the ones we've been waiting for.'"

Ava's body tingled, hummed. She pictured the spirit guides reading her light, saw the river, felt the current. She couldn't hold onto the shore now if she wanted to. "I feel it," she said.

Gary put large headphones over her ears.

Water. She heard the sound of water. Ava was in a rowboat with her dad. Her hair shone white-blonde, baby fine. Hands that had not yet formed knuckles clasped her soft knees. They were in the middle of the beaver ponds, a father-daughter outing, just the two of them, and she was having a good time.

"See there?" Dad pointed. Fish jumped intermittently, flashes of silver, the pond a giant disco ball. Dad reached down, ruffled her silken hair. "They're trying to get a peek at my girl."

Then darkness. The boat disappeared, the silver fish.

Another picture emerged, Dad at the shore, filling in a grave. A dirge plodded over the headphones. Ava looked down to see teenage knuckles clutching a shovel. Silently, they dug into soft earth mounds. But who is this grave for? Throwing another shovel full of dirt into the hole, she peered down. She saw her own teenage face looking up.

No! Panic rose in her throat. What am I doing here? Where are my spirit guides? Sadness thrummed an ache. Ava was alone, terrified.

Drums in the distance grew closer. There they are. The spirit guides took the shovel from Ava, and gave the girl in the grave a hand out. The one in charge motioned for her to follow. They walked away from the grave, beaver ponds, Dad.

Huge buildings. Ava looked around at a dirty, abandoned city. She was a little girl with a box. She wanted to share it, but not in an ugly, dirty, people-less place. Anger, disappointment slid down her throat. This is the journey? Fucking hippie.

She wandered into a big stadium. Wind blew through empty seats. A voice on the loudspeaker mocked her: God is not coming to solve your problems. God will not be bothered with you.

She felt the truth in that statement. She had been such a fool. No one took medicine expecting an answer for what to do with their lives. Stupid. Stupid.

"Ah!" her mouth became rigid, her tongue heavy. Words flew away. She was miserable, rejected by God, all alone. Ava turned on her side. In desperation, she whispered the only words she had left. "Help me. Help me. Help me."

Suddenly, the music opened up. A soprano came to the rescue, sang arias that tore holes in the darkness. Light shone in. Ava saw herself as part of a spiraling honeycomb, a luminous center.

Whispers enveloped her. Words in some other language—Italian? No, more ancient than that. She moved her lips to speak, vowels, consonants too heavy, wouldn't form. Why was it so difficult? Ahhh…Words, soldiers to the silence, were coming. Someone would teach her. But whom?

From the darkness emerged a familiar presence: Mama. Ava would have a lesson. "Is-a Mama," Mama instructed, a hand to her chest. She pointed to Ava. "Is-a Ba-a-by." Mama tapped her own chest again. "You lost? You hurt? You say, 'Ma-ma!'"

Ava whispered, "Ma-ma."

Green grass sprouted from earth thawing in the sun. A child took a wobbly step. A silver-haired woman donned tights, her first ballet class. A baby was born. An artist put wet paint to canvas. Yes. This was the reason why. In trying, new was created. And to create was life itself.

Mama pointed. "Ba-a-by!"

Ava got it. She was the baby, the new.

Mama's eyes shone. "More."

Ava would nurture the new. She would help others know what it is to love the first attempt, the new, the try. She was strong enough to expose her trying to others, show that it was okay to try--even when that meant looking the fool.

Mama spread her arms. Ava saw all of the caretakers, the nurturers, the Mamas. Stella. Cheryl. Ginny. Ruthie. We need to care for the caretakers. Yes.

A chill ran through her body. A new lesson: Papa. Ava turned away. She didn't want to feel that shame.

Mama put a hand to Ava's back, guiding her.

No! Ava stiffened.

Arms around her. Energy. A wave of protection. Love without conditions. Warmth emanated from the embrace. There was peace, calm, rest. Ava understood: Papas protected Mamas so that Mamas could nurture the new. Everyone had all of those roles within themselves: the new, nurturer, protector. Ava had not been her own protector, her own papa.

Mama nodded. We have to allow Papas their jobs.

Ava softened into the hug. Let go and let God. Tears soaked the blinders. This is how it feels. I had no idea.

She asked about Jimmie.

Mama looked into her belly. "He is good. He knows what is a Papa's job."

Ava asked if her children would be infected with mental illness.

Mama said, "No." Ava was a good Mama now. She knew her job. She wouldn't get out of balance again.

The music changed. Minor chords marched Ava down a dim stairwell. She saw how small she was on this interwoven spiral, how there are Mamas and Papas and Babies created without end. Then the source took Ava back to the middle, the inside of the grid, reminding her that Baby, love, is the meaning.

Mama pointed to figures in the distance. Ava recognized Ruthie's shape and felt familiar love blossom, spreading through her body.

"Only play with friends who love you," Mama said. She placed a loving hand against Ava's forehead. The wounded members of her tribe were comforted. Mama whispered, "Only play with thoughts that love you." A healer had come at last to relieve the comic. A sigh flowed down to Ava's toes.

Mama pointed to bottles of wine, Nyquil, and shook her head. "Only play with food that loves you." Ava saw a garden of vegetables, nourishment. Food was not supposed to numb.

Fatigue seeped in through Ava's pores. She had never been so tired. Or so hungry. She was ready, done. "Gary," she whispered, "can I come back now?" She took a blurry peek under the blinders. Gary's office was a neon maze of lines and colors: moving, shifting.

His hand, giving her water. "It's a little early to come back."

The liquid flowed cool and loving down her throat. Ava set the bottle down, shaky. She ate an apple slice, a lullaby in her belly when she lay back down. Closing her eyes, she rested.

Lying there contented, Ava fell into a deep state of restfulness. The journey is over. I get it now. I am here to expose my trying, the beauty of the new. Care for the caretakers. Care for the new. Be my own protector. I can rest now.

Then she felt something different. They were opening the box. A present. They were opening Ava. The box glowed.

Mama said, "Papa, is-a Baaabyy!" She was delighted.

Ava didn't see his reaction, she only felt his joy rising like gratitude in her own throat.

Water lapping a shore. Ava in a sailboat—Stella, Ruthie, Ava's mom. They all grinned.

Ava asked, "Where are we going?"

Mom said, "You're the captain. We've been waiting on *you*."

Stella hoisted the sail.

Ava took the wheel.

She opened her eyes, testing. The room, colors held still.

Gary sat next to her, offering a bottle of water.

"I don't think you charge enough," Ava said.

CHAPTER 49
YOU GOT CAUGHT

Pants stood in the front of the room, hands on polyester hips. "Blackboard Configuration. I'm not seeing it, people."

"I've got more important things to do with my prep time." Stella said loudly.

"More important than having your lesson standards on the blackboard? How are students supposed to know which standards they're working on? No. My expectation is for everyone to have the BBC up every day. Ms. Brill noted that we weren't complying with that directive, and she makes the rules, people." Pants perused her list of topics. "Okay. Next up, Hector Vasquez."

Ava zoned back into the conversation. Hector had missed class the past two days.

Pants frowned. "Got a call from YGC. He'll be in Juvie a while. Yesterday morning he was spotted leaving school as the first period bell rang. Apparently, he used that time to get drunk with friends—a nine am happy hour ending with him and his buddies beating up the father of a family of four on the man's break."

No! Ava's inhaled sharply. She was still riding the wave of her journey, the opening of the box. Mama. The sailboat. The new.

Now, Hector. Sweet Hector with the ponytail, lisp. The glassy eyes. Not Paco Taco. He attacked a stranger? This can't be happening.

Pants continued, "Two other men saw the beating. They tried to jump in to help the father, but the boys had knives on them. They cut the men enough to send one to the hospital."

Hector's homeroom teacher, Janice Randall, stared at Pants. "I don't understand. Hector wouldn't hurt anyone. He's got substance abuse issues, but violence?" She turned to Mary Kline, the Wellness coordinator. "What happened to his drug counseling?"

Mary grimaced. "We lost the guy who ran the substance abuse group…"

Cheryl sighed. "Shit. That man was so good with the kids, too. What was Hector thinking? What a stupid, awful thing to do."

A collective groan rose from the teachers.

Ava remembered Hector at the mock trial, tried to reconcile her student with a kid who could commit a violent crime.

"Anyone want to go with me to see him?" Janice asked. "He's going to be in there for a while. They usually don't get many visitors."

"Too pissed," Mr. Brennan said. "What the fuck was he thinking?"

Ava raised her hand. "We're allowed to visit?"

Stella grimaced, clay smudges on her cheek, nose. "If you're up for it. I stopped going to Juvie. Too many over the years. Makes it hard to come in to work, invest in other kids who may end up in the same place."

Three days later, Janice and Ava met up outside the Youth Guidance Center. Kids liked to call YGC "You Got Caught," crimes only counting if you ended up in handcuffs. Ava felt the place could as easily have been nicknamed, You Got Fucked. Getting caught was only the end of a process, beginning with a social and economic structure that passed along bundles of poverty and hopelessness.

Walking through the main doors, the women encountered metal detectors. Ava gave her purse over for inspection. Who were they there to see? A phone call.

Guards directed them to a series of long, narrow hallways, past tiny offices. As Janice and Ava made their way into the belly of YGC, the passageways grew smaller, darker. Soon, windows disappeared. Fluorescent lighting, listless walls. Off-white? No. Tan? No. Color had given up. All that remained were pungent odors. Smells of bodies trapped in spaces sealed too tight to dissipate. And still the hallways unfolded like a maze. How to get out? Panic pulsed inside her bloodstream. Breathe.

A second security checkpoint. Metal detectors again. The guard required the women leave their purses. Janice produced permission from Hector's probation officer. B4 housed the violent offenders.

Ava felt vulnerable without her keys, ID. She had nothing to hold close, clutch in her hands, let someone know she was not supposed to stay here. With surprise, she noticed the hallways becoming wider. Large doors bore the names of various cellblocks, leading off to their own wings. They were getting closer. When they passed the gym, Ava gagged. She switched to breathing through her mouth.

Finally, a dead end. Massive double doors labeled B4. Janice knocked on the heavy steel, and a man the size of an offensive lineman peered out. "Who you here to see?"

"Hector Vasquez."

The man nodded. He led the women into an open room with a raised librarian-style desk, flanked on the left by a visitors' area, orange and flesh-toned tables and stools bolted to the floor. The other side of the desk overlooked an open concrete shower.

The guard scanned his roster. He pointed to the table and stools. "Sit there," he said. "I'll send for Vasquez."

A few minutes went by. Janice and Ava sat at their bolted-down table on their bolted-down stools. "Every time feels as awful as this," Janice said.

Then Hector, flanked by another lineman, came into the visiting area. He held his cuffed wrists out from his body, shuffling in oversized flip-flops, gray scrub pants, and a faded sweatshirt.

The guard removed his cuffs.

Janice put her arms around him, and Hector hugged her tight.

After a moment, they settled onto stools. "I didn't mean to do it," Hector sniffed. "I didn't mean to hurt that guy. I wath just really, really drunk." He wiped his face with the sleeve of his sweatshirt.

Ava asked, "How is the guy now?"

"Mad."

"I would imagine," Janice said. "What about the other boys involved in the attack?"

Hector shrugged. "They're here too, but they keep uth apart."

Janice arched a brow. "Was the attack your idea?"

"I don't remember." He looked down. "We wath drinking tequila and gin and I don't know what all elsth and then one of my frienth looked at that guy, and the guy tharted mouthing off, and it all just happened. We didn't mean to hurt no one; the other men just came up on uth quick and I didn't even know what I wath doing then."

"Are you going to have to testify against the other boys?" Ava asked.

He shuddered. "I won't thnitch."

"What does your lawyer say?" asked Janice.

"I got a trial in a month. I got a fair judge. My lawyer hopeth that I'll get to go to Log Cabin, not CYA."

CYA was California Youth Authority, San Quentin for those under 18. Ava had read about it in the paper after two CYA teens committed suicide.

"We'll hope for Log Cabin then." Janice said, referencing the juvenile jail far out in the woods, miles south of the city.

Janice and Ava got up, prepared to leave Hector to the care of burly men in this oversized locker-room.

He looked at Ava, eyes holding back tears. "Mth L?"

"Yes?" Anything.

"Could you write me a letter for the judge?"

"Of course." A letter would tell the judge about the sunny kid she knew, the one who wanted to holler at college girls. She'd talk about his struggles with addiction, the complete lack of resources at the school to help him. The helplessness she felt and could only imagine he felt with the situation. The complete incomprehensibility of this heinous crime matching the student who came to class nearly every day.

Twenty minutes later, Ava stepped out into the free air, oppressive clouds unable to stop the sun's bright rays from filtering onto her skin. She breathed in, legs slightly unsteady. Holy shit.

Janice gave a sad wave. "Gonna find the nearest nail shop. After days like these, I just want to put my feet into some warm water and let someone else be in charge of my life for a while."

Ava walked up the street alone, her stomach churning. The smells of YGC still clung to her clothes. I don't know how to help him. She had known about the pot, the booze, but she hadn't known, didn't know now, what to do about it. If Janice hadn't gone to YGC, Ava wouldn't have known to go. The number of things she didn't know felt like they were piling up. The goal of helping students overcome adversity, move on to college, drifted further away. A mountain was rising, its shadow vast and ominous. "Mama," she whispered, wanting the warmth of her journey's guide to envelope her in her arms.

She stepped into her truck, buckled her seatbelt, and waited in the dull silence for Mama's wisdom. What to do now? She was too tired to go home, grade papers. A bus went by, shaking her truck with a whoosh. What had Mama said in the journey? Take care of the caretakers. What did that look like? Ava pondered a drive to the ocean. Or maybe just sit in the cradle of Dolores Park. She wanted green. Trees. She thought about Janice. Ava wouldn't have had the courage to go to YGC alone. She hated that she defaulted to coward when the going got complicated. Later, she would call up Janice, thank her for taking Ava with her, having the courage when Ava didn't. But for now?

Janice was right. It was time to rest. She fired up the truck and headed for the ocean.

CHAPTER 50

BUSINESS

March 22nd. A hazy Sunday morning. The phone rang. Stella. "Want to go for a bike ride? Wear good running shoes. And bring a towel."

Ava hugged her coffee mug closer, students' papers fanned out on the floor. "Bike ride and….? Spill it, Stella."

"I decided last night to start training for a triathlon. I thought we'd ride to the beach for a swim, go for a run after."

Ava pictured Stella's messy classroom, the overflow of ideas that couldn't keep up with the laws of time and structure. Stella's motto was "Ready, fire, aim." Of course her colleague had decided last night to train for a triathlon today. "Isn't the water freezing?"

"I've got something for that."

They drove on the gravel roads of Mt. Tam for half an hour, winding up and up and up. Stella parked her Nissan along a wooden rail fence. She got out, motioning to the dirt path on the other side. A sign nailed to a tree encouraged: *Keep Out*.

Ava helped off-load the bikes. "You sure this isn't private property?"

Stella pulled an old yoga mat from her car. "A friend told me about this place. Says it's only a few miles 'til you reach the Bay." Her brow furrowed as she cut out two circles from the mat. Then she pulled out two bathing caps from her trunk. "When we get to the water, put the piece of mat under your cap to keep your head warm."

Ava nodded. Yoga mats on their heads. Trespassing. Of course this was the plan. She looked at the bike Stella was setting up for her. It had been years since she had ridden. The seat looked way too high; her feet wouldn't touch the ground. "If I hit a rock and go off a cliff, please drag my body somewhere no one will shoot me for trespassing."

"Biking's about the bigger picture." Stella said. "If you're concentrating on the rocks, you're gonna hit rocks."

Ava nudged the pedal into position with her toe and began a wobbly course behind her colleague. The trail took them into the woods, short uphill stretches followed by fast-paced dips. The harder her legs worked, the more her body thawed. Really, she chided herself, jogging more than once a week wouldn't kill you.

"I can't believe you haven't gotten out in nature more," Stella called. "The Bay Area's got tons of open space for hiking, biking, swimming—anything you want."

Ava grew up in the woods. She loved the outdoors. But it wasn't until the weekend after her journey with Gary in which she'd met Mama, stood at the helm of the sailboat, that she'd finally driven to the ocean. Sitting on the sand at Half Moon Bay, she inhaled the sharp scent of eucalyptus, felt the salt spray on her skin. Why had it taken her so long? "Guess I've been a bit depressed."

Stella slowed down, then stopped, waiting for Ava to catch up. "You know, depression usually means *victim* and that kind of thinking never got anyone anywhere."

Ava bristled. "You don't know my story."

"Let me guess: Someone somewhere on down your family line messed up. Join the club. My family tells the story about when I was ten. My dad, sloppy drunk, offered to take me out, buy me a bike. I went. The whole family watched the two of us get into the car. He was stumbling, slurring his words. They thought it was funny to watch the drunk and the dupe drive away."

Stella held out her left hand, pointing to scars that hadn't healed, fingers that wouldn't straighten. "The car accident left me with permanent damage—radial nerve all fucked up." She looked Ava in the eyes. "But I don't blame him. I wanted the bike. I made a choice. Responsibility for yourself. That's all we've got."

Is she fucking kidding me? Ava heard the edge in her own voice. "I'm sorry about your hand, Stella, but I don't really need a lecture on parents who drink."

"Then what are you so depressed about?"

Don't say anything. Now wasn't the time for a heart-to heart. Still...It was the thought that had weighed her down since first starting at Ida B. The thought that made Sunny hard to bring up without a knot in her throat—"I can't save them."

"Them who?"

"Our students. I'm so far from saving any kids here, I'm a joke."

Stella stared. "And who ever told you that was your job?"

"What do you mean? Isn't that why we teach?"

Stella's laugh rang ugly. Ava turned away.

"Aww, don't be mad," Stella said. "Listen: there's a woman named Metta Annie. She said a long time ago that there's only three kinds of business: Mine, yours, and God's. Saving students? That belongs to the kids and God."

Ava bristled. "Not my business?" The image of Sunny—the girl's rage, her helplessness. She shook her head: Don't go there. "What about Hector? His drinking."

"Sorry to burst your bubble, but Hector's drinking is his business."

And Fuck. You. Too. Where was Stella when Ava and Janice were down in the pits of YGC? Ohhhhhh, that's right—she said she didn't go to YGC anymore. Life must be good when you ignore the shitty stuff. "Sounds pretty cold."

Stella began pedaling. "You report the drinking to Wellness. You talk to him about it. Then you let him figure it out. That's how it works. You think Hector is asking for someone on shaky emotional ground to be his guardian angel? Hell no! And you wouldn't want that either. Figure out your own life. You can't help anyone until you handle your own business."

That's it, bitch. Ava's voice came out hard. "Who are you to tell me I'm on shaky emotional ground?" She hesitated, then—fuck it. "The kids think you're on meth, did you know that? And you don't know me well enough to tell me what kind of ground I'm on."

Stella rode ahead silently, her legs pumping under her spandex. Ava didn't care. Stella obviously wasn't worried about sparing her feelings. She looked around, noticed the trees becoming sparse. Far ahead, a sliver of water glinted over the hillside. Great. We still have to swim after this.

The minutes ticked by. Ava considered that maybe her comment about meth had been out of line. You know what? No. I don't have to take shit from Stella. She had already said *yes* to this ride, a swim, a jog; she had taken her piece of the goddamn yoga mat.

"Cocaine." Stella called out.

"What?"

"They think I'm on cocaine. It's because I sing to them, act like a nut. Have you ever seen our students in art class? I give them a kid's toy—a plastic cow—and ask them to make one in clay. They sit there until I show them it's okay to mold four legs, a body. Put a round circle on top and call it a fucking head. They're so afraid to get it wrong. And it's a *cow*!"

Stella slowed. "So I sing to them, talk in funny voices, dance around the room, make stupid jokes until they see art isn't so serious. They can't fail it on an Exit Exam. Then, when they're working on those four legs on their own, and they're finally getting their hands dirty, I sit next to them and talk about feelings. That it's okay to have feelings. I talk about what we do when we can't handle feelings—drinking, smoking."

Ava didn't know what to say. She had seen it too—kids too afraid to put a period on a page because they might get it wrong. She sighed. The first leg of the morning's triathlon was already way more than she had bargained for. She wanted to go home. But she was on a bike. Stella was leading the way. She was stuck.

Gradually, her anger reduced to a simmer. Beneath resentment, curiosity lurked. "So what else does this Metta Annie woman say?"

"She says when you're upset about something, write it down. Ask yourself if it's really true. How do you feel when you think that thought? How would you feel without it? Then turn the thought around to its opposite, to yourself, or to the other."

The Bay was in full view now. Sparkling blue winked amid white-caps. Stella stopped at the edge of a steep hillside. Waves crashed onto a beach approximately twenty feet below. The art teacher dismounted her bike and looked around. She tested a frayed rope that had been left anchored to the ground, dangling off of the edge.

A rope? That's the plan? Ava shook her head. She watched Stella wrap the rope around herself. Cocaine. Cows. Metta Annie. This is what my life's come to. She asked, "So what would be a turn-around for the thought 'I'm supposed to save the kids?'"

"Turn the statement to the other."

She puzzled over that one, finally trying out, "The kids are supposed to save me?"

Stella gripped the rope tightly, lowering herself over the ledge. "Isn't that what they do?"

Ava stood a moment. The projector in her mind showed the kids singing. Ken in his silver sparkle suit. The General presiding over the courtroom. Her students asking about the homeless man, *Is he your boyfriend?* It was hard to imagine loving anybody more. Only play with thoughts that love you. Anger dissipated into the salty air.

She looked down at Stella who was using the rope to walk down the steep hillside. "Is there another turnaround?"

"Turn it around to yourself."

Ava snorted. "So I'm supposed to save myself. You bet. Let me get right on that."

Stella paused in her descent. "Isn't that more true?"

Ava saw her last interaction with Sunny. The mess she had made with Dan. The one-year time frame on living. The Nyquil. Her hands on the wheel of the sailboat in her therapy journey. Keeping herself from going too far off-course was a full-time job. She looked out over the thinning fog, emerging sun, the bay. "Maybe."

Stella grunted her way down, hand-over-hand, to the beach below. The rope strained, a few frayed cords snapping. Her long white hair blew in the breeze as she jumped the last few feet onto the sand.

Ava edged her feet toward the rocky drop-off. *Really?* It seemed way too steep to trust a sorry-ass rope. What if she fell? Far below, Stella waved encouragement—a woman who awoke in the mornings with ambitions of triathlons.

Ava felt the seven-year old in her take her hand. The little girl looked at her hopefully. "Yes." Ava said aloud. "Yes." Sitting down, she tested the prickly rope. Her palms burned as she gripped hard, lowering herself down the rocky cliff inch by shaky, slipping inch. By the time her feet hit the sand, exhilaration tingled. She was ready to climb back up, do it all over again.

Stella stuffed the circle of yoga mat inside her bathing cap. She wiggled out of her sweatshirt, then her tee shirt. She had nothing on underneath. "It's a nude beach," Stella said.

Ava looked around. "But we're the only ones here." Her colleague's bike shorts were off. Stella had gone commando. Why do I bother being surprised? Ava sighed. "Wait for me." She rummaged in her backpack for her circle of yoga mat, the extra bathing cap.

Stripping down to nothing, the wind hit her like a slap. Like covering my head is going to make a difference when I'm freezing my bare ass off.

Stella ran toward the water. "I'm going to try for a quarter-mile," she shouted.

Ava stepped tentatively into the Bay. Cold pierced her ankles. And after this we'll go for a run. She gazed pointedly at the clearing skies. "Let the record show, I *am* trying."

CHAPTER 51

IF I HAD A BOAT

Pants called the faculty meeting to inform the staff that this year, Prom would be held on a boat. She was still smarting from last year's event and wasn't about to have the same catastrophes repeated. As Cheryl described the scene, there were parents sneaking in the back exits to party with their kids, and students climbing out of windows to drink and smoke weed. The cops were called when an inebriated parent wouldn't leave. This year, Pants demanded a captive dancing crew. But a *boat*?

Cheryl raised her hand. "Ms. Sanchez."

"Yes?"

"Are you out of your mind? These kids don't know how to swim!"

Mr. Brennan raised his hand. "Neither do I."

"Are they going to have enough life vests?"

"Aren't there sharks in the Bay?"

Pants frowned, held her clipboard tighter to her chest. "That's why we'll stay on the *boat*," she said. "I'm still getting nasty phone calls from Jaleesa's mother about her daughter ruining prom photos by throwing up on her date. No one leaves to get alcohol or weed. No inside access to them either."

"I'd better prefunk," Stella muttered.

CHAPTER 52

SUNRISE

March 28th. Ava stumbled into the hospital, pajama pants inside out. Under her fleece, she was braless. "Ruthie Feinsilber," she told the nurse at the counter. Ava blinked. Sleep crust fell from the corner of her eye.

The nurse glanced at her outfit. "Third floor. Room 403."

The maternity ward was quiet, which somehow set Ava's world in order. She glanced at her watch. 4:45 am. All shouting should be over by 4:45 am.

Ruthie waved. "Hey." Her long hair hung in strings, face flushed, a tiny bundle in her arms.

Bill sat on the other side of the bed in a reclining chair. His face was shiny with sweat. His dark hair clung to his forehead. "It's been a heck of a night," he said. "I'd get up, but I'm exhausted."

"New papas get a pass on getting up to greet every visitor."

Shaun perched on a stool near Ruthie.

Of course Shaun's already here. What in the world was Ruthie thinking, making him Godfather?

He turned toward Ava, nodding at the baby. "He looks like me." Shaun's obviously new tee shirt still held the rigid creases from its former packaging. The lettering on the shirt read, *Paternity Test Says I'm the Daddy.*

"Classy shirt," Ava smiled at her friends.

"Ruthie almost didn't let me in the door, but the nurses wouldn't let me take it off on hospital grounds. All this nakedness, and I'm not allowed to walk around bare-chested. Their loss."

Ruthie motioned her over. "The deal was, he was supposed to turn it inside out. Come meet Benjamin."

Ava crept toward the manger scene. Benjamin's eyes were closed. His mouth moved in an incredible lip synch.

"He's been asking for you," Ruthie whispered.

Ava blushed. "I didn't realize I was such a heavy sleeper. I thought those first few calls were the alarm." She glanced at Bill. "Sorry to put you on snooze."

"Want to hold him?"

Ava felt steel bars close around her heart. "Oh, I don't think that would be a good—"

Ruthie pulled Ava to her and tucked the baby into Ava's arms. "He won't break."

She cradled the tiny human. He was wobbly all over, fragile. A pouted lip protruded over a chin that clearly resembled Bill's. "Hi there," she said, as if meeting a casual acquaintance at a bar.

"He's got my nose," Shaun said.

Ruthie frowned. "You're not supposed to say things like that. Now turn that shirt inside out—"

Benjamin yawned, a move that occupied ninety percent of his body. "He's perfect," Ava whispered.

Shaun puffed out his chest. "Like I said…."

Ava traced the translucent skin on the back of Benjamin's hand. That tiny hand. That thin layer of skin. He was so unformed. So new. Then the tears came. Ava's arms were shaky. She handed the baby back to Ruthie.

"What's up, slugger?" Bill asked. He got up from the chair. Ava shook her head, unable to explain the tears streaming down her face. Shaun put his arm around her.

Ava buried her head into his chest, heaving like a donkey. This is so inappropriate. Get it together. But the tears kept coming.

"You're not too old for kids, you know," Shaun said. "I mean, no mistake, you're getting old. You're no spring chicken. Plenty of women freeze their eggs—"

Bill hit him on the back. "Ava? Talk to us. This is a good thing. Benjamin's healthy. Shaun—you're out as Godparent."

"Hey, you said I'd get three strikes! It's only two—"

Ava pulled away from Shaun, her hair in her face, snot running salty over her lips. "What if someone hurts him? Who will protect him? He's so small." She turned to Ruthie.

Ruthie nodded, mouth set into a determined line. "I think it's good we're talking about this now. I propose that we make a pact to protect this one. We don't let anyone talk down to him."

"I will teach him how to be a good man," Bill said. "How to live on his own terms, with integrity.'

"I'll teach him that it's important to know your own worth," Ava said. "Everyone matters." She wiped her face.

"And I will teach him how to make sweet love to the ladies," said Shaun.

Ruthie groaned.

Ava leaned down to kiss the baby's forehead. "And I will teach him karaoke." She nodded toward Shaun's tee shirt. "You couldn't have washed it for your godson?"

"You've got pasta sauce on your fleece." Shaun gave her outfit a once-over. "You wear that to bed? I have a few ideas why you're single if you'd ever like to hear them." He took a longer look. "And no bra? Kinky. Probably normal for this ward. We won't even talk about the Karaoke comment. That's just sad."

Bill leaned in toward Benjamin. "Don't worry, kiddo; neither one of them has to be a godparent. It was just a suggestion. Your mom and I were probably drinking when we made that decision."

CHAPTER 53

NEED A DATE?

April 1st. "Quiet down," Ava called into the din of Homeroom. "I want all of you to hear the bulletin."

Melvin was still in the middle of a story, "Oh my God!" he shouted, "I told her she needed to—"

"Ms. L asked you to be quiet!" Charnikka barked. "I want to hear the announcements!" She closed her book, *Dear G Spot*, and looked at Ava. "Go ahead, Ms. L."

"Ok folks," Ava said, "If you're thinking about going to prom, you need to buy your tickets soon. We had to put money down for the space, the DJ, catering. If you wait to buy tickets, we can't pay the bills."

Sean raised his hand. "Which schools we going with again?"

She listed off a court school, an independent studies high school, and the school for pregnant teens.

"I don't wanna be going to no prom with pregnant girls!" Johntay protested. "We gone look ghetto!"

"You already look ghetto," Charnikka said. She had been out the past few days taking care of her daughter.

Ava held up her hands. "I'm sure they're very nice, friendly girls."

"*Obviously*," K'Ron said under her breath.

The girls had been buzzing about prom for weeks before the big event. They had borrowed money from relatives, earned it babysitting or, for the lucky few, saved up paychecks from jobs. Girls collaborated with grandmas or women in the community to design their dresses, they avoided Popeye's Chicken, and tried out various hairstyles.

Boys prepared by refusing to acknowledge that prom was fast approaching. This sometimes created awkward situations for girls who felt strongly that one needed a date in order to go to prom.

"Johntay!" Tanya shouted over Ava one day. "You wanna go to prom with me?"

Johntay looked up, startled. He shook his head slowly. "I'ma take my boo."

Tanya, unfazed, surveyed the room. Her neon green and yellow braids hung askew. "Sean!" she barked, "Wanna go to prom?"

Sean had been rooting around in his backpack. His head swung around, forehead forming beads of sweat. "Uh—I gotta pay for you?" he asked.

Tanya nodded.

"Uh, I don't think so. Thanks, though."

Ava took the opportunity to hand out the next assignment before Tanya was rejected by the rest of first period test-prep.

That evening, Ava's phone rang. Jimmie.

"I hear it's prom season," he said. "Need a date?"

"Does a bear sh—" she stopped herself. "Yes," she said, "but you realize you'll have to put up with teenagers, right?"

Jimmie laughed. "Trying to sneak in booze and necking in the corner?"

"Oh, wow. I don't think they call it necking anymore."

"Is it necking if I do it?"

Ava smiled. "We'll see."

She dialed Ruthie's number. "How's my Godson?"

Ruthie whispered, "Eating, sleeping, pooping. It turns out Ben and I have the same hobbies."

"He is the world's most perfect boy."

"Pretty much. The screaming made the Russian judge rank him a four, but I say this guy's a solid seven. Now, tell me about the world outside this house."

"Well, it's eleven years late, but I finally got asked to prom."

"Is this an April fools joke?"

"I'm pretending you didn't say that."

Ruthie squealed. "Whoohoo! Got a dress? Protection?"

"It's only a second date. I'll stick to needing a dress."

"Yes! I have the perfect one you can borrow. Marilyn Monroe."

"School appropriate."

"Whatever. I'm living through you now. I've spent the last week covered in spit-up and poo. Pick up the dress tomorrow?"

Ava groaned. "Yes, please."

CHAPTER 54

PROM

April 14th. He was taking her to dinner at a French restaurant. French *People,* Ava thought. She tugged at the hem of her loaner dress. It was teal, backless. Way too tight for a school event. What was Ruthie thinking? When she'd put it on, she imagined a fancy cocktail party. Ruthie gushed about the fit, the color.

Now, balancing in silver heels worn only at her sister's wedding, Ava felt like a cross between a hooker and a princess. She would stand out. "Like *Pretty Woman* goes to Prom," she said when Jimmie picked her up.

He smiled. "I don't care how you disparage it. I'm a happy guy just to watch you wear it." His suit stretched across his chest, yellow tie a nod to their beer ball team color.

He came around to open her door, a corsage behind his back. It reminded Ava of when she first started dating Dan, how he'd do small things, important things, like sprinting back to the car when she forgot her coat. She wondered what he was doing now, then felt guilty for wondering.

She focused on Jimmie. Give him a chance. "You might be thinking this is a bigger deal than it really is." She let him pin the corsage to her dress.

When they arrived at the docks, Pants assigned Ava the dubious task of checking the girls' purses for alcohol and illegal substances. Watching the first few kids arrive, some in limos, some dropped off by relatives or an older sibling, Ava pulled her wrap tight—she shouldn't have worn a dress like this. She looked ridiculous. And then to drag Jimmie into it—She'd assumed they'd find a nice corner, hang out, no big deal.

But no. She was in front, on purse detail. Jimmie stood by while Ava peered into clutches, apologizing profusely. However, uncomfortable as the assignment was, it could have been worse: Cheryl was on bathroom patrol.

The first student on the boat could have come straight from a runway in Italy: Niesha's long dress was slit to her hip, the orange and black fabric a cross between a basketball jersey and a slinky ball gown. Her date matched his suit and tie to her outfit.

Tanya's dress was defined by what wasn't there: fabric. Thin lines of green satin stood out against her bare chest, torso, hips, legs. Fortunately, she also carried a neon pink wrap. Pants told her she was allowed on the boat only if she kept her shawl on the entire time.

"Ms. L, you look fitted!" Tanya marveled, her shawl drooping a little to reveal a naked shoulder, the swell of a breast.

Tanya loves my outfit. Oh, God. "Thanks, hon," Ava said as she cringed, wondering what Jimmie thought. Please let there be a fire on the boat right now. We all have to evacuate, go home, get into comfy pajamas.

Tanya boarded the boat, wobbling in silver heels that matched Ava's exactly.

Johntay arrived in an all-white suit, white top hat, and silver-tipped cane. Like the rest of the boys, he stayed in his limo a minute longer to put on white sneakers straight from the box. The scent of pot hung over him like a cloud.

"Smells like college," Jimmie said.

"Look at youuuuu!" Johntay said. "This your husband, Ms. L?"

While Ava died, Jimmie shook his hand. "Just a date. Glad to meet you."

Francisco wore a pinstripe suit and fedora. He resembled an old-time gangster. The girl on his arm didn't go to Ida B. Her dress, tiers of white lace.

Jimmie stood back. "Classy."

It took a while for the kids to start dancing. The boat lurched and rocked on the open seas. Ava braced herself in what could have passed as a defensive lineman's stance.

Pants was looking green.

When Ava spied Tanya heading out the back door with Johntay and his date close behind, she put a hand on Jimmie's arm. "Excuse me."

Outside, cool night air blew salty spray onto the deck. To Ava's horror, Tanya was instructing Johntay to hold her out over the bow. "Like that white girl in *Titanic*."

"Tanya!" Ava shouted, "Get away from there!"

Mr. Brennan, the older history teacher, came toward them from the other side of the deck.

Johntay's eyes were cloudy as he took a grip somewhere around Tanya's bare midsection. When the boat lurched, they lunged toward the Bay.

"Noooo!" Ava ripped a life jacket from the wall, but Mr. Brennan was there, grabbing onto Johntay, pulling hard. All three fell backward onto the deck.

"Hey there!" a crewmate shouted.

Ava stared. Where were you a second ago?

The man wagged a finger at the tangle of legs, bare skin, white sneakers. "No one's allowed out here. You have to get back inside."

Ava hugged the life vest to her chest, heart pounding.

The history teacher brought himself to his feet. He wiped his face with his shirtsleeve. "I think I'll stay here awhile," he said, nodding at the deck hand. "You're going to need help keeping them out of the water."

Tanya, still hanging on to Johntay, gave a high-pitched laugh, oblivious to the adults, the raging waters below. "I'ma get me a boat someday!" she declared. "You want a boat, Johntay? I'ma get you a boat too. We gone get lit!"

Ava wondered if, in addition to the girl's shawl, Pants could stipulate Tanya also wear a life preserver the rest of the boat ride. It was going to be a very long night. Goddamn it, Pants.

Eventually, the ship's captain retreated to less turbulent waters. The staff breathed a sigh of relief. The kids were getting louder, eyes even more glassy. Ava worried that, if the Coast Guard pulled them over, the smoke wafting from the decks would be enough to put the adults in jail. Note to self: Never bring a date to Prom. Especially when it's on a boat. Especially when you both could end up in the pokey.

Cheryl wobbled over. "Whooweee! Had to take a break from bathroom duty. I'm in there reeking like a pot farm. Girls flush the evidence before I can nail them. I'm so high now, I'm moving in slow-mo. Besides," she smiled, "It would be a shame to miss the party. Who's your date?"

Ava smiled. "Cheryl, meet Jimmie. Where's your husband?"

"At home. Says after bathroom duty last year, he's still got a buzz." Cheryl skipped the handshake, enveloped Jimmie in a bear hug.

Another waft of pot, stronger, shrouded their section of the room. Ava hoped the captain was stuffing towels around his door. The last thing this ship needed was a captain hot boxing at the helm.

Hip-hop music pounded. Girls straddled their partners, the dance floor transforming into an underage strip club.

Ava froze. Oh, shit.

"Wow," Jimmie breathed, the future revealed to a hapless time traveler. "This is what they do now?"

Tanya dug her booty into a young man's crotch, backing him all the way across the dance floor.

Ava gasped.

"That's a really strong girl," Jimmie mused.

Cheryl started for Tanya. "Oh no she doesn't. No one's making babies on my watch."

Then Salsa music. Trombones, claves, maracas. The dance floor cleared. Ava stared as Latino students became ballroom dancers. *Thank you.*

K'Ron and Francisco were among those on the dance floor. Holding tight to their partners, years of practice shone in intricate footwork, spins.

The General took out his phone, videotaped K'Ron spinning and stomping. Later, Ava spotted the two of them dancing, swaying to one of the evening's three slow songs.

Near the end of the night, Pants crowned Ken Prom Prince. He wore a purple sparkle suit and a silver tie. His Mohawk was tinted with silver paint.

"Ken, you my boo!" Paris shouted.

A girl yelled, "You fitted, Ken!"

He preened. "I know."

When Pants called out Johntay's name as Prom King, he blushed scarlet. He shuffled to the center of the dance floor, protesting, "Ya'll who voted for me—we ain't cool no more!" But his beautiful grin was ear to ear.

Pants handed the king a microphone and music began.

Johntay shouted, "Clap your hands everybody!"

Kids and a few adults hustled to form three long lines, clapping to the beat.

Ava stared—a line dance that wasn't to a country song?

Johntay yelled, "Slide to the left!"

Everyone slid as if their legs were pulled by magnets under the floor.

"Take it back now, ya'll!"

The kids took a few large steps back, legs moving in unison. The General's face contorted from shy kid to a young man who knew how to get his groove on, *RIP Lil Eddy* painted on the back of his tux.

Stella sidled up to Ava and Jimmie. "Introduce me to your date," she said. "This man's so good-looking, you may just have to fight me for him." Stella paused, giving Ava's outfit a long look. "Wow. Was Vegas having a sale? That's a hot dress."

Fuuuuuuuuck. I knew I shouldn't have worn the dress. Why does Ruthie own a dress like this? Now everyone thinks I own a dress like this. But she was here. Prom was happening. Just don't look down. She took a breath. "Stella, Jimmie. Back off, lady. Now explain this dance that isn't a country song."

Stella said, "It's the *Cha Cha Slide*. DJ Casper."

Ava and Jimmie looked at one another. Obviously.

Johntay barked, "One hop this time!"

All shades of brown kids wiggled their hips. Even Fifty, the security guard took part, weaving and stomping. Johntay's grin spanned his entire face.

Ava smiled at her date, her dress horror forgotten. "I've died and gone to heaven."

"You like line dancing?"

"Yes, but I'm terrible at it. Give me a country bar and I'm a happy woman."

"What else makes you happy?"

"It's embarrassing."

"Guilty pleasures are the best kind."

"Karaoke."

Jimmie winced. "You had to say that, didn't you?"

"No pressure. It's just that Karaoke's the one thing where you're supposed to look ridiculous. It's freeing. I know it's not everyone's thing."

"Hey, I've got my marching orders. Line dancing and karaoke it is. I've just got to brush up on my DJ Casper. And my two-step." Jimmie looked her up and down. "All I ask is that you wear that dress."

Prom finally, interminably, over, the kids were picked up by family, limos, the city bus. Some simply walked out into the night, hanging onto their dates, laughter piercing the sleeping city. In this neighborhood, they were safe. And it felt good to be safe and young and pretty and loud.

Jimmie helped with cleanup before they finally retreated to the quiet, smoke-free sanctuary of his car. "You'll probably want to fumigate that suit before you wear it again," she warned. "And, now, your car too."

Jimmie leaned over, squeezed her hand. "It's much better than New Car smell. People will think I'm cooler than I am. I'm keeping it this way."

Ava was so glad when they finally pulled onto her street. It was midnight. Her feet ached. She couldn't wait to get out of this dress forever.

Jimmie walked with her to her apartment door. "That was fun."

Ava chuckled. "That was a disaster. I owe you. No more Proms on a boat." Then she wished the words back. Did he think she was implying they'd be dating next year? *Shit. Shitshitshitshitshit—*

Jimmie leaned in, gave her a hug. "I had fun. We still on for Karaoke?"

"I'm in if you are."

He squeezed her elbow. She wondered if he would kiss her again. She'd heard about the second date diss—men not wanting to bother with endings, explanations, so they'd give a non-committal,

"It was great," say good-night, and disappear. Is that what he's doing? She hesitated a moment by her door.

Then, like a bad movie, Jimmie waved, turned back to get in his car, and started the engine. Then he was gone. *Gone? What the fuck, gone?* Last time, there was a kiss. It was a cheek kiss, but it was a kiss. This was a hug and an elbow squeeze. They may as well have fist bumped. But he liked the dress. He made another date. She opened the door to her apartment, hopes sinking. What does this mean?

CHAPTER 55

STEP 9: STREET SWEEPING

Ava stumbled upon the workshop video one dreary afternoon mid-April. Metta Annie on *YouTube*, taking an angry woman though questions about her life, her resentments of her mother. Ten minutes later, Annie and the woman joked like old friends, the woman chuckling at herself and what she had believed for so long. Creases of fury around her mouth transmuted into laugh lines. Ava booked a weekend workshop just three weeks away. For the hundredth time, she wished that, even though her parents hadn't put aside money to pay for her college, they had the foresight to save up for her future therapy.

The transaction complete, her credit card winning the war, Ava looked out her bedroom window at the April fog threading through the city. She should grade a few papers while she still had energy, but there was something else she needed to do first to finish for her Adult Children of Alcoholics group.

Now that Steps Six and Seven were done—Church: Check. Asking God to remove all her shortcomings: Meh—Ava felt she was flying through the rest of the twelve steps. A little speed bump at Step Eight: Made a list of all persons we had harmed and be-came willing to make amends to them all. It was her own mini Mt. Everest.

"It's like cleaning up your side of the street," Lydia explained. "You're only worried about making amends for the harms you've caused—to yourself and to others. Besides, Step Eight is just ask-ing you be willing to make amends."

Ava got that. Willing to…Yes, I can be willing to.

And then, a full, screeching halt at Step Nine: Made direct amends to such people wherever possible. Shit.

She sat on her bed with the phone in her hands. You could just send her an email. But, no. Not for this. Lydia was sweet as a muf-fin most of the time, but failure to make progress on ACA Steps turned that muffin mean. Ava dialed her mom's number before her courage evaporated.

Her mom picked up on the second ring. "Sweetheart! So glad you called."

And Ava had to admit, Mom had always been happy to hear her voice. Even when she had pushed her mom away, taking Dad's side in the divorce.

"Hi, Mom," she said. "Do you have some time? I'd like to talk to you about something."

"Of course I have time for you!"

Ava smiled. That's my mom. She took a deep breath, and asked that God, Johntay, and Anne Lamott grant her the strength to spit this out. "Well, I…um…I'm sorry I was such a shit when I was a teenager."

"Oh," Mom breathed. Ava could hear the smile slide off her face.

"And I'm sorry I was mean to you about Dad."

"Oh."

"I didn't understand that it was hard for you, too."

"Oh, honey." Years of hurt were in Mom's voice.

Ava took a breath. "And I'm sorry about how I treated the guys you dated after. I shouldn't have written in permanent marker on that guy's car."

"What guy's car?" Mom sounded apprehensive, like she was finding an unopened bill years later.

"Your boyfriend. The court reporter."

"I didn't know you did that."

"Well…."

"What did you write?"

"*I'm stupid.*"

Her mom gave a shaky laugh. "Well, I guess you weren't too far off. Should I be checking your stepdad's car as well?"

"Naw, Randy's been cool."

"Well that's a relief. You're a writer, not a graffiti artist honey."

Ava was silent.

"Is that all, Lovey?"

Ava pushed her voice through the hard, painful block in her throat. "It was bad. With Dad. It was bad. One time, he had a gun. He was going to kill you."

The line went silent. Then Mom's voice, soft, tired. "I knew about the threats. He made them all the time when it was just the two of us talking. I'm so sorry. He loved you kids so much. I really thought he was better when he was with you."

Ava understood. It was what she had to think, too, when she fled for college and left Livvie alone. "I didn't tell you. You couldn't have known how he'd be without you there. If I had to do it over again, I'd speak up."

When she got off the phone with her mom, Ava wanted to be done, but her list still had a few more names. She dialed Livvie. Again, it felt like she was taking a step toward "warmer, warmer" in the Hot and Cold game. Warmer may be closer to the goal, but it still felt like shit.

"Hey," Ava heard her own voice on the other end of the line. She and Livvie looked and sounded so much alike, it was eerie seeing photos from family functions.

"What's up?" Livvie asked. Ava pictured her taller, thinner doppelganger on the other end of the line.

"You busy?"

"Making lunch. Leo's decided that he won't eat anything that's not purple. Makes for interesting cuisine."

Ava pictured her manly, three-year-old nephew. Upright walker. Master of fine motor skills. Lover of knock-knock jokes. Eater of all things purple. It was hard not to worship the kid. "I won't keep you long. Just have something I need to say about Dad." Ava felt the guilt stab into her chest, so unworthy of her angelic sister.

"Oh," Livvie's tone mimicked Mom's.

"I deserted you by moving out early. You were left alone with him, for almost a year. I didn't come back for you. I didn't even acknowledge that I left you behind."

Livvie sighed. "Oh, Ave. You don't have to apologize."

"No. I do. And an apology doesn't come close to what I owe you."

Livvie was quiet a moment. "I don't think about it all that much. I don't really want to. I chose to see it all as a play. He was acting a part. We all were."

"But you were alone." Ava hoped her sister couldn't hear her cry.

"Aww," Livvie's voice was sturdy, the family rock. "He was gone a lot—working, fighting fires. Besides, I have a lot of good memories. That's what I tell Leo. His grandpa was eccentric. I don't go there with the bad. Don't you remember how Dad would hide things around the house? Make a treasure hunt with clues. Then he'd tell us to hide things from each other, make our own clues. It wasn't bad all the time. He loved us."

Ava had no memories of the treasure hunts. She wished she did. She listened to Livvie describe Leo's latest adventures, his love of dinosaurs and *National Geographic*. Like Ruthie's Benjamin, Leo would grow up in the safety of his parents' love. He was lucky. He didn't have to be on a list of kids Ava worried over. Anyway, she was beginning to see that Stella might be right; other people's lives weren't hers to save. It was enough to clean up her own. She hung up the phone, letting her sister get back to lunch and Leo.

Lying back on her bed, she searched for a good memory of their dad. Mostly, she remembered him driving hours to every ballgame, every school function whether he was in the mood, or, more often, not.

And what else...? She remembered driving the old red Ford down their dirt road, Dad teaching her how to use a stick shift. Alan and Livvie were at her mercy in the truck bed. Her brother and sister lurched and slammed against the wheel wells as Ava hit the gas, then the brakes. She and Dad laughed and laughed, alternating between flying, then screeching to a dead halt, down the dusty road toward home.

She also remembered those rare instances of driving with her dad alone. In silence, he kept one hand on the wheel, holding out the other. Ava took it. She felt his loneliness. They spent the whole drive that way, not saying anything, the radio off, just silently holding hands. One time, Dad confided, "You know, Ave, your brother told me something that really hurt."

She held her breath, waiting for the storm to rain down.

"He told me that he loved his dad, but he hated J.W." Dad began to cry. "I hate J.W. too."

Now, in San Francisco, the landscape was different, and so was the truck, but the memories leapt up as though Dad was here now. While she couldn't take Livvie's rosy view, Ava allowed some of the good memories to float to the surface. He hadn't wanted to be sick. Or mean. Yet he was. And that was still so, so sad.

The phone rang. Livvie? No—Jimmie. She let it ring another time. She didn't want to answer. He likely wanted to break plans for their date next week. But, still, it was better to know. Her stomach turned over. "Hello?"

"I'm a little worried about my two step."

Ohhhh. He's gonna cancel. "Don't worry. We don't have to go. What's said at Prom can stay—"

"I want to go. But I got assigned a business trip."

Riiiiight. He wants a way out. Ava wanted out of the discomfort. "No worries. Okay. Well, then, I'll let you go—"

"No, I want to reschedule. Three weeks. Will that work? I'm really sorry."

He still wants to go. With me.

"Yes," said Ava. She hoped he couldn't hear the grin that spread like forgiveness across her face.

CHAPTER 56
FIRE II

A few days later, schools started hearing news of lay-off notices not being rescinded when the new budget was approved. Ava's pink slip from March sat on her desk at home. Maybe if she held onto it, its threat really wouldn't come true.

Ida B and other schools in San Francisco were asked to use up the last of the year's budget before they lost that too. This meant that Ava would receive fifty dollars as reimbursement for the eight hundred or so she had spent that year on school supplies.

The secretary handed out the money in envelopes, her air sending the knowing message, "Don't spend it all on drink."

After school that day, Ava and her colleagues went to the pub down the hill, toasting to the unexpected cash and those who may not be back the following year.

Ava wondered what she'd do if she didn't work at Ida B. in the fall. Math, science teachers were in demand, not English teachers. She could waitress, find work in a department store, but teaching was her only honed skill, what she had gone to school for all those years. It was the only thing she wanted to do. When their beers came, she looked into the foam for an answer.

"It's looking like we'll have to strike," Cheryl said. "I'ma get out my signs from '91." You remember how bad that one was?"

"Thirty-six days," Stella said, picking up her beer. "I thought I'd starve before we ended it."

"But we got a two percent raise."

Cheryl sighed, raised her glass. "To taking care of the caretakers."

Ava toasted. Only play with friends who love you.

CHAPTER 57
IS IT TRUE?

April 27th. Friday. She took the day off to drive down through Big Sur's redwoods, the ocean opening up like a book as she crested the hills outside of Monterey. Winding down the two-lane road that hugged the rugged coast, she marveled at the towering hillsides to her left. A sign for a hermitage led up to a dizzying peak. On her right, foamy waves crashed into rocks far below. Then the forest swallowed her up for an hour. Threading her car through tall trees, a tiny sign: *Esalen*.

The retreat institute sat on a cliff overlooking waves, whales, and miles of ocean. She found the cabin she would share with a stranger, set her bag inside, then walked back along a dirt path past the communal farm, the small houses overlooking the water, searching for the space where Annie's workshop was held. She had expected a large building, a conference room, but all she saw was a string of people marching like ants into a large tent. Watch where the people go in. Ava joined the line.

Taking a seat on a folding chair inside, she watched the tent fill. She marveled how normal the other attendees looked, able to cope with their lives and not, say, impose a one-year time frame on living.

Hippie music played overhead: flutes, a lulling melody. The crowd murmured as Annie took the stage. She sat on one of two white, overstuffed chairs, a silver-haired grandma whose living room happened to be in front of a hundred or so people. Annie closed her eyes. The hippie music trilled on. When she opened them, she smiled.

Okay, Ava thought.

Annie was silent.

C'Mon. All around Ava, people shifted in their seats.

Annie scanned the crowd, her gaze steady, luminous, like a beacon. Nervous laughter trickled through the hushed room. People glanced away. They looked down at their shoes, not wanting Annie's pale blue eyes to lock on theirs.

Ava ducked her head as well—Annie wasn't here to see her. But after a minute, she felt silly. Was she going to sit through the whole thing with her head down? This workshop cost her two hundred and fifty dollars. A strike was looming. Shit. There'd better be more to the retreat than this.

She glanced sideways at her fellow workshop attendees. People had grown bolder and were meeting Annie's gaze. A few snickered at the awkward silence. Then they were openly laughing. Ava willed herself to lift her head. Annie's eyes found hers before moving on, and she felt recognized. Like she belonged there.

The hippie music stopped. The grandma on stage clapped her hands together. "Now, who's ready to do The Work?"

From the front row, a balding man with a spare tire raised his hand.

She beckoned him. "Welcome, honey. Come up here and tell us: what's the first thought that's kicking you out of heaven?"

The man's face was weathered. Ava pictured long days out in the wind, sun, cold. Heavy work boots thudded the stage as he walked up. He sank into the chair, one of Annie's helpers handing him a microphone. His shoulders slumped. "My wife doesn't appreciate me."

Annie nodded. "That sounds painful. What an awful thought to live with." She turned to the audience. "I'll bet all of you have had someone in your life who didn't appreciate you the way they should. Think of that person. Do the work with us." Her face held compassion for the man. 'My wife doesn't appreciate me': Is it true?"

He paused, closed his eyes. "Yeah."

Ava felt his hurt, her own chest constricting. She thought about Dan, his jabs, the video games. Their final fight. Dan didn't appreciate me.

Annie repeated slowly, "'My wife doesn't appreciate me'; can you absolutely know that it's true?"

Light reflected off the man's forehead. He thought a long time, the corners of his mouth turning down as the seconds ticked by. "Yeah."

"'My wife doesn't appreciate me:' How do you react, what happens, when you believe that thought?"

Ava saw Dan mocking her in front of their friends. She saw how she shrank inside. She saw herself yelling at him.

The man on stage said, "I wonder what my life's been for. I think about the long hours, how I'm worried all the time about providing, then I see her looking at me like I'm choosing to be at work so late at night."

Annie asked, "And then how do you treat her when you think she doesn't appreciate you?"

"I want to tell her that I'm afraid, but I don't want her to think I'm weak. So I get snippy. I shut down."

Annie nodded. She looked up at the audience. "Snippy and shut down. And we wonder why they aren't appreciative?"

A few people in the crowd chuckled.

"And who would you be without the thought *my wife doesn't appreciate me?*"

Ava tried that one. To be without the thought, Dan doesn't appreciate me—That was new. She saw him opening his mouth, making a comment. She could see that in his head, he was expecting her to laugh. That was Dan. Jabs were what he did: he made jabs at people all the time, including her. Fish swam. Dogs barked. Dan jabbed.

In his overstuffed chair, the man sighed. The tightness around his forehead eased. "I'd feel lighter. I'd feel better about being a provider. I might even hear what it is she's so unhappy about."

"So with the thought: stress, snippy, shut down." Annie ticked off her fingers. "Without the thought: lighter, open, listening. I'm just noticing. Why don't you try a turnaround now to the thought, 'My wife doesn't appreciate me.' Try turning it around to the self."

The man hesitated a moment. "I don't appreciate me?"

"Can you find a time when that's been true?"

His big shoulders shook. He covered his face with his hands.

Ava took the thought inside. I don't appreciate me. Not giving herself credit for making it work at school, calling herself names, assuming she wasn't wanted at ballgames, with Jimmie. She put herself down all the time. She didn't need Dan to do it.

Annie gave the man some time. Then she said gently, "I like the part where you think her appreciating you is so easy. Really? You try it."

He laughed, wiped at his face with a tissue.

Annie smiled. "The only person whose job it is to appreciate you is you. Can you find one example?"

He nodded. "I took in three foster kids."

"Well! I think you could have three reasons right there," Annie chuckled, "but where there's three, there's four."

"I spend every weekend taking the kids to their soccer games, ballet practice."

"Yes. I think you'll find a lot to appreciate when you let yourself sit with it a while. Let's try another turnaround now. Can you turn around the statement to the other?"

He thought a moment. "Hmm—I don't appreciate my wife?" His face fell. Slowly, he nodded. "Huh. Yeah. I can see how it could be true that I don't appreciate her. I guess I don't think about what it takes for her to get our kids to school, to their sports. I don't appreciate that she works too, wants to spend time with me."

Ava thought about that a moment. I didn't appreciate Dan. After the put-downs, the Dominoes game, she found it hard to acknowledge Dan's appreciable qualities. She closed her eyes. She saw him supporting her efforts in the classroom, wanting to visit her in San Francisco, coming home with her for Christmas when they both knew it made him uncomfortable. And what else? Another way she could appreciate Dan? She saw him popping out of bed in the morning, suggesting they go camping, loading sleds onto his car, making reservations for white water rafting. When he stopped suggesting fun outings, she blamed him. Ava realized with a shock, I never initiated those things myself.

Annie nodded. "Can you turn 'My wife doesn't appreciate me' to the opposite?"

"My wife *does* appreciate me." The man's shoulders softened, Atlas permitted to rest a moment. Sisyphus allowed a union break. "I can see that," he said. "I can see the things she does to show me she loves me, like making my lunch, rubbing my back. She's watching the kids this weekend so I can be here. It's true. And...it feels better."

"Yes," said Annie. "Maybe you can tell her in detail how much you appreciate her when you get home."

Ava nodded. She and Dan weren't compatible, but that didn't mean she couldn't appreciate him. Some of her anger, resentment dissipated. She remembered the phrase from her mushroom journey, Mama's words. Only play with thoughts that love you.

The rest of the day was a deluge of turnarounds, feelings, and the growing feeling that Ava had some apologies to make. Annie said that when you realize that the fault lies with you, it feels better to find a way to make amends. Which is what Steps 8 and 9 of Adult Children of Alcoholics said too: Take responsibility. Clean up your side of the street. And, in her mushroom journey, Ava supposed that was what the end of the journey was all about—Stella, Mom, and Ruthie in the sailboat, telling her that she was the one who had to steer. "*We've* been waiting on *you.*" Ava needed to take responsibility for her past with Dad. For her present with the kids and Jimmie. And for her future as a teacher. Nyquil, Ambien were for people who wanted to sleep. She was ready to be awake now.

She gave a small smile to her roommate when they met in the yurt. Then she corrected herself, held out her hand and looked the woman in the eyes. "I'm Ava. So glad you're here. Is this your first workshop too?"

CHAPTER 58
COLUMBINE LOCKS

It took just four days back at school for Metta Annie's peaces.

Ava was teaching her afternoon senior English class on a quiet, sunny afternoon marking the end of April when she heard shouts and screams from down the hall.

Her students were at the door in an instant, scavengers to a bleeding carcass. Ava fought her way to the front.

In the hallway, Fifty and several teachers were breaking up a fight between three boys and two grown men.

Outsiders, Ava thought, adrenaline pounding.

Fifty had a grip on a thirtyish black man in a white tee and work pants, but the man yanked free from the aging security guard and took off down the stairs. His companion followed.

Mr. Brennan, the history teacher, had his arms wrapped around one of Ida B's warring male students. Blood poured off the student's lip, a black eye forming.

Another kid took a swing at the boy, the punch glancing off the side of his bruised face.

Students in the hallway roared like Roman spectators in The Coliseum.

Bursting out of the throngs of shouting kids, Charnikka barreled toward the boys, yelling, "Get yo hands of my cousin!"

A girl Ava recognized stepped out, clothes-lining Charnikka with one long, bony arm. "You tell your cousin he's gone get fucked up by my brother, bitch!"

Charnikka rocked for balance. She grabbed the girl's shirt, ripping it halfway off, Kenya's bra on display for the entire second floor.

The hallway pulsed with students hoping to see blood.

"Oh, shit!"

"Hit the bitch!"

"Pull her weave!"

"Charnikka!" Ava shouted. "Let her go!"

Fifty and another teacher now had hold of the two boys, wrestling them down the stairway.

The vice principal held Charnikka tight while Ida B's janitor grabbed for Kenya.

Wrenching free, Kenya slashed her nails across Charnikka's face.

Ava knew she wasn't ever supposed to touch a student. *Still...* She wrapped her arms around Kenya's waist and pulled. It was like hanging onto a carnival ride in a hurricane. "Help me!" Her fingers slipped. "Somebody grab her!"

Kenya swung her around, and Ava fell on her butt, spinning from the velocity. Her fourth period let out an "Aaaahhhh!" as though watching a fireworks display.

She looked up into a forest of jostling arms and legs. The kids above her pushed in toward the girls. Then Tanya's neon braids were in Ava's face. She grabbed Ava's arm, dragging her away from the fighting in the hall. "Don't you push my teacher!" she yelled at Kenya.

The vice principal managed to hustle Charnikka down the stairs while Fifty and another teacher wrestled Kenya to the floor.

Lacking a show, students reluctantly shuffled back into their classrooms. Because the fight began with outsiders, Pants called for a whole-school lockdown that lasted an hour. *A bit too late for that*, Ava thought. Police were called. Students were buzzing, restless, thrilled.

After school, Pants called an emergency faculty meeting to debrief on the day's events. It did not help Ava's confidence to see the principal had been crying. "First of all," she said, "I'd like to thank everyone, especially Mr. Brennan and our security team, for staying calm in a crisis."

Mr. Brennan did not look like he felt calm. He face was pale, his hands shaking as he held onto a cup of tea from Wellness.

"By now many of you may have heard that we had outsiders on campus today—men came in to Mr. Brennan's third period class, apparently looking for Will Bozeman and Trevor White. When the first man saw Trevor, he picked up an overhead projector and threw it at Trevor's head."

The faculty drew a collective breath.

"Thankfully, it missed, but the other man started attacking Will, and did some damage before Mr. Brennan and security were able to break them apart. We think Devon Smith was involved in calling the men to come into school. He's been suspended for fighting and for having a knife."

Cheryl said, "This is why I keep saying we need Columbine locks."

Pants threw up her hands. "And there's still no money to pay for them. What can I say?"

Mr. Brennan put his mug down slowly. "If either man had had a gun on him, or if the boys had…"

Ava remembered last fall when the homeless man had wandered into her classroom, and now burly thugs had barged into the classroom down the hall. There was nothing to prevent someone coming into her room with a gun and…She felt a chill.

"That's exactly what I'm talking about," said Cheryl. "Columbine locks can be locked from the inside—no one could get into a classroom unless they're let in by a teacher."

"Thanks for pointing that out again, Cheryl," said Pants. "And we are all so thankful that no one today had a gun. We'll all just have to be hyper-vigilant in the coming weeks."

Ava watched Cheryl stew: Cheryl was the only faculty member who had been on staff eight years earlier, when a man with a gun had come into the computer lab. The teacher in charge of the class at the time stood between the man and the students while the gunman fired a shot into the room. The bullet skimmed the teacher's head and lodged in the wall. Cheryl showed Ava the divot during her first week at school. "Lock your doors whenever possible," Cheryl said then. "It's technically illegal and pisses off the principal, but I think this reality has far more serious consequences."

"So let me see if I have this right," Cheryl said loudly, slowly. "We don't have money for another security guard, Columbine locks, metal detectors, or security cameras. We don't have money for a PE teacher, music teacher, or college and career counselor. There is barely money to cover our counseling interns, and no money to supplement kids' snacks, which I bring from home every day. There is no money to pay for the supplementary materials I buy for my classroom, and the school district negotiated away our cost of living raises two years ago so they wouldn't fire a hundred more teachers."

Ava's future came into view. It was terrifying.

Cheryl collected her things. "I'm sorry," she told the room, "but I've got work to do in my classroom." She turned to Pants. "Emilia, I'ma need you to tell the school district we need some help here 'cause right now they're asking me to conspire with a system that I get no say in and do not condone."

She stood up. "When someone wants to start talking about putting social services back into schools, giving teachers back our professional autonomy, funding all schools like brown kids matter too, and ending this goddamn school segregation, I'm your woman." She walked out of the room. "Until then, you can tell the superintendent exactly where he can place his joy."

Pants glared at the remaining staff. "It's not my fault."

Mr. Brennan put down his tea and rose. "I'm going to excuse myself as well. I need to get my lessons together for next week. Maybe, as tomorrow's a furlough day, we can all use that time to ask ourselves and our voting neighbors, how did we get into this mess?"

Ava sat silent, as did the rest of the faculty. She was embarrassed for Pants, upset for everyone in the room, and angry at herself for not having the courage to also speak up. *What do I have to lose?* Her job was likely over by the end of the year anyway.

Still, the thought lingered: what power did Pants, in her polyester slacks, serving at the pleasure of the superintendent, really have?

Absolutely none.

The superintendent and his army of assistant superintendents, for all Cheryl's high-minded speeches, hadn't come into office last year wanting Pants' opinion, let alone teachers'. The school board, the only oversight for administrations, was made up of seven busy people with other full-time jobs. So where do I protest? Ava sat frozen, silently fuming, until Pants dismissed them all.

CHAPTER 59
THE DANCE

May 5th. On Wednesday, union members voted to strike. Thursday, after school was over, Stella opened up to the art room to make picket signs. Cheryl brokered deals with local businesses to use their bathrooms.

Ava had never been through a strike. The idea of not even going into the building to use the restroom was strange. The idea of not being paid for an indefinite period of time while she was on strike made her skip a breath. She traced the lettering on her sign: *Care for the Caretakers.*

Mark Jeffries poked his head in the room, lounging in the doorway. The young Teach for America teacher had recently been giving speeches at TFA meetings, talking about the challenges of urban education. "Looking good," he said.

Stella waved him in, "Come join us."

He shook his head. "I'm heading out the door," he said. "Besides, I can't afford to strike. I'm saving up for the move—PhD program, here I come!" He turned into the hallway, whistling.

Cheryl closed her eyes, her jaw clenched. "And those of us who make teaching our careers can't afford not to strike."

That night, at a local bar in the Mission with Jimmie, Ava heard the first notes of her song begin. The old tug-of-war waged in her mind. She shouldn't like the attention, singing in front of a crowd. It was so not her to be up on the stage. She looked a fool.

And that was exactly why she loved it. It was permission to act the fool. Somewhere deep inside, a buttoned-up part of her took the glasses off, let her hair down.

Ava first cut her Karaoke teeth in Olympia, Washington. Going out with her roommate after two bottles of rhubarb wine, she found herself on stage, staring down into the sea of jaded hipster faces. She'd never make it playing it straight. Besides, she couldn't do straight. She'd give 'em a country song—a ballad so uncool it rocked them out of their skinny jeans. And for God sakes, girl-friend, you better shake what your mama gave you.

Ava laid it on, only really understanding mid-verse that the song she'd chosen was about spousal abuse. *She tried to pretend he wasn't drinking again, but Daddy left the proof on her cheek.* There was no turning back now.

She shook harder, sang louder: *Well she lit up the sky that fourth of July/ By the time that the fireman come/ They just put out the flames, and took down some names/ And sent me to the county home/ Now I ain't saying it's right or it's wrong/ But maybe it's the only way/ Talk about your revolution/ It's Independence Day.*

The audience roared. Ava left the stage holding the key to ka-raoke gold: make it absurd. Shake it like the rock star you took the stage to become. It doesn't matter what you sound like, they wanna see your moves. They want to believe.

Now in the heart of the Mission's hipster district, Jimmie right be-low her, she surveyed the crowd. Like shooting fish in a barrel. She assumed her karaoke stance, back to the audience. It was more ridiculous that way.

A man in the front hooted.

Ava raised her microphone in the air.

She spun around. "People are talking, talking 'bout people," she rasped, Bonnie Raitt mixed with frat boy air guitar. Ava hit her knees. "Let's give them something to talk about, a little mystery to figure o-o-o-o-ut."

The crowd pulsed. A hipster waved a five. Ava tucked it into her boot. She dipped the microphone toward Jimmie. "I feel so foolish/ I never noticed/ you act so nervous." She turned to the crowd. "Could you be falling, baby?"

The audience was shouting, dancing, believing.

Ava slinked across the stage, then slid, Tom Cruise in *Risky Business*. An odd feeling spread across her chest, rose into her throat, flooded her senses. *Joy.*

From Mission Karaoke, they drove miles out of town, heading away from hippies, hipsters, and urbanites to find the rednecks. Ava explained the strike to him on the way.

Jimmie looked puzzled, "But isn't cost of living an automatic raise?"

"You'd think so, right?"

When Jimmie pulled his car into a parking lot in the middle of podunk no-where, Ava knew she was home. The country bar was crowded, couples on the dance floor. Jimmie purchased a couple of Coors Lights. He guided her to a seat courtside. Ava heard the slide guitar, saw the cowboy boots and hats. She looked at her date, smiling with her whole body. "I'm a pig in shit right now."

"Such a romantic." Jimmie held out his hand. "Dance?'

"I'm terrible," she warned.

"So am I. Dance?'

She took his hand. It was rough, cool. Her fingers felt safe. His other hand found the small of her back. They slipped into the round of couples two-stepping clockwise. George Strait sang in the background *I'm a fireman, that's my name.*

Fireman. Fired. The strike. Ava could be spending her last few weeks on the picket line, sinking deeper into debt, only to be fired at the end of the year.

She shook her head. Buck up, Buttercup. That would be another day. This night was happening now.

Jimmie looked down, pushed the hair away from her eye. "Did I tell you I'm a volunteer firefighter?"

"Imagine that." His scent, smoky. Solid. She knew something had to be wrong with him. This was a bit too perfect. The fall was going to be hell. But, just for tonight, Ava let go of the fear. She felt the music, boots shuffling on the dance floor, her karaoke alter ego. It's the freakin' weekend, Baby, I'm about to have me some fun. She rested her head against his chest. She leaned in.

Jimmie pulled her tight, spun her around. "Now, I didn't spend the past three weeks on YouTube learning to two-step for nothing, boss." He whispered, "Let's give them something to talk about."

Later, outside her apartment, Ava finished her story, "…I thought the car was going to explode, so I just ran. I should have mentioned it to the people walking past, but sometimes that's when you know you need to work at being a better person."

Jimmie smiled, his eyes on her face. They were at her door. Time slowed. He leaned in. She held her breath as his lips touched hers, a sweet kiss, then not so sweet—hard, soft, and everything in between.

His hands slid to her waist and pressed her to him.

A shock ran through her. Ava dropped her purse onto the sidewalk, ran her hands along his back, felt the muscles flex in his shoulders.

After twenty minutes, he whispered, "Take you out tomorrow?"

She came up for air. "Yes."

CHAPTER 60
DEM BONES

Mrs. Collins had agreed over the phone to come this morning if Ava would pick her up. It was the very last thing Ava wanted to do. Picking up Ms. Collins made it real. She would rather worry about the strike coming up on Tuesday, losing her pay and maybe her job.

No, Ava most definitely did not want to go to Hunter's Point. She wanted to stay here at home, a strong cup of coffee steaming comfort into the air, light streaming through her bedroom window. She wanted to think about it being mid-May, school almost over. She wanted to think about her evening with Jimmie, going to a movie, his hand taking hers in the dark, the make-out session in his car, her nerves humming, thrilling.

She'd rather think about the hippie weekend she spent at Esalen retreat, using *The Work* to turn around stress and transform it into empowerment. But there wasn't any empowerment in what she had to do today.

She glanced at her watch: it was time. She GPS'd the address, stepped into her truck, and drove into Hunter's Point for the first time since moving to the city.

Soon, bustling Mission streets, shopkeepers calling out to mid-morning customers transformed into Potrero neighborhood's empty sidewalks. She passed a Payday Loans storefront, a pawn-shop, and a liquor store before she hooked a left onto Third, the gateway to Hunter's Point.

Ava had been vaguely aware of Hunter's Point before today; most of her black students either lived here or in the Fillmore neighborhood. People spoke of The Point as a place to avoid—drugs, gangs, and violence. Ava took them at their word, but other information had filtered into her consciousness through faculty conversations.

It turned out that Hunter's Point was notorious for having been a Naval shipyard in the 1940s. The Navy had used the area as a living laboratory to decontaminate submarines exposed to radio-active materials, in addition to experimenting on the effects of radioactive materials on living organisms. By the time it shut down Naval operations thirty years later, water, soil, and dust from the site was toxic. In some places, fires burned continuously under-ground, chemical reactions that couldn't be extinguished. Ava wondered how the families living so near to a Superfund site man-aged to avoid its dust. How could the Navy allow housing so close to toxic waste?

She turned off the radio as she drove through streets lacking trees, any greenery. Instead, bars grew like vines over buildings, turning homes and businesses into steel fortresses. A group of young black men hung out on a corner, staring from under dark hoodies. She locked her doors as she drove closer, then felt a wave of shame. The young men could have been any of her students. The click as she unlocked her doors echoed in the silence.

She turned up the hill onto Palou where a broken-down Datsun sat on blocks in a concrete yard. An old man walking his dog stopped to watch Ava as she drove past. It was all so still.

Pulling onto Mrs. Collin's street, she searched for the house number. Was it the light pink house with the broken bottles in the cement yard? Or the one beyond, two cars parked on the sidewalk, against the house, neither of them looking like they had run in the last ten years. Ava checked the number. This was it.

She parked her truck and let out a long breath. Turning off the engine, she closed her eyes. She didn't want it to be real, and getting out would make it real.

She got out.

A pit bull lunged against the neighbor's chain link fence, teeth glistening.

She jumped, putting a hand on her truck. The dog reached the top of the fench with its front legs, barking its intentions.

A woman came out of the pale pink house. "What's going on out here?" She glanced at Ava, then back to the dog. "Get down!" she shouted. "I said, Get! Down!" The dog gave a few more warning barks then quieted, moving toward the back of the house. The woman put her hands on her hips, taking Ava in. "He's harmless," she said. "He won't be if you get in there with him, but he can't get out. You lookin' for Ms. Collins?"

Ava nodded.

"You the teacher?"

"Yes. From Ida B Wells."

The neighbor thought a moment. "Well, I guess he done with that school now. A real shame. My boy went there for a minute, too."

"Ida B?"

"No. YGC. Lot a good it done him. Got shot the week he got out." The woman pointed down the block. "On this street."

Ava looked at the bleak stretch of road. "I'm sorry."

"Me too. Them drug dealers around here lure them kids in like they're Santa Claus. Handin' out cash like it's nothin.' Takin' my son's life like it's nothin.'" The woman sagged a moment, staring down the block. Then she straightened up, waved an arm. "I'll let you get to it. Don't let Jackson scare you."

"Jackson? Is that your dog?" But the woman had gone back inside.

Ava walked up Mrs. Collins' cracked concrete steps and rang the doorbell. She waited a minute. A car drove slowly past, the passenger turning toward Ava. She rang the doorbell again.

From inside, a man yelled, "Get the goddamn door!"

A child wailed.

Ava waited.

The door swung open. "What?" A man in his 60s stared her down.

"I'm Ms. Llewellyn," Ava said. "From Ida B?"

He looked at her. His white undershirt was stained, black sweatpants bagging on his hips.

"I said I'd swing by this morning and pick up Mrs. Collins—to visit Sean."

Finally, recognition dawned. The man grunted, leaving the door open as he walked back into the living room and sat down on the sofa.

She took it as an invitation. The bare bulb in the living room made the off-white walls stark, dingy. A huge flat screen TV took up most of the room, a sagging green couch and rocking chair the only furniture. A few children's toys littered the faded linoleum floor: colored plastic donuts on a yellow cone, a plastic doll with ratted blonde hair.

Ava stood while the man on the couch stared at the movie on TV, an action film with lots of shooting. Who was he? Sean hadn't mentioned a man in the house. Mrs. Collins' husband was dead. Two boys, about nine or ten, poked their heads out from a door to another room. They stared at her. Ava smiled, but they didn't smile back.

Sean's foster mom came into the room, her hair tied up in a scarf. "Goddammit, Jackson, I been asked you to get some milk from the corner store. I ain't making nothing but cereal for break-fast, and that damn CPS woman best not catch me without food in the house again."

Ava stared at Mrs. Collins. The woman's face was angry. A child about two hid behind her leg, wearing only a diaper.

Mrs. Collins' face softened. "I meant to call you but couldn't find the number. I can't go today. Too much to do here. Got a CPS call. This one—" she nodded toward one of the boys hiding behind the door, "told his teacher he was hungry. Woman teaches third graders and she never seen hungry kid before? I asked her, 'Why didn't you just feed him? He done had cereal, we just ran outta milk.'" She looked at Ava. "She coulda called me. She coulda gave the kid a cracker." Ms. Collins sighed. "Now I got to clean up the whole damn place. No time to see a kid who's too stupid not to get hisself locked up." She nodded to the man on the couch. "I see you met Jackson."

Ava nodded.

"My brother. Come to live with us for a while. Laid off after fifteen years with his company."

"I'm sorry," Ava said. It sounded weak, even to her. "And I'm sorry about CPS and that all of this is happening today. Maybe if you wanted to write Sean a letter—"

Mrs. Collins laughed. "I don't think a letter's going to fix stu-pid. No, he can just stay in there, think about what he plans to do now. I got three more boys to take care of, and in this neighbor-hood, that's a full-time job."

Looking around the room, remembering Mrs. Collins' neigh-bor and the neighbor's son, Ava couldn't disagree. "I'll tell him you say hi," she said.

Mrs. Collins only grunted.

The quiet air outside was a relief. Ava stepped into her truck and sat for a moment. This was the neighborhood in which Johntay lived, too. The neighborhood in which many of her black students lived. Being here, seeing it for the first time, she realized nothing about that was right.

Sean was blinking back tears when the guard led him out to the visiting room. He shuffled in flip-flops, a grey sweatshirt, scrub pants. It was like seeing Charlie Brown in handcuffs.

"I'm…I'm not going to make it, Ms. L." He looked so lost, so sad. "Why do bad things keep happening to me? What's wrong with me?"

Ava shook her head. "Not one single thing."

Sean sat on a bolted-down stool. "Then why doesn't anyone w-want me?"

"You're wanted," she said, but it came out weak.

"No. My mom didn't want me. She'd leave me by myself. That's what my foster mom said. When CPS came, I was two, in a messy diaper, all alone. Mrs. Collins says the police couldn't find my mom for three days." Sean's voice was wooden. "I would've died."

Ava felt desperate. "Mrs. Collins wants you."

"Naw, she's too busy."

"Well, she's got those other kids she's worried about too. I stopped by your house this morning. She said to tell you hi."

Sean looked up. "She did?"

Ava nodded. "And you know that I want you, and your teachers at Ida B. want you." But wanting isn't the same thing as taking care of you, loving you like a mom would. "You know, you were the first student to make me laugh at Ida B. Star Wars. You were imitating Darth Vadar, "Ms. L, I ammmmm youuuurr faaathaaaa." But something about that made her sad. "You made me feel welcome when I was feeling new and scared. And your classmates like you—you know they do. Shoot, Tanya invited you to be her date for prom."

Sean shook his head. "She asked Johntay first."

Ava thought a moment. "Well, we have to forgive girls for not always seeing the best guy as their first choice."

A small smile spread across his face. Finally, something that stuck.

Ava looked him in the eyes. "You are the best choice. You were my first choice today. And many, many days in that classroom, you're my first choice. I just don't tell you." Until you get locked up. "I'm sorry for that."

A round tear rolled down Sean's cheek.

Ava handed him a tissue. "Your teachers at Ida B are rooting for you. We are all hoping this turns out okay. But it was a pretty big thing that you did."

He nodded.

Ava sighed. "What happened?"

Sean shook his head, bewildered. "I just wanted them neighborhood boys to leave me alone. It was almost every day."

And for the first time since meeting Sean last August, having just come from his house that morning, Ava had a clear picture of him making his way home on those silent streets. She saw him walking amid the toxic dust of the Superfund, past the concrete yards with houses behind bars. She thought about how he must have felt, stepping off the bus, knowing that someone was waiting near his home to beat him up. She wondered if the boys were drug dealers or just bullies. What had they wanted in harassing Sean? What he was resisting? "Why were they bullying you?" she asked. "What did they want?"

Sean kept his pathetically round, shaved head focused on the floor. "I can't snitch. I didn't have that gun very long. I was just gonna show them boys I wasn't gonna take it no more."

Ava thought a moment about how brave he must have been, how alone, and scared. "But having it on the bus, Sean." Her stomach turned over. "That woman's in the hospital. What if someone had been killed?"

He shuddered, his face grim. "Surprised me when it went off. I thought the safety was on. I never owned a gun before."

"Where did you get it?"

Sean twisted his Kleenex in his hands. "I can't snitch." He looked at the floor.

Ava boiled. She wanted to shake him, yell so loud, he'd finally hear, Why the hell not? You're going to go to jail, Sean. Who were the assholes that gave you to gun? Then she heard her colleague, Cheryl's, voice: These weren't her rules. Ava wasn't a teenager in Hunter's Point. She didn't live with the threats. She didn't live with the poverty, racism, or thwarted opportunities. She stuffed back her words.

Sean had one more request. "Will you ask my foster mom again to come visit? She won't take my calls."

Ava nodded. "Of course." They both knew Mrs. Collins might not show.

Walking out of YGC, the transition from claustrophobia to the cool, free air left her dazed. She had spent two hours in jail, now she was out. Sean had to stay. She would drive away.

She would visit Sean on Sunday, but she wasn't his mom. Neither was Mrs. Collins. It dawned on her that she didn't know the first thing about helping a child who was in foster care. She remembered when Haiti had been devastated by a hurricane. She'd clicked on *Donate*. Fifty seconds of barely helpful effort, but better than nothing. Sean? She didn't even know where to start. How was that possible when she worked with foster kids every day?

Mama, she asked, tell me what to do.

She got in her truck, hung her head, was still. She sat silent a long time, just breathing. Amid the traffic noises, the hum of busses passing by, a line from a poem by Edna St. Vincent Millay. The poem was about the inevitability of death, but it still rang clear outside YGC: *I know. But I do not approve. And I am not resigned.*

Ava thought about Sean's trajectory to Ida B. It had been a long road. She remembered a song from when she was little, belted out in kindergarten, "The hip bone's connected to the thigh bone, the thigh bone's connected to the leg bone, the leg bone's connected to..." A two-year-old, alone and hungry in Hunter's Point. CPS. Mrs. Collins. The neighborhood boys. Gun. YGC. Some things just followed, like the leg bone to the knee bone.

But I do not approve. Ms. Collins had taken on four foster kids in Hunter's Point. Boys. Four of them. In Hunter's Point. Sean had made it this far. They were not resigned. Ava didn't know what it would take for Sean's circumstances, for the circumstances of all her black students in Hunter's Point, to change. Would it be a long, plodding movement or an explosive retaliation? Things couldn't go on this way. The weary resolve in Ms. Collins' expression revealed that much.

But I do not approve. And I am not resigned. Ava took one last look at the cinderblock building of YGC and the teenagers locked inside. She started up her truck.

When she got home, she called her mom.

"Honey!" Mom said. "It's so great to hear your voice."

CHAPTER 61
THERAPY DOGS

Monday morning. The visit with Sean on her mind, the strike looming, Ava listened to the radio as she got ready for school. A shooting on Mission Street. A seventeen-year-old young black man dead. No name had been released. She had heard about shootings, or stabbings in the Mission before, but they had always seemed removed. Now, she thought about Sean, Johntay, Melvin. Francisco. Hunter's point wasn't the only neighborhood her kids lived in that wasn't safe. It could be one of ours.

She scrambled for her laptop, searching for the details online, but it didn't make the local beat. Cheryl said that only a few of the murders made the news. There were just too many.

Ava walked to school thinking about Sean, the shooting in the Mission, and about the strike. Tomorrow she would again take this route, but she wouldn't be going in the school building. She would stand outside the school holding a sign and shouting slogans.

A small black child wearing a backpack, no older than six or seven, stood at a public bus stop. He was waiting for the 49 or maybe the 14. By himself. There were no yellow busses to take the general population of kids to school. Busses were reserved for special cases, extreme disabilities. And yet there was no money for this boy's parent to take him either. So he took himself to school. Waiting at bus stops where kids like Johntay's friend, Trey, had been shot in the face. The same streets on which a teenager had been killed only the night before.

Ava didn't know whether to be upset at the parents, the school board, the superintendent, or if she should point the finger first at herself. She would walk past this six-year-old boy this morning. She wouldn't see him onto the bus, wouldn't ride the bus with him to his school, wouldn't tell anyone, including Ruthie, about him because the problem was just too big. Even as she prepared to rise up to strike.

At school, three girls huddled in the hallway near her room. "Three times! In the chest!" one girl told her friends. Her braids shook with...what? Fear? Anger?

Ava sidled up to the conversation, aware she was, as students called it, "ear hustling." She asked, "Who was it?"

The girl turned, pausing a moment before answering. "My cousin."

Who was her cousin? Not Johntay. Not the General. "I'm so sorry," Ava said. "Your cousin?"

"My play-cousin." The girl shrugged. "We been friends for a minute. He come over and chill. Now he dead." She pointed to a boy's picture on the placard around her neck. "Bookie. My cousin."

Ava stared at the boy. Not one of her kids. Someone's child, someone's world, this girl's play cousin, but not one of her kids. Thank you. "I'm sorry."

That morning, Wellness brought therapy dogs in to visit classrooms. Though the special education teacher down the hall was one gun law away from a rampage after students put M&Ms into his fish tank, Mary Kline said that that was an unfortunate, isolated incident, and the students deserved another chance at bonding with animals. Therapy dogs had gained a reputation for having a calming effect on those suffering from PTSD and other traumas.

Ava wondered if Wellness could bring in therapy dogs every day. She daydreamed about a therapy dog keeping her company on the picket line tomorrow. And the next day. And, quite likely, the next. In fact, the more Ava allowed herself to play out how long a strike could last, the more therapy dogs sounded like a good idea.

"This is Maya, everybody," Mary told the class, introducing the yellow lab with a blue *Therapy Dog* jacket. "Maya's owner, Anne, is going to walk her around the room. If you'd like to, Maya loves to be petted."

The kids looked at Anne, a volunteer from the community, standing cheerfully next to her furry, pedigreed social worker. They glanced at Maya.

"You should let Ms. L pet Maya first," Paris said.

"Yeah," the rest of the class agreed.

"You go first, Ms. L," said Melvin.

Ava wondered if they were afraid of Maya, or just too raw from news of the shooting to let in even a dog. She bent down to give Maya a scratch behind the ears. Sometimes the kids were more generous of spirit than she gave them credit for.

Johntay nodded. "You work hard, Ms. L." He sounded concerned.

Okay, now this is getting suspicious.

"Did you get enough sleep last night?" Tanya asked quietly.

Ava sank her fingers into Maya's thick fur, a downy warmth against her skin. "I think so," she said. "Why?"

Tanya looked down, uncomfortable. "Well—something's wrong with your hair."

Ava put a hand to her head, looked around the room for explanation. "What do you mean?"

The kids suddenly became very interested in studying the tables in front of them. Johntay finally said into his hoodie, his twisty dreads poking out, "It's all...messy."

Ava put a hand to her hair. A tuft stuck up in back. Had she really not looked in the mirror that morning? Heat rose into her face.

"That's not nice," Melvin said. "You shouldn't say things like that to Ms. L."

Paris surveyed her teacher. "Yeah, I think it's her clothes. Her hair looks like that every day."

Big Moe, back in school after a week in the hospital for chest palpitations, gave Maya a good rub under her belly. "It sure is hard to keep yourself up when you get older, isn't it, Ms. L?"

Ava looked around at the class, tables strewn with Food Bank apples and their own breakfasts: hot Cheetos. Moe's compassion, two days after monitors and IVs. They want to help me.

She glanced down—she'd missed a button on her sweater. And, in the early morning light, mistaken one black shoe as the pair to a brown one. Not huge in the fashion world, but not a look to inspire confidence, either. And why should I inspire confidence? Who was inspiring her confidence? She was tired.

Ken held up his sparkle purse, "I've got some accessories like this at home I'm not using any more, Ms. L. I could bring some in and you could share them with the other teachers."

"Yeah, like Ms. Wilson," said Paris.

"Or Ms. McGinnis—she really needs a makeover!" declared Tanya.

"I could bring in some earrings," K'Ron said. "You'd look good in big hoops."

Ava nodded. "I'd like that." Accessories. It was a sweet gesture. They wanted her to pull herself together so that she could be there to—to what? Help? No. She couldn't help, not in any real way. Not Sean, not the small boy at the bus stop, not Bookie who was shot, and certainly not these kids in front of her. She would go on strike so that she could fight another day, so that she and other teachers could try, but the problems were so far beyond the classroom, it was enough to make her want to give up.

But they want you to try. You came here to try. She saw these kids, many of them, much more than their parents did. It was Ava's job to model what it was to speak up, to stand tall, to believe in better. Someone had to keep it together. Comb her hair. Know black from brown. She nodded. "You're right, Moe. Some days, it is harder to keep my self up. I'm lucky I have all of you here to help me."

She stood up, smoothed the front of her slacks. "Now," she said, "who's going to pet Maya next?"

That night, news stations carried stories of the strike.

A grim reporter stood in front of the school district headquarters. "Parents are starting to panic. Moms and dads of elementary school children have been calling the mayor's office all day. They don't know what they will do with their children during the workday. With the economy already making those of us in the private sector suffer, is it really the time for teachers to be thinking of fattening their wallets?"

Ava willed the reporter to interview someone who would explain what the strike was about, but the camera cut to the school district spokesperson, a thin woman in a cashmere sweater. "I wouldn't call the teachers greedy exactly..." the spokesperson said.

"Just unwilling to compromise?"

The woman gazed into the camera. "Yes. Sometimes adults have to think about the children. Put their own interests aside."

The camera cut to the mayor. His tie hung askew. "It's been a long day, and it it'll be a long night, but we will find a solution."

Ava wanted to believe. As long as elementary school parents, fearing childcare nightmares, kept calling the mayor's office, there was reason to hope.

She went to bed that night dreading what would be on the news the next morning. I shouldn't have bought that new skirt last week, she thought. She didn't need a new date skirt when she was going to be pounding the streets, waving a sign. If the strike went longer than two weeks, she had no idea how she'd pay her rent.

She awoke around 4:30 and checked the news on her laptop. The strike was off. Relief poured over her like water on a fire. An eleventh hour stay of execution.

She read on: The mayor, in contact with district and union negotiators for weeks, had miraculously found funding at two a.m. in the city's Rainy Day coffers. The union and the district had clashed until three in the morning before brokering a deal: three quarters of teachers who'd been pink-slipped would be granted clemency. Teachers without credentials would be let go, possibly hired back in the fall. Ava would stay at Ida B. No raises over the next few years. More furlough days. All administrator layoff notices were rescinded.

Walking to work that morning, Ava passed the same little boy at the bus stop. He had made it to school yesterday, made it home. Of course he had. Until he doesn't. Today she had to go to school, do her job. She couldn't see him onto the bus or worry about him on a daily basis. It was too much. Still, she was here to try. She saw Sean shuffling in grey sweats in Juvie. *And I am not resigned.*

Ava brought to mind Maya, the therapy dog, how good it had felt to sink into that soft fur. And, just for a second, she was nine years old, the cats on her lap. Pumpkin's raspy purr conveying love, security, a sense of belonging to the world. You have to care for the caretakers. If she was going to teach another year, it really was time to get a pet.

CHAPTER 62
J.W.'S BUNDLE

May 20th. The school year was drawing to a close. The sun now reliably lit up the green hillsides of Marin, but Ava wasn't in the mood to appreciate the scenery. Her mind was on the topic her ACA group had tackled two weeks ago. It was part of Step 8: How do you make amends to someone who's dead? Today, Ava was going to try.

Hiking up Mt. Tam, Lydia huffing some distance behind her, Ava barely noticed the smell of Eucalyptus over the pounding of her chest. But still, when Lydia forced them to take a breather, the older woman wheezing, Ava had to admit she loved the oversized redwoods and the ferns curled around the morning dew. Going for a hike with her dad in the woods had felt like this too: undiscovered country.

One year, Ava thought she saw the figure of a bear high in a tree.

Dad peered at it through his glasses. "Let's take a look."

They tromped through the forest, looking up, assessing, moving on until they stood directly beneath the tree. "It's mistletoe," Dad said.

She was enchanted.

"It can be deadly to the tree. Sucks the nutrients out, but it sure is pretty, isn't it, Avers?"

Ava had stood there with Dad, staring at the tree for a long time, surrounded only by snowflakes falling in the silence of winter.

Now, on Mount Tam, she thought about how little she'd known about her dad. In fact, there were only two stories he'd told her about his past. In the first one, he was eight years old. The bigger boys on the playground had stolen his hat. It was a round felt cap he hated. It made him look like a baby. Arriving back home without the cap, Ava's grandpa silently went to a small tree in the backyard and hacked off a switch. He handed the switch to Dad. "Don't come home without your hat," Grandpa said.

Dad went and found the boys. He beat them until they gave him back his hat.

"Weren't you afraid of them?" Alan asked.

"I was more afraid of your Grandpa," Dad said.

When Dad was in high school, Grandpa became moody, unpredictable.

"He was a maniac," Dad told Ava and her siblings. There was a note of pride in his voice.

"Manic," Mom corrected. "Bipolar."

One day, Dad returned from school to find Grandpa crying. A distant relative had sent him his mother's diary. Grandpa's mother had married a Mr. Llewellyn, a homesteader in Minnesota, after moving to the United States when Grandpa was a baby. His father was not his father.

"He howled," Dad said, the shock of the scene still incomprehensible so many years after Grandpa had died.

Ava's dad had been an actor, a trail boss, a bull rider, a son, and a father. Still, the only movie of him that played in her mind was her dad as despot. He was the terror she had feared, and that fear still ruled her life.

She changed the reel. Another, older picture emerged:

"I want quiet back there," Dad warned, backing the blue Subaru out of the theater's parking lot.

Ava, bedded cozily on the folded-down backseat with Alan and Livy, sighed with contentment. The stars were coming out; she could see them clearly though the rear window, the defroster lines sectioning the night sky into horizontal stripes.

Mom, in the passenger seat, fussed, "It's going to be a long twenty-four hours."

"I know." Dad sighed, putting an arm over her headrest. "Just try to get some sleep. I'm going to want a relief shift tomorrow morning." He still had stage makeup on his jaw.

Mom wiped it with a finger. "We'd better get our story straight before Minneapolis. I'd hate for you to arrive there exhausted only to get an earful from your dad."

Dad laughed, but he didn't sound happy. "Got a standing ovation tonight. The crowd was with me, did you feel it?"

Mom nodded.

"And my old man tells me not to bother calling if I want to dabble with theater in my off-hours. Work a 40-hour week, rehearsals at night, a three-week stretch of performances, and I got to sneak away in the Goddamn night to make it there on time. Like I'm doing something wrong. Fucker."

"J.W., the kids can hear you."

"Better to know their dad didn't let his father run his life."

A hard, unflinching dad. Bundles.

Ava rested against a log. The hike up Mt. Tam had taken them longer than anticipated, but Lydia was a trooper.

Sweating in her tracksuit, Lydia put her hands on her hips. "Phew! That took care of some cake."

Ava unzipped her backpack. "Thanks for doing this. I don't think anyone else would get it." She took out a slim notebook, opening the cover to two familiar photographs. Hi, Dad. She looked up at Lydia.

"I'm an ACA. I'll always get it." Lydia gave Ava's shoulder a squeeze. "Now you do your thing, and I'll pretend I'm meditating instead of having a heart attack."

For the thousandth time that day, Ava was grateful. Only play with friends who love you. She gazed at the photo of Dad's headstone, a bronze circle stamped to look like a rodeo rope. How do you make amends to someone who's dead? Lydia had said the directions were the same: You clean up your side of the street. In the notebook, Ava wrote down what she didn't want to even think: You didn't really love me.

She asked herself the first question Metta Annie posed: *Is it true?* Ava heard Dad growling, "I hate your mother more than I love you." Yes. It was true.

How does it feel to think that thought? She waited a moment. Tears welled up. Defeated, tired, sad. That thought had made certain that every day of her life, she felt unworthy.

Who would I be without that thought? She let her mind go still, set aside the video of his raging, the vein bulging in his temple. With the image gone, it was a transformation, light opening up the darkness. A relief from the heaviness that seconds ago had overwhelmed her. He was just there: Dad. Like Livvie said, it was a play. He was playing his role. It wasn't personal.

She checked her Metta Annie cheat sheet. *Turn it around to the opposite:* He loved me. Ava sat with that for a while. Through all the resentment and sadness, it was hard to even—wait for it. Wait for it. Then she saw it: He cooked us breakfast every weekend. She saw the eggs, the muffins, the bacon steaming on the table. That was one reason why it was true. She remembered what Annie had said: "Where there's one, there's two...."

He rented movies and baked pizza on Friday nights. He came to all of my games. He told me that I was a writer. He played with us. Ava saw her dad, stiff from working outside all week in the cold, tying the sled to the back of the truck. She bumped along with Livvie in the plastic sled up the long driveway, then they flew down those powdery mountain roads. Their turn over, they sat in the truck bed watching Alan grip tight to the sled. Dad couldn't really afford the gas money, but he drove them around on the sled all afternoon.

She could see it: He loved me.

The thought made her more sad than the idea that she wasn't loved. He had loved her. He had loved her siblings too. And he was sick and said mean things. The one didn't negate the other. She sobbed.

After a while, Ava consulted her cheat sheet again. Turn it around to the other: I didn't love him. She waited. Then she felt it. It's true. Not when he said those awful things. And she never told him how much he hurt her. She had been too afraid he would leave.

To the self: I didn't really love me. Yes. She let it go on and on and never told. She should have said something so that Livvie and Alan wouldn't have suffered either. Now, so long after he'd been gone, she still held the thought that she wasn't lovable. She dated jerks who said unkind things to her. I don't love me.

She thought about a poem she had read years ago in college, a line by Mary Oliver: "Someone I loved once gave me/ A box full of darkness./ It took me years to understand/ That this too, was a gift."

What gift had her dad given to her? Ava knew it immediately, from a place inside that was beyond language: Not everyone gets to wake up every morning and decide what mood they will be in. Not everyone gets to love their children as they would like, or, for that matter, be in charge of how they speak to those they love. It was a gift to wake up and have choices. It was a gift to have the ability to choose to be kind.

She took out a lighter she'd confiscated from Francisco. She remembered what Lydia had said: "You can make a living amends. Promise yourself a new behavior you would have liked to have practiced with him."

Ava took a deep breath. I'll tell the truth. Other people have a right to hear the truth. I have a right to the truth. I can clean up my side of the street. She burned the paper. She took responsibility. She accepted the gift.

The next morning, she headed out on a new jogging route. She walked up and over the hill separating the Mission from Noe Valley, aptly nicknamed Snowy Valley for the clear racial boundary. Once out of the crowded, dirty, Mission streets, she jogged down the wider, more jogger-friendly sidewalks amid Snowy's greenery and high-priced shops.

The motivation required for jogging mimicked the delicate negotiations she had seen her sister employ with her toddler nephew: Just put on the jogging clothes. You don't really have to go, just see how you feel with the clothes on. Then, Well, putting on shoes never hurt anyone. You can dance around the room if you don't feel like leaving the apartment. Then, How about just going outside and walking for a bit? You don't have to run if you don't want to. Finally she arrived at, Doesn't this walking feel good? You could start jogging, and if you don't like it, go ahead and walk again. Ava was emotionally exhausted by the time she broke a sweat.

Transitioning into a trot, she felt the heaviness of getting air into her lungs fast enough to fuel her muscles, heart. Her legs pumped, thighs ached. Sweat rose to the surface of her skin. She thought about Sean in YGC. She thought about calling his foster mom, offering again to drive the woman to the jail. Her heart beat faster, lungs working. Ava began to breath heavily.

"Get a room!" a teenager called out.

Asshole. I try to get some exercise and some little shit wants to—Then Ava felt something odd. Someone huffed right beside her, a friend.

That deep, aching loneliness eeked out with her sweat, rolled down her body, dripped to the sidewalk. She looked over at the guy. She wasn't frightened or creeped out. She had a jogging buddy, one with baggy sweatpants, a headband, a few extra pounds. She heard him struggling, saw the sweat. Connection.

Ava knew about an extra roll here and there. "Kinda hard, isn't it?" she gasped aloud between breaths.

They guy just nodded, saving energy for breathing in and out, one foot hitting the ground at a time. It was enough to sweat and jog and breathe.

Several blocks down, he peeled off, nothing personal.

She kept going. The warmth of companionship stayed with her for days.

CHAPTER 63
GREAT AMERICA

May 28th. One week until the end of the school year. Mary Kline, the Wellness counselor, stood next to Ava. They glanced around at the students all lined up, ready to ride the "Terminator" at Great America's theme park. Ava smiled. The kids were counting off in pairs so they all could get on the same ride—finally, some unity. A month ago, Ava's class had softened Mary to the idea of this trip, got her to convince their naïve new teacher to take them. Wellness shook down local businesses and community organizations to pay for the bus. Students negotiated with the theme park for discounted tickets that they paid for themselves.

Watching them now, Ava relaxed a little. To see them all lined up in pairs at the gates, K'Ron and the General holding hands—it made the trip worth having to pull the bus over to ferret out the pot smoker that morning. Except that now the kids were straining forward to see—

"Who that with Johntay?" asked Paris. In the hot sun, she still had on her shiny pink puffy jacket. She squinted toward Johntay and his mystery woman, already boarding the ride in front of them.

"Johntay!" Paris yelled. "Johntay…I know you see me! Who you think you is?" She turned to Melvin, "He probly told her he has a Lexis or some shit."

Melvin looked disgusted. "He isn't even allowed to drive his mom's van."

Paris continued, "Hey Johntay, yo class is right here!"

People began staring.

She hollered louder, "Don't forget, we gotta get back on that bus, Johntay! Our bus is number 201! Remember our bus? Ms. Kline paid fo' that bus! You got on that bus fo' *free*!"

Ava shook her head. Now that girl is doing some cock-blocking.

The class was cracking up.

"You came with your class Johntay! Yo teacher is right here!"

Other kids began getting into it.

"Whoop! Whoop! Who you cupcaking Johntay?"

"You ain't got no Lexus, Johntay, you got yo'self a bus! A big, yellow bus!"

Fortunately for Johntay's dating life, the ride began moving before Paris could say any more.

The rest of the afternoon, Ava watched as students raced from one ride to another, grabbing friends to mug for photos. She marveled how their grins seemed to morph from wary teenagers into elementary school children thrilled to play.

Play. Despite her willing against it, Dan's face appeared in her mind. Dan had known how to play. She didn't. He had been clever and charming and mean, but most of all, she'd stayed with him because he'd known how to play.

So I better get on it, Ava thought. I can't wait around for someone to show me. She buckled herself into a seat behind Melvin.

He turned around to give her a thumbs up. "It's 'bout to be an epidemic on this ride, Ms. L. I'ma lean over if I throw up so it won't hit you."

She smiled. "You're a good man, Melvin." The ride started moving, and Ava found she couldn't think too much about failed relationships, lesson planning, drive-bys, or Juvie. As her turn to crest approached—click….click…click, she took a shallow breath and looked around. The sun sparkled over the bay in the distance, the people down below in the park tiny specks—

Click, click, click, click…Oh, God. All thought erased. Gravity wrenched her downward with exhilarating speed. She let it all go. Her screams merged with Melvin's in the air.

When the day was finally over, the kids dragged themselves onto the bus, dripping with feather boas, overstuffed bears, and foam gloves, favorites from Great America's gift shop.

"Wow," Ava said, surveying their haul, "you really must have saved up for this trip."

Charnikka rolled her eyes.

"What town you from again?" Francisco asked.

Tanya shook her head. "Bet Ms. L pays for all her stuff."

"Yeah, like, here's my money—can I give you more?" said Charnikka.

The kids cracked up.

Ava felt sick. "Um, folks? Anyone have a receipt that they can show me?"

"Lost it," Paris said.

"Me too," said Johntay, donning a feather boa.

"They didn't give me one."

Francisco shook a foam finger. "No hablo Ingles."

"Unh unh."

"Don't gotta show no receipt."

Ava glanced around. Almost every kid was wearing or carrying something that they did not have when they boarded the bus that morning. Since the Wellness coordinator seemed paralyzed with either fear or disbelief, Ava surveyed the crime scene and reviewed her options alone.

"Everyone accounted for?" asked the bus driver.

She envisioned many calls to parents and an evening at the police department. Fingerprinting. Mug shots. Juvenile, or—for some—adult records. Cold concrete benches. The hours spent waiting. Pants' reaction and the feeling Ava would have when she heard the words 'You're fired.'

A year in, all those lessons learned, and Ava felt like she had the first day of school when the students rebelled against rule number one: No Swearing.

Shit. Next time, tell them they can't get back on the bus without an effing receipt. "Yup," she told the driver. "Let's get out of here."

CHAPTER 64

GRADUATION DAY

The last faculty meeting of the year, teachers sat back in their chairs, joking. Months of hard work behind them now, their faces reflected the light of summer ahead. Fifty-two students would graduate this year. More than half of Ida B's two hundred and fifty students had sophomore and freshman credits when they transferred. Catching up after being so behind on credits required a commitment to do more, work harder. Some students made up the credit quickly. Others took the full two years.

Pants handed out a sheet of duties each teacher would be responsible for during the graduation ceremony. Some staff were assigned the task of handing out programs while others would herd and confine the excited graduates to one location until it was time for them to march. Ava's role included "Help guard the stage." She turned to Cheryl, pointing to the list.

Her colleague shook her head. "You'll have to experience it to believe it."

Graduation fell on a warm day in early June. Pants negotiated the use of Mission High School's auditorium, big enough to accommodate graduates' entire families. The fact that it was also in rival *Sureño* territory meant families wouldn't linger on the other school's property after the ceremony was over.

Jimmie parked his car on 18th Street, taking Ava's hand as they walked toward Mission High. Seeing the school's stucco fortress rise against the backdrop of the city, Ava felt a sense of pride that she, too, had made it through this school year.

Melvin stood outside the school building, flanked by his parents and sisters. He had new shoes and slacks under his graduation robe. Around his neck, leis stacked up like a multicolored mane. One lei was made of candy wrapped in plastic; one included a string of folded dollar bills; another, a chain of purple orchids.

"Good morning, Ms. L!" Melvin sang. His mom, tiny in her dress and heels, beamed. She said something in Filipino. Melvin reached into a bag near his feet.

"This is for you," He handed Ava a yellow lei, cold petals startlingly fresh.

His mom extended her hand, "Thank you."

Ava asked Melvin help get the lei over her head. "It's beautiful," she said.

Melvin blushed. "Awww, Ms. L, you know how we Filipinos roll."

Johntay's family was also out front, a large group all wearing white tees, Johntay's face blown up on the front. *Black Man Graduating* was printed under his mug.

The family's tee shirt, its assertion, gave her pause.

Ava remembered how she'd lit up seeing Johntay at the drive-thru window after her stint at church, how he put extra fries in her bag. She remembered his tee shirt assertions over the past year: *I Am a Man*, *Don't Shoot This Man*, and, the one he wore to his own mock trial, *Innocent Black Man*. She thought about him losing his best friend, Trey, and the blood stains Johntay couldn't get out of his white tee. She thought back to the book she'd read in preparation for teaching at Ida B: *Courageous Conversations about Race*. Johntay could write a far more instructive version of the text.

Not far from Johntay, Paris strutted like a runway model in stilettos and a sequined dress. Ava asked her to stand close with Charnikka and K'Ron, also in four-inch heels, for a photo. The girls beamed into the camera, posing this way and that. Ava promised she'd put the pictures up around the school for new kids arriving in the fall.

When the graduates walked in to Pomp and Circumstance, the audience reacted like home team fans at the World Series. Parents screamed, friends tooted horns, and cousins rang cowbells. The graduates took their time strutting down the isles, all smiles in caps and gowns. Some of them would be getting certificates of completion when the ceremony was over—they hadn't passed the Exit Exam. Others would receive the diploma coveted by generations. The audience radiated pride.

These are my kids, Ava thought. She took Jimmie's hand, not knowing what to do with the happiness swelling like a symphony inside. She settled for a grin that spread throughout her whole body.

The graduates took their seats in risers on the stage, waving to families and friends. Half had their phones out, texting. Ava was embarrassed about the kids' lack of etiquette until she glanced around the audience to see that moms, dads, cousins, friends also had their phones out. They were texting, taking pictures, and calling friends and family who weren't there to celebrate with them. Ava pulled out her own phone for a picture of the crowd.

After numerous reprisals of Pomp and Circumstance, the song cut off abruptly. K'Ron walked to the microphone, teetering in sky-high heels. "La bienvenida a la familia y amigos," she said, blushing.

Melvin high-fived her as he took his turn at the podium. "Welcome pamilya at mga kaibigan." He waved to the audience all the way back to his seat.

Ken was next, a purple tie and silver sparkle suit beneath his gown. He bowed. "Kangei, kazoku ya yūjin."

Pants gripped the podium with both hands. "Welcome family and friends to our graduation ceremony."

The audience tooted horns, screamed, rang cowbells—ecstatic fans about to get a win. Enormous balloons blocked everyone's views, got batted about. No one minded: the crowd was just warming up.

When the noise ebbed, Pants shouted into the microphone, "We have a wonderful gradation program for you today, beginning with student speakers who have been chosen by their peers to say a few words. Can you welcome our first speaker?"

The General stood up, tall in his cap and gown. He solemnly made his way to the podium amid the crowd's roaring approval, their vies for graduates' attention.

"General!" Johntay boomed.

"Francisco!" Someone in the audience screamed.

"Gooooo Johntayyyyyy!" Johntay's fan section piped up, cowbells and horns deafening.

"Ronnie!"

"Gabriella!"

"Goooo K'Ron!"

Ava glanced around, anxious for the crowd to let her student speak.

The General, undaunted, waited.

"Quiet, ya'll!" someone yelled.

A woman's voice. "You folks have no manners!"

"Shhhhhh!"

The room grew as quiet as it would likely get. The General began, "Good afternoon," he said, a preacher to his flock.

"Good afternoon," the audience responded.

"First, I'd like to thank my family, especially my mom, for all her support. I also want to give love to my brother, Lil Eddy, who died two years ago," the General said.

"Lil Eddy! RIP!" someone shouted from the balcony.

"Ed-deeeeee!" a teenager's voice belted out.

Several people shook cowbells for the deceased.

"My mom always said that she wanted her kids to be the first in our family to graduate high school," the General said. "But when my brother died, I just stopped caring about all that." He paused a moment.

Ava gazed at the skinny young man with the shaved head composing himself at the podium. How far he had come from the shy kid in a hoodie she had met her first day at Ida B. She felt an overwhelming sense of love.

A woman in the front row shouted to him, "Awww honey, that's all right—you just speak from your heart."

"Say it, baby!" called the General's mom.

He took a deep breath. "But I didn't give up. I came to this school, and I made some great friends, and now here I am." He spoke louder, "I'm 'bout to graduate. I made it."

Cowbells again.

"And I want to go to college now, maybe go to school to be a lawyer or even a judge."

"That's right! Supreme Court, here we go!" someone yelled from the balcony.

"And I want other people to know that if I did it, you can do it too." The General looked into the audience. "I'm a graduate."

He walked back to his seat amid applause, horns, and cowbells.

Ava looked into the crowd of parents, grandparents, family, friends. There was so much hope in this room. Generations clinging to a foothold.

She squeezed Jimmie's hand. She loved the faces on that stage. Graduates. They had worked hard, many taking the Exit Exam over and over until finally passing. They had followed her into the ballet and the courtroom. They had learned essays and algebra and chemistry, completing the required 230 credits. They had earned their diplomas.

Ava felt that she, too, had earned the right to be here. In her mushroom journey, the mystic Mama said that life was in the try, and Ava had tried so much this year—in the classroom, working the steps of Adult Children of Alcoholics, on the ball field, and in putting herself out there dating. Her students had taught her about forgiveness after she ruined their papers with red ink, and they also had taught her about gratitude—Paris promising to send Jesus back to get her at world's end. They had given Ava a chance to try again.

Four students came down to the front of the stage, Johntay and Tanya among them. Johntay was wearing his usual white sneakers, but, to Pants' chagrin, he had broken the rule on graduates refraining from writing anything on their robes. He had used paint. Large block letters reiterated his tee shirt's plea, the hope that it would mean something: *Black Man Graduating.*

Johntay cleared his throat, tossing his long twisty braids.

The top of Tanya's cap spelled out 'RIP Sonny B' in purple glitter.

Johntay began, "How do I-I-I-I, sayyyy good byyyye—"

Tanya and the rest of the group joined in, "To what we haaaaad. The good tiiiiiimes that maaaaade us laugh outweigh the baaaad…"

It was a beautiful a cappella rendition of a Boyz II Men song, something the students had rehearsed after school and at each other's homes for the past few weeks. Ava wished Sean, Hector, and Kabernay were up there on stage too. She had wanted college for them, a brighter future. Only it turned out Stella was right; their lives were their business. Still, Ava felt she could do more for them than this….

The song over, Pants took the stage again. She had been nervous from graduation's outset. She now looked green. "Okay, I don't want to put a damper on anyone's celebration," Pants said, "But I need all families to refrain from rushing the stage when your graduate walks across."

"Boooo!" yelled the crowd.

Pants continued, "You're welcome to send representatives to the front stage area for photos, but please be aware of the people behind you wanting pictures of their graduates too. Please stay low. Don't hand items up to students as they make their way across the stage." She gave a signal to the staff in the front row.

"Here we go," Cheryl whispered. She stood up and blocked the center isle access to the stage. Ava stood up next to her, bewildered. Other staff blocked the side isle entrances.

All over the auditorium, parents and friends began to get up, those with balloons unconsciously whacking others in the face as everyone jockeyed to be closest to the stage.

"Will the front row please rise?" Pants motioned to the graduates. They had practiced standing as one on cue for thirty minutes the day before. The front row stood in unison, except for Paris, who was lost in a text.

"Hey ShayShay! Pay attention!" A woman yelled from the audience.

As Pants called Johntay's name for his diploma, he strode across the stage in a new pair of Jordan's, pumping his fists in the air as he strutted.

"Go baby!" his mother screamed. She pushed past Ava as if a running back focused on the end zone.

Johntay bent down to collect a dozen floating balloons. With the other hand, he raised his diploma high, like a heavyweight champion hefting his belt for the world to admire.

Melvin blew kisses all the way across the stage. "This is what sexy looks like when it graduates!" he yelled. The cowbells shook their approval.

"Melbinnnnn!" his mom cheered.

Ava touched the lei around her neck. She remembered Melvin's work as a defense attorney in their mock trial, when he had called

Moe a liar for saying girls drank Hennessey. Would she have had the thrill of this trial with other students? Likely. But there was something about these kids that couldn't be replicated.

Charnikka's family also blew right past the human barricade. Ava stepped aside to let Charnikka's mom, Janice, wheel by.

Janice held up the student's three-year-old daughter along with a bouquet of roses. Charnikka's pink cheeks matched little Iyanla's as Charnikka juggled her toddler and flowers to also shake the principal's hand and grab her diploma case.

Big Moe, who had missed the last month of classes because of lung problems, stood behind Ava in the audience. He rattled a cowbell. From his huge grin, no one would know his disappointment of once again failing the Exit Exam.

After the ceremony, Pants invited everyone to the school's cafeteria for a cake and punch reception.

Francisco's mom walked up to Stella. "I am so thankful for all you have done for my son," she said. Francisco had thrived in art class the past quarter. Stella secured him a scholarship for a summer art institute, but remained doubtful about whether Francisco would actually go.

Ava caught Francisco's gaze.

He waved his diploma.

K'Ron tapped Ava's shoulder. "Will you take a picture with me, Ms. L?" Teetering in stilettos, she wrapped an arm around Ava's waist while Jimmie snapped their picture.

"You look beautiful," Ava said. She was sorry she'd never asked K'Ron how to draw on Cleopatra eyes.

She walked out into the late afternoon light, graduates and families milling about on the stairs of Mission High School. She gazed out at the kids, their caps and gowns, their parents. A school year completed. They had made it. *I made it too.*

Jimmie stood beside her. "Now that was a whole new graduation experience."

Then a car full of *Sureños* drove past slowly.

Francisco's and K'Ron's family and friends keep an eye on them, tense. But the car kept going, a reminder of overstepping territory. The grace period of graduation over, the *Sureños* were warning it was time to leave.

Jimmie touched Ava's elbow. "Can I take you to dinner, Ms. L?"

CHAPTER 65
"GOOD MORNING, MS. L."

September. A month into the new school year. Ava was still re-living the summer road trip with Jimmie. They had driven up Highway 1 overlooking the icy Pacific to the rocky coastline of Oregon, cutting in at Seattle to head toward the Bitterroot Mountains. By the time she and Jimmie stepped out of her truck at her dad's old house, the huckleberries on the wild hillsides were ripe.

And now she was back at Ida B with Stella, her advisor and com-ic relief in the art room, and Cheryl, her constant mentor across the hall. Mr. Jeffries was in Philadelphia, Teach for America hav-ing sufficiently boosted his chances of getting into a PhD program for Educational Policy. He was a spokesperson for TFA on the side. Amid faculty protest, Pants hired another TFA teacher to take his place.

K'Ron stopped by the school to let Ava know she was starting community college. So was Melvin. Hector was still doing time miles south of the city. Sean had been sentenced. He was serving a year in the California Youth Authority Prison. Ava thought of him often, writing him letters and occasionally getting one in return. It was a tough prison. It was hard time.

That morning, so early on a crisp September day, Ava was at the copy machine. Mr. Brennan walked in. His eyes looked tired. "Ms. Llewellyn." He pointed to a newspaper clipping. "Did you see this?"

"Good morning." She took the paper and read the first few paragraphs, disbelieving every word. No. Nononononono.

She crumpled the article and let it fall to the floor.

Mr. Brennan nodded. "Your first one? I wish I could say they get easier."

"No," Ava said. She felt dizzy. There was a ringing in her ears.

"I'm sorry. I know he was a favorite."

Ava shook her head. "You can tell Ms. Sanchez I fucking quit."

Mr. Brennan grimaced. "Just give it a little—"

"No. I'm done."

He left the room.

Leaning against the copier, Ava closed her eyes. She tried to grasp what the paper claimed was real.

Cool night air. A streetlight out in Hunter's Point. Darkness. Sirens in the distance. A friend's front porch overlooking a concrete yard. Johntay lounging against the doorframe, joking. His hoodie pulled over his twisty braids. That big grin. Maybe he was laughing about Gutta, his racket escapades. Maybe he was telling racket stories of his own, making plans for his new life after high school. What statement had his tee shirt made that day? Likely, *Graduated Black Man*. Did he even realize he was in danger?

It would have been another teenager—Cheryl said that's how the O.G.'s did it. Teens were assigned the executions. Lighter sentences. Just another hoodie moving in the darkness.

Then, Johntay, mid-sentence, mid-smile…Did he even see the gun? Was he afraid? Did he think of his friend, Trey? Or of his mom? If he had time to think at all.

Noooooo, Ava breathed. It wasn't real. He hadn't worked so hard go out like this.

The grin was gone, the boy who'd loved his friend, washed his friend's blood out of his own white tee. The young man who'd held it together, kept himself alive long enough to graduate.

The reporter quoted the homicide investigator: "He wasn't the intended target, but he resembles the intended target."

Lots of people in the house that night. No witnesses. Johntay's murderer would go free. Snitches end up in ditches.

Another quote, from a neighbor, a Reverend: "It devalues life when so many cases go unsolved. It's bragging rights to kill somebody. I'm up to my waist in this. I've been dealing with it for fifteen years."

Ava swallowed through a hard knot. Resembles the intended target. Really. A black teenager in a doorway, head covered by a hoodie, darkness. She tried to imagine a reality in which she could be killed because, at midnight, in a coat, she resembled another, short white woman. There would be outrage, arrests. A mother-fucking conviction.

Pants sent Fifty to counsel Ava. The security guard ambled in, grimacing. He leaned against the doorframe, Don King hair straight up, observing. "This just happens sometimes," Fifty said.

"But it's *Johntay*." Johntay stubbornly asking to leave class five minutes early. Johntay poking her belly on the stairs, telling the class she had lost eight hundred dollars. Noting that Mina's shoes were only Eccos, giving his testimony on the witness stand, Leaning out the drive thru window, giving her extra fries, calling out the Cha-Cha Slide in his Prom King crown…

The tears spilled over. "He *knew* he couldn't be out in that neighborhood late at night. It's so stupid! Why would he be so *stupid*?"

Fifty shook his head. "He was probably out visiting a buddy. He's probably had that buddy since he was in kindergarten. Why would he stop visiting his friends? It was an accident."

Ava glared. "An accident is emailing someone something you didn't intend to send. It's bumping into a car in the Target parking lot....It isn't getting *shot* at *midnight* because you *looked* like some-one *else!*"

Fifty held up his hands. "That's what it means to teach these kids. You want to cry about it? Cry. That won't help your students, and it won't help you." The corners of his mouth turned down in distaste. "I'm getting too old for this shit. You have your class in two minutes. Why don't you clean yourself up and get ready for school?"

In the bathroom, formerly a closet in the copy room, Ava looked at her face. Mascara bled into crow's feet. The kids were right: it was getting harder to keep herself up. But how do I go into that classroom? How could she look at them and not see fos-ter moms, group homes, Sean sitting at the visitor's table in juvie, Johntay standing in the doorway at midnight, visiting a friend and then.... Ava had no idea what to do. From her mushroom journey, she heard, You lost? You hurt? You say....

"Mama." she whispered.

The last bell rang.

She stayed a while in front of the sink, the morning's work-sheets on the copy room floor. It didn't matter: what the kids need-ed most wasn't going to be found in packets on comma rules or teacher-proof textbooks.

She splashed water on her face, rubbed off the last of her mas-cara with a paper towel. She gazed into the mirror. Those eyes could easily have been his staring back. "I'm so sorry," she mouthed. You can't be dead. But he was. He can be dead because he is. She shook her head. Fuck you, Metta Annie.

Turn it around: I can't be dead. She shuddered. It was the truth. Quitting wasn't life. She couldn't do anything for Johntay, for herself, for anyone, if she was dead too.

She took her time walking up the stairs to her classroom. She didn't know what she'd say when she saw her students.

On the stairwell, someone had tagged the name, *Gutta*. Kids were always trying to leave their marks on the school; a reminder that they were here—they did exist. Until they didn't. So what the hell am I doing here? I can't teach them just to watch them die.

Ava remembered a quote from Edward Everett Hale. It was one of her favorites: "I can't do everything, but I can do something. The something I ought to do, I can do."

What something could Ava do? She searched through her set of skills. She was an English teacher. She was a writer. She was a right fielder. She wasn't brave enough to tell the kids she loved them. But maybe she could write it in a book. She could let Johntay know, too late, that he mattered. Tell Sunny she was trying. Be a witness.

A book. Who would read it? And really, would it matter in the end? She had no idea. But she could try. Mama said that life was in the try. That in every brave moment, we are created and re-created anew.

That's what she had done this past year. She wasn't the same person who had driven into the city from that tiny town in Washington. Now she knew *Norteño* from *Sureño*, where to find Latino *People* M*agazine*, and how to get students to follow Rule #1: *No swearing*. She had learned to let Dan go. Learned to let her dad go. She saw tie-dyed Gary twice a month for hippie therapy. She had Lydia and the ACA group, Cheryl, Stella, Ruthie, Jimmie. She had a loving family and her dad's dark gift: the ability to choose to be kind.

But what would she write? She smiled, light breaking though on such a dark day. That part was easy. She'd write about her first day at Ida B, how the kids got up to leave when she read out Rule #1, Ava nearly shitting her pants. She'd write about Sean making her feel welcome with a Darth Vader impression, the General coolly waiting out the chaos, Melvin asserting into the fray, "I'm professionally sexy." Charnikka, clearly the only one in charge.

She would write about Johntay's story and, especially, his smile. She would write about Ken at the ballet, his eyes holding the light of heaven, and Tolly's triumphant, messy, mock trial. K'Ron's brass knuckles, her thick cat's eyes, and Hector stealing Snapples from the back of a Walgreens truck. She'd write about parent conferences, the pain in family members' faces, how hard they tried. The hip bone's connected to—Hunter's Point, Mrs. Collins, Sean. You Got Caught.

She'd write about her roommate, Pedro, giving her a soft landing in the city, and Cheryl and Stella, the veterans she'd leaned on to teach her how to teach. She'd describe Pants and Assistant Superintendent Brill's mandate for "joyful" test-takers, and how the kids had found their own joy despite that mandate, the class sing-along ending with *Mazel Tov*.

She'd share the triumphant celebration of graduation, Johntay holding his diploma above his head like a champion.

Ava knew it would take years to learn to tell the story right. Fine. Just like Cheryl said about teaching, it should take more than five weeks to learn an important skill. It would mean that Ava had more time to spend with her students, to settle into her life here. They were worth it. So was she.

Coach John had taught her that, standing in front of his twelve-year-old little leaguers, loving each one—the kid who comes to practice dirty, with a borrowed mitt; the clumsy kid who can't stop even a weak grounder; the star whose parents scream obscenities from the bleachers; the shy kid no one sees—Coach John saw them all and beamed behind his logger's beard: Everyone is important, and everyone—everyone—matters.

She thought back to the words Gary had read before her mushroom journey, the Hopi Elder: *You have been telling people that this is the Eleventh Hour. Now, you must go back and tell the people that this is THE hour….We are the ones we've been waiting for.*

It wasn't anyone else's job to write about Johntay. It was hers. The something she ought to do, she could do. It was time.

Ava could hear her students long before she reached her classroom door.

She walked into the chaos of her barely supervised classroom. Fifty was visibly relieved.

"Ooohhh! You're late, Ms. L!" sang out Brandon. He held a stapler high above another student's eagerly outstretched palm.

Princess asked, "Did you read that story I wrote?"

"Good morning, Ms. L!" said Mariella, waving from her seat. Her eyeliner was drawn into Cleopatra eyes.

Ava looked at her students. They were still forming their personalities, talents, and aspirations. At the end of the day, it wasn't about the Exit Exam or teacher-proof texts. It wasn't about raising the next tech genius or banker. It was time to set a higher bar, one with some humanity in it. She didn't know how to take on bad policies or the big kahuna, the country's Secretary of Education. But then, he had never been a teacher. He'd been the President's basketball buddy. A forward. She shook her head: He didn't stand a chance. I'm an English teacher *and* a right fielder.

And I am not resigned. She smiled at her students. She would fight.

"Good morning," she said. "Sorry I'm late. Let's get started. I'm ready."

ACKNOWLEDGMENTS

I'd like to thank my husband, Franklin Dorin, for his unwavering belief in me and this project from the beginning. It was Pamela Feinsilber's narrative nonfiction class that birthed the first chapter and Pam and my classmate, Scott Elder saw it through to my first shitty, joyful first draft. Leslie Keenan's class (and book) You Can Complete That Book took up the cause and helped me to, indeed, give shape and narrative arc to this book. Thomas Centollela's brilliant writing class took the novel, two pages at a time, week by week and, over the years, helped me learn the craft of writing. Blossom Plumb and Genyne Long made a writing group into a place where I belonged. Beth Franks shared her beautiful YA novels with me and gave me invaluable insights into this one. Natalie Eaton shared her impeccable writing and critique. My mom, brother, sister, and stepdad were generous with their support and, always, love. I'd also like to thank my dad for his dark gift. I didn't know the kindness in the darkness. I know it now. Thank you.

68304367R00224

Made in the USA
San Bernardino, CA
02 February 2018